The Legend of Levitika:
THE CITY OF ANGELS

by B.D. Weddell

The contents of this work, including, but not limited to, the accuracy of events, people, and places depicted; opinions expressed; permission to use previously published materials included; and any advice given or actions advocated are solely the responsibility of the author, who assumes all liability for said work and indemnifies the publisher against any claims stemming from publication of the work.

All Rights Reserved
Copyright © 2022 by B.D. Weddell

No part of this book may be reproduced or transmitted, downloaded, distributed, reverse engineered, or stored in or introduced into any information storage and retrieval system, in any form or by any means, including photocopying and recording, whether electronic or mechanical, now known or hereinafter invented without permission in writing from the publisher.

Dorrance Publishing Co
585 Alpha Drive
Suite 103
Pittsburgh, PA 15238
Visit our website at *www.dorrancebookstore.com*

ISBN: 978-1-6470-2285-3
eISBN: 978-1-6470-2852-7

This is for Cambry.
Who chatted my ear off to no end
Just to express her love for her brother.
Love ya, sissy

Contents

The Innocent 1
A Tragedy 5
The Boy 19
The Elf 29
Legends of Old 45
One Blood 59
The Street Rat 65
A Dream 73
The Witch and the Hunter 83
The Fate 89
Escape 99
Open Season 107
Camping 115
The Xerxe Encounter 125
The Heartless Machine 137
The Lost World 147
Savages 159
Pursuit 165
The Dark Forest 181
Evolution 189
Man in Wolf's Clothing 199
Forest Fire 209
The Inferno 219
Freak of Nature 231
The Keeper 241
Agony 251
Loss 261
The Queen of the Sky 269
The Princess of the Sky 281
The City of Angels 295
Revelation 311

A Choice	323
The Spies and the Hypnotist	333
Departure	349
The Dreaming	355
Small Doorways	375
Creation	387
Guests	397
The Storming of Heaven	409
Angels and Devils	419
Abomination	431
A Bond	443
Possessed	455
Falling Angels	463
The Prophecy	473
From Another World	485
The Cyborg's Fall	499
The Legend continues in...	501

~ The Innocent ~

Markus

It was not the first time Markus had ever seen a dead body, but this was the first time it ever being a woman and her child.

He had gone out as night was beginning to fall, to the Market Place in the city of Nineveh for some firesticks and to deliver a package he had forgotten about during his rounds earlier that day. It was a cold winter night; the harshest winter Nineveh had seen in years. Snow was falling down in massive clumps, looking like falling feathers that would cover the entire city in a blanket of white. Most of the shops were already closing down after Markus and his sister left, and the miners would be returning to the city under the watchful eye of the drones and the Hellhound hovercraft the Ninevite Guard used throughout the city.

Earlier in the year, a satellite had fallen from the sky and crashed into The Narrows, the district in the city where the family lived. Many homes had been decimated, and a lot of people wound up dead. Many homeless were still slowly dying away.

Just like the mother and her child, sitting huddled together in an alley behind a dumpster. Markus had come into the ally in order to relieve himself and got frightened at the sight of the ghoulish blue skin prickled with frostbite. They both wore dirtied rags that were now carrying clumps of snow and already a rat had gone for the little boy in his mother's arms. It wasn't big enough to be a Badrat, but it was still large enough to not get scared away by some kid wearing a thin coat and welding goggles at the top of his head of blonde hair.

Markus noticed that on their chests were blackened splotches that upon closer inspection was a burn straight down to the chest cavity of their ribs. They had been shot by an energy weapon, probably by one of the Guards. A small and homeless family, out in the cold, and probably found in this exact spot before being shot and left alone. At least these bodies weren't hung up along the powerlines like many others for both show and warning by the Ninevite Guard. But still, what a cruel fate to just be left next to a garbage dumpster ready to be taken away like the rest of the trash left in this dirty alley.

"What is it?" his sister asked impatiently at the mouth of the alley. "Are you done yet?"

"Just picking a spot," Markus answered. While Ruth exclaimed her repulsion and exasperation, he went on to the other side of the wall away from the corpses. He didn't want to do it so close to the dead, it felt wrong. When he finished he stepped out just as a member of the Guard came walking by, his black and crimson armor gleaming and his rifle held tight in his hands. They got stopped and asked what they were doing and when they answered they were returning home, the man in the electronic helmet told them to move along.

"Curfew's in about an hour or so. Better hope we don't catch ya after that."

"Yes, sir," Markus said taking Ruth by the arm. "C'mon." He led her away under the watchful eyes of the Guard. In the distance, the high city walls were blaring an alarm, announcing the arrival of the transports bringing in the miners from the Bronze Mine to the east of the Northern Wastelands.

"Daddy's gonna be home soon," Ruth said tightening the strings holding her hood together. She had short and dirty blonde hair just like her brother. They both actually appeared almost alike, except for their eyes. While Ruth's eyes were as brown as ripe walnuts, Markus' were as blue as polished sapphires, the kind that only the richest lords of the Wastelands could afford to obtain.

"Yeah, he is," Markus said happily. "And early this time too, it seems." He never felt safe when Father wasn't around. He could never leave Ruth alone, even in their own home.

Nineveh just wasn't the place for a child to be alone, and even two was pushing it. They hurried the rest of the way home, their feet sinking into the deepening snow with every block they crossed. Somewhere above them, a drone buzzed across the sky and somewhere in the city, a gunshot rang out. The two stuck together still, keeping their heads on a swivel their entire walk.

The bundle of firesticks that Ruth carried under her arm slowed her down and so Markus offered to carry it for her. When she let him, she surprised him by scooping up a ball of snow and throwing it at his back. The snowball exploded against his coat in a thick spread of clumps, with some snow sticking to his back after a majority of it fell away.

"Hey," Markus said turning back slightly annoyed. "Seriously?"

"Gotcha!" Ruth said laughing as she sprinted forward and out of her brother's grasp.

"Oh, you're gonna get it," Markus warned her as he picked up his feet and chased after her. They kept going to their house, never sidetracking or stopping even for a moment. Because like the Guard had said, Curfew was about to begin.

And it was not safe to be out in the cold at night.

~ A Tragedy ~

Markus

Markus' father, being a mechanic for the miners, had been allowed to come home early and was about to cook a stray dog that he had found dead in an old ally near the Underground, another district in the city.

The city itself was under a heavy ration shortage, with a majority of fresh food going only to Baron Ovid and those who served directly under him. Even potions and common medicines were difficult to find anymore and as a result, hunger and sickness was a common problem in the area. Still, the man was always trying his best to provide for his son and daughter who loved him dearly.

They were just about to eat their meal when a heavy pounding at the door made them all jump in their seats. Their father opened it to the old bartender, Jim. The cyborg was panting heavily, his metallic arm made crudely of corroded titanium pipes and copper wires magnetized to the nerve-endings on his stump and upper-right torso. His dirty white hair was dripping in sweat and soot, and his wrinkled face was strained to a point where Markus thought the man's skull would tear through his very face.

The cyborg looked at Markus' father, his one good eye wide with fear and his replacement scope-eye flashing red as he looked at him. "John!" he gasped.

"Jim, are you okay?" Johnathon asked the cyborg who looked on the verge of collapsing. "What's-"

"It's the Hunter, Black," Jim said quickly. "He's coming for you."

Markus' father immediately went serious. His bearded face hid a lot of his expressions but his eyes flashed bright and dangerous at the mention of the Baron's lead assassin. The Hunter Black, a known bounty hunter who had just recently been taken under the Baron's wing. Anything the Ninevite Guard couldn't handle or something that the Baron wanted taken care of quietly (or publicly in some cases), Black was always sent to take care of it. The news of his coming to find his father filled Markus with a great fear that sent shivers down his spine.

"How far out is he?" Johnathon asked. "There any word on why?"

"I don't know," Jim answered. "The boys who were at The Drunken Badrat said something about treason. No warrant for your arrest, just a public execution."

Johnathon's eyes narrowed. The news of treason had to be a lie, but then again it wasn't uncommon for innocents to be wrongfully accused of treason with the neighboring kingdom of Xerxes, just like the witches of Salem. Markus knew his father would never become a traitor, but that would hardly matter to Black or the Guard.

Johnathon asked, "Why him though? Why not The Guard?"

"They're coming too. But the Hunter has been hired to get you specifically. Apparently, they want no mistakes and want to show off their most valued warrior via a duel."

"A duel? Ahh, hell, they wanna make a show of it… They must have found out what I did…" Johnathon mumbled before saying, "Thank you, please come inside."

"John-"

"If you help me the Guard'll kill you too. I need you here with my children."

"Daddy?" Ruth said now worried, her small fist curled around her ragged blonde hair. She and Markus had kept quiet, standing by the little fire pit in their 'living room' as they listened to the adults' conversation.

Johnathon looked to his children helplessly. "Daddy's gotta go baby-girl." He crossed the room and gave Markus' sister a hug and a kiss upon her brow. "Stay with your brother," he told her. "I love you."

He then walked past his son, not saying a word as he went into his quarters. He came back out carrying his bladed staff. What caught Markus' eye every single time he got to see the remnant of his father's past occupation was the wired sapphire-colored stone connected to the base of the blade. He never knew where his dad got the stone, but whenever an electric pulse went through the crystal, a concentrated beam of static energy would shoot out, sometimes obliterating wooden carriages into ashes. The blade, made of Radio-Bronze would cut through the bone of any beast, and the metal of almost any machine.

Johnathon then came up to Markus and opened his arms. His son ran to him, hugging him tight and burying his face into his coat. He didn't know what it was his father did, but he didn't care. Markus did not want him to go.

What will happen to Ruth and me? Markus wondered. Though he knew his father planned to fight back, even if he won there would be nowhere for him to go. The Guard would just shoot him dead if he got lucky enough to slay the Hunter. No one had ever dueled Damion Black and lived to tell the tale. No one called to duel with the Hunter or any of the Ninevite Guard's elite soldiers survived.

"I can help," he said wanting to help his father desperately. It was the first words that passed his lips since Jim's arrival.

Johnathon smiled and pulled away before patting Markus' head. "No, son."

"Dad, please, I-"

"I need you here. To take care of Ruth for me. Can you do that for me?" his father looked his son dead in the eyes with his icy blue spheres. "Promise me, Mark."

As a tear trickled down his cheek and onto the dirty wood floor, Markus nodded reluctantly.

Smiling, Johnathon ruffled up his son's long blonde hair with his hand. "That's my brave boy."

"You'll die." Markus said as his father brushed past him.

Jonathon smiled again, for his son's sake. "Maybe I will. Every man dies. But I will die, if it means to protect you and Ruth." He showed his staff to Markus, his son's reflection glistening in the polished metal of the blade, the sapphire stone twinkling in the candlelight. "This is yours as soon as this is over. Okay?"

Markus didn't understand at first. "What…"

"Remember to deliver your packages, okay?"

"Yes, Dad."

He placed a hand on Markus' shoulder, his smile warming his son's heart better than the fire in their pit. "You're the best flyer I've ever trained son. I want you to know that."

The compliment while bringing Markus incredible joy, brought with it terrible dread that he may never hear such a thing again. Still, Markus bobbed his head and said, "Thank you, sir."

"Love you both." And before Markus or even Ruth could say the same, he walked out the door, the harsh cold and snowy wind greeting him in its cruel embrace.

Not willing to just let him go despite what he said, Markus ran outside, following him before Jim could call him back. The boy left the cyborg and his sister inside the shack as he ran to the crowd which had gathered outside and circled around his father and another man, trapping them inside with nowhere to run.

Citizens, androids, and the Guard all watched the two men who faced each other in front of the old church building. The church was condemned and marked, for the building itself was falling apart piece by piece, and the out-of-order monorail that had once been used for transportation hanging above it was a constant threat of one day falling upon the building and crushing anyone who dared to go inside.

Within the crowd before the church, Johnathon and The Hunter Black stood before one another, eyeing each other with a predatory look in their eyes. Neither of them moved as the snow fell upon them. The many buildings and shacks stood towering above them; crowded, dirty, and falling apart as if decaying before their very eyes. Clotheslines passed from window to window, where a raven sat squawking at the two men in the circle below, its three eyes blinking like flickering black beads.

The androids and Guard shoved the crowd back as well as kicked the trash bags and rotten parts aside for more room. Jim hadn't been kidding when he said that the Guard wanted to make a show out of it. One even shot the rope of a hung body against a power pole, letting it drop to the ground. The skin was gray and covered in frostbite. It looked to be a man. He too was kicked among the trash to make room in the cracked street for Johnathon to duel the Hunter, Damion Black.

The Hunter Black had the same build as Johnathon; his black armor covered by a dark cloak which billowed in the wind like a mighty flag, and his face was covered by a shroud of midnight. At his hip was a Nine-Banger shotgun. In his hands at ready was a sinister blade which represented a samurai sword; its handle wrapped in black and red cloth, and a bluish glow seemed to emit from the silver-steel. The faint smell of ozone was in the air, revealing it to be a shock-sword.

Johnathon stood across from the bounty hunter, his staff at ready while The Guard took aim at him again to make sure he didn't try to flee from the duel.

"Well?" Johnathon demanded his voice low and loud for all to hear, a tone Markus had never heard his father use before. He laughed out loud at the Guard surrounding him. "What's wrong? You boys don't know what to do or something?"

Ignoring him, the Hunter Black spoke loud and clear for the people watching to hear. "By the order of his majesty Baron Ovid, you are to be executed for the crimes of treason against his Lordship, and for the deaths of the seven officers sent to arrest you. Johnathon, you are hereby sentenced to death by my hand be it willingly, or by duel."

All around them, the people started chanting 'duel, duel, duel!' like a horrible chorus of a dreadful song. Markus hated to hear so many people wanting to watch such a show.

"You sure like making a scene out of it." Johnathon commented. "I'm surprised your men hadn't noticed they were gone when I came back to the mines the last seven nights."

"Let's just light this son of a bitch now!" one of the soldiers shouted.

"Put your weapons down." Black commanded in a stern voice while never once taking his eyes off his target. "Do not shoot unless he tries to escape. Johnathon, your head has a hefty bounty, and these men will not interfere with whatever you choose."

"You afraid I will escape if it was only you?" Johnathon jeered.

Black's jaw began to twitch. Was he nervous? It was hard to tell, especially from where Markus stood. "What will it be, Johnathon? Will you lay your staff down, or will you fight?"

"What's it like, Damion? Taking the Barons orders like a whipped dog?"

Black remained stone-faced. "Any who oppose Baron Ovid, or even myself within these walls, is a traitor; and a traitor's fate, is death. I will ask you one more time: will you surrender, or will you fight? It matters not to me, but if you value your honor, stand down."

Johnathon smirked again at the man. "I would rather die with it in my hands."

Black's expression remained neutral, indifferent. "So be it." he said, like he didn't care otherwise. "I will not regret what is to come, John."

Johnathon nodded, seeming satisfied. "I would expect nothing less of you, Damion." He then readied his weapon, and he bent his knees and rested his weight on the balls of his feet. "Shall we?" He asked as if he was challenging not a hired killer, but an old friend.

The Hunter readied his sword in both hands, its sinister edge glistening like the snow. "Let's."

The Hunter charged towards Johnathon with such speed that the snow flew aside in a wave-like spread as he lunged forward; his sword point heading straight for his target's heart. Johnathon brought his staff up and the two collided with a thundering *clang*! Then spinning his staff around and knocking the sword back, he struck the Hunter in the knee with the butt of his weapon. In the same span of the second it took he then lashed out with the bladed-end, the bronze ready to slice through Black's throat.

The Hunter however leaned back, dodging the blade which missed his chin by a hairs-width. He then grabbed his enemy's staff with a free hand, and turned his body, throwing Johnathon over his back and sending him a good ten feet away.

Markus watched as his father tumbled in the snow kicking up powder, but then he steadied himself and managed to land on his feet, his weapon ready again. He panted heavily as the Hunter got back into his stance, his weapon raised across his chest.

Johnathon then aimed his staff at the Hunter and his thumb clicked against a button where his hand held the weapon. The Hunter's eyes went wide and he dove to the side as a bolt of red electricity shot out at him and blasted snow in a hot radius of where he was once standing.

Johnathon fired again and again, but this time the Hunter was ready. Shifting his blade into different positions, he caught the bolts of red, blocking them and deflecting them away and into the snow. As he deflected each shot, he walked forward, unrelenting with such determination towards his target. Markus found himself clenching his fists in anxiousness as he watched Black draw closer and closer, the suspense as to what would happen next making him dig his nails into his palms to the point of nearly spilling blood.

Suddenly metallic arms grabbed Johnathon from behind and held him up and still. He kicked at the android who stood unmoved by the force, waiting for Black to finish the man off.

The Hunter however stopped his advance immediately, his weapon now at his side. "Release him." he commanded the droid.

"Just kill him." the android said, his humanoid face showed no emotion but his glowing red eyes seemed to glow the brighter. "We do not have time for this."

"You are interfering with a duel. Release him."

"Just kill him." the android said again in its emotionless voice. "What difference does it make?"

The Hunter then suddenly reached for his shotgun, rose it towards Johnathon, and fired. Markus had looked away, but after a second of silence, he turned back.

The android's head had been completely blown off. Sparkling wires crackled and belched smoke within the stump and a whirring sound hummed through the air as the robot began to shut down. The hands released Johnathon, who fell to a crouch at the ground. He quickly got up and got out of the way as the android fell forward into the snow with a *poof* of powder.

"He is my prey." the Hunter called out to everyone shoving his gun back into its holster and raising his sword at ready again. "Anyone who interferes shall pay the same price." The Guard immediately lowered their weapons which were trained not only on Johnathon, but the Hunter as well. Markus watched again as his father set his staff again, his stance already steadied.

Black acknowledged his opponent. "Shall we continue, John?"

"Yes." Johnathon said, and then this time, lunged at the Hunter himself. Markus clenched his fist tightly around the scruff of his coat, now excited to see how the fight would unfold from this point on.

The Hunter parried Johnathon's first attack, and blocked the second before the two then grappled with their weapons, swinging each other around and around, each trying to get a foothold in the deep snow. The Hunter shoved Johnathon back and swung his sword, which he in turn blocked the attack and deflected it so that it would strike the ground at his feet. Johnathon danced with the staff in his hands as if he had done this a thousand times before, holding his own against the assassin.

The Hunter then struck out with a gloved hand, backhanding the man away. Followed by a sharp swing of his sword again, cutting a deep gash in Johnathon's favorite coat, but not hitting anything vitally important. However, Markus *did* see a small speckle of crimson spread across the snow as his father leapt further back and out of reach of that hungry blade.

The Hunter leapt up into the air and with both hands, sliced downward with all his strength. Johnathon had gotten his staff up just in time to catch the sword just before it could slice him in half. The Hunter then flicked his wrist slightly and Johnathon was suddenly blown backward with a loud zapping sound. The smell of ozone was suddenly stronger now, and the man crashed into the side of the old church building.

Sliding down the side and collapsing to his knees, Johnathon shook his head in a daze as the Hunter walked casually towards him. The sound of his boots crunching the dense snow was the only audible sound for everyone had held their breath- including Markus who was biting the knuckle of his index finger to the point where he actually spilled blood in his fit of worry.

Johnathon, using his free arm for support, pulled himself back up. The Hunter stopped about five yards from him, waiting, taunting him almost it seemed.

"Do you need a moment?" he asked irritatingly casual.

Chuckling, Johnathon stood up, and when he was back in his stance, his right foot supporting himself against the bottom corner of the church, his weapon aimed at the Hunters chest, who saw this and held his weapon up to catch the shots. "Don't make me laugh. I'm good." the man said with a smirk of defiance.

Black's brow softened slightly. It was as if they were two kids fighting in the alley and yet at the same time concerned for each other's health in the assurance that it would still be a good fight.

"You *do* realize this could go a lot quicker if you simply surrender?" Black then asked. "The Baron just wants your death; you can have it quick and painless, or slow and painful, as I've said before. Think about your son. He's been watching this entire time."

When he said that, Markus felt his blood run cold. He had no idea how the Hunter even knew he was there, watching in the crowd. Markus wished he could just disappear, but his feet would not move. He was planted there, wanting desperately to see if his father would win.

"I *am* thinking of him." Johnathon then said. "And if he were to see me back down and cower, what would he think of me?"

To this the Hunter had no reply but instead asked, "Why continue to fight then? Is it just because of your pride? To show off for your son?"

"No," Johnathon said shaking his head. "To show the people of Nineveh that there are men in this city, willing to fight you and that tyrant of a leader!"

Now Black *really* had nothing to say.

"Have you no tongue, old friend?"

"I do what is expected of me, as I always have." Black said spinning his sword in hand as easily as if it weighed nothing at all. "You were the one always causing trouble. Be reasonable John. What will you accomplish, even if you kill me?"

"Well, for starters, I would be removing a stain who should have never been born."

Black remained stone-faced at this comment.

Johnathon shook his head. "Well, now it seems I will pay for my troubles. And I shall pay in full, or none at all."

Black truly looked disappointed at this. He sighed, "So be it." and the Hunter lunged forward again, his blade swinging to the side faster than humanly possible.

Johnathon leaped up over the blade which sliced through the wood of the church. He shot out a bolt as he came back down, missing the Hunter who sidestepped out of harm's way. Johnathon then swung his staff, but the Hunter grabbed hold of the weapon and spun the man around before slamming him right through the wall of the church and leaving a gaping hole in the rotten wood.

The Hunter leapt into the hole after Johnathon. There was the sound of clashing weapons inside, and a couple of shots were fired, lighting the interior. The back of the church had soon caught on fire, and was now being eaten away by the flames that quickly rose up to the rotted ceiling. More flames erupted within, obscuring any sights through the windows with flame and smoke. Still, everyone watched in silence, waiting to see what would happen next as if the entire district was frozen in time.

Even Markus feared the worst as the church was slowly eaten away by the flames. But then he saw his father leap out one of the windows and then grabbing onto the overhead shingles he swung himself onto the roof. Markus was relieved to see that his father was alive, but he could see even from the distance he was at that his father was hurt.

His arm was cut and was bleeding slightly. Even from far away Markus and everyone else could see the crimson glistening on his arm. He swiveled his torso, his staff aimed everywhere his eyes turned as he searched the rooftop. Suddenly the Hunter burst out of the roof, kicking up splintered wood and landing on the chimney of the church as the flames and smoke rose around him, making him appear more sinister like a creature of the dark.

The Hunter then grabbed the necktie of his cloak and untied it, letting the black cloth sail through the air towards the snowy streets below. It flapped through the sky like a pair of Ahool wings until it landed beside the Guards who were staring in awe at the two on the rooftop.

With the cloak now gone, the Hunter's build was revealed in its entirety. He was well-defined, the black armor of Sand-Dragon leather edged around his torso; each muscle easily visible in the crevices of the armor. He was not particularly big and strong, but his lean figure was muscular and etched like a perfect painting. The skin that was visible, which was only the thin opening in his shroud was deathly pale and the fingers which were visible in the leather gloves he wore, were long and pale like a skeleton's hand. With them he gripped his sword again, ready to attack again.

He leapt into the air and as he came down upon Johnathon, his target fired more bolts which the Hunter deflected; making them hit more sections of the rooftops and causing more pockets of flames to appear around them. When he was closer he swung downwards at Johnathon, who deflected the blade yet again, causing it to embed into the weak shingles. He kneed the Hunter in the nose, knocking him back with a sickening *crunch*; and Black's hand tightened around the hilt of his weapon, wrenching it out as he fell backwards.

Johnathon took another shot but the Hunter spun back, rolling down the side of the roof and off the edge. He quickly grabbed the edging and swung himself back up, propelling towards his target, the sword aimed right for his heart. Johnathon leapt back, dodging the attack, and the two once again struck out and parried, keeping up with each other's attacks and defenses. It was like watching two pirates have a sword fight, with each swing of one, the other blocked and vice versa.

The two warriors' swords then clashed against one another, and they held each other at the crossing-point, both trembling at each other's strength as they pushed against one another. The Hunter seemed to be saying something to Johnathon, but at the distance of the churches rooftop, no one could hear anything from the streets below. Johnathon had replied something and then pushed with all his might, kicking outward with his foot and causing the Hunter to jump back so that they were only mere yards from each other. When their weapons were back up, neither seemed ready to attack the other as the church burned around them.

Johnathon had swung first, and the two began to fight again, parrying and stabbing at each other, trying to get an angle on one another. They eventually disappeared as smoke engulfed them, but their shadows were cast by the flames against the city wall. They danced and slashed at one another, their shadows moving like demons revealed in the cursed light. Johnathon had struck the Hunter, and he in turn got a few good swings into him in return; Markus and everyone else could tell by the way his shadow reacted as opposed to the Hunter's. For a moment at that time, it had seemed as if Johnathon could really beat this assassin. Markus himself, actually felt a small spark of hope ignite in his heart.

But his heart sank as he witnessed what happened next.

The shadow of the Hunter lunged forward, and the shadow of the sword seemed to slide through Johnathon's own just before the staff could block it. The shadow arched back and everyone heard the distinct stifled gasp as the blade slipped out and then Johnathon's figure twisted and fell into the smoke. Then the shadow of the Hunter dipped down into the smoke to follow.

It then became deathly silent, save for the muffled roar of the flames and the falling snow around them. Everyone held their breath, even the Guard it seemed as the seconds rolled by. They all watched the burning church in silence as they waited for the inevitable. What were mere minutes felt like hours, dragging agonizingly slowly.

Then after what felt like forever, Markus saw something coming out of the burning building: The Hunter was walking out of the smoking doorway, his sword now in its leather scabbard across his back, and behind him he dragged the unquestionable resemblance of a body bag in one hand. In the other, his father's staff rested in his bloodied hands. Markus' eyes swelled with tears as the Hunter dropped the bag in the middle of the street before the crowd as he walked over to the boy. The crowd dispersed like water before a rock as he stopped before Markus, and held out the staff.

"Here," he said simply. His cowl had fallen off at some point during the fight, and his face was now visible. A pale angled face with high cheekbones and lips red with blood that had dripped from his nose and now stained his teeth.

In his anger, Markus slapped his father's weapon into the snow at his feet. Powder went up in a flurry as the weapon made contact with the ground. The boy seethed as he clenched his teeth. "You monster, you killed my father!" At this point hot tears had escaped Markus' eyes, dripping down his cheeks and freezing in the cold. He stumbled forward and started pounding on the Hunter, hitting him with all his might.

"You murderer."

A member of the Guard started towards him but Black sent him away with a silent hand. He merely watched the pitiful child beating on his chest. He didn't even flinch when Markus kicked him in the leg and even went as far as to jump up and try to punch at his face. Black merely sidestepped and allowed Markus to fall flat on his face.

Black turned to the nearest officer. "Place Johnathon's home under a deterrent. The home is now under my protection, including the residents."

"Sir?" the soldier asked, wanting Black to be sure as to what that would mean for himself.

"Do it." Black said without hesitation. He then looked down at Markus who was glaring up at him with such hateful rage. He then turned his back on the boy and walked back to the body bag. "Let's go." he said to his men. He had absolutely nothing else to say to Markus, nothing that would either make it better or any worse.

An android who had caught the cloak Black had discarded took it back to the Hunter; who then slipped the cloak back on before shouldering the bag that contained Johnathon, Markus' own father and walking away. Not a word was uttered from the Hunter's mouth as the crowd made a hole for him to walk through, and one by one members of the Guard followed him, while some lingered to tend to the citizens, telling them to move along.

Markus, now pushing himself up off the snow-covered asphalt screamed out "You murderous bastard!"

The Hunter didn't even look back once. Some of the Guard did, but he told them to keep going- and for all citizens to heed the Guard's warning.

Eventually, the entire street was once again vacant, and desolate as before. All the cowards who simply watched as Johnathon fought for his life and lost, returned to whatever matters they were attending to earlier. Such was normal within the city of Nineveh, but Markus now felt the true pain behind the hiding faces.

They left him all alone, with a staff at his feet, and the crimson stain where his father's body had laid before Black had taken him away. Markus would never see his father again, he realized. First his mother, and now his father, was truly gone from sight, forever. The weight of this reality kept him on his knees as he cried for himself.

The crows from the lines above were Markus' only company as the snow continued to fall lightly upon them. They cawed and cackled as if they were laughing at the pathetic little boy crying for his father. In the distance, a clock tower from its iron lungs breathed the first hour of the new day, and still, Markus stayed on his knees. He remained still, looking down at the weapon as the church burned across the street. No one would come to put the fire out. No one cared about the burning building anyway.

At some point, he had stood up and walking away he stooped down and picked up his father's staff, not wanting to believe that he was really gone. He hoped that it was all just a horrible nightmare, and that he would wake up from it come morning. But this was no fantasy, despite how much he begged it to be. It had happened, and there was nothing he could do to change it. Another life, fallen into ash.

Markus cried for his father, for his sister, Ruth, and even more-so for himself. He wondered about what would happen now, and feared what the future may hold.

He then felt a hand on his shoulder, and turning his head he saw that Jim was there. He nodded some condolence before walking away. Maybe he didn't know what to say, but then again, maybe it wouldn't have mattered anyway. No words could heal the wounds inflicted upon his soul.

He eventually turned to see Ruth standing in the doorway of their shack, her face full of innocence, but her eyes full of tears. The tears of a human being broken by the cruelty of reality. Such a thing should never happen to a little girl. She must not have seen the fight, but she knew what the outcome was. She was bright like that, always had been since Markus could remember.

He walked over silently and hugged her with a free hand, burying her sobbing face into the front of his jacket. He then looked back towards the empty street where the Hunter had taken his father away; disappearing behind the rotting buildings of The Narrows. In the pit of Markus' heart, a seed had been planted. A terrible desire, of a lost child.

He wished the man dead with all his heart. It was the first time Markus truly wished for a man to die, and he would wish that every day since that fateful night; which still haunts the boys' dreams even today. Always caressing him with agony and misery.

This event, brought upon the ashes of sorrow that bound Markus. But, it also planted the seed, which would eventually grow seven years later, when he would be faced with a challenge, unlike anything he had ever experienced in his life.

~ The Boy ~

Markus

In the late spring years later, Markus was working as a tax collector for the Nineveh Guard.

It wasn't the best part-time job, having to deliver notices to civilians and being The Guards errand-boy, but he needed the money for the basic necessities, especially for his sister.

Ruth had gotten sick about a month or so ago, with some common cold symptoms. He didn't know what it was, but it hasn't gone away and according to the few people who knew anything about diseases and medicine, it wasn't a normal sickness. Unfortunately, all remedies including the alchemists and doctors who made them belonged to Baron Ovid now, and they remained in the Nineveh Tower and out of public reach. With nothing much to go with, all Markus could do was make the necessary money for watered-down remedies and care for Ruth and pray that someday she would get better.

But still today, it hadn't gotten any better.

It was around mid-afternoon and he was making his rounds for those who hadn't paid their taxes yet. The 'necessary funding' would cripple business and lead many families into starvation, but 'Your sacrifice today will make for a better tomorrow!' Or so Baron Ovid says during his rotational broadcasts throughout the city.

Thanks to the Hunter Black's word, Markus and his sister were given Immunity, which meant no taxes and no mandatory searches from The Guard.

But as for the rest of the kingdom, the people suffered from seizure of all their funds, or worse if unable to pay. Markus being the Guard's errand-boy and given that he and Ruth were untouched compared to many others, didn't go well with his neighbors. In fact, everyone within The Narrows had grown to despise the boy and his little sister.

At this current point in time, Markus was having difficulty with the last home he had to visit in The Narrows. He was on the third floor on one of the industrial buildings. The hallway had broken away and there was a massive gap in the floor which opened up to the streets beyond. The building had been collapsing for years, and the debris had been cleared away before the new season had settled over the city. However the opening in the side of the building allowed the bitter cold winds of winter to enter and billow around Markus as he stood in the broken hallway, waiting for the man in the doorway to finish counting his coins.

"Here ya go, ya bloodsucker." the man said with a toothy scowl while dropping a couple of copper coins into Markus' hand from his own seven-fingered hand.

"C'mon, man," Markus said beneath his scarf that covered his head. "I just make the rounds; I don't decide the taxes. And it's either me, or the Guard."

"Lotta good that does me." the man said taking a tin of tobacco from his overalls and shoving a pinch under his lip. "Get the hell outta here." Then stepping back he slammed the door in Markus' face, leaving him out in the howling hallway.

"Thanks." Markus muttered distastefully as he started for the end of the hall, nearly jumping out of his skin as a chained dog slammed against the chain-link fence that held it in the room it was in. It's saliva sprayed through the fencing and its bald and pink face was snarling with hungry rage.

Deeper inside the opened room was a mother and daughter huddled by a small trash can fire. Just another poor family living off the scraps found wherever they could in The Narrows. When they saw him, the mother scowled and ignored the snarling dog's barking. Markus kept clear away, not wanting to cause trouble as he made his way to the edge of the hall where it broke away and started to climb down carefully. It was like that wherever he went. No one wanted anything to do with him, and treated him like crap wherever he went.

It wasn't like he wanted to be treated fairly by the Guard- least of all working with them. But he needed money, so it helped him to think that anyone else would do the same thing in his and Ruth's position.

After leaping off the first floor and grabbing onto a pipeline that hung on the side Markus slid down and landed onto the side of the roadway. He then passed by one of the towers that used to carry the monorail until the Guard took it all down to provide more room for the drones and Hellhound hovercraft that would fly overhead. When Markus reached his Hoverbike which was parked by one of the sirens that the Baron used to give announcements to the people of Nineveh, he kicked it into gear just as another announcement came on.

"People of Nineveh!" Baron Ovid's voice boomed on the speaker making the wall it was attached to shake. "Remember: report any suspicious people you see in your district! Xerxe soldiers have been reported to be spotted throughout the city, and must be detained! Failure to do so will result in your joining the spies in their demise!"

Ignoring the rest of the speech, Markus started off down the road with the hover-disks lifting his bike off the ground and carrying him to his next destination.

By late afternoon Markus had made it through the Market Area; a long passageway making a square-like encirclement around the castle. The narrow streets were littered with fountains and drains, and before them, shopkeepers would set up booths; selling any goods they had. Food, water, medicine, tools, and even the cybernetic horses or parts for machines used to travel the Wastelands- if one dared to. Sadly, any of the medicine sold here were either painkillers or buck-weed which was mainly used to just simply escape the horrors of the city if you were willing to pay the price for the hallucinate drug.

Because of this, Markus was unable to find any legit medicine for Ruth, and he refused to talk to any of the mages or witches that are said to be wandering in the Market Area. The last thing he wanted to do was get involved with magic. He didn't want to get caught should the Guard happen to know the truth and are waiting for a slip-up, or even run the risk of getting cursed or some other danger when it came to the unnatural.

He rode through dodging pedestrians and small business carts at breakneck speeds. Most people would wreck their bike, or worse kill someone going as fast as he was. However, his experience with his Eagles Wings' which he would use for vast travels throughout the city made Markus an expert in riding hovercraft; hence why The Guard asked for his help in everyday deliveries. As he did so, he spotted a couple of merchants being harassed by members of the Guard. Men garbed in the usual black and crimson power-armor tipped over the cart spilling fresh produce everywhere and when the owner tried to defend his stuff he was shot in the back by one of the captains. Another then unsheathed a metallic sword from his gun, sticking out like a long bayonet and beheaded the man, finishing him off.

Markus was tempted to rush in to help the man before the unfortunate happened, but no one should risk standing against The Guard, especially if they were Captains. Apart from the traditional power-armor that most of the soldiers wore, the Captains would have a gold band around the base of the neckline where the armor broke apart to carbon leather to make it easier to move in. If you ever saw a soldier without his band on, you could tell if they were a captain or not, based on the black lined tattoos on their cheeks- if they took off their helmet at all.

Markus didn't need to have the helmet removed to see that the captain was *smiling* as the shopkeeper collapsed to the ground with a hole in his head, the matter inside now spilling into the slushy roads. The thought, knowing that the Guard enjoyed what they did made him sick, and he wished desperately that he could whip out his concealed pistol and put a stop to them. But between the numbers as well as the Behemoth mech nearby, he knew that it wouldn't be long before he was run down and shot as well.

Many people around the area screamed and started to flee, forcing Markus to slow down to avoid hitting anyone. He watched as the keeper was kicked aside like a sack of garbage as the group of Guard started to go through his things. He watched as the soldiers began gathering up the produce and loading it into a crate that would soon be taken by a nearby Behemoth who stood ready. The man operating the mech kept watch over the citizens who were in a hurry to get away from the grisly scene. The Guard just left the dead man lying there as his blood began to soak into the snow-ridden curb. Those who remained in the Market Area stared somberly at the man and in hatred towards the Guard, but would immediately turn away when the crimson helmets looked their way. Even two years later, the Guards' cruelty to the people of Nineveh hadn't changed.

Markus hated working for them, but money was money, and he needed it. But Markus didn't like to dwell on it too much. He just had to focus on finishing the job, and getting back home as soon as possible. He had to believe that Ruth would be better by the time he turned eighteen and had to leave every day to work in the mines. That was in only a year from now which certainly wasn't a long time. If Ruth wasn't better by then...

No. It wasn't good to think things like that. He had to keep looking ahead, and watch where he was driving to avoid any more present problems. When a clearing finally opened up, he pushed the Hovercraft to go faster, so that he could get further away from the horrible scene he had witnessed.

The city was still covered in a shroud of fear and darkness. The war had not let up in the whole year siege, and on top of that were the whispers that spies from Xerxes had gotten into the city. Assassins have soon been reported, now hunting generals, commanders and servants of the Baron. One had even tried to assassinate the Hunter Black who to Markus' dismay had cleaved the young teen in two like it was nothing. Every time another spy or assassin was spotted- or in most cases accused -the Hunter Black would be called in. On more than one occasion Markus would see him walking about or riding his cyborg horse through the street, sometimes with a body bag across his saddle. He remembered seeing one person he recognized as a regular at Jim's bar, being dragged away by the Hunter Black after having a bounty on his head for suspicion of giving information to Xerxes spies. Markus had never known what a human being looked like on the inside, and he never wanted to see the intestines dragged behind someone ever again.

More bodies had been hung in the street in the past week in general, all now reduced to bones and leathery skin eaten away by the frost. All of them constant reminders of what happened to those who were traitors to The Baron. More people were being caught and tried, and more citizens were found in the crossfire; being accused of aiding Xerxes by spying for them. Jim had been accused several times by officers but they had no proof; and the Baron had never called to have him brought in so the bullying officers had no foothold to torture the old man. Even Black didn't seem interested in the old cyborg in the slightest. But more and more bodies of Xerxe 'spies' were being put out on display; a warning for all who dared to illegally enter the city of Nineveh.

At this point Markus was passing through the district known as Hell's Kitchen. It was here where the so-called 'rich folk' lived. People who could actually afford medicine, food, and even a decent home in old apartment buildings unlike the shacks that were so common throughout the city. Some waved at Markus but he kept going without looking at them. His eyes peered through his special goggles as he eyed his last stop for the evening. He soon slowed down and pulled up alongside a large building a couple of blocks away from the base of the towering castle. Black smoke belched from the chimney, and as Markus hopped off his bike he caught the distinct smell of cooking meat. His stomach growled in his belly but he suppressed the thought of food as he walked up to the front door and pushed his way inside.

The inside of the barracks was dark, lit only by a hazy lightbulb that hung above a desk, the rest of the room lit with small candles that flickered strange shadows upon the walls. Behind the desk sat a man who was typing into an old computer connected by a cord to a small battery. He wore the standard Guard uniform, but his crimson helmet was off, revealing the symbol of Nineveh; a snarling shadow of a wolf's skull with a gun and a sword crisscrossed behind it as it screamed on his left cheek. All members of The Guard were branded as such, so that even when out of uniform the people would know *exactly* who they worked for. But he didn't have any of the branded lines to mark his rank, revealing himself to be a mere grunt. Beside him, a doorway leading to the inner rooms where The Guard slept.

Markus walked over to the desk, the floorboards creaking as he stomped the snow off his boots and removed his scarf. He then slid his goggles off his eyes and over his forehead, holding his long dirty-blonde hair up. The officer looked up at Markus for a minute and then immediately returned his attention to his console. "Gimme a minute." he grumbled, his fingers flying across his keyboard.

"Yes, sir." Markus said in mock kindness. *Respect your Guard as you would respect your Baron, boys and girls.*

As he waited, Markus looked at the door leading to the sleeping quarters and inner offices. It was open and the smell of sweat and the sound of snoring was immense. This was where the human guard slept. The androids which required no sleep patrolled the city day and night, never stopping except to recharge at the battery stations placed in various parts of the city. That was a job Markus himself sometimes had as well; upkeep the stations so The Guard could recharge. It was dangerous work, having to cross some gang territories, or worse, in The Narrows. His reputation was bad enough with what Blacks' protection on his home, if anyone saw Markus helping with the charging stations they would throw rocks or even shoot at him. Thankfully some members of the Guard who stood nearby would end the shooting, but at a terrible price that caused even more outburst towards Markus and even his younger sister. Thankfully, everyone left him and Ruth alone; fearing the wrath of Black or any Guard that might catch them. It didn't make life any easier, but Markus didn't care. As long as he got back home to make sure Ruth was safe and getting better, he would overcome any hardship, even if it cost digging a bullet out or being chased by rabid dogs. He didn't care about anyone in The Narrows', or in the rest of Nineveh for that matter.

As long as Ruth was safe, and got better, that was all that mattered to him now. The rest of the world could freeze over for all he cared.

When Markus heard the striking of keys stop he turned his attention back to the man who was now standing up and holding his hand out, a look of impatience on his face. Markus slipped his backpack off and reached in, pulling out the large purse which held the tax money. He held it out and dropped it into the man's huge hands. The clinking coins jingled in the bag as the man pulled back. "Thank you." the guard said tiredly as he dumped the bag onto his desk.

Markus nodded waiting patiently as the man counted the money. Spilling all the rough-looking coins of copper on the table, the guard counted it out, mumbling under his breath. When he saw that it was all accounted for, he typed it all into the system before scooping it all back up into the sack. "I was promised a chicken, and some water." Markus reminded the man.

"That you were, kid." the guard said. "Says so right here. Kyle's a generous guy that's for sure. Waste, if ya ask me, but, a deals a deal." He stood up and disappeared into the barracks. He eventually returned with a two-gallon jug of water that actually looked clean compared to the water from the fountains throughout the city, which would spew black-sometimes green. He sat it on the desk and held up an old chicken by the leg out to Markus, its body wrapped in foil.

Markus took the chicken and the water gratefully, ignoring the smell coming from the foil. "Thank you." he said.

"Anytime kid. You live in The Narrows, right?"

Markus looked at the man. It was never good news if the Guard ever referred to where he and Ruth lived. "That's right." he answered.

"What's that?" the man asked in a low and threatening tone.

"That's right, *sir*." Markus quickly corrected himself, biting his cheek to keep from adding anything else.

The man nodded with a taunting smirk, making Markus want to punch his in and create a dent if he could. "You look like you're from The Narrows. I have another job for you to do on your way there."

Markus did not want to work anymore today. It was dark now and he had to get to Ruth and cook up some soup for her. But to disobey an officers order was like disobeying the Baron himself. And the Hunters promise would not bind the tyrant.

"What?" he asked unenthusiastically.

"Excuse me?"

"What is it you want me to do, *sir*?" Markus said not bothering to hide the irritation in his voice.

The officer gave him a toothy grin, his gold tooth flashing in the dim light. "Watch your mouth, boy. The other guards ain't as... lenient as I am. I need you to drop something off at the Drunken Badrat."

Markus felt relief flush through his body. He knew the Drunken Badrat well, and he wanted to see if Jim was okay anyway. Maybe the old cyborg will offer him a drink, or even some leftover food someone couldn't finish. Whatever the case may be, it was on the way home so Markus decided he might as well. "Okay." he answered to the guard. The man reached under his desk and held out a glass canister full of an amber liquid. Markus noticed that the bubbles in the liquid were falling to the bottom, instead of rising to the top.

"That's raw Radio-Bronze ore, son." the man explained. "Very volatile when processed into a liquid. So I wouldn't drop it if I were you. That would be... a waste of good money." He chuckled at himself.

Markus gave him a grin which held no joy nor emotion. "Yes, sir."

"Ahh, the boy can learn!" the guard said mockingly. "Well, off with you then! And have a good day too."

After taking the cylinder of volatile ore, Markus turned and walked to the door. "You too, sir," he threw back, and as he stepped outside he heard the man once again typing onto his computer. "Ass." Markus muttered under his breath as he closed the door and tightened his scarf around his neck. He then pulled down his goggles before hopping back onto his bike and riding back home to The Narrows'.

Just another day in paradise.

~ The Elf ~

Markus

Markus reached the Drunken Badrat just a few minutes before the sun finally set beyond the wall.

At this point the streets were now lit by terribly flickering lampposts, casting eerie shadows with the bodies of the deceased against the walls of the nearby buildings. Some beggars, gangsters and even members of the Guard were still in the streets, either loitering or on patrol. Watching the Guard suddenly turn to the beggars demanding for their papers, Markus took his chance to slip away. Keeping his eyes on the ground, Markus killed his bike and walked inside the bar, the flickering sign buzzing above his head. The canister had wobbled the whole ride here so he had to go slower to avoid dropping it. Raw ore was always volatile, but who knows how bad it would be for Radio-Bronze? Markus had not wanted to find out today and he was eager to get rid of it as he pushed the screen door opened and stepped into the warm bar and out of the cold.

He was met with the warm air tinged with the smell of sweat and alcohol. The bar was not full, but there were a few men playing cards at a nearby booth, and some old music was playing on a broken-down jukebox found in the Wastelands. He walked past the few dusty chairs and eyes of both men, women and taxidermy monsters followed him as he walked up to the bar table where an old miner sat drinking from a coffee cup. Judging by the smell there was no coffee in the mug. He took one look at Markus and scowled, turning away and taking a seat further down the bar table.

Didn't want to sit with you anyway. Markus looked at the bartender who was cleaning something behind the long bar table with three of his arms. "Hey Aventis, where's Jim?" he then asked to the mutant's back.

Aventis turned around and gave the boy a lopsided grin. His head was deeply malformed due to radiation, but what made the mutant really stick out was his black eyes and his four arms. He had two normal arms, and two more which stuck from the top of his shoulders. He reminded Markus of a spider almost. Other than that though, Aventis looked completely human, but his four arms would scare many customers away from the bar. But The Narrows had accepted him as one of their own, and Markus had to agree, for Aventis had helped him many times before and Markus the same for him. Aventis smiled and held one hand out to shake, which Markus shook gingerly. It was wet and smelled of spilled booze.

"Marky! Long time no see!" the mutant said with a toothy grin that had stretched from ear to ear.

"How's it going, A?" Markus replied warmly while wiping his hand on the leg of his pants.

"Just dandy. Work, and work. Sorry to say, but Jim's not here at the moment. He was tired so I sent him home."

"You sent *him* home?"

Aventis shrugged sheepishly. Jim was the owner of the bar, and hardly anyone could tell him what to do- save for his daughter Kaltrina, who was a waitress here at the Drunken Badrat. "Old codger has been working himself to an early grave, especially with the walls shakin' at night and such."

Markus understood that. Every so often the city walls would shake due to the Xerxe army on the other side shooting shells at the base, or even the towers along the wall. It always caused quite a stir, especially in the middle of the night.

Markus said, "Okay, well The Guard wants me to give him this." He pulled out the canister of ore for Aventis to see. "Could you...?" He shrugged.

"Of course!" Aventis said grasping it carefully with two hands. "Dangerous stuff, this is."

"Yeah." Markus was glad to finally get it off his hands. "What's it for anyway?"

"Oh, that's a secret." Aventis said with a wink.

Markus raised an eyebrow. "None of my business anyway, I guess."

"Oi, you hear about the army outside?"

"No, Aventis," Markus replied sarcastically. "They've only been hitting our walls for the last few years now, why would I have heard anything about that?"

Ignoring him, Aventis continued to speak. "Well get this: the bastards are running out of options. They are planning a full assault- if they do, they're all dead! The Baron's got an army of Behemoths ready to launch with his androids, they'll run over that army and crush 'em like beetles and then continue to destroy their camps outside! The Baron will make sure they are all either dead or driven back to Xerxes."

"Fascinating." Markus said. It's not like he would have gotten to see what was happening outside the walls anyway. Inside Nineveh, all you did was hear things, not see them. The walls have separated them all from the battle outside for a long while now, but that didn't mean you couldn't occasionally hear the distant thunder of cannons. There was no telling how bad it really was out there; it was anybody's guess.

"Isn't it though?" Aventis agreed, then sighed in contempt. "I'm just tired of the war. It's gotta end soon. Thing is, it's gonna be worse for those who are inside. If word gets to the men who broke into the walls already, they'll warn the army, and they'll just storm through the sewers!"

"They're using the sewers?"

Aventis gave Markus a small wink. "How do you think they got in, in the first place? When it comes to war, one side always falls. Maybe it will be us, maybe it will be them. Either way, us common-folk will be caught in the middle."

"You think that's a way *out* too?" Markus then asked.

Aventis nodded once. "Absolutely. Although, I don't recommend it. The place is sure to be crawling with mutants, Badrats and of course there may still be Xerxe soldiers inside. That, and then there are the Wastelands beyond." He looked at Markus more seriously now. "You're not still thinking of leaving, are you?"

"What if I am?" Markus had been thinking of leaving for the longest time now. To pack up and take Ruth far away from this horrible place. He was getting nowhere with Ruth's illness, and he would be turning eighteen soon. One year may feel like a long time, but what point will it be by then? Besides, he found that even today he was still plagued by what could possibly be out there in the world beyond the walls.

Aventis sighed. "Look, life here sucks, I know that, you know that. But Ruth? You and her won't make it. You're too young, and you don't even have anywhere else to go. Everything out there is a wasteland of tarnished destruction. If the beasts and weather don't kill you, starvation and thirst just might. If you thought of running to Xerxes, forget about it. They would shoot you dead with zero warning. I hate to say it, but it's better in here than it is out there."

"She'll die here anyway." Markus shook his head. He was tired of everyone saying that inside the walls of Nineveh was better than the alternative, but it was pointless to argue with Aventis or anyone here. "But no, I don't plan on leaving any time soon. Don't have the time. But I don't know what to do here."

"Well you know Jim and I are here for you two to help best we can. I wish we could do more, but Jim has his own family, and I don't have much to give at all." Mutants weren't allowed to live in The Narrows. They had to live in concentrated areas close to the tower in the center of the city for The Guard to keep an eye on them. It seemed kind of stupid to Markus, but what did he know?

"I understand. Don't worry."

Aventis meant well. He had a good heart, and Markus respected the mutant tremendously. "Thank you, A."

He gave Markus a small smile. He then reached up with one arm over the shelves and it came back with a tin can with the top welded on. "Here. Soup for the little sick pup."

"You sure you can spare it?"

"Take it." Aventis insisted not going to be taking no for an answer.

"Thank you," Markus said, taking the can with such gratitude. "But what about-"

"Don't worry about it. I gotcha." Aventis gave Markus a wink. "Just don't tell Jim. Come back tomorrow. I got a job to do, but I'd like your help."

If it was a friend, even if they didn't understand, Markus was more than willing to help. In a city where he was on his own, he was willing to do anything for the few friends that he had. "Will do, A. Thanks again!"

"Go on, get out of here," he said waving all four hands and laughing that hoarse laugh of his. Markus, laughing as well, turned and left the bar. He then hopped onto his bike and drove for home. All the way there, Markus could not help but feel ashamed, for his laughter was full of lies and falsehood.

He looked in the direction where the beggars had been, and all he saw was the bloodstains that covered the walls of the buildings they had stood right by. Their corpses, now food for the stray dogs that snarled and gnashed at the beggars with bloody teeth as their shadows were cast onto the walls caused by the trash can fire which continued to burn.

Markus quickly turned away, and hurried on home.

When he finally got home a light snowfall had begun to sprinkle against the metal shack Markus and Ruth called 'home'. He parked the bike into the crowded garage and killed the engine. The battle bot Markus had once worked on stood like a sentry, overlooking all the failed projects that Markus' father would never again finish. Anyone could come in to steal the stuff, it was all just useless machinery at this point. After walking around Markus then stepped inside front door which led to a dark room.

He closed the door behind him and lit a match so that he could light a candle. When the room was illuminated with dim flickering light, he stepped past the small table where he and Ruth would eat their meals. Behind it was a fire pit, a smoke grill hanging above it. Passing the little work desk where he would work on small projects, Markus then grabbed some logs by the stove to his right and then dropped it into the small pit in the middle of the room. He lit another candle and burned some old newspaper before tossing that too onto the logs. Soon he had a little fire going, the smoke drifting towards the grill which would direct it through the hole in their ceiling into the snowy night. When the flames were big enough, Markus crossed over to the door in the back of the shack where he slept with Ruth. He opened the door, and the sliver of light was cast onto the face of his sister.

She looked tired and worn, bundled up in two blankets frayed and worn from years of use, but her smile was full of joy when she saw who it was. "Hey, Mark…" she croaked. Her blonde hair was a rat's nest, and sweat beaded her forehead. She smiled sickly, her brown eyes closed to keep out the glaring light behind her brother.

Markus walked over and gave her a light hug. "I got you some soup today." he said pulling away.

"I'm starving…" Ruth looked at him with glistening eyes as green as the sea, or at least how the sea was described in the books that Markus had read. He figured they had to be as shiny and as green as the great sea, but he figured he would never truly find out.

Markus released her, nodding with a consoling smile. "I know. It'll be ready soon. Do you need anything else?"

"Water…"

He reached into his pack which was still on his shoulders and pulled out the canister of water. He opened the cap and held it up to her frail lips where she sipped delicately. Markus pressed his hand against her cheek. She was burning to the touch despite how much she shivered. "I'll get some soup in you and you'll be a little better." he said. He lost count how many times he had told her that.

"Okay…" When she took another sip, Markus sat the canister beside the cot where she slept before heading back outside.

He reentered the 'kitchen' and placed a pot onto the raised racks they used to boil water. Markus then poured some of the soup he got from the Guard, and he placed the can Aventis gave him earlier into the small cupboard under a small wooden basin. They would use that soup later.

He grabbed a wooden spoon and began to stir the broth of noodles and carrots. He added a pinch of salt. Ruth needed as much water stored in her as Markus could get into her body. After taking the half-rotted chicken he was given, he chopped it up and tossed the chunks into the broth as well. When the soup came to a boil and the meat was cooked, he grabbed a dirty bowl from the cupboard and ladled the steaming broth into it. He then went back into Ruth's room soup in hand, and as soon as the aroma was caught in her nostrils she began to sit up.

"Easy," he said holding her steady. Markus held the bowl out to her which she took with shaking hands, letting the hot bowl warm her small hands. She then blew against the surface of the liquid and began to slurp it up, taking breaks every once in a while to chew the soft noodles and meat.

"The Guard… know how… to make soup." she said between slurps.

"That they do." Markus agreed, helping her down the last of her soup careful not to spill on her. When she cleaned the bowl he asked if she wanted more.

"You should eat." she said.

"You need it more than I do." he answered. In all honesty, Markus was *very* hungry. Any scraps he could gather he would give to Ruth, leaving himself next to nothing. This soup was by far the most decent –and well needed- for Ruth. She needed the food more than Markus. Not only to survive, but to get better. Her sickness was getting worse, and Markus was hoping the soup would help break her fever after it burned whatever was inside of her.

"You need to eat too, Mark."

At that his stomach started to growl again. But he pushed the thought from his mind as he replied with a weak smile. "I'm more worried about you."

Ruth wasn't fooled in the slightest. In fact she looked Markus right into his sapphire blue eyes, not breaking away as she stared him down and said, "You eat a bowl of soup, or I won't have another bite."

"Good grief, Ruth…"

"Get yourself another bowl." she insisted still staring like a mother expecting a child to listen.

Markus shook his head in surrender. "Alright, alright."

Ruth smiled weakly, the weight of her eyes finally lifted from Markus'. "Thank you."

Markus left the room and then came back with two bowls of soup this time. His was less full than hers, but as he promised, Markus got some. He handed Ruth's bowl to her, and sat down on the floor with his back against the wall. They both slurped in silence. The soup tasted great compared to all the scraps and rotten food they've been eating the last few nights. The burning broth cleansed Markus' throat and filled his belly, warming him up from the inside out. When he had cleaned out his bowl, Ruth handed him her empty bowl.

"I'm good." she said.

"There's still a little left in the pot." Markus said to her.

"I don't need anymore." She reached down and took the water canister which she drank. "I honestly just want to sleep." She then laid back down into the bed. Markus got up and pulled the covers over her. He kissed her forehead softly. It burned his lips before they even touched her skin.

"I love you, Ruth." he said.

Ruth smiled as she closed her eyes. "I love you too, Mark." Nothing filled he brother with more joy, than hearing his baby sister say such words. In a world so cold and cruel, those words always lifted Markus' hollow heart.

"Hey, Mark?"

"What is it?"

"Did it snow again today?"

"Harder than last time."

Ruth nodded, her eyes focused on the dark ceiling overhead. She loved the snow, ever since she was a little girl. "I wish I was feeling better."

Markus agreed completely. "Me too." He smiled at her and then flicked her forehead, making her eyes snap down upon him. "As soon as you do, the first thing we'll do is build a snowman together."

That made Ruth smile. "Remember when we used to build forts and have snowball fights?"

"How could I forget?" Markus remembered Ruth so young and full of life creating her ammunition which they would both use to pelt their father with. "I remember you wanting to build a slingshot to hit the signs on the side of the walls."

"That was *your* idea."

Markus chuckled warmly. "You're right, it was."

"Remember the last snowman father built with us?"

Markus smiled but he felt his heart waver slightly. "I do. It was what, twenty feet tall?"

"Ten. No one makes snowmen that big." Ruth coughed in her throat. "But, that was the tallest we ever built one."

"Well, we'll build a bigger one as soon as you are able. This time, it *will* be twenty feet tall."

"Promise?"

"I promise."

Ruth stuck her pinky out and Markus gave her a look that clearly asked if she was kidding. When her expression didn't change, Markus relented his pinky to hers and they shook on it. "I promise." he said again.

"Can't break it now." Ruth smiled victoriously. "None of that 'I'm too old for this' okay?"

Markus laughed. "Okay."

Ruth yawned again, and closed her eyes. "Can you tell me a story, Mark? Like the ones that Daddy used to tell us?"

"Aren't *you* too old for those now?"

"Pfft, you're never too old for stories. Come on, it'll help me sleep."

Markus smiled amusedly and nodded. "Alright, what do you want to hear? The spaceman who tries to come home? Or maybe about the half-vampire who hunts a witch?"

"Tell me the one about Taiyou the Groundling Elf." Ruth smiled tucking her blanket tighter under her chin. "I like that story."

"That one is a fairy tale though."

"So?"

Markus chuckled, remembering how he used to enjoy hearing about the fairy tale when he himself was a little boy. "Alright. Let's see if I can remember it correctly…"

"I'll remind you."

"Then why don't you tell the story then, if you know so much?"

"I want *you* to tell the story."

"Alright, alright." Markus laughed. "Alright, let's see here…" He gathered his thoughts as Ruth tucked herself deeper into her blankets, her eyes set on him in excitement to hear the story.

"There once was a Groundling named Taiyou, who had lost his family in a fire. The young elf was taken to the king, to be cared for until an appropriate foster home was found. The princess, who was a Noble, played with Taiyou like he was a little brother of hers. This caused quite a stir in the castle, for everyone in the royal family was a Noble with beautiful wings that shined like their beautiful eyes, while the Groundlings, the lowest race of elves had no wings and they all feared princess Tsuki's friendship with the boy. Eventually, a home was found for young Taiyou, and he was to be sent away from the castle. Unable to say goodbye, the two friends made a pact, and they promised that one day they would meet up again, and get married. Princess Tsuki gave the Groundling a pendant of an iron rose, as a symbol of their promise. The two then separated, and Taiyou went to the farmland that was separated for the Groundlings away from the Nobles of the kingdom. Time passed, and eventually Taiyou has taken it upon himself to join the kingdoms' army, to earn the royal families trust to become a royal guard so he could be with Tsuki once again.

"However, no Groundling had ever joined the army, for the army was mostly made up of Noble Elves. Any who dared to, risked discrimination and bullying. In fact, the last one who had joined was run out by the soldiers, while the generals laughed at the misfortunate elf. But Taiyou, he wasn't afraid. He was determined to see his princess again, and prove his worth to not only the Royal family now, but to all Nobles in the kingdom. So he fought hard, and trained despite the treatment he received. He trained, and trained, and refused to quit, in hopes of one day achieving his ultimate goal."

Markus paused his story to look at Ruth. The silence beneath her soft breathing proved that she had fallen asleep. He smiled down at her, and reached out to touch her cheek. It burned to the touch, but it proved that she was still here. His own princess, who he vowed to protect.

"Goodnight, Ruth." he whispered. After taking the now empty bowls from supper, he then stepped outside and closed the door, shutting her into darkness. He wished her sweet dreams, and sighed happily that she was alive another day.

Markus then walked over to his workbench and removed his dagger from his belt. It was simple with a leather handle, but it had the same blade and crystal from his father's staff. He had the weapon modified so that it would telescope and collapse into a large dagger. The staff bit would slide down to the size of the handle, where the blade and blue crystal would stick out. It made carrying it a little easier. After setting the dagger onto the table, Markus crossed the room and also sat the empty bowls there where he could wash them in the morning. He walked over to the pot and looked inside where the last bit of broth was. He thought of just letting it simmer throughout the night so Ruth could eat in the morning.

But at that moment Markus heard the sound of a Guard whistle outside his shack. Three short blasts. They were chasing someone. A thief maybe, or a Xerxe soldier. Or just another poor soul they wanted to torture. Markus shook his head, ignoring the whistle blows. He turned to head for his work at the desk.

He had just reached it when the door to the shack slammed open, blasting the room full of cold air before it slammed shut again. Markus shot up in a flash and he flicked a switch on the dagger and it extended into the same staff his father once used. Then holding the staff up, he then aimed the blade and the jewel at the intruder who had trespassed into his home.

It was a girl.

She about his height, with dark auburn hair, scraggly and undone. Her moon-shaped face was dirty and stricken with fear, and her clothes were ragged and worn out. She had no boots on her bare feet, which were red from frostbite. Markus recognized her. She was a girl he had seen in the Market Area. She was a street rat; a known thief. Her green eyes were wide with fear, and in her dirty hands she held a half-eaten apple. She was panting heavily, and when another whistle was sounded her head darted towards the sound. *She* was the one they were chasing.

"Get out." Markus said immediately, his eyes set cold and threatening to the girl.

"Wait! Please…" she begged turning to him. Her voice sounded so afraid and fragile, as if she was made of glass and might possibly shatter. "I gotta hide. Please, you gotta hide me!"

Markus wasn't going to have any of it. "I don't want any trouble. My family and I don't need you bringing the Guard in here. Get out of here. Get out!" he said much sterner than before. He lifted his staff a little higher, flicking a switch and making it hum to life in order to show her that it was loaded and ready to fire at her.

The girl continued to look desperate. Looking between Markus and the door behind her. "Please! I'm begging you, please help me." she looked so pitiful and scared that Markus almost felt sorry for her.

"Just get out of here!" He flicked the switch on his fathers' staff and the sapphire crystal began to hum and glow. "I'm sorry, but it's not my problem. Get the hell out of here, *now!*"

"Markus!" Markus looked through his peripheral vision to see Ruth standing in the doorway, covered with a blanket and holding a closed fist close to her lips.

Why are you out of bed!? "Ruth, get back to bed." he said turning his attention back to the street rat that barged into their home. "She is leaving before the Guard comes in and takes us all away."

"Sir, please!" the girl begged now starting to cry.

"Don't 'sir' me! I want you out!" Markus said. "I don't need you getting us in trouble when the Guard comes in. It's either you, or all of us. So, I'm warning you right now: get the hell out of my house!"

"Markus!" Ruth cried pleading. "Please. We can help her!"

"No, we *can't* Ruth." Markus said in a low and impatient voice. "If they find her in here we'll all get shot. You know the Guard has no mercy- especially for children."

"But won't Black's sanction protect us?"

"For the love of- That won't matter if the Guard finds her here!"

"What about the basement?"

"What about it?" The whistles were getting louder and Markus heard voices coming towards the shack, but he kept his focus on the girl before him.

"We can hide her in there!" Ruth exclaimed.

"And if she gets caught?" Markus demanded trying to make his sister use her head. "Then what? We'll get arrested- or worse! She needs to leave, Ruth!"

"If you hide me," the girl said. "I'll leave as soon as they do and never come back again. If I get caught, I won't say a word about you. I promise!"

"How do I know you'll keep your word?" Markus demanded. "You can't trust anyone anymore, not in this armpit of a city."

"Please, I'm begging you!" Her tears were now dripping onto the floor. "You're my only hope!"

The door shook as fists began to bang on the door. "Open up in the name of the Baron!"

On some strange whim, Markus cursed and threw up the rug beneath him where a trap door was hidden, leading to the basement. He opened it up and jerked his head towards it. The girl ran inside quickly and quietly, her eyes thanking Markus as she hopped into the hole in the floor.

"Do *not*, make a sound." Markus hissed as he closed it and threw the rug back on top. As soon as the rug was straightened out and he stepped back, the door banged again. "I'm coming!" he called out sheathing his weapon back into a dagger which he placed on the table. "Go to bed Ruth. *Now*."

She nodded and ran inside closing the door silently behind her. His hand barely touched the old knob when it was kicked open by a droid.

"Hey!" Markus spat as he leapt back to avoid getting hit. "What is this?!"

The droid ignored him and began sweeping the house, its eyes scanning the entire room. It went over to Ruths' room and kicked it in. Ruth began to scream. "Hey!" Markus was about to run to the droid when a hand grasped the neck of his coat. "Get away from her, you bucket of bolts!"

"Mind your manners." said a gruff voice that belonged to the hand that grabbed him.

Markus looked back to glare at the Guard holding him. Her head was covered with the Guards uniform helmet which would encase the entire head into a shell of black metal. A hiss came from the neck and the helmet peeled back and folded to reveal her face. The woman's head was shaven and her tattoo was fresh on her cheek, joined by many others that seemed to cover a good portion of her skin. She was a captain; a higher ranking officer in charge of the manhunt for the girl Markus gathered.

"We're looking for a thief." she said giving Markus a look of disgust. She released his coat and allowed him to turn to her. "Neighbors say she ran in here."

"There's no one here," Markus said jerking his coat out of the guard's hand. "Just me and my sister. And now, you two."

"Watch your mouth." the Guard said as she smacked his cheek. It stung and there was now a ringing in his ear. Markus gave her a dirty look as he rubbed his face. The droid came out of the room alone.

"Clear." It said in its mechanical voice.

"Mark!" Markus then heard Ruth cry out.

"It's fine, Ruth." he said still eyeing the Guard with murderous intent. "They'll be out soon."

The Guard looked down at Markus and gave him a smirk. "Say," she said. "Aren't you Kyle's delivery brat? Ha!"

"Shut up." he said without thinking.

"Excuse me!?" The woman smacked him again, harder this time and making him fall to the floor. As he began to push himself back up she then kicked Markus in the belly, knocking all the air out of his lungs. Markus gasped and groaned in pain as the foot came back down on his body, crushing him into the floor. "You mind your manners to your superiors, kid. You'll live longer."

"Enough, Akira." an emotionless voice said behind her. They all looked and to Markus' horror, there in the still open doorway stood the Hunter Black, His black armor shone dimly in the firelight, and his cloak billowed in the snowy wind. His head was still covered in his black shroud, and at his hips were his guns and his thigh pack. Across his back was that dreadful blade he used to slay Johnathon. Markus forgot all the pain in his stomach as he glared at Black with a look of hatred and anger.

"That's enough." the Hunter said again to the Guard.

"Yes, sir." the girl said backing off. The pressure of her boot gone, Markus was able to breathe again. "Stand up." she told him. Markus coughed and struggled to get up, using a chair for support, his eyes flashing still at Black, bearing right through his armor and through his very soul.

"The thief is not here?" Black asked the android standing by quietly.

"No, sir." muttered the droid as it shuffled its foot nervously. The R.U.R models were so life-like it was hard to believe that it was artificial it looked so human- aside from the skin that was just a shade paler than normal.

"Then we have no reason to be here." Black then said. The Guard who had kicked Markus had noticed the soup simmering in the pot and had dipped one of the bowls into it. She scooped some up and drank from it noisily. She looked at Black and offered the rest, but he shook his head. She shrugged and drank the rest.

"I apologize for the intrusion." Black said to Markus.

"Sure you do." he snidely replied.

"Hey, nice." the Guard, Akira, had found Markus' dagger on the table and flicked the switch, extending it into the staff. She was startled at first but then she looked it over with impressed eyes. "Very nice."

"Hey!" Markus said starting towards her. She flicked the staff up, pressing the blade against his throat, stopping him in his tracks. The point had stuck the skin lightly but it was sharp enough to draw a small trickle of blood down the boy's neck. Markus didn't move an inch as he glared at the Guard. She merely smiled back, daring him to keep coming.

"That's enough." Black said again in a harsher tone. "Put the staff down."

Akira looked over at her superior. "C'mon sir, you know the rules about weapons. Guns swords or-"

"Put it down." Black said. "I have given this man complete permission to keep that weapon."

Markus shifted his eyes over to the Hunter. "A promise you made to his dead father." the Guard argued.

"Would you like to discuss this outside?" Black said placing his hand at his hip where his shotgun hung. The Guard went pale and retracted the staff back into a knife.

She dropped it onto the table with a slap. "*Fine.*" she said.

"Do *not* disobey me again." Black said. His words were so cold that they brought a greater chill than the snow outside ever could.

Akira glared at him. "Just because you like these brats does not give you-"

"Silence!" Black said in a low but stern voice. The droid began to shift uneasily. It was as if the cold atmosphere had completely engulfed the group. "Argue with me again," Black said in a calmer tone of voice. "And I'll relieve you from your duty. Permanently." It was not an idle threat.

Akira stared at Black unbelievably. "Why you…"

"Yes?" Black asked his hand now gripping his shotgun in a gloved hand.

Akira lowered her eyes like a dog who disobeyed her master. "Nothing, sir." The Guard said quietly with her head lowered. "Nothing at all, sir."

"Good." Black said stepping aside and leaving the open door clear. "Now you both check the other buildings. I'll catch up."

"Yes, sir." they both said and ran back out into the night, eager to leave the sight of the Hunter. Akira gave one last look at Markus and whispered to him, "Someday I will make you sorry." She then disappeared with the droid into the harsh cold that continued to blow outside.

Black looked back at Markus, his face emotionless and his voice when he spoke just as indifferent. "I apologize, again."

Markus sneered at the man. "Whatever." Black said nothing to that comment. He looked past Markus and he turned to see Ruth watching them from her room. "Go to bed, Ruth," he said.

Ruth began to pull the door shut. "Okay…"

"Thank you."

"Goodnight, Miss." Black said to Ruth.

When Ruth was gone Markus turned back to Black. "I didn't need your help."

Black's eyes drooped slightly. "Could have fooled me."

"I don't *want* your help."

Black said nothing for the longest time. It amazed Markus how quiet the man was.

"Do you really hate me that much?" he finally asked, his voice soft with curiosity or mere spitefulness, it was hard to tell.

Markus had nothing to say. Honestly, there was nothing he *could* say. He *did* hate Damion Black. Every fiber of his being, he *hated* him. Markus cursed the Hunter from the heavens above to the depths of hell where he belonged.

Outside another whistle was blown. Black turned his head to the sound, and then he then looked back to Markus. He nodded his departure, and left closing the door behind him, shutting out the darkness outside.

Markus sighed in anger and turned to the rug. In his anger he tore the rug away and threw open the trapdoor to reveal the girl who cowered behind her hands. "They're gone," he said to her. "Get out." Lowering her hand's, the girl climbed out thanking him over and over again. Without a single word, she crawled out the broken window, took one last look at Markus, and then disappeared into the night. Markus cursed again and then blew out the candle. He locked the door and then closed the broken window. He then took a pail of water he and Ruth would use to wash in, and poured it over the flames of the fire pit, extinguishing them in a flash of steam.

What a night... He eventually thought to himself as he stood in the smoky darkness.

He walked into his and Ruth's room and laid on the little pile of blankets he had set aside for himself to sleep in so Ruth could have the whole bed. He could not afford to get sick too. Markus zipped his coat tighter and curled up into his blankets. He heard Ruth say goodnight and that she loved him. He replied as such, and then they both fell asleep as the sounds of the never truly sleeping city sounded around them. The day's tasks and the final situation at hand had worn Markus out worse than any other day. The break-in, the Guard, Black, and then that girl. All this he just wanted to forget in the land of the dreaming. And as he closed my eyes, Markus slipped into the black and disappeared into his own world, where his dreams flew free and full of memories full of both happiness and monstrous images.

His dreams were like that; caged beasts that tore at his mind every night even after a whole day of suffering with his sister.

There was never any peace, not even in his own world.

~ Legends of Old ~

Markus
The next morning would be known as the day the war was over… for the time being.

    The armies of Xerxes, fearing for the lives of their soldiers, retreated further into the wilderness as they attempted a final stand. For what Aventis told Markus and everyone last night was true: The Baron had sent his legion of androids to wipe out the men who stood and fought, while sadly unbeknownst to them, he had also sent his Behemoths out to hunt down the deserters. The giant battle-mechs, some standing over a hundred feet high of Bronze alloy and armed with missiles and lasers, ran the deserters down like roadkill. The men were slaughtered by the droids and the Guard, while the other side was crushed under the heels of the Behemoths. All the while the Baron watched in his Firefly chopper high above the bloody battlegrounds. When the last Xerxe soldier was killed, cornered by the droids and mechs, the Baron reclaimed the fields beyond the city walls. The mine north of the city, where Ebony-Bronze Ore was mined, was also reclaimed. The Baron, took back his prize, and immediately, mere hours after the enemy was annihilated, sent some miners and droids to those very mines to dig. It was a victory for the Baron and his men, but misery for the civilians.

    In retaliation of their army's annihilation, the Xerxe soldiers that had managed to make it into the walls through the sewers attacked the Guard within the city itself. Soldiers were found hiding in the homes of some of the civilians inside the city. And whether they meant to hide them or not, those families were burned along with the soldier or runaway in their own homes. Some smaller Behemoths were also dispatched to reclaim order within the walls as well; and to keep watch over the soldiers dealing with the remaining rebellion. Some who had begun to run from the mechs' were immediately gunned down by the Behemoth's Gatling's, the bullets tearing through their flesh and painting the snowy streets crimson.

Some suicide bombers had taken refuge in The Narrows' and would run up to one of the Behemoths and blow themselves up in hopes of taking as many of the Crimson Guard as they could. Throughout the day the sound of explosions and gunshots rang through the district, taking with them many lives and resulting in the destruction of many homes and shops. It was a constant battlefield, and anyone caught in the middle of it be it citizen or otherwise was gunned down as well. The infiltrating Xerxe soldiers made a final stand near one of the collapsed buildings close to where Markus and Ruth lived. To kill them all, The Guard blew up the base of the building, making it collapse into the streets. Any Xerxe soldier unfortunate enough to still be alive was shot where they laid crushed in the rubble, making their blood flow like a river down the frozen roadways.

To the Baron and the castle, this was the day of Jubilee, the dawn of a new day. To the civilians, this was the day the snow fell red, for many were sacrificed, or taken away never to be seen again. All day Markus hid with his sister, not caring about the job Aventis had. Markus just wanted to stay under the covers with Ruth, hiding with her from the horrors of the world. While the city was ravaged and burned- 'cleansed' as they called it, the Baron had his army of robots return to the castle. The Guard were now celebrating in their barracks, while little Ruth coughed beneath the covers with Markus who kept alert. For the day was not over, and any rebel or Xerxe soldier that could possibly come in, he would have no choice but to do what was necessary for his and Ruth's safety. He did not rest, even when the last gunshot took the life of the last spy in Nineveh.

When night rolled by all was quiet once more. The sounds of gunfire and the smell of smoke slowly faded away, and Markus decided to creep outside to check what was up. Most of the buildings were liberated, some families and businesses were attempting to fix them up before the evening cold blew in.

Overhead, Firefly choppers and Hellhounds buzzed over the buildings; and a stray Behemoth marched down the streets, it's robotic head on the swivel as well as its Photon Rifle. It had appeared to look at him, but the driver kept the mech moving. Markus didn't dare to breathe until the robot was out of sight. He turned to the building that had been brought down, seeing many people digging through the bloodied rubble for their loved ones. But many had been taken for Xerxe soldiers and had been killed when the Guard shot up the rubble. One woman in particular, the same one that Markus saw in the apartments with the dog and daughter, was holding a broken figure in her arms, howling in despair at the moon that shined on overhead. No one moved in to help her, no one seemed to care. They had to care for their own, and search for their loved ones- or whoever was left.

From one of the sewer drains a broken figure had crawled out. He had a laser rifle in one hand, while the other was missing completely at the elbow. It was a kid, no older than Markus and having black hair instead of blonde. He wore a torn up and dirtied trench coat, and beneath the opened flaps Markus was able to clearly see the black armor from Xerxes. Blood stained the front, dripping into the snow and steaming in the cold. The boy turned his head to Markus who stood planted in front of his home, and opened his mouth which was spilling blood.

The Guard was now doing a sweep of the sewers, making sure that no more rats had attempted to hide in the sludge. This had to be one of the last survivors, and he was hurt, *badly*. Markus took a step back, reaching for his concealed pistol which was tucked in his belt.

"He… help me…" the boy croaked, spilling blood all over his front. He dropped his weapon, and reached out to Markus with a bloodied hand. "Help me…"

"Get back." Markus said gripping his gun with a tight hand. "I don't-"

Whatever he was about to say was cut off when a bolt of concentrated energy struck the boy in the chest, sending him falling back as a smoldering mark hissed smoke from the shot. He laid there dead, his guts cooked by the shot. Markus looked to the side to see a Guard coming his way. He hunched over the boy and checked for a pulse. Then as what must have been just an insult, the man even stomped down on the kid's head, smashing it like a watermelon. Markus forced himself to look away, not wanting to look at the gruesome scene. In his final attempt to survive, the boy had been shot dead with zero warning.

Markus didn't know whether to feel relief that he didn't have to deal with it, or disgust with the death of the kid.

"You okay, civilian?" the Guard asked his voice robotic beneath his beetle-like helmet.

"I'm fine." Markus said eager to get away.

"Stay clear, we'll be done here soon."

"Right," Markus didn't need to be told twice as he backed up and returned to his home.

He then decided to check on Jim and Aventis. Anything to get rid of the gruesome image in his head. Markus ran into the garage and pulled out his Eagles Wings; The glider-like pair of wings made of bronze suppressed into a small backpack until they were released. The booster rockets could help him travel clear across the city in nearly no time at all. Flying overhead was risky, for the Baron's forces were known to shoot anything in their airspace-or worse- run into the flyer with their own choppers or cruisers. If a drone caught wind of him, he would definitely be captured and questioned. Markus had his share of close calls in the past, but he wanted to see how bad the carnage was when the purging of the city began on his way to the Drunken Badrat.

He strapped the backpack-like container onto his shoulders and kicked on the rocket boosters. After he was launched a good fifty feet into the air, the wings emerged from the pack and extended as a nerve-connector clipped onto the back of his head. Once he was stabilized in the air, he propelled forward and then took off, flying into the night while the snow beat against the wings and the parts of his face where his scarf did not cover. To the people below him, they probably thought he was some giant bird flying overhead. Hopefully that kept them from asking the Guard to take a look.

After a minute or so of flying over the devastated city, the smoke rising to the heavens too much for his nostrils to handle, Markus landed just outside the Drunken Badrat. Snow kicked up as his wings retracted back into the small black backpack. He then ran inside and closed the door behind him, shutting out the cold and harsh snow. He felt the nerve connector finally come loose and then it too folded back over the backpack.

Members of The Guard sat in the back corner of the tavern, toasting their victory. One of the waitresses- Kaltrina, Jim's daughter- was serving them large mugs of draft beer which foamed over the top and fell to the floor to be licked up by the rats. The Guard Captain and lead commander, Veegar, stood among them, giving out a speech. Something about victory for the Baron, death to the Xerxe scum and vermin outside the walls, victory for Nineveh etcetera, etcetera. Around the room typical commoners were sitting drinking and eating with their heads lowered as if to avoid attention. What caught Markus' eye however was who was sitting in the back corner of the bar alone with a pint in his hand, sipping gingerly with tight lips.

It was the Hunter Black. His cloak was laid to the side and hanging off the edge of his seat, his shroud lowered for him to drink and Markus could clearly see his features. His face was still untouched by radiation or sickness, leaving it smooth and as pale as freshly fallen snow. His eyes were dark and brooding under a pair of trimmed eyebrows. What surprised Markus was the fact of how clean-shaven he was; not a single hair protruded his handsome face. Black turned and caught the boy staring at him, and Markus quickly turned away and went over to the bar table where Aventis was pouring drinks with two hands and serving dishes with the others. Jim stood behind the register counting up orders and handing some to the cooks in the back along with shouting orders to Kaltrina who looked on the verge of collapsing. Markus said hi as she darted past him and then he took a seat in front of Aventis who smiled.

"Still alive, I see?" the mutant asked in a tiresome voice.

"Somewhat," Markus answered. He couldn't get the face of that boy to escape his mind. "Our side didn't get hit as bad as the north wall, but the soldiers that got in started bombing themselves in The Narrows' closest to the taller buildings, where the monorail used to be. They're all dead now, I think. Ruth finally fell asleep again."

"Good, good. I'm glad you guys are okay. How is she anyway?"

"Same. I wasn't going to leave until the noise died down." He left out the story of the kid who died right in front of him. The less he tried to think about it, the more likely the memory would go away- at least that was what Markus hoped.

Aventis nodded solemnly. "Hey, on that particular subject… I know you don't like help, but there's a sorcerer, here in Nineveh. A woman who knows the arts used in the ancient times, thousands of years before the war. She could possibly heal Ruth..."

Markus wasn't going to have any of that. "No." he said immediately.

"Listen, Marky, she ain't one of those witches who call upon the demons to cast their will. This woman, she knows potions. She knows medicine and healing magic. She could help."

"I don't want her help." Witches were nothing but trouble, demonists or otherwise, and Markus wanted no part of it. Whether this sorceress was a witch or not, it wouldn't do him any good to ask for her help. They were rumored to always expect a payment that no one could afford. Many have lost their lives or the lives of others because of their asking for help with the dark arts. That was just tempting fate, and he wasn't going to test his fate any more than it already was.

Avenits held two hands up as if Markus had been holding a gun to him. "Okay, okay. Just wondering." He lowered them and then added, "She said she used to live in Eden."

"The lost gardens?"

"The same. Says it got overrun by pirates and mutants. It's gone."

"Like many of these 'magical places' it seems. I wish I could see it."

"Don't we all." He leaned in close to Markus. "You want anything to drink?"

"I don't have money." A lie, but he definitely didn't have enough to spare for a drink.

A hand rested on one of Aventis' shoulders. "It's on the house. One drink." Said the owner, Jim. He smiled at Markus under his whiskers. "We got some old Cola off of some of the dead rebels."

"What's that?" Markus asked.

"Here." Jim reached under the counter and came back up with an old can. It was dirty but Markus could still see the red and blue colors and the words that read 'Cola'. "Try it."

He popped the can open and took a small sip. The drink stung for a moment from the sugar but Markus found it delicious. He felt bubbles pop and rise in his stomach and escape through his throat, making him burp. He drank some more and then sat it down on the bar half-empty. "That's *really* good. I'll take the rest to Ruth to try it."

"Make sure you do," said Jim. He gave a small smile which disappeared when the sound of a glass hitting the ground came to their ears. They all turned around to see the guards staring at a spill of shattered glass and bubbling beer.

"Hey waitress!" A guard called. "We need another! Hurry up!"

"Coming!" Kaltrina said running past Markus again with a fresh mug in her hand. Her face was beaded with sweat and she looked simply exhausted.

"Busy much?" Markus muttered to the two bartenders.

"That's for sure." Aventis said. He winked at Markus. "Snuck some sleeping medicine in the beer. They'll be out soon."

"Not soon enough." Jim muttered. "But the sooner they fall asleep the quieter it'll be. They still got a huge mess to clean up out there. Do they have any idea how many homes were destroyed? How many lives were lost on their little witch-hunt for Xerxe soldiers?"

"You think 'his majesty' cares?" Aventis asked.

The cyborg grumbled. "Good point."

"By the way," Markus said. "Why's Black here? I've never seen him in here before."

"Neither have I." Jim said. "I'm just as surprised as you are. He said he was tired and needed a drink. Naturally, he ordered one and Kaltrina gave him one. He's been silent most of the night and only asked for one refill. He's a lot easier to deal with than those grunts over there."

"Weird." Markus said wishing The Hunter wasn't here. "He's not welcome here."

"Not to you anyway." Jim pointed out. "But he ain't causing trouble. Besides, beer ain't cheap." The cyborg leaned over to him, his false eye seeming to zoom in on the boy in front of him. "Besides, you've got to let that go, Markus."

Markus stared at the man. He felt a spark of anger light up in his heart. "How can you tell me that? He killed my father, Jim."

"I know, I know. But he had his orders from the Baron. You really think he wanted to?"

"He's a Hunter. It's what he does. He murders people."

Jim fell silent. He couldn't disagree with Markus.

Yes, Black had his orders. Yes, he's skilled in the art of hunting and killing criminals and monsters that threaten 'the good of the city', but there was no way Jim could convince Markus that Black was the victim. He lived for his job. To assassinate anyone the Baron wanted gone. He took Johnathon, Markus' own father without a second thought and many more before him. What's worse; he actually made a huge show of it for all to see. Deep in his heart, Markus hoped that when his time did come, Black would die a horrible, horrible death. He deserved it.

His thoughts were broken when Markus was shoved to the side, causing him to fall to the ground at the feet of the Guard member responsible. The disgusting wooden floor was sticky with dried beer and crumbs of rotten food. He turned and glared at the Guard venomously.

"Move it, kid." he grumbled down to Markus. "Hey, you old coot, gimme another beer."

"Yes, sir." Jim said reaching behind him for the drink. He flashed a senile smile, but Markus could see right past the teeth that he was pissed at the Guard. He filled a mug and handed it to the man who gulped it down fast before slamming it onto the table shattering it. He then turned to Markus who had pulled himself up. "What a'ya looking at?" he demanded.

"Nothing, sir." Markus muttered clearly showing his anger. He wanted to wipe the smirk off the mans' face, and rip off the mustache over his lips.

The man turned and looked at the boy, picking up on the detest in Markus' voice. He reeked of alcohol and his nostrils flared with rising anger; as if he could smell the lies. "Got a problem with me, boy?"

"Not that I'm gonna say." Markus said. Aventis was giving him a throat-slashing signal but Markus ignored him; his eyes never wavering from the Guard in front of him.

The Guard sneered. He grabbed the scruff of Markus' coat and lifted him off the ground. "You need a beating, boy? Learn a little respect for the men who saved you?"

"And destroyed half the city?" Markus said defiantly, holding the man's wrist to prevent himself from getting choked by the scruff of his jacket. "Yeah, thanks a *lot*." He cringed when he saw the mans' fist come up to his face.

"That's enough," a low voice stopped the guard. He looked past Markus who looked back likewise. Black was still sitting there unmoving. But from his lips came more words. "Leave the child alone, Gru."

The guard let Markus go and snickered at the man who sat quietly taking another sip. "Whaddya care?"

"Leave the child alone." Black said again in his unexpressive voice still sitting as still as a statue. "He has done nothing wrong. You know I hate repeating myself."

"He's disrespecting my authority. My honor!" Gru argued.

"A man with no honor *can't* be disrespected."

A few members of the Guard chuckled at the remark, but Gru gaped at the Hunter. "How dare you?" Gru growled. Behind him, Veegar had stepped forward, and the Guard behind him had also stood up. "You say I don't have honor eh? Veegar, tell'im he's in the wrong!"

"Gru, take it easy," Veegar said with a calming hand but making no attempt to leave his spot. "You're drunk."

"And he's an asshole!" Gru snapped pointing at the Hunter.

"You have been under his command for a *month*." Black continued not looking at the man. "Yet you now feel the need to harass the very citizens you 'protected' in today's battle."

"This coming from a *Hunter*." Gru spat on the floor before Black. "You have no right to accuse me of only doing what is my right."

Black turned his head to look at the man. "Under the circumstances, I'm sure the Baron would *love* to hear what you have just said. And this coming from me will not only harm your reputation worse than you have already, but he might make sure you can never embarrass the Guard ever again."

Captain Veegar went pale and Gru began to shake; his face was blood red with anger. "You spineless creep!"

"That's enough, Gru." Veegar said. The old man's voice was stern but not unkind. It was full of concern and worry of what Black might do. "He's being as patient with you as it is."

Gru turned to the old commander and laughed in disbelief. He turned back to Black. "You think you're so high and mighty Black? After being found in the Wasteland by the Baron, you think yourself better because you know how to clean up messes and scare the living daylights out of people. Well not me, no sir! Screw that!"

He then clicked a button on his armor and the suit began to shift into scale-like plates, making him seem larger. A helmet popped from the back and strapped over the man's head. In his now fully-engaged power-armor suit, he seemed twice as big as he once was. His helmets glass face revealed his gruesome grin along with little lights and gauges where he could see hydraulics and armor damage as well as different weapon systems built into the suit.

"You think you're so tough, pal?" Gru demanded loudly his voice low through the speaker. "Standing up for a useless brat like him? Against a man like me, I'd like to see you actually earn your title, 'Hunter'."

The Hunter didn't even bat an eye. "Your incompetence is only embarrassing your commander." Black said setting his mug down now empty. Immediately, Veegar retreated back to his tables nervously. Everyone else just stared in wonder, eager to see what would happen next. "I suggest you power down before you embarrass Veegar any further." Black continued. "You have already dug your hole deep enough. You really want to dig any deeper?"

"Ha! That's a lot of talk, for a scrawny bastard like you."

"Gru!" Veegar exclaimed almost comically frightened. "That's enough. Stand down, soldier!"

"Yes, please," Jim said eager to make sure nothing happened in his bar. "Please, enough."

Gru aimed a fist at Jim, which opened up to reveal a plasma gun, capable of leaving no mark on the body but cook it from the inside out with its concentrated energy. "You stay out of this, you old fart." He turned back to Black, his fist still aimed at Jim who began to whimper. "I'll be damned before I let a lowlife like *you* boss me around. Everyone else might be scared, but I ain't! I'll beat you to a bloody pulp!"

"Then why do you look so tired?" Black asked suddenly. Behind Gru, Veegar had taken a seat, his head in his hands. His men around him were likewise now falling asleep at their table. Gru, who did not notice his comrades, began to sway. He staggered for a bit, using the bar table for support. As he tried to steady himself, he saw Black coming his way slowly and calmly as if he knew what was happening. "I will deal with you when you awaken." Black said as Gru fell face-first onto the floor with a thundering crash.

Black laid some coins onto the table, then walked over to Gru and hit the disengage lock at the neck of the suit. The suit retracted back into the normal armor. He then took the now sleeping Gru by the arm and began to drag him to the door.

"Thank you for the drinks." he said to Jim as he walked by. "Next time, try to avoid putting a sleeping drug in my beer, if you please."

"Um yes… Of-of course." Jim said flabbergasted. Markus couldn't help but stare at wonder same as everyone else who was still awake.

"Thank you." Black said and with that he dragged the sleeping Guard outside into the cold, leaving the others to sleep peacefully where they sat or laid.

"Wow." Markus said, clearly impressed despite his hatred for The Hunter. "What will happen to him? The Guard, I mean."

"I don't know." Aventis said broodingly. "But it cannot be good."

Jim nodded, looking at the men who continued to sleep with beer-drenched armor. "At least it now got quiet…"

"Indeed." Markus said, slightly disturbed at what he had just witnessed.

"I swear, he is like a legend," Kaltrina said coming up to the group dreamy-like. "He is so handsome and brave, like one of the heroes from Levitika."

Markus had to swallow bile at that comment.

"Hero?" Jim said with a sneer. "Pah!"

Also irritated, Markus grumbled to Kaltrina. "He's no hero."

"He *could* be." she argued. "He has the demeanor for it."

"Next thing you'll be saying is that he's some sort of angel," Jim snorted. "Some godsend dressed in wolf's clothing."

"He certainly has the face of one." Kaltrina said now just teasing her father. "All he needs is a pair of wings- maybe golden wings!"

"Ha! Just like the old legends," Aventis muttered with a sigh.

"Yes! That's right!" Kaltrina said smiling at the mutant. "Just think what it would be like if he was a descendant from the City of Angels."

Aventis sighed again. "The City of Angels… Haven't heard anyone say that name in a long while."

Curious at the mention of the name, Markus looked at the mutant. "What's that?" he asked. "Another fabled city full of magic and dreams, like Eden?"

Aventis looked at Markus as if he had not heard him. "Beg your pardon?"

"The City of Angels," Markus asked again, this time being a little more serious than he had been before. "What is that?"

Aventis released a puff of air from the corner of his mouth. He turned to Jim who cleared his throat. He leaned on top of the bar to Markus, making himself comfortable.

"The City of Angels is said to be a 'magical' kingdom which floats high above the Wastelands on a stone island. You ever heard of the floating isles?"

Markus nodded. The floating isles were known as masses of earth that were lost high in the earths thinning atmosphere, whether by the radiation in the soil or some strange sorcery or even some strange new technology which kept them afloat. Some floating cities of metal were made to represent the floating isles, until they fell back to earth one by one, decimating entire villages. Some villages even lived among them high above the world, only to be sacked by pirates or Ahools who plunder the skies in search of prey. They used to be common, but since the war, many floating cities have fallen back down to earth where they belonged.

"Well," Jim continued. "The City of Angels, was once a city near the Razor-Back Mountains known as Levitika. It had defied The Capitol back in its Golden Age, and in the end, it is told that the city had taken flight, and now resides in the clouds as a floating city. No one knows how it happened, but no one ever laid eyes on the city again. They call it 'The City of Angels', because those who claim to have spotted it, said they've seen men with wings. Kind of like you and your Eagles Wings, except, they were of pure gold like a true angel of old. Many have tried to find the city, but none have found it- or returned at all. Some say the people who find it are never seen again. Whether they died trying to get in, or succeeded in entering and ended up staying there, is still a mystery."

Markus was deeply intrigued in the description of the floating city in the sky. He had often dreamed of great castles in the clouds, and wondered if it would ever be possible to live in a place far away from here.

"Is this real, or a legend?" he then asked.

"Oh it's a real legend." Jim winked at his joke. "But it's as old as the war itself. Your father was actually an explorer before being forced into The Guard and the mines, before he met your mother I believe."

"Really?" Markus knew his father came from the Wastelands, same as his mother but he never knew his father was actually an explorer.

"That's right. He said he saw a castle, enveloped in the clouds as he was sailing to one of the old compounds in the north. He said he saw a whole community of people up there, humans, mutants, droids; all of them living in peace away from the rest of the world. When John had returned and told everyone, no one believed him."

"Sounds hard to believe anyway." Markus admitted.

"Sure does. But he swore on his life that it was real. In fact, his last voyage he took a detour to try and find it again. He was gone for two years. He then returned with you, and your sister."

"What? But, Father said I was born here…"

"No." Jim said. "You were very, very young is all. Your sister, a newborn."

"I never knew I wasn't born here…" It relieved Markus to know that he was not born in such a horrible place like Nineveh. "But where did I come from?"

"Your father said you came from a village where he met your mother. He never said more." The cyborg tilted his head. "He never told you?"

Markus shook his head. This new information he was hearing was overwhelming. "Why *didn't* he tell me?"

"Maybe so you would not hate him, or leave." Aventis said behind Jim with a shrug. "Who knows for certain?"

"Did he ever say if my mother was alive?" Markus asked. He had been told that she died when he was young, just after giving birth to Ruth. He wondered if any of it was actually true, and if he really knew who his father was.

"No, he didn't." Jim said shaking his head.

Markus nodded, sad at this news. He then asked, "And the city? Did my father ever find it again?"

Jim shook his head. "He said he hadn't. And the Baron, tired of his lack of effort and waste of time sent him to work in the mines. He questioned your father for what seemed like years." The cyborg then leaned forward. "Your father once said that he held the key to the city's secrets."

"Secrets? So you're saying it *does* exist?" Markus asked trying to get the story straight. "That he lied and the city does actually exist?"

"No, he didn't lie, at least I don't think. I just remember him once saying, the city is lost, and must never be found. Neither denying the city's existence, or not. But he told everyone and their mother that he just couldn't find it again."

"This is confusing." Markus sighed. He wondered if it was just a waste of time to be speaking of such things.

Jim shrugged. "Still confuses me. Since he never spoke of it I never asked again. And we all took it as a fable, once told by the Wastelanders."

"Typical." Markus said sitting back into his stool with a *thump*. "Wouldn't it be incredible, if only it was true?"

"I suppose." Jim leaned back and sighed. "Your father came back with many stories, and trinkets. New ways to improve our technology, and the Barons army, but after that he was sent to work in the mines. Typical 'thank you' from our great leader."

"Explains why he left the garage to me." Markus said.

"He had a way with machines, just like you. You basically completed his work. Your bike, your Wings, even your battle bot suit."

"Some use they are." Markus said. With the depression taking over the city, hardly anyone was willing to buy it if they could. "I would sell them if I could."

"Well the Baron owns most of the vehicles, and sells the parts anyway. Makes it hard for a young boy to make a living off of his creations."

"Too right." Markus nodded. He looked at Aventis. "Do you believe the city exists?"

"I wish it was," he said. "It would be great to live there, if all that is said about it is true. Escape from the horrors here on earth."

"Me too." Markus said. It *would* be nice if Levitika was real.

But here in the real world, fairy tales only dragged you down; merely something to hide what the harsh reality was. Here in the real world, Believing that an entire kingdom actually escaped the once-glorious Capitol by vanishing into the sky no less was simply foolish. There couldn't be anything any different outside Nineveh's walls than what was in. Not if the kingdoms of the Northern Wastelands were still fighting for the scrapes of the long-dead empire.

~ One Blood ~

Black

Damion Black stood silently in his normal spot in the Baron's throne room, hidden in the shadows as he watched the meeting taking place before him.

The throne room was a long archway of stone with pillars holding up the sky-windows; which were now blanketed in snow that plunged the room into total darkness. The only light came from the gas-fed torches on each pillar and the two fireplaces on either side of Baron Ovid's stone throne. Black stood behind one of these pillars, the shadow of the tall stone and bronze obscuring him in black as if he was Death lurking in the shadows. He watched closely as the Baron who sat on his throne spoke to his guests. They were foreigners, two of them. Lameika and Lee, brother and sister, who had come before the Baron with such grace of a prince and princess. But they were far from royalty, Black could sense this even from far in the shadows.

Lameika, was a witch who said she was from the foreign city of Eden, which was now desecrated by pirates. She had learned her powers from the dark teachings of her mother; how to draw energy from her very soul unlike other witches and warlocks in the Wastelands who rely on the four elements and even demons to give them power. Lameika, Black could tell was a true witch, the power that emitted from her body brought chills to his spine, though he did not let it show. He eyed her garments of gray, which were tinged in black, and had a blue diamond hanging by a chain over her bosom. Her pale face and high cheeks gave her a beautiful stature, with her small lips, hair as black as midnight, and deep gray eyes tinged with a light green that made her appear even more beautiful. They were cat eyes, Black decided, sharp and cunning.

Her brother on the other hand, being no warlock or magician, was completely different from his sister. Lee wore a body of black armor tinged with yellow; light and yet durable. Black noticed the heavy gauntlets on his hands, and wondered what many weapons were stored in that armor. Hover-rockets were strapped to the heels of his massive boots, and by the size of the man's torso, Black figured him to be well-fit, like himself; with broad shoulders underneath the armor, and a neck roped in muscle covered in pale skin. His face was similar to Lameika's, but with dark green eyes with a wide nose and dark eyebrows. His hair was shaven off, revealing a deep scar across his bald head. He was the same height as his sister, and Black wondered if the two were twins. He kept his opinions and judgements to himself however, as he always had. These two were here on business with Ovid, and nothing more. So, he remained out of sight with his back pressed to the pillar in the shadows, listening, ready to protect the Baron if the need arose.

"I am glad you two made it safe from your travels." Baron Ovid said his voice deep and rich, but also cold as if Winter's breath was passing over the back of one's neck. His face was hidden in shadow, but his strong torso garbed in a dark tunic covered by a cloak of fur that was pinned by a golden broach on his left breast. "We had just finished wiping out some… nuisances, from Xerxes, trying to break through the walls of my great city. I swear, their leader will not rest until she has more land. I am glad you two were able to join us after being gone for so long. But tell me, have you figured out how to find it?"

Black listened to this in silence. This was the first he had heard of the two once being here before. That had to mean that they knew each other longer than Black knew Ovid.

"My dear Baron," the one named Lameika said in a voice that was soothing and yet mischievous as that of a Siren. "We are happy to say that we now know for sure what Johnathon was researching on his earlier quests. A key. A powerful key, powerful enough to find the city."

"A key you say?" asked the Baron, never moving in his seat leaving him in the darkness and hiding his large features. "And how, pray tell, does this 'key' help me find the forbidden city?"

Lameika explained. "You see, the island has some kind of force in it, whether it be spiritual or technological we haven't a clue. But when it comes into contact with specific compounds, namely, a type of crystal, the island seems to beckon it, bring those who possesses one closer to the kingdom. We have managed to fool the force with fool's gems, but we only catch mere glimpses before it disappears into the clouds. But according to Johnathon's notes, he may have an actual crystal in his possession from his travels- so his journals say which we found buried near the pits."

"Interesting," the Baron said with chilling interest that sounded closer to greed than anything else. "And so where is this gem? With it, I could lead a legion into the city and take over. With the treasures of old and the advanced technology with a fresh army of slaves, I could rule further into the Republic. Vast cities would crumble at my feet. I would be unstoppable against the Capitol…" He went silent, lost in his thoughts. He then cleared his throat and continued. "Forgive me. Where is this fragment, my dear?"

"The notes do not say my lord." Lameika said softly. "However, as I have said before, Johnathon may have had one in his possession. So, I need to talk to John himself."

"He's been dead for years." the Baron said. "Died nearly a decade ago, at the hand of one of my… subordinates."

Black chuckled humorlessly, silently at the word.

"Does he have family still?" Lameika asked.

The Baron's chuckle sounded throughout the hall. Strong, deep, almost inhuman. "Yes, as a matter of fact: they still live here in the city. They have been living under the protection of my dear, Hunter Black. You'll have to forgive him; he doesn't like being close to strangers."

Lamieka looked over to the spot where Black stood and smiled coyly. "The Hunter Black… I've heard of you out on the Wastelands. I must say, your reputation speaks wonders of yourself."

"Thank you." Black said uninterested. He did not care for praises of the witch before him. She seemed to notice his feeling, and her smile turned into a smirk.

She turned back to the Baron, her smile returning. "Well, who says we cannot just demand information from his children? I am surprised you didn't search the home before letting them live, but no matter. My learnings from the Wasteland had granted me the power of great... persuasion. If Johnathon told his children or close friends anything, I could find out. The process is... painful. But I would be able to find out everything the children would know."

"That is out of the question." Black said immediately.

"And why, pray tell?" Lee demanded, speaking for the first time since their arrival. He sounded like a teenager almost; just a kid.

"My young Hunter made a promise to the deceased Johnathon." The Baron explained. "Those children are not to be harmed by anything- until appropriate age of course. And I doubt Black is the kind of man he is willing let a witch from the Wastelands enter their minds."

"And you allowed this." Lameika asked, not mockingly but it certainly not a question either.

"How can I deny the desires of my closest... subordinate?" Ovid asked. "Why, I never really gave it that much thought. I never particularly cared for the children, and in the near future I would need more workers to mine for ore. So to put it bluntly: it never occurred to me to deny Black's wishes."

Lameika smiled, seeing something that she could use to her advantage. She turned to Black. "You promised them no one under the Baron's rule could harm them, correct?"

Black's mouth twitched slightly. "Yes."

"My brother and I are not under the Baron's rule. We are merely guests. So, we have full authority to do so." She turned to the Baron, giving him a sensual smile. "If my lord wants the information to the Forbidden City bad enough."

"And if the children don't know anything?" the Baron asked coolly but still obviously interested.

"Our minds are like the bank of the soul, my lord." Lameika explained which Black thought sounded absolutely rediculous. "A part of Johnathon lives on in the children. From there, I can see through them, and hopefully find the key to the Forbidden City."

Black stepped forward. "My lord, you aren't considering this, are you?" It was horrible luck to trust a witch, but he was more concerned about Johnathon's children than the fate of Nineveh's leader. "In all due respect, she is a witch."

Ovid sighed. "I understand your honorable code from your experience with The Brotherhood," The Baron said this calmly—dangerously so.

"However I want the location to the city. And what does it matter if the lives of two orphans are lost? People die all the time, and if we find The City of Angels, then we won't need as many miners anyway. And in a way, you are not breaking your 'code'. I will allow them to do this. The treasure and power held in the city will grant me the very weapon and power needed to control the entire region. And you, my dear Hunter can be my right hand still. You will achieve greater power than what you already have."

If you only knew… Black thought to himself feeling the weight of his crystal in his pocket.

Ovid continued. "Do not worry yourself with children, their lives are no longer in your hands."

Black nodded unhappily. "As you wish, my lord."

The Baron seemed to nod in the shadows. He looked at the siblings before him. "Do what you must. Those children mean nothing to me."

"It would be our pleasure." Lee said with a sinister grin to his sister.

"Indeed." Lameika said in agreement.

Black returned quietly into the darkness, not saying another word as the Baron finished his meeting with his guests of 'honor'. He didn't say another word for the rest of the meeting, his mind turning like Clockwork, wondering about the future of Nineveh- and its citizens.

~ The Street Rat ~

Markus

Later that night, Markus was working on another project in the living space when Ruth started to have a terrible coughing fit, another one of many she had been having the last week and a half.

It was hardly an hour after feeding her and giving her the remainder of his soda, and he was working on a little firefly robot at this time. Just like the big ones hovering in the city, it looked like a large bug with a bronze thorax and wings so light but so strong it could carry a good ten pounds in its six legs of titanium. He was fixing up the motor in the little guy while Ruth enjoyed the bubbling drink. That was when the violent coughing began.

Her coughs had been bad before, but they sounded terrible at this moment. Deciding to check on her, Markus got up from his desk, crossed the room and looked inside the bedroom to check on his sister. She was hunched over her side on the bed and spitting onto the floor as she coughed, and in the light that shone through the door and past Markus, he saw droplets of crimson on the floorboards, joined by many more as Ruth began to cough again.

"Mark...?" she croaked, her lips stained red.

"Ruth!" he exclaimed in shock as he ran towards her. He dropped to his knees beside her and began to pat her back, not sure of what to do. He then reached under her bed and held out her bottle of water, spilling the soda in the process. "Here, drink." She did as he said but immediately began to cough again. A dribble of blood began to seep from her chapped lips and into the water.

Oh no, Ruth... "Don't move!" Dropping the bottle of bloodied water, Markus shot up and ran to the door. After tearing through the kitchen in search for any medicine, he cried out in frustration when all he found were simple painkillers; nothing that would help her. He then tore across the room to the front door and upon opening it to the blizzard outside, he called out for help.

"Hey! Anyone! I need help!" Lights went on, but would then immediately go out. No one would come he realized; as soon as they realized who was calling they were no longer willing to lend a hand. His reputation with Damion Black was going to get Ruth killed...

He begged again, louder this time as the desperation arose at an alarming rate. "Please! Somebody! My sister's dying!" No answer. "Help..." he said, his voice now giving up as well. It was no use. No one was going to come to his aid. They were happy to see him and Ruth suffer.

When still no one came to answer his cries still, he swore violently and ran back inside to Ruth. He started to panic. This had never happened before, not this bad, and he didn't know what to do. He didn't want to do nothing, but nothing he would do felt like it was helping, even as he got back to her side on the bed.

She was coughing uncontrollably now. He reached for her and held her in his arms across his lap. "Ruthie, I'm here, sis, I'm here..." He patted her back trying to calm her down- but to no avail. He felt so useless it was heartbreaking. Tears began to fall on his cheeks as he feared the worse. "Please Ruth stop coughing... I'm here." She let up for a bit but continued to cough. Markus held her for what felt like forever. He held her and was never going to let go. *Please no... Not you too, Ruth...*

He was eventually aware of another presence in the room. He looked up to see Jim standing there in the doorway with his daughter. Kaltrina rushed over to Markus and pried Ruth from his arms. Jim then came up beside Markus and helped him up and kept his hands on the distraught boy's shoulders while Kaltrina calmed Ruth down enough to take some medicine they brought. For many minutes that felt like hours, Ruth kept coughing.

But then her fits began to slow, and then stop. After a few more minutes on intense silence, she was soon asleep, and breathing normally again. Her face was wiped clean with a rag from Kaltrina's pocket, and Markus never felt so much relief in his life.

Setting her onto the bed and covering her in her blankets, Kaltrina then stood up and walked over to Markus, a grim expression set on her face. She then motioned for them to leave the bedroom, and when the door was closed, shutting Ruth into darkness, Kaltrina turned back to him. "Hey, Markus." She tried for a smile.

"Thank you," Markus said looking past her at the door where Ruth slept peacefully despite what she just went through. Gratitude filled up his chest like a balloon, as well as the fear of what would happen should the fit come upon her again. "Is she gonna be okay?" he then asked, prepared for the worst.

Kaltrinas expression turned to dread. "Mark, she's really sick. The potion I gave her only dulls the pain and lessens the coughs. She's bleeding from the inside out. She's… she's not gonna…"

"Don't say it!" Markus exclaimed in a shriek.

"Not so loud, son." Jim cautioned him placing a hand on the boy's shoulder.

"Please…" Markus begged in a whisper as he jerked his shoulder away. "Don't…"

"Son," Jim said. "She may not make it. Winter is still here, and it's getting colder which is not helping her. She's coughing blood, there's nothing more we can do for her."

"There's gotta be *something*; anything!"

"Mark." Kaltrina said placing her hands on his shoulders. "I've done all I can which is mask the pain, but it *will* get worse. She could die really soon."

She didn't mean to hurt him, Markus knew this. She was just simply telling the truth. The cold, hard, damnable truth.

"Oh, God…" Markus said crying. "No not Ruth too…"

Kaltrina looked at her father helplessly. Jim sighed and hugged Markus from behind. "We're here for you Mark. I'm sorry we can't do anything else. Maybe a healer in town, but it's a long-"

"Get out." Markus then said suddenly and then sniffed. If his last resort was a witch, he wasn't going to take it. But still, a little part of his brain had thought of going through with it, despite the risks. He didn't need Jim to tell him again.

"Please..." he then begged. "Thank you."

Frowning, Jim nodded. "If it happens, send her again. We'll come as soon as possible."

Markus looked at the old man. "Her?"

The old cyborg tilted his head. "Yeah? The girl who came to get us... She said you needed help, and so we rushed here."

"Oh." Markus said with realization. *She's still around?* "Okay..."

"We need to go." Jim said pulling her daughter outside where a blizzard started to blow again. "It is late. Try to relax, okay? Goodnight, Mark..." He held the door open for Kaltrina, before following her out into the storm.

"Goodnight." And just like that, Markus was alone when the door shut the world out. He drifted over to the chair in a trance and fell into it. He then allowed his head to fall into his hands and he allowed himself to cry.

He couldn't lose Ruth, He just couldn't! Markus sat there on the floor and trembled. He had to get a grip. Crying wasn't going to solve anything, but he felt so helpless it was painful. Tomorrow he had to find a doctor, if there were any *legitimate* healers left. His last resort was the witch in the other side if the city- The Courts. He had to at least go see her. She had to know *something* or at least have something for Ruth. If it wasn't for the cold he'd take Ruth to her himself. But she had to stay here in the house where it was warm and dry.

Not only that, but the fear of repercussions made him extremely weary of what could happen. To trust a witch, was tempting fate, and he wondered if the risks would be worth it in the end. He was stuck with nowhere else to turn to. He felt as if the entire weight of the world had fallen upon his shoulders. Ever since Father died and he was left in charge of taking care of Ruth, the weight had gotten heavier and heavier, and now that Ruth was possibly fatally ill, that weight just became too unbearable.

She has to stay warm, and alive.

Markus then felt as if he was being watched and he looked over at the broken-glass window to see her again. The girl who he and Ruth had helped hide from the Guard. She ducked out of sight as soon as Markus saw her. With a sigh and wiping his tears, he stood up and walked over to the window. He stood there for the longest time before calling out silently. "Hey, um... if you're out there... thank you, for getting them."

Minutes passed, the only sound being the flickering of the fire pit and the whisper of the wind outside the shards. And then in a quiet voice, soft, and afraid said, "You're welcome."

Markus coughed into his sleeve before talking again. "Why'd you get them?"

Her face came into view. She was pale, and her long scraggily hair blew in the wind, and she shivered in the cold. "You helped me." she then said.

"So?" he asked peering into those eyes of hers, deep, and green.

She looked down, and then back up again. "You helped me, I help you." she said with a shrug. "Isn't that... isn't that how it works?"

Markus stared at her for the longest time, as if trying to read some hidden meaning behind her words. "What's your name?" he asked finally after moments of uncomfortable silence.

She pursed her frozen lips. "Ashlyn."

Ashlyn... Markus nodded and then sighed. When he looked back at her he said. "Are you... hungry?"

She looked at Markus skeptically. But then finally admitted, "A little...." She looked away as if embarrassed to even mention it.

"Come in." Markus said. Ashlyn blinked and then disappeared from view. He waited for her, not moving from his spot. The front door then swung open once more, and Ashlyn came inside closing the storm off behind her. He told her to make sure no one saw her and she did so with a peek outside. She was still deathly thin and pale, and her face and clothes were filthy with dirt. Her feet were still bare and red from frostbite. Nothing seemed to have changed since the previous night. She looked around the house as if afraid to touch anything.

"It's okay." Markus said beckoning her to sit by the fire.

She took a tentative step inside, then another. When she was close to the fire she stooped down and rubbed her hands near the flame. Markus went over to the pot of left-over stew from supper earlier. He was going to eat earlier, but Ruth's coughing made him feel too sick to eat. Besides, Ashlyn looked like she needed it more. She deserved it anyway. It was still warm so he just filled up a dirty bowl and handed it to her. She looked at the food, and then looked at Markus. He waited patiently, saying nothing as she slowly reached and took the bowl from his hands.

"Thank you..." she said.

"Don't mention it." he said to her before walking away and taking a seat in his chair at his desk like before, his project still laying across it. He pushed his bangs out of his eyes as he watched Ashlyn hold the bowl to her lips and slurp ravenously.

How long had it been since she actually ate? Markus wondered as he watched her practically inhale the broth and meat bits. When she finished her bowl she sat it at her feet and continued to warm herself by the fire.

"Thank you." she said again after a moment of silence.

Markus nodded. He scratched the back of his head nervously. "Look I… I'm sorry, about the other night."

He saw her look at him out of the corner of her eye. "Don't be." she said.

"Still," he replied. "I was rude, I just… I just had to protect my sister." He looked at the door hiding little Ruth inside. "She's all I got left."

"I understand." Ashlyn said nothing for a long while, and then nodded. "You're lucky, you know?"

"Why is that?"

"Cause at least you *have* somebody to worry about." She looked away. "Sorry, that was mean. I'm the one who caused you trouble anyway…"

Markus let her words sink in for a bit. He turned back to his project, not really feeling the motivation to finish it. Instead he took his father's staff-blade out of its sheath and began to polish the blade end. When satisfied, he flicked the switch to extend it into the staff and began to check the wiring and battery life for the crystal which launched the particle beams. He wanted to be distracted, so that he didn't have to talk too much.

"Is that your father's?" he heard Ashlyn say behind him. "I heard the Guard talking about it the other night when I was here." Markus turned to see her standing *right* behind him and he unconsciously tensed up. If she were to attack him, he'd be ready.

"Yes." he said stiffly. "He died a couple years ago."

"How?" Was she just being nosy, or just honestly curious?

He bit his lip. "The Hunter."

Ashlyn's brow softened. "I'm sorry."

He shrugged it off. "It happened. Can't do anything about it now."

She pulled up a chair and sat beside him, watching Markus check the staff out. It made him uneasy having her study him so close like this. It felt…

strange. *If she is waiting for me to lower my guard, I won't lose. Two can play the waiting game.*

"What kind of crystal is that?" she then asked pointing at the glowing sapphire-rock at the base of the blade.

"I don't know really," he said setting the staff down. "My old man never told me what kind of mineral it was. I even had it scanned at the nearest mineral deposit and it doesn't show up anywhere on the periodic table."

"Interesting." she said eyeing it like a jewel thief.

He looked at her for the longest time. When she looked back down he spoke again. "You should sleep." She gave him a look to which he shrugged. "You look tired," he explained. "It's safe here. Besides, it's warmer too." *Then I can keep an eye on you better than you on me.*

Ashlyn pursed her lips. "How will I know you won't kill me? Or send in the Guard while I sleep?" she asked.

Markus shrugged. "Guess you'll have to trust me."

"Do *you* trust *me*?"

He fell silent. He got up and went into his and Ruth's bedroom, returning with a spare mat and blanket. "Here." he said setting it in the corner of the living space. "Sleep. I'll… keep watch."

Ashlyn eyed Markus warily as she crossed the room and then crawled upon the pad. As soon as she laid down and covered herself in the moth-eaten blanket she closed her eyes. "You didn't answer my question." she said eyes still closed.

"No, I didn't," Markus replied. He resumed sitting in his chair with his blade across his lap, watching her.

For an hour her breathing did not change for she was still awake; probably to keep an eye on him. Eventually, her breathing became deeper and slower. Eventually, her moon-shaped face relaxed and she was soon fast asleep. Markus, who then felt safe enough, rested his head back and closed his eyes. He listened for any movement, just in case Ashlyn was still awake. Eventually, he could keep conscious no longer and soon then slipped away from the real world and into The Dreaming.

As he slept, he was unaware of the crystal upon his blade, which began to glow brighter in a blinding blue light that illuminated the room hauntingly.

~ A Dream ~

Markus

Markus was dreaming about his father again.

He watched in mute terror as his father was stabbed with many blades with shadows that represented The Hunter Black. Again and again he watched as his father twisted and turned in agony as the blades pierced his flesh and shed his blood, turning the darkness misty with crimson. It swirled around him like blood-red fog, hiding a darkness more sinister than anything Markus had ever felt. He tried to run to his father's aid, but felt as if he was running through syrup. He tried to call out but no sound escaped his lips, and as his father fell into the blood-drenched snow he began to cry out. As he reached out to touch his father, the entire dream faded to black, as if a flood of darkness passed through his mind.

He stood there, able to move freely and speak in both confusion and terror. "What is this?" he asked to no one in particular his voice echoing throughout the abyss. Before him somewhere in the darkness, two large eyes opened, and peered down at him. They were dark soulless eyes with black iris' and glowed blood-red. The laughter that came from the eyes was deep and sinister, like something out of the stuff of nightmares.

"I see you." it growled which made Markus cower to his knees and shield his eyes from the horror before him. Around him whispers of demons penetrated his ears and grabbed him with violent black claws.

War will tear your home apart,

To return, all must play the part.
The Twelve will be one once more,
And they shall bring the Destroyer
Death
Salvation
Wolves
Kill.

For what felt like hours he sat there, hoping the monsters would go away, unwilling to look up to see for himself.

And then he smelled something. Something clean, something fresh. Like freshly grown apples in an orchard, or a field of daisies. The smell and the feeling of the sun against his skin caused Markus to look up, and see that he was indeed in a small field. He stood up, marveling at the scene before him. The sea of grass that swayed in the 'wind' that appeared to come from everywhere and nowhere. The small clusters of flowers that stuck up from the sea smelling sweet and clean. He had never seen a field like this before, only in books and stories told by his father was he able to see what a field would look like. And now he was here, seeing all of this with his own eyes.

"Wow." he said.

"Amazing, the difference between what is considered a good dream and a bad." a voice deep and rich spoke out, making Markus jump. He began to look around, his head on the swivel as he tried to find the source. But no one was there. He was all alone- or so he thought.

"Do not be alarmed, Markus." the voice said again. "You are not alone. The Nightmares will leave you be, for now."

"Who are you?" Markus demanded. "Where are you- and where am I?"

"You yourself are still asleep at home, sitting in a chair with your neck aching from where you laid back. Your sister, Ruth, is in her own bed dreaming of seeing her mother. And young Ashlyn, is dreaming as well… poor thing."

"Who are you?" Markus asked again still desperately searching for the owner of the voice. "Where are you?"

"You cannot see me, for I cannot hold you here and personally see you. My power is weakening day by day, and it is hard to reach out to you this early."

"Then *who* are you!?" Markus called out his voice echoing over the fields of daisies and other flowers. "And where am I?"

"You are in The Dreaming." the voice said. "A world beyond what the normal eye can see. But you, are special. I have decided Markus, that you are the one. And you may call me Abner. I am a spirit, trapped in this realm."

"Realm?"

"Please, I do not have much time. *He* hinders my calling to you, and I must hurry."

"He?"

"Just listen, son of Johnathon." At the mention of his father's name Markus then felt really cold, as if a fist of ice was now clenching his thundering heart. "A great evil is on the horizon, threatening to break free of his bonds."

"Enough with the pronouns!" Markus screamed. "What is going on!?"

"Just listen." The voice said sternly, desperately it seemed. "The war in your world now, is about to awaken a force more evil than anything that has crossed this land. A terror so terrible, that it still haunts the memories of those who witnessed it. The forbidden city, Levitika is in dire peril. Within their walls, a source of power so evil, so dark, is hidden and must remain. For if your world is to survive, it must be contained. Only one who can wield the power of The Dreaming, will be able to shackle the awakening beast."

Markus laughed. "The City of Angels? You're saying it exists? Ha, what a load of crap."

"Your father did not think so." the voice said which silenced Markus completely. "He spent his life hiding Levitika's secrets from the forces of your world for so long; in fact, he is the one who was supposed to be The Keeper, until you were born. You now hold the power to contain the monster that threatens to escape and wreak havoc upon your world, and I will help you. Only you have the power, to end the never-ending wars your land is scarred by. Only you, can save The City of Angels, and eventually the world."

"You got it all wrong pal," Markus said with his hands raised towards the blue skies above. "I'm just a kid, a delivery boy. I got nothing to help anyone."

"You have your father's crystal, and within it the power to find the city."

"You are saying I have to find it? What, out there in the Wastelands?" Markus laughed again. "Sorry, but I got better things to do. I need to stay and protect Ruth and-"

"Her blood runs dark and diseased." the voice said, his words cutting deep like a dull knife. "She will not survive in Nineveh. Only through the healing of the Levitikan's will she be able to survive. Only they, can heal her. If you do not venture out there, and find what your father had kept hidden for many years, not only will your world most likely become razed by The Dark Master, but your sister will fade away."

Markus cried out, a tear threatening to spill from his eye. "No! I don't believe that! I'm just a kid, I can't do anything!"

"You must go. Do not worry, I will guide you on your journey… He is near… I must go." the voice said. "Even now my energy fades. Go to the city Markus. Only they can save your sister, and only you, the Keeper, can save *them*. The Prophecy has begun.

"You are their only hope."

"Wait!" Markus shouted. "What prophecy!? Answer me! Wh–" Suddenly an owl, large and golden emerged from the darkness that had shrouded the field of daisies and flew directly at Markus at break-neck speeds.

"*Awaken!*" it shrieked as it collided into him.

Markus awoke with a cry and covered his mouth quickly hoping that no one had heard him. He looked over to see Ashlyn still asleep on her mat; the morning sun that peered over the great walls and shining through the shattered window of the shack now illuminating her face. Markus frowned as he rested his chin on a closed fist in thought. His eyes went to his blade and was surprised to see that the blue crystal was glowing. He placed a hand on the handle, and brought it up to his face as he peered at it.

Go. he heard a voice from nowhere in particular, and realized it was the same voice he had heard in his dream. He now stared at the crystal with newfound interest and uncertainty.

Was it real? Did that all really just happen?

"Hey," he heard a croak and looked up to see Ruth standing in the doorway.

"Hey," he said to his sister as he sat the dagger back down. "How are you feeling?" He tried to not let her notice the terror he felt as he saw thin droplets of blood on her chin.

"Same," she said shuffling her feet.

"You should be resting."

Ruth shook her head. "I had a bad dream."

"Oh?" Markus said standing up. He crossed the room over to her and placing a gentle hand on her, he steered her to the bed. "Look, you need to rest. Come on. What was your dream about?"

"I was dead." she said her voice shaking as if she was still witnessing the horrible nightmare. "Mom was there, and I was just dying, next to her skeleton…"

That stopped Markus' heart in mid-beat but still he pretended to smile. "It was just a dream. You're still alive though."

"A man was there." Ruth then said. "We were in a hot place, where I was dying, but he was holding my hand, telling me it would be okay. He made me feel better, and he said it was just a dream…"

That's interesting… Markus thought to himself. "That's nice then! Who was he?"

"He said his name was, Abner."

That stopped Markus dead in his tracks. He stopped Ruth and turned her around to face him. "Excuse me?"

The ferocity in his voice frightened Ruth a bit. "Abner?" she said unsurely.

"What did he tell you?"

"Wha…?"

"Ruth, what did he tell you?" Markus asked again. "It's… it's important!" He wasn't sure why he was overreacting, it was probably just a coincidence.

Ruth gulped. "He said, you and I would be leaving. Leaving the city." She tilted her head when she saw the look on Markus' face. "Mark, is that true?"

"Wha…?" Markus asked still in disbelief,

"He said, we were going to a castle in the clouds…"

"Oh my God…" Markus took a step back and started to walk away. He then fell into his chair again with a hand to his head. *No way…*

"What?" Ruth sounded worried now. "Mark?"

"Ruth," Markus said trying to keep his voice calm and collected. "This is going to sound crazy, but, I had the same dream. Except he told me to take you there." He did not mention the prophecy or the dangers because he felt them to be irrelevant. He did not care for what he was supposed to do, all that mattered to him was Ruth, and he didn't want to frighten her as much as he was frightened himself. *This has to be a coincidence. But…* "He said… that we are supposed to go to The City of Angels." he eventually said.

Ruth's eyes widened at this. "The one Daddy used to tell us about?"

"Wait, Dad told you about it?" Markus asked. His father never told *him* about the story.

Ruth nodded. "Yeah, he used to tell me the story before bed."

Interesting... "Yeah." Markus then said trying to push the thought out of his mind. "That's right. There is supposedly a cure there for your sickness."

A large smile spread across Ruth's lips. "That's great!"

"Maybe," Markus was never one to believe in dreams and fate. In fact, he hardly ever heard of a dream coming true. But if Ruth indeed talked to the same person...

He heard a sound and turned to see Ashlyn sitting up and staring at them. She looked flustered and embarrassed. "I wasn't eavesdropping..."

"It's okay." Ruth said which the exact opposite of what Markus was thinking.

"If I may..." Ashlyn said pursing her lips. "I... dreamt the same thing."

"What?" Markus said completely bewildered now. *Her too?*

"Yeah, he said that I am the one to *lead* you out of the city..." She looked away. "You think I'm crazy, don't you?"

"Why you?" Markus demanded. He *did* think it was crazy though, this was all too much too soon. But if she dreamt about the same person as well... No. This had to be a coincidence, there was no way they could leave. Not with Ruth's condition.

Nothing can save her here though. The voice reminded him.

Shut up, Markus thought back.

"How are you going to get out?" Ashlyn asked looking back to the siblings. When Markus had no answer, she continued. "We... We can use the sewers to break out. There are pipes that lead to waste dumps outside the city walls."

"You make it sound like we've already decided to go." Markus said crossing his arms. "We're not going."

"Why?" Ruth asked her brother.

"Seriously? You're *sick*." Markus told her stating the obvious. "If the monsters in the Wastelands don't get us, the chill in the air will kill you."

Ruth frowned and looked down. "I always wanted to see the world outside the walls though..."

"I know," Markus said running his forehead in frustration. To be honest: he felt the same way. "But it's too dangerous..."

"But..."

"No. We're just *kids*, Ruth. We can't go. Besides, it's not like we can get passed the front gates without a pass anyway, which only the miners and soldiers have."

"Then we use the sewers, like I said," Ashlyn said. "Also, if you're worried about the cold and the monsters, I have an idea for that as well."

"Do tell." Markus said crossing his arms sarcastically.

"Well, we would most likely be using your bikes, right? If we do leave, we would use them to cross the Wastelands, right?"

"Right, my Eagles Wings wouldn't carry all of us." Markus said. He had actually thought of trying with Ruth but was afraid if the wings failed to carry them. He would most likely bring them anyway just in case *if* they do indeed go. What made Markus wonder was how Ashlyn knew that he had more than one bike but he didn't ask. *Also, why am I thinking that we are actually going to go anyway?*

"Right, so listen to this," Ashlyn said standing up and stretching her body. Markus then noticed how lean the girl was. She really was terribly thin. "The witch that came into the Market Area? She has some potions and pelts that we can use to keep warm. We could 'borrow' some of them as we get more rations."

"You mean *steal* them." Markus said.

"More or less…"

As to be expected from a street rat. "You sound like you have this all planned out." Markus pointed out.

"You got a better idea?"

Markus had none, but he still had his doubts. *Was this a good idea?*

"It might be worth it." Ruth said. "It's not like I'm going to last long here anyway…"

"Ruth…" Markus whispered honestly frightened by how straightforward she was.

"I'm not dumb, Mark." Ruth said crossing her blanket around her body. "I'd rather try something than just lay here and do nothing. There's nothing here that can help us. Besides, I want to go out there. I want to just see if there is something better out beyond the wall before I… you know."

Markus looked at Ashlyn and the street rat shrugged. "I'm in for trying." She said. "It's better than being in here."

"What if we're wrong?" Markus asked.

"What do you mean?"

"What if it was all just coincidence? A mistake?" *What if we do go out there, and being out in the cold wilderness only lead to our deaths?*

"Why would it?" Ruth coughed.

"What if we go out there, and there is no city? What if The Baron sends men after us or we get captured by pirates? What then?"

"He said we would find them." Ruth said. "That we would make it there."

Markus couldn't help but laugh. "You believe him? Some guy you saw in your dreams?"

"Yes."

Markus was silent for a moment. Shocked by her blunt response, he stared at Ruth for a long while and he was happy that Ashlyn remained mute so that they could all take it in. When he finally spoke he was still uneasy, but a little more confident.

"Are we actually going to do this?" he asked. "We are escaping Nineveh and heading out to the unknown?" He looked back at Ruth. "Risking you?"

"I guess so." Ashlyn said. "We might have a better chance."

"Are you sure you want to come with us?" Ruth asked her.

"Yes," Markus said looking back at the street rat. "It's not like you *have* to come…"

"You won't make it through the sewers without me." Ashlyn argued. "And I *hate* this city, and want to get out as soon as possible."

Markus nodded understandably while Ruth spoke. "So, it's settled?" she asked.

"I think it's too risky…" Markus said.

He was scared, scared about losing Ruth. But if they went out there into the Wasteland in the middle of winter, there was a chance that he would lose Ruth faster than he would by staying here. But, if they do stay here, Ruth will die one day and they will accomplish absolutely nothing. He would receive no sympathy from The Guard, and no one would be able to help him. They would both die under the rule of Baron Ovid and never taste true freedom. Besides, Ruth wanted to see the world before she… before she leaves. Markus didn't want to risk taking her out there, but it would be an even bigger risk to risk nothing and simply wait for the inevitable. And if they succeeded, she would live…

You want her to live, do you?

With all my heart. "I guess so." Markus stood up after answering both his own thoughts and the girls question. "But we should leave soon."

"Agreed." Ashlyn said. "Let's go get the stuff now."

"Now?"

"I'll start packing what we have here." Ruth said without waiting, turning to head back to her room.

"You, rest." Markus said standing up. Ruth tried to argue but he was firm. "Rest up best you can. We'll pack up and then go get the stuff. We will wake you as we get closer to actually leaving."

Ruth, unhappy but being as understanding as she usually was nodded. "Okay."

Markus shook his head as he looked at Ashlyn. "I can't believe I'm agreeing to this." *This is more likely to get ourselves killed than anything else…*

"I can't believe that we actually have a shot." she said in return. "A chance."

Markus looked back at Ruth who had entered her bedroom again and disappeared into the darkness. "A chance…" he repeated.

~ The Witch and the Hunter ~

Lee

The next day Lee walked in on Lameika in her bedroom just as she was quickly putting a fire out from one of the basins in her room. What Lee caught was that the flame was bright green, and the air within the room felt cold and prickly as if someone was running their cold fingers along his spine. He smiled cruelly as he slammed the door, announcing his arrival to his sister.

She jumped at the sound and turned to him furiously. Her eyes were more cold than the room itself. "What do you want?"

"How'd you sleep?" he asked innocently.

She sneered at him. "Fine."

"That's good, that's good," he leaned against the doorframe, taking in the elegant bedroom. The stone walls were lined with the Baron's bright banners and the large bed was covered in satin linin and pillows as large as children. The gas-fed torch above the desk on the back wall made the room feel more full as he saw the dancing shadows of whatever spirits shared the room with his dear sister. "Doing good in here, I see?"

"Yes." Lameika said dismissively.

Lee wasn't about to let her have her way, yet. "Who were you talking to?"

"None of your business, brother."

"C'mon Lay-lay, we in this together or what?"

She eyed him, piercingly. "Do not call me that. And yes, we are."

"Then show me, Sis. I may not have magic like you but I still wanna know what's going on." He crossed his arms patiently as he waited for his sister's response.

Lameika sighed, relenting to his desire. "The Master calls to us."

Lees expression went serious. "You don't say?"

"He still sleeps. But he is there, he is still reaching."

"And the Baron?"

"A pawn, he says. His time is short."

Lee smiled again. "I like it. And these children are the key?"

"Yes."

"Well, let's go get them."

"Later this afternoon. I've got some business to take care of first."

"Well I'll go then. I'll get Tank and maybe Pyro. Have 'em here before the sun hits its highest."

"No. You will wait for me, brother."

Lee scowled. Lameika was always like this. It had to be done her way, to the key. She was so controlling like that it irritated Lee to no end. But still, he relented to her this time, as always. "Very well, if you insist, *Sis*. I'm telling you though, I can do it."

"I do not question your ability to do so, Lee." Lameika said shortly. "But Tank and Pyro? Can they be trusted to keep the brats alive? Or even Slitzar? They *are* Hunters after all. You cannot trust any of them."

Lee nodded still unhappy. Considering the fact that he himself was a Hunter, it irritated him that his sister would treat him like a common criminal, despite all that the two of them had gone through.

"Just like Black? Or even me?" Ever since becoming a bounty hunter, he was never trusted by anyone or anything. Not in his village, and sadly, not even in his own family; even now, he could see the resentment in Lameika's eyes. "I see your point."

She nodded once. "We do this the right way- *my* way. You got it?"

"Fine. You promise to tell me when and how?"

"Yes."

"Swear it."

Lameika rolled her eyes but placed the sign of The Oath across her chest. "I swear under the stars and moon. Satisfied?"

Lee nodded, "Gladly." he lied. "However I am not patient, especially for this mission. Damion Black... I want him."

"All in good time." Lameika said brushing past him.

"I don't think you understand." Lee said turning around to face his sister who waited within the doorframe. "I am impatient, Lameika. I want my chance."

"It won't matter." Lameika said. "You are a great Hunter, Lee. I will not deny that. But you will never gain our family honor. You are born without magic, born without the gift. That is something that will never change. Do you really believe our father- or even The Master will accept you? Ha! Don't make me laugh. You are born to follow, nothing more, nothing less. I will make sure you have your chance at Black, Lee. I promise you that much. But if you truly believe that you will even come close to me, then you are pathetically mistaken. Head to the ship. I will command you what to do when I get back, brother." she spat the last word out like it was bile before turning and leaving down the hall.

"Bitch..." Lee swore, slamming a fist into the stone wall with enough force to crack the stone and leave a small crater. *Tempting... bitch.* "I'll show you. I will show you, and Cath. Just you wait, witch." One way or another, he would gain his honor and make his family proud.

He, not Lameika, would have the last laugh.

Lameika
Lameika laughed as she strolled down the dark hallways of the Baron's vast and magnificent castle, her destination nearing swiftly and silently. "What a fool." She said cheerfully as she went alone after talking to Lee. He was to wait for her in another section of the castle until she arrived. She didn't want him to get in the way- like he always was while growing up.

Looking out the windows, high above the city, Lameika could see the citizens far below in the streets of Nineveh. Every single one of them looked like ants- the simple creatures that they were. The Baron and the patrolling Guard that passed her as she crossed the halls were even smaller. Mere pawns for a greater purpose. She smiled at the thought as she bowed her head to each passing Guard who in turn would nod back or their eyes would linger as she passed by.

Every single one of you, pawns, insects, destined for a greater purpose: to serve me.

She soon found herself in front of a large door with a white hand print placed in the middle. She adjusted her bosom slightly and took a deep breath.

Why was she so nervous? It wasn't as if this wasn't her first time. She knocked on the door, and waited patiently with her hands rubbing together anxiously. After a minute or so of silence, she knocked again.

"Enter." a flat voice finally said on the other side.

Lameika pushed the door open to reveal a darkened room lit by a single candle which sat upon a desk where the man she came to visit sat. He appeared to be writing something on a piece of parchment, and she saw his sword resting against the table's leg. His cloak was off, revealing his black armor and physique which she noticed was strong and hardened after years of obvious use. His plasma blaster laid across the table, but his shotgun rested against his leg in its holster. His cowl was off as well. The man's hair was undone, tumbling in shrouds of black over his face and shoulders. Lameika smiled and walked over to the silent Hunter.

"What do you want?" he said without looking up from his paper. Did he know that it was her, or did he think it was someone else? His eyes still hadn't moved, even as his pen danced across the paper, leaving ink in many shapes and forms.

Lameika released a silent sigh and pushed the thought from her mind. "I wanted to apologize." she said.

The pen stopped in mid-stroke, only to resume before Black spoke again. "For what?"

"If I have upset you during the meeting last night. I understand your code of honor, being with the Brotherhood and all."

"A past I would like to keep buried." he said simply. "I am no longer a member of the Brotherhood."

"Understood." She took a tentative step forward. "But in all honesty, such honor of *the* Hunter Black should not be idly given to an orphan child."

Black said nothing. In fact, it seemed like he had not heard her at all. The pen refused to stop writing.

Lameika squinted, wanting to say something but caught herself and managed to smile. "What I mean, milord, is that, so much has been said about you. I never would have…"

"Save your apology." Black said indifferently. "If you cannot understand then there is no point in me explaining."

"Hmmm." she said irritated but hiding her feelings inside. "I suppose you think your honor is more important than your loyalty, to your Master? Protecting a couple of rats from an Eagle?"

Black turned to her, and she felt an icicle pierce her heart the glare was so dark. *How can such a beautiful face, appear so hostile?* When Black *did* speak, his voice was cold and heartless. "What I do, I do for the glory of Baron Ovid. So forgive me, if I do not think he will achieve such glory from sending a *witch* to murder some children."

Lameika couldn't believe her ears. "How dare you?" she spat venomously. "Do you even know who I am?"

"No. And I do not care."

"Hmmm." she growled. "You've got a lot of nerve. While I was going to compliment you on your beauty, considering all I have heard about you since I was a child, I was kind of hoping to find out more about you- maybe even steal your attention. Maybe, even a kiss. But I see now that you are a disrespectful swine no different than the slack-jawed men who guard this castle. Your blood is as thin as a peasant, and your honor is wasted on *trash*." And with a flick of her gown she exited the room. "Good day."

"And to you as well, 'milady'." she heard him say as she stepped outside the door.

She threw a glance at him. "The Baron will hear about this." she threatened, trying to scare him.

But to no avail, Black remained indifferent all the same. "He is in his chambers asleep for his nap. If you wish to wake him up, then by all means. Otherwise you're going to have to wait until he wakes up to state your complaints."

"The nerve!" Lameika said furiously slamming the door and shutting the dark room from her sight. "Arrogant, heartless, ass!" She swore as she furiously stomped away from the incompetent bastard who dared defied her. The sheer nerve that man had! Despite his beauty and strong nature which Lameika found quite attractive, her anger for him was like venom in her veins. *He made me appear, like Lee!* "Asshole!"

No matter. He would rue this day for his rudeness, one way or another. She realized as she stormed down the hall to her chambers that her clenched fists were crackling and small flakes of snow had begun to fall, which she extinguished immediately before her anger made her hands shoot the next guard who shied away from her venomous but silent rage.

~ The Fate ~

Markus

After the long morning of packing up supplies as well as ammo canisters and fuel tanks, Markus checked on Ruth to find her still asleep. He whispered that they would be back soon and then left her.

He then stooped to the floor and gripping a damaged floor board under his workbench, he removed a couple of wrapped items from the depths of the shack. When he unwrapped the dusty rags, he revealed two Laser Pistols and an Old-School sawed-shotgun to go with the ammo canisters he and Ashlyn had packed earlier.

"You have guns here?" Ashlyn asked. "Where'd you get them?"

"Found them one day in our bedroom." Markus answered. "The one Ruth is in now. It was under Dad's old sleeping cot."

"And you kept them all this time? I'm surprised the Guard hadn't discovered them yet."

"Pray for the best, prepare for the worst." Markus said taking the guns outside and carefully without being seen, shoved them into the saddles to strap onto the Hoverbikes. The saying was one of his father's, and saying it made his heart feel heavy.

After locking up the shack, the two then entered the garage and emerged with one of the Hoverbikes stored within. Markus then started up the vehicle and when it was in hover-mode, he beckoned Ashlyn to sit behind him. She seemed nervous at first, but she climbed on nonetheless.

"Hold on." he said as he gunned the bike forward. Ashlyn's arms shot out and wrapped around his torso, nearly crushing his lungs within. She cried out for a bit but then the scream turned to laughter in an instant. Markus thought she had a nice laugh.

They were going fast, faster than Markus would normally go for deliveries. By the way the bystanders cursed at them as they whipped past them, he figured they were going *way* over the limit. The local Guard however paid them no heed but shouted words of vulgar extremities as the two zoomed past them. Snow billowed behind them and every once in a while an updraft from the sewer drains would make them jump. At this rate the two would be there within a half-hour maybe less; and eventually back to Ruth and out of the God-forsaken city within the hour.

I still can't believe that we're actually doing this... Markus thought to himself. The entire morning was spent packing and preparing for their departure from Nineveh. It was all one thing after another, bam, bam, and bam. But for some reason, he now felt hopeful, like their endeavor could be actually done, but a small bit in the back of his mind thought otherwise. *I hope this is not a mistake...*

When they finally arrived at The Market, Markus slowed down the hover-boosters, making him and Ashlyn slow to a stop in the center among the tents and booths of different shops. He looked over his shoulder to see a queasy-looking Ashlyn. He had to bite his tongue to keep from chuckling at her. "You okay?" he asked.

"I'm fine." she insisted despite how she looked. "I'm just not used to being on this kind of stuff." She pulled up the hood of the cowl that Markus had given her before they left. If any of the Guards or worse yet any of the people she robbed spotted her, it would all be over.

"Well, when we leave the city we'll be using them." Markus reminded her. "But you can ride it at your own pace."

"I only rode a bike once..." she said getting off while Markus extended the kickstand. "Get off my back..."

Deciding to let her off the hook, Markus relented. "Don't worry, it's easy. I'll teach you as we go through the tunnels. You'll get the hang of it like that." He snapped his fingers to prove his point. With that they began to walk through the crowded Market Place over to a tent made almost entirely of Werecat pelts. They made sure to keep their heads low as to avoid attracting attention. The thick white fur that made up the tent offered much needed protection from the cold for the darkened interior. "What's the plan?" Markus then asked Ashlyn near the mouth of the tent where the smell of herbs and strange decay emitted.

Ashlyn pointed towards the entrance flap. "You talk to the old lady, seem interested in a potion or particular subject, or something."

"She's a witch, what could I possibly be interested in?"

Ashlyn shrugged. "Not my problem. I'll sneak in and steal some medicine and that potion I mentioned."

Markus still didn't like the idea of stealing from a witch, but he needed the medicine if it would help Ruth on their journey. "Alright fine. Just, be careful." he said.

Ashlyn winked. "Likewise." The two then departed, separating in the square, and Markus after some mental encouragement, entered the tent.

When his eyes adjusted to the dim light of a single candle on a table near the center of the tent, he got a good look of the interior. Different plants and species of dried animals hung from the ceiling, and on the make-shift shelving were many glass jars of liquids, some with body parts of animals, and some shelves were full of elegant bottles of different color of concoctions. As Markus approached the table in the center the eyeballs in glass jars seemed to follow him, giving himself a feeling of unease in the place. It was creepy, unnatural, frightening. His hand subconsciously went for his knife, the blue crystal glowing faintly beneath his jacket.

"Come in." a frail voice said beyond the candlelight, which before his eyes seemed to grow brighter until the features of an old woman came into view in the flickering light. "Ahh, Markus, son of Johnathon." The witch, Madame Zerona said in a low and soft tone, her eyes which were like polished silver bearings rather than human eyes staring at him. Her toothless-grin made his spine tingle, and her wrinkled skin looked like tattered leather. Her dead eyes sat on Markus, empty and emotionless as he took a seat on a little pillow before the woman, thankful for the table between the two of them. Behind him, Markus felt the rush of wind against the nape of his neck. Whether that was Ashlyn or some freak coincidence was beyond him. Markus could not help but look into those creepy eyes as if he had been caught and trapped in a trance.

"I'm sorry," he said when he finally found his voice. "But we have never met before. How do you know my name?"

Zerona grinned. "Are you sure, dear?"

He nodded. "I'm sure."

She nodded unconvinced. "You know me though."

"Well," Markus said scratching his head. "When you hear about a witch in the city, you tend to hear things- ma'am."

"You hear a lot of things, when you have the ability to hear." Zerona then held out a hand to the candle, which seemed to be as thin as bone as if the skin upon it was pulled tight. "Nevertheless, how can I help you, my dear?"

Markus swallowed in thought. *How can I keep her distracted long enough?* "I heard... you do fortunes?" It was the only thing he could think of.

She squinted at him. "I do read *some* but not as good as an actual fortune-teller from the Wastelands. Who told you that?"

"Um, a Guard mentioned it, I think." *Not very convincing...*

"Ahh," But Markus could tell from her tone that she did not believe him in the slightest. "Did they now? That's funny, because I've never had a Guard come in here. They don't... appreciate my talents."

Markus shrugged. "Maybe he was lying?"

"Hardly. I *can* read a *little* bit, Dear. However, how would you be able to pay for it?" Zerona turned her eyes to Markus, those ghostly eyes bearing right through his very soul as if threatening to consume it.

"I can't." he answered simply.

Zerona tilted her head. "Why is that?"

"All my money goes to food and medicine for my sister, Ruth."

She nodded again. "Tell me about this, Ruth."

Markus pursed his lips in thought. "She's a few years younger than me." The words seemed to fly out of his mouth. *I don't want to give out too much information though.* "Hair as blonde as fresh wheat. She was like a second mother to me after my father was killed. She is now sick with some disease which eats her from the inside out as we speak." Markus looked down at his feet which was shrouded in shadow. "She's dying, everyone tells me."

The old woman was silent. When she spoke again, it was like a pick breaking through the ice. "What is it you want to know?"

Markus took a deep breath and looked up at her. "Will she survive?"

The woman seemed troubled as she reached out and took his hand. Her bony fingers started to write imaginary lines along his palms and fingers. "I cannot see the answer to that. I see many things happening in her life... A long journey. But it is hazy with the shadows of possibilities. The Dreaming itself is even muddled by chance and possibilities. The future is always different, always ever-changing. No one on this earth can clearly predict what will or might happen in their life- or the next." She peered at Markus. "What happens in the present, can always change the future however. For example, presently, what could happen in the next few seconds can change in an instant what your original plan would have resulted in."

"I don't think I understand..."

"Well, what if I told you that you can tell your friend that what she seeks is on the top shelf next to the jar of Ahool claws?"

Markus froze, not knowing what to say. *Oh crap...*

The old woman smiled. "Do not be afraid. That medicine will keep your sister warm on your journey. May I suggest a mix of herbal tea? It would help with any chills or fevers she has."

Markus nodded dumbfounded.

"Did you get that, dear?" the old woman asked looking behind her.

"Y-y-y...yes ma'am..." Ashlyn's voice carried somewhere within the darkness.

Zerona released Markus' hand and waved it. "In my chest. It's labeled with an 'H'.

After a minute of sitting in silence besides the shuffling of Ashlyn, she finally came into the light and presented a small plastic bag of grasses and other ingredients. On the side, a black 'H' rested in black ink.

"Is this it, Ma'am?" She asked sheepishly, obviously just as nervous about the fact that she was caught as Markus was.

"That's the one." Zerona claimed without taking a second look.

Ashlyn gulped. "How did you..."

The old woman merely smiled. "I see all that happens in my tent. I may be blind, but I can see clearly that what you are doing is for a good cause." She looked over to Markus. "I may not be able to see clearly what will happen to Ruth. But I can say, that your journey is shadowed with doubt and endless possibilities. And at the end of your journey, I see a lot of pain, suffering, but it all adds up unto great happiness and joy. Remember this always; gold does not take form without fire. Whatever your path leads to, you will prevail, and you will find happiness- all of you."

Markus swallowed hard. "Thank you." he said not knowing what to say.

She turned to Ashlyn and then to her said, "You keep an eye on this boy. He saved your life, in fact I see it many times on your journey, but I see you helping *him* more than you let yourself see."

Ashlyn nodded without a word, still dumbfounded. Even Markus himself was surprised at this. He wondered just how close the two of them would become once they- *if,* they reach their destination.

The witch then turned back to Markus. "Before you leave, I suggest you give little Ruth some tea. And, please, take that blanket by the barrel. That is Werecat fur. That should keep her warm on the coldest of nights. Winter still plagues this land, it is best to not let it claim any of you."

Markus nodded. "Thank you." He said this though he was not getting up just yet. "We should probably pay you with something… huh?" He felt bad for trying to steal from her in the first place, he felt he had to do something to compensate for it.

"You already have." Zerona said to his surprise.

Markus tilted his head in confusion. "What do you mean?"

"You give me hope." she smiled. "This city might just survive because of you."

Markus blushed slightly. "Ma'am, I don't understand. I only wish to save my sister."

"Then I hope you succeed, young Markus." She winked. "A word of advice from an old woman: Never give up. No matter what life throws at you, no matter what happens, trust in your friends, and trust in yourself to keep moving forward. You will run into times of trial and turmoil, but it all ends well in the end. Gold does not take form, without fire. You just need to keep going."

Still unsure of what Madam Zerona meant, Markus merely nodded. "Yes, Ma'am."

She then waved her hand at the two. "Now off with you both. Before I call The Guard." She winked, and for the first time since Markus entered her tent, he smiled back as well.

As the two rode back to the shack, Ashlyn was quiet behind Markus for a good couple of minutes. She held him close and the warmth from her body made it easier to bear the ride. They were riding slower this time so the humming of the bike didn't keep Markus' words from reaching her when he decided to break the silence.

"That was... interesting." he said back to her.

"Yeah," She leaned forward to speak into his ear, her breath hitting the base of his lobe through the chilled winds. "What did she mean?" she asked. "That you give her hope, and the city might survive?"

"I don't know." he called back. Ashlyn fell silent again and did not speak until they stopped back at the shack. They climbed off and Markus pulled the bike to the side, determined to put the encounter with the witch in the back of his mind.

"Get the gear," he told Ashlyn. "I'm gonna grab a few more things." He then left for the garage without waiting for a reply. In his pack which served as his Eagles Wings carrier, Markus shoved some ammo and fuel canisters into the pack, as well as a couple knives and bags of dehydrated food packets.

You never know when you might need more. Those were his father's words back when he was still alive. Satisfied he slung his pack on and then grabbed the second Hoverbike, which unlike his own which was bronze with a jet-black stripe, this one had a hot pink stripe. It was meant for Ruth to ride, before she got sick. He took it outside and parked it beside his. After checking the bike to make sure it was still good to ride, Markus then went inside the house, happy to see Ruth wearing the Werecat cloak and sipping from a cup which smelled of berries. She smiled despite her weak posture and sickly face. Ashlyn too looked at Markus, a smile on her own as if to say *Got her to drink some.*

Markus smiled back at the two. "Hey, Sis." he said to Ruth.

"Are we really going?" she asked in a raspy voice. "This is real?"

Markus sighed and nodded. "We're gonna get you better, Ruth." he said then looking at Ashlyn who was putting on her pack which was full of extra blankets, water and food. A knife hung at her belt as well as one of Markus' father's laser pistols. "We have to."

Ashlyn nodded. She looked at Ruth with a confident smile. "We'll make it."

Ruth nodded, a smile tugging at her own lips.

"Hey," Ashlyn crouched as she said to her. "By the way, thank you, for keeping your brother from shooting me."

Ruth chuckled. "Thank *you* for helping us."

"No one I have left to help other than you guys."

Ruth smiled at this, genuinely this time.

"Ready?" Markus asked eager not only to end this conversation but get a move on.

Ruth sipped the last of her tea and sat it on the counter, where her teddy bear sat. She had that bear for a long time, but she didn't pick it up. She was leaving it behind. Markus wanted to ask about it, but decided against it. They were both leaving things behind here. Ruth then turned to Markus and nodded her reply.

"Okay." he said following with Ashlyn close behind. "Let's go."

"Alright," Markus called from his bike to Ashlyn who was steadying her craft, moving slowly and trying to get a hang of the different gears and knobs. "You all set?"

"Ready." she said without confidence. "This is a *little* easier than I thought though." She had been practicing by moving around slowly in the street. She only fell off once but in no time at all she was able to maneuver the bike with ease.

"Good," he called. He then looked back to Ruth who was strapped to the backseat of his own bike, her torso bundled in the pelts. "You ready, Sis?"

"I guess so." she said teeth chattering as she tightened the Werecat pelt around her.

"Keep your face warm." he said. She responded by covering her face. "Alright." Markus called. *We're actually doing this...* "Let's-"

Whoosh-pissss!

A shot sounded, making Markus jump. Beside his bike was a splotch of black soot with smoke rising from it. He looked up to see a woman in gray standing in the street, a blue pendant around her neck with her black hair flowing in the cold breeze. Next to her stood a tall lean man with black and yellow armor, his face hidden by a helmet of smooth black steel. One of his gauntlets held a gun, the barrel smoking.

"By the order of his majesty, Baron Ovid," the woman said smiling sinisterly. "You two are to be arrested and questioned for measures his majesty wishes to pursue. Surrender, and you will live." She said this as her hand rose with crooked fingers, and before the children's eyes they watched as a jagged shard of ice grew from her palm.

"Oh crap," Ashlyn said wide-eyed.

A witch! Without thinking, Markus looked back to her. "Floor it!" he screamed and gunning it, he propelled forward, making Ruth cry out behind him. Ashlyn, breaking free from her own trance launched after him and Ruth.

When she came up alongside Markus, he looked back to see the man in special armor taking flight behind them, his rocket boots billowing smoke. Beside him, another man, this one in an armor of gray steel and a jetpack appeared from behind one of the abandoned buildings and soared after them as well; his helmet in a beetle-like shape. In his hands, he held a large gun with a pipe leading to a tank on his lower back. Markus didn't know who these people were, but they were definitely not normal members of The Guard.

"What do we do!?" Ashlyn called out to him.

A laser beam shot past Markus, blowing apart the wagon they had passed by, the man standing beside it being blown back a good ten feet into the snow-covered street. Markus then looked back to see the two Hunters were gaining up on him and the girls. The one in gray armor clicked the trigger and puffs of flame erupted from the barrel of his weapon.

Not good. "You know how to get through the sewers?" he called out to Ashlyn.

"Yeah!"

"Head straight there, and DO NOT STOP!"

She nodded and gunned ahead of Markus. He in pursuit followed and maneuvered as blasts exploded all around him. He and Ruth heard maniacal laughter above them, and looked up to see the soldier in gray right above their heads.

"How about a little heat?" the robotic voice called down. "You look cold!" From his gun, a pillar of fire shot down towards them. Ruth squealed slightly and Markus jerked the handlebars to the side, avoiding the splash of flames that melted the snow around the spot. "I like it when my prey runs!" The man called out still following the other man in close pursuit, his gun flashing with every shot and laughing like a maniac.

"Markus!" Ruth screamed.

"I'm going, I'm going!" he cried out following Ashlyn while going as fast as he could, his drive to keep going being driven by fear, and fear alone.

~ Escape ~

Lameika

Lameika growled as she appeared out of thin air in a flash of frost on the rooftop of one of the Guard towers stationed on various buildings in the area.

The smoke that curled above the chimneys made it difficult to see, but she was still able to make out the kids fleeing on their bikes. She had called the Guard to block the section of the city the brats were now driving through. She watched with keen eyesight how close her brother and the Hunter known as Pyro pursued them. Despite how fast they were however, the kids would bank through alleyways and even through various street kiosks. At the rate they were going, Lee and his partner were going to take forever. Not only that, but the response-time for The Guard was just plain pathetic. Despite how many Hellhounds were converging on their position, they would take even longer to catch up and assist in the capture of the children. So Lameika reached up to her ear, where her earpiece was and spoke. "Tank."

"Go ahead." a robotic voice answered.

"The brats are heading for the Eastern wall. They just passed one of the barriers, wait for them near there. The Guard is moving too slow."

"Yes Ma'am."

Lameika then said, "Slitzar, get ready to pounce."

A snarl more than a voice answered, "Aye, milady."

"Captain Veegar."

"Yes." the Captain of the Guard said over the radio, his voice sounding rushed and nervous.

"The brats have fled. Have some of your men check their shack. Turn the place inside out if you have to."

"Roger."

"They are *not* getting away." Lameika hissed to no one in particular, and in a flash of crystalized frost, she disappeared again.

Markus

As Markus and the girls passed alley after alley, building after scorched building, men and women hid behind locked doors while the Guard marched out in unison; all trying to corral the fleeing children. They were forced to run right through a group of Droids who popped out of nowhere, and Markus nearly fell off his bike as he crashed through them, their human escorts retaliating as they were trained to do so. Their rifles flashed red as they shot at him and Ruth, who ducked and swerved as they felt the shots buzz past them like angry hornets. Above them, following on either side were the two Hunters who were still in pursuit, their own guns thundering above their heads.

"Don't hit them!" the man in black called out. "The Baron wants them alive! Hit the bikes!"

"Yeah, yeah," the man in gray said letting loose another pillar of fire towards Ashlyn, who swerved to the right and slowed down as a trash bin was consumed by the flames. Markus and Ruth had passed her, and it was then when Markus had gotten his blade out and extended it into the staff. He would then turn back and fire a bolt of energy back at their pursuers, but they dodged every beam he shot at them.

"How much further!?" he called out to Ashlyn turning back to face where he was going.

"Almost there!" she cried out pulling back in front of them.

They drove for what felt like forever, dodging bullet's and taking detours whenever a roadblock came up. Above them the Hunters continued to chase them, and more gunfire thundered around them. Some drones were even airborne, following the bikes like a bad smell. They were almost to the East wall when Ashlyn suddenly screamed. Markus, who had just fired at one of the Hunters returned his attention to the front and saw why.

Ahead of them, was a large robot. Standing tall in strong steel-armor and painted green, it stood with a rocket-launcher for one hand and a large broadsword for another. Its massive head was bucket-shaped with glowing red eyes and no mouth. He beeped and clicked as he raised his launcher at the oncoming children.

"Freeze." he echoed loudly through its speakers, and Markus knew his shots would not be able to hurt that thick of armor. They were losing options, and fast.

"Do we go back?" Ashlyn asked worriedly as she slowed to match Markus' speed.

Markus looked behind him past Ruth to see something more terrifying; a large creature with rough tan skin as large as the robot blocked the only way out. Whatever it was, it had a large tail, and massive hands which curled into black claws. Above its leathery head, the two Hunters flew past it towards them. They couldn't go back, and looking around, Markus saw no other way out. The buildings were too close together, and the time it took to raise to a higher hover-zone would take too long and make them a better target for the Hellhounds hovering overhead. Even now more troops were zoning in on them like ants to a dying wasp as they closed in on the robot up ahead.

Markus swore vulgarly. "No! Where's the entrance? Ashlyn!?" Behind him, Ruth clenched her brothers jacket in terror.

"Right in front of that thing!" Ashlyn called out to them. "Go forward!"

Markus turned back to the robot who had not moved. "You gotta be kidding me!"

"Just gun it! When I say so, swerve right!"

"Ahh!" In unison, they all propelled forward faster than ever, the snow pelted Markus' face but he kept forward. The buildings passed them by in a blur, and the shots coming in from behind missed more and more often.

"These things go down!?" she called back to him.

"Yeah!?"

"When I say 'now', push down!"

"What!? Oh man..." He pulled up alongside her. The bullets whizzed past them and the laser and fire beams exploded around the two bikes, but they kept at it. The massive robot kept his gun up, ready to fire. As he came closer and closer Markus began to panic. "Are you sure it's here?"

"No!"

'No'!? "Oh sh…"

The robot squared up; his sword-arm held out, preventing the children from going around. "Stop or I *will* shoot!"

"Aren't they doing enough of that already!?" Ruth called out to her brother.

"Ready!?" Ashlyn screamed, her hair a halo of billowing darkness.

"No!" Markus exclaimed.

"Now!"

Markus screamed as he slammed his handlebars to the right. Following Ashlyn, they swerved away from the robot and zoomed towards an alley where a slanted opening to the sewers sat. Ashlyn shouted at them to duck and at the right moment, Markus and Ruth ducked beneath the archway as they dove down beneath the streets and into the sewers. Most of the drains or entrances such as this were covered by a thin grate which gave in easily as both bikes plunged through it and down the pipeline.

Darkness enveloped them except for the faint glow of their bikes and Markus' staff. The Hoverbikes automatically leveled themselves before they struck the bottom of the sewers, which left their stomachs somewhere in the sewage beneath them. They were then propelled forward, all zooming fast down the maze of tunnels beneath the massive city. The circular brick-layout smelled horrible and Markus was sure some of the sludge beneath them had splashed onto the bike as well as his boots.

"Follow me!" Ashlyn screamed. Markus and Ruth followed, and the three traveled through the tunnels as fast as their bikes could go. Sewage rushed beneath them and as they made sharp turns down the tunnels Markus could feel his own stomach turn and bounce around inside of him. After a few more turns, a faint light began to appear at the end of the smelly and damp tunnel.

"There it is!" Ashlyn called again up ahead.

Markus gunned his bike and rolled around the tunnel across the ceiling and back down in front of Ashlyn. He then pressed a button, jutting out the built-in battery-ram on the front of the bike.

"Hold on!" he called behind him. As the light became brighter, he soon came aware of the iron bars appearing within the light. He screamed out as the bike made contact with the bars, and smashed right through them, the bikes now flying out of one of the waste pipes leading outside the city. Dull sunlight struck them before the deep snow did as they landed on the other side of a toxic waste dump.

"Go, go, go!" Ashlyn called out as they steadied their bikes all gunned it again, hovering fast over the plains of snow. As they continued their escape, they would sometimes pass a destroyed vehicle of war used by the Xerxes army, and the occasional burned skeleton in the snow but they would not stop to survey the true horror lying beneath the fresh snow. Behind them the city alarm continued to blare, and more Hellhounds came over the walls after the children. Passing the massive aircraft were the two Hunters who sped up as they dived down the length of the wall and swooped back towards Markus and the girls, releasing more gunfire, which would pellet the snow around them and occasionally strike the metal of their bikes. They were definitely not being more careful this time.

"They're catching up!" Ashlyn cried.

Markus' eye then caught a fallen building covered in snow. "Over there!" At the same time two Hellhounds had closed in near ground-level zone and were speeding up behind the pursuing Hunters. "Hurry!"

They propelled to the building, and Ashlyn followed close to Markus and Ruth right through the gaping doors which were hanging on their hinges, revealing a dark room with another pair on the other side. They zoomed through it, past the darkness and out the other side. One Hellhound stupidly smashed into the building in a blast of fire and burnt shrapnel. The other zipped past it and gunned after the kids, passing the two Hunters and making them wobble along their path. Markus then clicked on the autopilot and turned around with his staff. Ruth ducked as he took aim at one of the aircrafts turbines and fired. The machinery exploded and the Hellhound spun out of control before crashing into the snow. Ruth cheered but her praise was short-lived, for the two Hunters were upon them now, passing through the smoke and snarling angrily.

"End of the line, runts!" the gray-suit called out holding out a sphere of black matter, a small red light blinking against the side.

"Bomb!" Markus screamed and shot another bolt up at the Hunter. He dodged but a sliver of the beam caught one of the wings of his jetpack, scorching it. He growled and tossed the bomb at the rear of the bike. Markus returned fired again, hitting the bomb and setting it off. A large ball of fire expanded and blew apart, propelling him and Ruth forward with its intense heat and wind. Markus felt the heat on his neck and was worried for Ruth, but by the looks if her she seemed okay. He regained control of the wavering bike just as the other Hunter closed in on them, hands extended with a grapple-hook on one of them- and aimed right at the bike in the area beneath Ruth. At that moment Markus looked over at a selection of trees that were close by.

He had a plan. He jerked to the right leaving Ashlyn going forward. "Mark!" she called.

"Keep going!" he called. The Hunter continued to follow him and Ruth, leaving Ashlyn to drive away dumbfounded.

Ruth and Markus came up to the trees fast, and Markus looked back to see the Hunter taking aim. He waited, and waited, and as he drove into the tree line the man fired. Markus leapt back over Ruth, letting the claw grab *him* instead of the bike. He turned his body around as he was jerked back, being pulled towards the Hunter, and at the same time whipping out his staff. With a sharp turn, he swung it, letting the blade-end slice through the wire pulling him up. The wire was cut clean and when the staff was aimed right at the Hunter, Markus pulled the trigger. A blast of red lightning shot out, and caught the man dead-center in the chest, throwing him back and landing far out into the snow with a large splash of powder. The other Hunter, turned and went to help his partner as Markus fell down and landed into the snow. He was stuck for a moment; having sunk chest-deep, but he eventually managed to claw his way out and trudge quickly to his bike, which Ruth had stopped a good fifty feet from where Markus had been grabbed.

"You okay?" she asked worriedly while scooting back as Markus hopped back on.

"Never better." he lied. His leg was hurt from the fall, but it mattered little. They had managed to lose their pursuers- for now. "Let's get back to Ashlyn." Markus fired up the bike again, and the two propelled the same direction Ashlyn went only to find her waiting at the base of the hill.

And she was scowling at Markus. "Don't *ever* do that again." she said as they pulled up alongside her.

Markus shrugged. "Had no choice." He pulled out the knife and brushed his finger across the crystal. As if by accident, something strange happened. The crystal glowed for a moment, and it seemed that something was coming inside Markus who suddenly closed his eyes. In his mind he had a vision, a sign. A small lake… After studying the image in his head for a moment, he shook it and then looked back at the dagger. Then putting it back into his sheathe he looked at the girls.

"This way." he said jerking his chin to the right. "We'll ride until nightfall then camp somewhere."

"Where?" Ruth asked.

"It's hard to explain." Markus said. "I… have a feeling."

Ashlyn didn't look convinced but she didn't argue. "So… did we really make it?" she asked.

Markus said looking back in the direction the Hunters had crashed. "For now." For the time being, they were safe. They had escaped Nineveh, and now they were out in the wilderness. He had a strange idea of where he was supposed to go, but he was still weary. At the same time however, he was also glad to be free of that horrible place.

Maybe they *did* have a chance after all. "Let's go," he said. "The more distance we put between ourselves and the city, the better."

~ Open Season ~

Black

Black stood on the walls of the city, observing the carnage happening in the Wastelands far below. Behind him, the city continued to blare loudly in chaos, there had never been an escape of this magnitude before, and the Guard were simply not prepared for it. Outside, it didn't appear to be any better.

Two Hellhounds and eight men were lost; and the two Hunters, Lee and the other one those two troublesome siblings brought with them were on their way back. Despite the damage to the city, losing some men and the fact that the children had escaped the clutches of the Guard, Black smiled. He felt in both his heart, and the crystal he played with in his pocket, that this was going to be interesting. *Very* interesting actually. He wondered just how Baron Ovid would react to such an event, and what would happen to the twins in the process. He knew without a doubt that he was going to be roped in; all of this trouble could not be avoided at this point. But he was used to it. If there was one thing that Ovid and his precious city was capable of, it was to regain control. Soon all the citizens within the city would be sent back to their homes, and the Baron would have a plan to eliminate all rumors that someone had managed to slip out of the city and escape The Guard's clutches.

And hardly anyone ever escapes the reach of Baron Ovid.

Which made this situation, all the more interesting.

He was eventually found back in the Baron's hall, listening to the sibling's story to Baron Ovid, who sat dangerously silent in the shadows, not making a sound or movement. It was almost déjà vu; the scene was so similar to the last meeting. Black just sat quietly back as the story unfolded to the part where the children escaped through the sewers. Ovid remained silent, but Black knew this silence all too well. The Baron was livid, and he was just biding his time. Part of Black hoped that they would just do something; that he would just eliminate the failing duo. To just get rid of the rogue Hunter and his witch of a sister.

Still, they continued to talk as calmly as possible, making it almost impossible to actually be upset with them. "We have sent the Guard out there," Lee said. "But only a few came back. They're gone, sire." the Hunter said, his helmet resting in his arms.

"You *lost* them." the Baron stated, straight to the point. His voice appeared dangerously calm. Black had heard this tone before as well. It was more dangerous than the silence. Ovid was known for his temper, his fits of rage, in fact there were times he would kill men in his anger. The silence, followed by this deathly tone, it was a force to be reckoned with. But it was the silence itself, the eerie calmness that was worse. Much worse. "That, is what you mean, correct?" Ovid demanded.

Lameika nodded without showing the slightest bit of fear. "Yes." Black had to give it to her, she was indeed strong-minded.

The Baron mumbled to himself and then said, "If you were my subjects, I would have my servant Black throw you out the nearest window."

"Yes, sire." Lee said. Lameika, said nothing.

But Ovid then said, "I want that crystal. I want the location of that city. But we need those children- more importantly, that crystal. It is safe to believe that they took the crystal with them. Why else would they leave with such vigor? None of my men were able to find anything in that rat-hole of a home for them. I shall question them myself when they are brought back. I did not become Baron by mere wars and chats. The dark arts I have been taught thus far has helped me become… tremendously persuasive."

That was another thing about the Baron that Black knew about that no one else did. Baron Ovid had been taught the basics of hypnotism, a magic force once thought lost up until a few years ago. It was once outlawed and marked as a taboo, nearly as bad as witchcraft. That is, until Ovid came to power. It was one of the reasons why Ovid had so many loyal followers, and why the Baron himself respected Black as such. He was one of the few people in the world who could resist his lord's control, and Ovid seemed to find this very respectful to find such loyalty without the use of force. Black still didn't know how the Baron could do it, and maybe no one did. But he could feel it, some form of energy coming from the man whenever he stared directly into the Hunter's eyes. He wondered if that was the source, but he never dared to reveal what he knew about the Baron's hidden magic- or that he believed that his tricks wouldn't work on the siblings either.

"And those children are the next piece of the puzzle." Ovid continued. "I will bet the entire kingdom that they took it with them when they fled. As soon as I get my hands on them..." Ovid then raised his head slightly. "Black?"

"Yes, my lord?" Black said stepping out of the shadows. He knew this was coming, it was only a matter of time.

Ovid grumbled. "It seems fate has given you a chance to redeem yourself from your worthless 'code'. You are to bring the children of Johnathon to me, at *any* cost. Dead or alive, alive if you are able. If by chance they do not have the crystal, I want them alive to find out where it could be."

"And the girl with them?" If Black was told correctly, there was three children, not two.

"I don't care about her."

Black pursed his lips before answering. "As you wish." As expected of his master.

"Whatever you need, get it. Whatever it takes to bring those children and get that crystal, I want those two brought to me *screaming*. No 'code of honor' bullshit. You bring me those children, or I'll have you shaking hands with the Reaper himself."

"As you wish." Black said without hesitation or fear.

"You and your damnable courtesy." The Baron sneered and with a wave of his hand he said, "Go."

Black bowed before his Baron and exited the room with a flap of his cloak. His boots clicked across the stone floor as he stepped out, and ventured down the hall already heading for the Baron's garage under the city. Hidden among the Hellhounds and Fireflies was his own Hoverbike, which he had not used in so long. He didn't need to go to his room to retrieve his stuff, for his gear was already with him, as well as his cowl and scarf, which he pulled up when he exited the castle and into the cold. As for the matter of food and water he would hunt and use the snow when he made camp, which he would do little of. He would ride as long as he could so he could catch up to the children who had a day's advantage on them. He had no time to lose, he had to find them. He *would* find them.

No one escapes the Hunter Black.

Lameika

"As for you two," the Baron said after Black had left. Lameika and Lee both looked at the leader of Nineveh, concerned of what Ovid would do or say now. "You have failed me." Ovid continued. "But, I will offer you both *one* chance of redemption."

The nerve of this man! Lameika thought. *Does he even know who we are?* "What is it we are to do, my lord?" She said cautiously. One false move, and she knew that her and Lee's days would be numbered. Years of preparation would completely go to waste.

"My Hunter will no doubt track down those children." Ovid said somewhat proudly. "However, I *am* concerned. His own code of self-righteousness has costed me years of work as it is. It has made him blind."

"What is your point- good Baron?" Lee asked.

The Baron sighed broodingly. "I have faith in my servant, but I do not believe he will harm those kids, no matter what. And seeing as they put up quite a fight for you, young Lee, I do not think they'll just go that easily. I am afraid, that it will take too long for Black to obtain them and the crystal simply because they are children, and his 'code' prevents himself from bringing them to harm."

"And he won't bring them if it means to hurt them." Lameika said distastefully.

"That is what I fear." the Baron agreed. "He is resourceful, but I cannot risk any mistakes or delays. Too much has been put into this to delay it any longer. If *you* are able to get them however- alive, then not only will your own honor be restored, but you will also become my most powerful servants."

Lameika nodded. They would be granted permission to lick the boots of the Baron, or they would die, is what Ovid meant to say. "And what about Black my lord?"

"I do not care what it takes." the Baron said. "I want those kids brought to me screaming if you must, but you *will* do whatever it takes to bring them here. And if Black keeps you from that, then I'm sure you being from the barbarous Wastelands, you have a few ways of handling such difficulties."

Lee's lips curled into a cruel grin. "It would be our pleasure."

"I do not like it, but I see no other way. My men will help you if need be."

"That won't be necessary, my lord." Lameika said behind her own smile. "My brother and his gang will be more than enough." *This man,* She thought to herself. *Willing to sacrifice his own men so that he will get what he wants. Greediness in government knows no bounds it seems, even after years and years of examples made by leaders of old.*

"Very well," The Baron said seeming much more relaxed than before. "Then please, take our fastest Hellhound, large enough to fit your whole group, but fast enough to catch up to them. Dr. Lich, will be more than happy to assist you in preparing for your trip to redeem yourselves. How soon will you be prepared to leave?"

Lameika and Lee looked to one another and nodded. The very thought and pleasure of what was to come was a blissful taste in their mouths and minds. Their Master would be freed, and the prophecy destroyed. And this, *fool* of a leader was leading them right to it.

They both turned and to the Baron in unison, the siblings said, "Immediately."

Lameika was in her room while Lee went downstairs to prepare for the journey. In a small basin, a pillar of purple flame was lit in the utter darkness of her room as she spoke into it.

"My Lord." She felt a cold wind brush her cheeks, tickling her ear. She felt his presence, whispering into it like a long-lost lover. All around her, she felt crooked hands cold and evil crawling across her skin. "We will find the child. We shall.... Yes. Yes. It shall be done."

She listened to him; heeding his words. The words of the ancient prophecy echoing in her head, and her very conscious being brushed by a hand that was not really there. Her hair stood up on end, and gooseflesh erupted from her skin.

"You shall be freed of your prison." she assured him. "You shall… Yes Master. It shall be done… The Baron is a fool. He shall not receive the glory of the great city's destruction… By my word."

She shuddered as she felt his own pleasure against her body. The sensation, the cold excitement, it was enough to make a man go insane, yes it was. The time has come, the new world was just beyond the cold horizon. Soon, unimaginable power would be hers, the rightful hand to serve the Master along with her subordinates. Nothing could stop her now, not those children, not Ovid, not Black; no one. No one at all.

The time has come.

Ovid
When Lameika had finished her packing she headed down to the launch pad and boarded the Hellhound with her brethren before they took off into the frozen sky.

The Hellhound Dr. Lich had issued them was jet-black, with thrusters as large as plane turbines and a sharp wingspan. It was also equipped with the most advanced Gatling Laser which hung beneath the hull of the vehicle. It was a wicked-looking thing but still flew with the grace and agility as a Firefly. Once they were off the ground they shot off into the night after their prey. Baron Ovid, watched them disappear from his window high in the castle. Behind him, his dear Captain Veegar stood beside him, watching as well.

Veegar, who was at the meeting hiding in the shadows, did not like the twins or the plan. In fact, he figured it all to be a hoax Ovid had come up with to trick them, and Veegar was sound enough to voice opinions earlier. Ovid had been kind enough to at least hear the general out, and in the end he was happy he did. Though none of his own men were with them, he would know exactly what the twins were up to, and where they were. "Shall we follow them, my lord?" Veegar asked.

"No." the Baron said to which seemed to surprise the Captain. "Our dear professor has taken the liberty of placing a bug and camera on the bulge of their ship. We will be able to track where in the district they are, and if need be, actually see what they see."

"Brilliant." Veegar grinned yet still looking unconvinced. But he was not about to question the Barons motives. At least, he had better not.

"Indeed." Ovid said crossing his arms. "Those Wastelanders are nothing but barbarians, they won't be able to pull anything without making it too obvious."

"You believe me then? That they would betray us?"

"My father once told me, to never trust a witch- especially if she came from the Wastelands. If they do deem untrustworthy, we shall punish them with no prejudice. If they find the city without us, our legion shall go and take it by sheer force."

"And Ninevah?" Veegar asked. "What of the city?"

"I have already made preparations, my dear and faithful Captain." Ovid assured him while stroking his heavy black beard. "If the plan goes well and I venture out to take the legendary City of Angels, you shall take over Nineveh." When Ovid said this, it made his Commander of the Guard's jaw drop. "I shall take the strongest men, with the most advanced weaponry and ships to take the Forbidden City. And you shall rule this section of the kingdom by my side. Our empire will grow with the lost and ancient technology at our will. Together, we will become unstoppable. And you, my friend, shall receive the reward of total dominance in the western region, and more to come. Under my rule, soon, the entire Wastelands shall be ours. First we shall take Xerxes, and make that wretched queen of theirs suffer at our hands this time, and from that point on, the rest of the country."

"I like it, my Lord." Veegar said with a greedy gleam in his gray eyes.

"So do I, my General." the Baron added along with a cold laughter that echoed through his dark halls, as he watched the fresh snow fall come down upon his dark city.

"Although, Queen Lamia might not take kindly to us advancing on The Capitol after Xerxes," Veegar pointed out.

Ovid grinned at the thought. In fact, he *laughed* at the misery of the people below him, and laughed more at the thought of complete and utter control over the entire country; and eventually, one day, the world. It made him break into fits of ecstasy, laughing to the point of coughing fits. He rubbed the bushy eyebrows above his steel blue eyes. There was still so much to do, and so little time. Veegar was right: the Dark Queen would not like what he would be doing, not one bit. But in the end, it wouldn't matter at all.

Soon, the forbidden city of Levitika, would be his.

~ Camping ~

Markus

When darkness had fallen Markus and the girls decided to camp out in a small dugout at the base of a large tree. The space under the roots trapped the heat of their small fire, keeping them- especially Ruth, warm. She laid beside the fire, sipping on her tea and chewing on what little jerky Markus could give her.

Ashlyn, sat beside her. Her boots were off, and her little toes were wriggling by the flames for warmth. Her auburn hair was pulled back, as to not get singed. Even though she spent most of her time as a street rat, Markus could tell she once knew how to act like a normal child, the way she stuck a stick into the fire and drew on the rocks with the soot. Definitely childish still, despite the horrors she probably went through. What could be going through her head? Why did she push on when she clearly had no means to live on?

Why am I even thinking that? Is that really the world we live in? Markus pushed the thought from his head as he stood at the mouth of the dugout, watching the two girls, listening to the howls of the Snow Wolves beyond the dark and snowy horizon. As the blizzard moved in, the howls died down, and only the wind remained. Markus tugged on his coat against the cold, his head spinning with thought. *We made it. We almost got killed, but they had made it. I wonder how long it will be before the Guard tracks us all down?*

He wondered. Would they even bother for a bunch of kids? He didn't know for sure. No one had ever escaped Nineveh before, at least not in his memory. Where exactly would they be going? Would it be worth the trip?

What about Ruth? So many 'what ifs', and 'whys', it began to hurt Markus' head. He rubbed the bridge of his nose in frustration. *Could I keep them safe at least? What would my father do in a time such as this?* He decided to push that thought out of his head as well. He did not need to think about such un-pleasantries.

"Markus?" He turned to see that Ruth had finished her tea. "You okay?"

Markus smiled, turned and walked back over. He then took a seat on the ground opposite of her, the fire sitting between them. "I'm fine." he said, despite the thinking making him worry himself sick. "How are you, sis?"

Ruth shrugged. "Been better, obviously."

Markus chuckled softly. "What do you think?"

"Of all this? This trip we are going on? I think it's crazy."

He looked at her. "Do you want to go back?"

Ruth gave him a funny look and laughed. "Back to that place? Not on your life."

A smile tugged at Markus' lips. "Then forward we go, I guess."

"Do you think it's real?" she then asked, referring to Levitika.

"I don't know." Markus admitted but then added, "I'd like to think so."

"How do you think the city floats?"

He shrugged. "Floating Islands? They've been seen before. Heh. My guess would be machines."

"Or magic." Ashlyn chimed in.

"Magic." Markus repeated skeptically. "You can't honestly believe in that, can you?"

"A lot of things have changed since the war." she pointed out playing with her scraggily hair. "Anything is possible. Besides… how can you explain that witch?"

"Which one?"

Ashlyn rolled her eyes. "Zerona, smartass."

Markus chuckled. "I dunno…"

"How did you think that old gypsy found me?"

"Lucky guess?"

"Okay, how about that witch from earlier? The ice on her hands?"

That was easy. "Gloves. They *do* make that, you know."

Ashlyn nodded. "You don't believe in magic then?"

"No. I don't."

Ashlyn grinned slyly. "Then explain how you have a *feeling* that we are going in the right direction."

Markus was stumped at that. He didn't want to believe that there was such thing as some magical force that could alter how the world works. Witchcraft was nothing but talking to demons and getting into trouble, and whatever wizards were out there were only capable of conjuring tricks and lies. The world was all too brutal for something like magic to just come to light, and the thought of it even being possible was just… childish.

"I believe in magic." Ruth then said with a weak smile. "It *could* happen. Just like in Daddy's stories!"

"If there is such a thing," Markus said amused at the conversation they were having. "Why do so many not use it then?"

"It's a personal thing." Ashlyn said. "Some are granted through spirits, others potions or chemicals, or even radiation some claim. Sometimes, it's just the person."

"Oh really?" Markus said resting his body against a propped arm. This really was too funny to just stop.

"Really." She looked down at the flames. "My mother was a magician. She did not use potions, mutation, or spirits to create her magic. It just, *came* from her. The pureness of her heart, and the cleanliness of her soul maybe made her powerful. Honestly, even she didn't know how she could do it. She could do small things. Warm up the room, make plants grow faster, take away pain. Just, little things that seem to make the world a better place for my little sister and I."

"You had a sister?" Markus asked truly intrigued. *Guess we have more in common than I thought. But…*

Before Ashlyn could even reply, Ruth piped up coughing slightly as she did so. "That's incredible!" she choked.

Ashlyn smiled. "Yeah. It was. She always made the day a little better…"

Markus looked down at a small patch of dirt in front of him, studying the little rocks within the mounds of compressed earth. "So she wasn't like a witch?" he said.

"No, she wasn't." She smiled amusedly. "She would show me many things. Said if I caught a little bit of her power from birth, I would learn soon. Like I would feel it." Ashlyn laughed, then looked at her pale hands. "Not that I have been able to feel anything however. She would tell me the differences between her and witches too." She laughed more to herself than to Markus and Ruth who continued to listen attentively. "I remember her saying, 'If I ever hear you turned into a witch I'll slap you silly'."

Markus laughed. Even Ruth chuckled behind a cough. "Say, what happened to your mother and sister?"

Ashlyn's smile immediately vanished into a frown of despair. Markus could see the memories replaying behind those sad eyes. She seemed on the verge of tears at the thought, but she held them back like she has done a thousand times before. "They died," she said somberly.

Ruth got the message and covered her mouth in remorse. "I see."

Markus cleared his throat, anxious to put an end to the conversation before Ashlyn broke down. "Ruth, you need to sleep. We need to leave first thing tomorrow."

Ruth yawned. "Okay." She turned and tucked deeper into her Werecat pelt and then turned back to Markus. "Can you finish your story, Markus? I fell asleep before the good part…"

"Story?" Ashlyn asked.

"I-It's nothing." Markus said feeling suddenly embarrassed.

"Please?" Ruth said her eyes wavering. She was giving him the puppy-dog eyes.

Unable to resist, Markus relented. "Alright, fine. What was the last part you remembered?"

"Taiyou joined the army, trying to earn respect so he could become the princess' guard."

"Oh, right." Markus said remembering now. He felt the eyes of both Ruth and Ashlyn weighing down on him as he thought of where he had left off. When he got his mind in order, he continued his story from the previous night.

"Alright, so Taiyou was in the army to gain his chance to reunite with princess Tsuki. It was his dream and his promise to return to her, one way or another and the only way to do that was to become a Royal Guard- the first Groundling Elf to surpass any Noble and join in the princess' courts."

"He wouldn't be in the courts." Ruth pointed out. "Guards don't go to court."

"Alright, alright, sorry." Markus chuckled. "Anyways… However, one of the lead commanders didn't like how Taiyou was still around. They were nearing the graduation ceremony, and the Groundling had refused to give up, even with all the Nobles treating him like trash. So, deciding that it was necessary, he told Taiyou that the princess was waiting for him at the base of the mountain by the training grounds. Excited, the naïve Groundling followed the Noble, having to run to keep up with the flying elf. But when they made it, Taiyou saw that the ship waiting near the base of the island was not one of the kingdoms', but of pirates. Before he knew it, he was taken prisoner, and sold to the pirates. The last thing Taiyou saw of his home island, was when the pirate ship took sail and flew away into the night skies, their new cargo in stock. For weeks, Taiyou was taken from place to place, ready to be sold as a slave to some buyer somewhere. It seemed that all hope was lost, and Taiyou would never see his home, or his princess ever again.

"That is, until another pirate crew, stole him and a few other slaves away to give them back to their original owners. After sneaking them all away, they all boarded the ship called *The Black Rose*, and after raising the sails, the pirate crew took Taiyou and the slaves to another island where the slaves were originally from. When the crew saw that Taiyou was not of that group, they asked him where he was from. As Taiyou described his home, he noticed that the pirates were of both races of elves. Both were of Nobles, and of Groundlings, all working together under a Groundling captain. After telling the pirates what happened to him, the captain, Arturo, made a deal with Taiyou.

"He says, 'Tai, you help us get pardoned so we can become free, then we will take you home to your princess'. Tai says 'why would I help a pack of pirates?' The captain replies, 'Because you won't find anyone else willing to go to the enemy for yer sake'. So Taiyou agrees, and they all set sail back to the kingdom, and the hopes of seeing his princess again lifted Tai's heart. Upon reaching the mainland though, Taiyou was dismayed to see that an army of Orks had come to the kingdom, wanting to claim it for their own under the rule of the witch who lead them. Wondering what he could do, he watched from the deck of the ship, worried about what exactly he could do to stop the monsters from breaking through the walls and destroying his home and all the Groundlings and Nobles from within."

At some point, Markus turned to look at Ruth, who was already sound asleep, warm in the firelight and lost in the land of dreams. Ashlyn turned to look the same direction he did, to see the girl sleeping pleasantly, without a worry in the world.

"How does she do that?" Ashlyn asked rubbing her eyes.

"I don't know." Markus said now studying the flames. "I envy her."

"Me too." Ashlyn laid on her side against her pile of blankets. She looked at Markus through the flickering flames as if in deep thought. "That was a good story. Where did you hear it from?"

"My father." Markus said. "He loved telling fairy tales to us."

"How did the ships fly?"

"It's a fantasy world, if he could imagine pirate ships flying in the sky, it was possible." Markus shrugged. "I guess the short answer would be... magic."

"I see..." Ashlyn said thoughtfully, smiling at him. "I think that would be cool. Sailing on a ship in the sky. You're a good story-teller."

"I suppose." Markus then turned back to Ashlyn and saw that she was now staring at him. "What?" he asked.

She didn't answer at first. Markus felt her eyes seem to dive into his own. "That night," she finally said. "When The Guard was after me... would you really have pulled the trigger?"

Markus sighed. Now *he* was the one silent in thought. *Would I have? I suppose I would. It was Ruths' safety that was more important compared to a street rat I did not know or care about.*

"I don't know." he finally said instead.

Ashlyn nodded. She grabbed ahold of a blanket and covered herself. She tucked herself in, and then returned to facing Markus. "Be honest with me. Do you think we'll make it, Mark? To the city?"

Since when did she start calling me 'Mark'? "My honest opinion?"

"Please." she nodded.

"I wish I knew."

Ashlyn pursed her lips. "You still think that? After we escaped that terrible place?"

"Look where we are now Ashlyn." Markus said looking at the shadows flickering against the walls of dirt and roots. "We're in the *Wastelands*. You really think we'll survive out here?"

"We have to. For Ruth's sake."

Markus looked at her credulously.

She shrugged. "I guess I always wanted a sister to protect. I had no one to protect me so I know what it's like to feel all alone. I don't want her to feel

and made the entire place look like it was on fire, blinding those who were awake. He yawned and wiped the tear that had frozen upon his cheek. He looked over to the girls, who were still asleep beside the smoldering ashes of the fire from the previous night. Markus smiled at Ashlyn and Ruth, despite that he was still dwelling on his father's words. He was telling Markus to have hope. Did he have hope? He didn't think so.

But I have to try. For Ruth's sake.

He got up and took out a can of pork n' beans from Ashlyn's pack. He popped the top off with his knife and sat the can over the mound of hot coals. As the food heated up Markus stood and stepped outside.

The sun felt nice on his skin; it felt as if the rays were opening and cleaning the pores in his face and breathing life into his body. In the distance Markus saw a Snow Wolf with its cubs playing near a submerged Xerxe tank lost in time. The beast stood as large as the tank itself, and its cubs as tall as a person at the shoulder. They cooed and wrestled in the snow under the watchful eye of their mother. Her head turned and Markus could see those intense blue eyes looking right at him. Not threateningly but curious at the figure watching them from afar. She then nosed her cubs away, and they disappeared into the frontier.

Markus smiled and turned back to the girls who were still asleep. He decided to let them sleep a little longer. Maybe there was hope for them yet.

~ The Xerxe Encounter ~

Markus

Markus was studying the map the following morning he had tucked into his bag. Though he still had that strong 'magnetizing feeling' coming from the east, he wanted to see if there was a chance that there was a village nearby. It would be risky to approach, but he wanted to refuel and see if there was a trading post that could at least spare some extra water and blankets.

Ashlyn eventually emerged from the dugout and joined beside him. She watched him trail the blotted and torn map with his finger where many figures of distant kingdoms were marked in a language she didn't understand. Markus didn't understand them either, but he had memorized at least what each blot represented and from there determine where exactly they were located. Not precisely by any means, but close enough.

"I believe we are here." he said to Ashlyn making a circle to the north of the Bronze Mines. "We escaped through the northeastern tunnels, and we are to go east."

"Because of this 'feeling' you got." Ashlyn stated. It was clear that she still found it a little unbelievable on how Markus was leading them to the City of Angels- *If* it existed, he reminded himself.

"That's right." Markus then pointed at a little blotch that looked like a house. "This here is Lakeshire I think. I'm thinking we should make a stop by the village."

"You think that's a good idea?"

"Lakeshire is under the wing of Xerxes. There's even a Xerxe outpost I think, if I remember correctly. We shouldn't run into any Ninevite soldiers there. However, I'm not sure how they would react if they found out we are from the city…"

As he was talking, he thought he had smelled something off about Ashlyn. She had a strange smell to her, something burnt like ash that definitely was not from a fire. It was sweet, similar to tobacco. Not thinking too much about it however, he ignored his nose and proceeded to explain that the Xerxe soldiers might not take too kindly to them but he wanted to risk making a stop.

"Do you really think we should stop in town?" Ashlyn asked.

"We need to make sure our bikes are full of fuel. Besides, I also want to see if we can't get extra blankets or fuel. Last night was freezing, and I wanna make sure Ruth has everything she needs. Who knows, maybe their laws on potions and medicines aren't as strict as Nineveh."

"Good idea…"

Markus looked at Ashlyn, hearing the hesitation in her voice rake the back of his head. "What are your thoughts?"

She pursed her lips. "It sounds risky. We have enough fuel canisters, but at the same time, some real food and fresh water would be nice. Who knows what we might get in this snow?"

"Exactly. Besides, Ruth needs fresh food and some real medicine."

"We have some stuff from Madam Zerona still."

"I want something else to go with it. Before we get any further from any civilization, I want to be absolutely sure we have what we need to travel."

Ashlyn nodded in understanding. "What would be our story? I've never been in a village before."

"Neither have I. I suppose we can make it up as we go. We can say we're all siblings trying to catch up with our caravan."

"Markus, you and Ruth are the only other human beings I've seen out here thus far. With the risk of bandits and raiders out here as well, I think the only kind of people we'd meet are people like them."

"Maybe. But do you have a better idea?"

"We could just keep going." Ashlyn offered. "But if you think we should check in at Lakeshire, I say let's do it. Let's be smart about it, but let's do it."

"Okay. As soon as Ruth wakes up we'll hit the road."

"The sun's already up. Shouldn't we wake her?"

"Let her sleep. She needs it more than us."

The two of them let Ruth sleep for another hour until she finally roused. When they all packed up they set out into the Wastelands again, their current destination a village under the protection of Xerxes; Nineveh's current arch enemy.

They rode for about three hours before a large black blotch appeared across the white horizon. About an hour later they came across a large compound completely fenced off by a large wall of fused metal. The walls stood about twenty feet tall with guard towers covered with satellite dishes and antennae's. The trio had to circle around until they finally came across the entrance that was in-between two large towers with a group of soldiers searching what looked like an actual trading caravan.

The caravan consisted of a few men wrapped in furs and armed with heavy Old-School weaponry. They had a large cart drawn by a pair of Leaper Dragons who were hissing and growling at each other, baring sharp teeth and hitting one another with their long tails. Behind them, sitting on a mechanical tread was a cage and inside was a Werecat. The humanoid body was covered in fur, but its snarling cat-like face was pressed against the bars and its claws were scratching at the floor of its cage. It looked malnourished and incredibly angry, especially at the trader who prodded it with a shock-stick. When the Xerxe soldiers told the men to head in through the opening, one of them approached the now-parked teens who were waiting patiently.

The solider was garbed in sleek black armor with a helmet that looked insect-like with its oxygen piece and blazing yellow eyes. Markus figured that the lenses' would have different focus-modes as well as different vision options. In his hands was a large Gunsword, an energy assault rifle with a large steel blade following along the barrel and passing it by about a foot in length. Even the stock that rested in the crook of the soldier's arm was revealed to have a special grip so that the man could just swing the weapon around like a berserker if he wanted to.

He addressed Markus and the others with a brisk nod. "What is your business here in Lakeshire?" his voice was garbled by the speaker in the helmet, but by the sound of it he sounded young. Younger than a member of the Ninevite Guard had to be to even attempt to join.

"We are travelers." Markus said dismounting his bike and standing before the soldier who stood just a little taller than he. It was impossible to tell the age but he doubted that it really mattered. "We are here to trade on our way to Bronzeshire." He knew that the village was just along the border of the Southern Sands south of the Nothern Wastelands, and he figured it was a safe risk to tell the soldier.

"I don't recognize you." the soldier said shaking his head. "Besides, you all look too young to be just travelers."

"We got separated by our caravan." Ashlyn stepped in still sitting on her bike. "We're trying to catch up with them. Besides, we've been out here all our lives."

"So you are Wastelanders." the soldier stated obviously in disdain. "I bet. Which caravan was it?"

"Uh, the mechanics traders?" It was all that Markus could think of.

"I don't recognize that name." The soldier was obviously not believing them.

"We're, uh, new." Ruth said with a cough.

"Right." The soldier then nodded at Markus again. "You all appear heavily armed with weapons more than tools."

"Gotta keep ourselves safe." Markus said hoping that the soldier wouldn't search them or anything.

"True, true. How about this then, what tribe are you from?"

"We don't have a tribe." Ashlyn said. "We all travel only with our family."

"You all are form the same family?" the soldier said looking between the three of them. He then gestured to Markus and Ruth. "You two, I can believe that. You however…"

"Our father had many wives." Ashlyn said. She was a pretty fast thinker to come up with that.

"Now it sounds more believable that you are Wastelanders." the soldier said seeming to relax his shoulders a bit. "Either that, or you're escaped slaves or royalties, given your age."

Markus didn't even have to fake his own laughter. "That'll be the day."

"Well, you all don't appear to me as folk who mean harm." the soldier admitted. "However, I find your story hard to believe. Therefore, I cannot let you inside Lakeshire."

"We only wish to trade, sir." Markus said trying to offer the same sort of respect he would present to a Guard back home. "We have money for food and water. Besides, one of us is sick, and we'd like medicine."

"I'm not letting you in." the soldier said. He paused for a moment and then said, "How about this, give me a list and I'll count what you have. Then I'll have someone buy the stuff for you. Then you can be on your merry way. Sound fair?"

"That's fine." Markus admitted. "Has it been that bad with security around here?"

"Heh, 'fraid so." the soldier said now lowering his weapon and letting it hang in his hand. "Metalheads have been growing bold out there. Now we only let in soldiers and known caravans in here. We also have to check on farmers who have fields outside the walls."

"We didn't see any farmland." Ashlyn said.

"It's closer to Xerxes, north of here."

"Makes sense." Markus said. And then with the soldier's permission, he gave the man a small list of necessities.

The solider tilted his head curiously. "You gotta be more specific when you say 'medicine'. Just what exactly do you need?"

Markus scratched his head, somewhat embarrassed. "We really don't know, sir."

The soldier looked at Ruth who had started conveniently coughing and then back to Markus. "How about this then, I'll have a medic come and check on her. She can determine what you need and we can proceed form there. Is that okay? I don't want to give you the wrong thing and make it worse."

At least the man had courtesy enough to offer and express concern for their well-being. He wasn't entirely heartless. "That would be great," Markus said. He was a little disappointed that he wouldn't get a chance to actually visit Lakeshire, but he didn't want to arouse any more suspicion than they probably already had. Looking back at Ruth, he could tell she was a little disappointed too. She was ecstatic when told they were stopping at a village. However, she was also understanding, and probably got why the soldier was being so cautious.

While the soldier was speaking into his earpiece, Markus took the opportunity to look around some more. The other soldiers had gone back to the entrance where three of them now sat around a crate playing cards while the forth was sitting up against a Hellhound. The hovercraft was completely black instead of red, and it had a longer wingspan with what looked like a more advanced anti-gravity plating. The ship sported the Xerxe emblem, a woman surrounded by the ouros boros circle. The craft had a large sign saying that it was for sale, which only made the craft look out of place outside the walls of the village.

Markus turned and pointed at it while looking at Ruth, trying to tell her how awesome it looked in his eye. But Ruth wasn't looking at him. She was looking up and turning around Markus looked up towards the top of the wall and saw something he hadn't noticed before: a body.

The body was strapped to a large pole and propped up with some chains connected to a nearby tower. The body was completely charred to a black husk, the skeleton visible in the shriveled flesh. It made Markus' stomach crawl, and he looked to see that the soldier had noticed him staring and was looking at the body himself.

"That one of the Metalheads you mentioned?" Markus asked.

The soldier shook his head. "No. Witch. Village council declared her to be burned and displayed as a warning to all witches who enter."

"Looks pretty harsh," Ruth said, her voice quiet.

"Magic is not something to mess with in the first place." the soldier said. "Not under Xerxes' gaze."

"Xerxes is anti-magic?" Markus asked, intrigued.

"Has been for years."

"Interesting." Markus decided to just keep the man talking, to avoid any awkward silence. "How long as Xerxes operated in Lakeshire?"

"Couple of years now. Been based here since I was a kid."

That meant the soldier had to be young still. "Do you just work here?" Markus then asked.

"That's right. I'm still technically a grunt. Only soldiers who undergo more training join the actual army or become the Queensguard. Don't know if you three have heard anything, but our armies just got walloped by Nineveh."

"We did hear about that." Ashlyn said leaning forward on her bike trying to look intrigued. "What happened exactly?"

The soldier chuckled humorlessly which sounded funny coming from his helmet speaker. "Just a load of bad luck. Lots of miscalculations and bad calls.

We lost a lot of men, and I'm betting me and the rest of the platoon here are going to be drafted. The queen isn't going to give up, she wants that region."

"Why does Queen Psyren want Nineveh?" Markus asked.

"Why does any nation attack another?" the soldier then pointed up three fingers for each item he listed. "Land, resources, and control. Just like a chess board. Royal pieces want more control of the board, but they need to send the pawns first. Sadly, between that bastard Baron and our queen, things just haven't looked good since King Mikhail died."

Markus remembered hearing about King Mikhail. He was once the king of Nineveh, and had a solid relationship with Queen Psyren and the two nations traded and worked together in harmony. But when the king died with no heir, his only successor, Baron Ovid, succeeded the throne. Ever since then, Nineveh was cut off from the rest of the world and both the Kingdom of Coal and the Industrial Kingdom had been at each other's throats for years.

"That's a shame." Markus said crossing his arms. "You say Queen Psyren plans to attack again?"

"Sooner or later." The way the soldier said that made Markus nervous. He decided to stop asking questions about the war. He didn't want to get arrested on suspect of being a spy.

Thankfully, he didn't have to think of anything else for a girl was brought out through the entrance by another soldier. The girl was cute, just about Markus' age with no hair and a face that made it look like her head was the moon. She was garbed in white and had a stethoscope around her neck. She approached Ruth and asked her to get off the bike. She then proceeded to do her check on his little sister.

The entire time the 'medic' did her work, Markus watched her like a hawk. He watched as she took Ruth's temperature, listened to her heartbeat, and then shined a light into her eyes, nose, and then into her throat. After a few minutes, the medic stepped back, disappointed and stumped by the looks of it.

"I cannot tell what she has." she said in a soft tone. "All I know is that her lungs are full of liquid."

"Liquid?" Markus asked, hoping for more of an answer.

"Yes, and unfortunately I do not have the equipment necessary to do a more thorough check."

"Is there anything that could at least help her?"

"Staying out of the cold would be one idea."

Of course it is. "We don't really have that luxury right now. Is there anything else we can do?"

"Bundle her up best you can. You said you were here for medicine and supplies? Well, I'd recommend cough syrup and maybe a Clearing Potion to see if it does anything to help her body fight whatever it is it fights. It'll help break up any blockage and help her breathe better."

Markus looked to the soldier. "How much would those two things and a couple of more blankets cost?"

"Let's see your purse." the soldier said holding out his hand after thanking the woman and sending her back inside in a hurry. After Markus handed him the little purse of coins the soldier counted them up and sighed disappointedly. "You don't have enough, not for either of those remedies. Just enough for a moth-eaten blanket."

"Seriously?" Ashlyn asked surprised.

"Sorry, but that's all we can give you for this much."

"Oh c'mon, have a heart, sir." Markus pleaded. "Anything to help us?"

"My job is to help my kingdom, and protect this village. Those two things come before helping any Wastelanders. I'm sorry, but there is nothing I can do."

Bastard... Markus grounded the thought in his mind as he wondered just what to do. "Is inflation seriously that bad?"

"You aren't going to try and haggle me, are you?" the soldier asked in a cold tone of voice. "That would be a bad idea, especially coming from people who don't seem in the slightest bit trustworthy. I've been patient enough with you as it is, and was kind enough to have someone check on you. That is where my pleasantries end."

Thinking fast, Markus looked towards the Hellhound still parked behind the soldier's buddies. Having an idea, he asked, "What's that?"

The soldier looked at the hovercraft and snorted. "A piece of crap, that's what it is."

"What's wrong with it?"

"Engine's blown. Can't fix the damn thing. Everything inside looks fine, but nothing fires up when we turn it on. So we're scrapping it. If any trader who we *do* know wants scrap metal and parts- and I know they do, then they can buy it from us."

"What if I fixed it?"

The solider looked at Markus as if he had not heard him correctly. "You?"

"We are mechanics, sir. I've worked with a Double-H Hawkeye model before, maybe I can take a look at it and get it running?"

"You know what model that is? That's kind of impressive, coming from a Wastelander. Far as I know, only kingdom that makes these models is Xerxes."

"Well, I've never been in Xerxes before, but I can promise you I am not lying. I might have a chance to fix it if you want me to."

The soldier thought about it for a moment. "It would be convenient if you can get it running…"

"If I do, would you get us the medicine?"

The man thought about it some more. "If you can, I'll give you the potions and more."

"Deal." Markus said holding his hand out. The soldier reached out and shook it and then took him to inspect the vehicle with both Ashlyn and Ruth in tow.

"You sure about this?" Ashlyn asked.

"Do you have any tools I can borrow?" Markus asked the soldiers at the crate, ignoring her.

They shoved a toolbox over to him and Markus opened the bottom hatch and stuck his head inside. He used a flashlight to look around, seeing a lot of the general parts in place. He asked the soldier if he would be willing to turn on the engine. Once the man was in, he turned it on and the inside of the Hellhound started to hum with very faint breaths of life.

Tick-tick-tick-clunk! Tick-tick-tick-clunk!

Markus knew immediately that it was a power deficiency somewhere in the hydraulic mechanism that brought the anti-gravity panels to life. He told the man to stop the engine and he came back out asking for a wrench and a screwdriver. With the two tools in hand, he crawled deeper into the machine and wriggled like a worm to the very back where the engine rested beneath the cockpit of the hovercraft. From there, he shined his light underneath the pistons and beneath it he found the crankshaft. It looked to be in good condition, but Markus' trained eye working under his father's wing, proved otherwise.

"Right here." Markus said taking his screwdriver and shoving it into the space between one of the gears. He twisted until it came loose, and then getting his wrench in there, he loosened the gear and then adjusted the pistons above it. When it looked about right, he scooted back and when his feet dangled in the air, he felt relief and pushed himself completely out of the hull like he was being born a second time.

"Found the problem." he told the soldiers waiting patiently. "You had tightened the p-98 crankshaft too tight and it was choking the piston, not allowing them to turn and let it churn the battery to bring power to the anti-gravity panels."

"Do I look like a mechanic?" the soldier from earlier demanded. "Just tell me, did you fix it or not? It didn't take you very long."

"I have an ear for these things. C'mon, fire her up. Trust me."

The soldier humored him, and called for another who crawled back up onto the Hellhound. With the front hatch still opened, he turned on the engine which hummed to life and beneath the hovercraft, a faint blue glow brightened. Seeming startled at first, the man clicked something and the Hellhound rose a good foot in the air. He then took it higher into the air and started to hover around; slowly at first but then he started doing faster maneuvers. As it flew the first solider just stood there so flabbergasted that he took off his helmet and revealed his shocked features; handsome, stern and strong, and as Markus assumed, very young still, not even a man by Nineveh's standards.

"Holy shit, the kid did it." one of the other men said.

"That's my brother!" Ruth squealed very much pleased. Her praise lifted Markus' heart.

The soldier who had removed his helmet, turned to look at Markus. "Your caravan is new, you say?"

"Something like that." Markus said laughing, enjoying this reaction. "Should fly fine now."

"Have to admit, I'm impressed…" the man said with his helmet now resting at his hip like he was a biker himself. "We could certainly use hands like yours. But, a deal's a deal. You'll have your potions- no charge."

"You sure?" Markus asked.

"Keep your coin. You might need it. You've saved us a lot of headaches with that." As he said that, the Hellhound disappeared within the walls of Lakeshire, out of view entirely. With that taken care of, the man called in for the supplies Markus asked for to be brought out- "On Xerxe's tab." he said.

The solider then turned to Markus with a genuine smile on his face. "Thanks for the help, kid. Name's Uzzah."

"Uzzah?" Ashlyn asked, intrigued with the name.

"It's southern. I'm from a village in the Southern Sands Region. Moved up here when my Da got a job in Xerxes. From there, joined the army."

"Interesting," Markus said just as the very soldier who took the Hellhound (Markus guessed that was the same soldier) came out the front with a blanket folded like a sack. Upon opening it he revealed the two vials of cough syrup and the Clearing Potion. He gave both to Ruth who was back on the bike and then to Ashlyn he handed her an additional fuel cartridge for their Hoverbikes. Inside the heavy blanket stitched with stuffed jeans there was also some dehydrated food packets.

"You sure you can spare this?" Markus asked.

"If you want fresh food we can bring you some." Uzzah said. "Thing is, doubt you trust me with fresh food any more than I trust you inside the village walls."

"Understandable." Markus wouldn't have accepted any food or water offered by the soldier unless it was all sealed. He didn't suspect them of any ill towards him and the girls, but he wasn't about to risk it. He knew Ruth would check the potions at least, but the blankets and fuel would be most helpful.

"What is it like in the Southern Sands?" Ashlyn then asked loading the dehydrated food packets into the saddles of her bike.

"Cold in the winter, and hot as hell in the summer." Ussah answered. "Least down there it never snows during winter. Never even knew what snow was like living in the desert. I wasn't used to the snow when we first came up here. Back then though, those were simpler times. Certainly didn't realize how big the world really is."

"I don't think anyone ever truly realizes how big it is." Markus said thinking back to Abner and what he had heard in his dream. He then mounted his bike and thanked the man for his help.

"Of course." Ussah said. "Bring your father back here, and then maybe we can fit your caravan into the route. Hope your journey goes well. May the stars shine bright on your road."

Knowing the saying to be a farewell common in the Southern Sands from what his father had taught him, Markus returned the blessing. "And may the sun and moon always points you in the direction to the oasis."

Ussah appeared pleased. "Been so long since someone returned the blessing as such. Farewell, uh… what are your names?"

"Deegan." Markus lied. "And these are my sisters, Jasmyne and Ofelia."

The soldier nodded. "Farewell, Deegan, Jasmyne, and Ofelia." With a final wave, Markus kicked his bike into gear and Ashlyn followed close behind. They rode in silence until Lakeshire was nothing more than a black blotch once again on the white horizon, the smoke of the village still reaching towards the sky.

"Guess Xerxe-folk aren't so bad." Ruth commented.

"Yeah," Markus agreed. "Makes you wonder what else we are missing out here." He wondered if he would ever get a chance to see Ussah again, maybe in another time. Maybe, actually, in another life.

But the voice of Abner spoke and said to Markus, *You will see him again. I foresee it.*

Black

The Hunter Black had spotted the children at Lakeshire, but before he could head to the village, he sensed something coming in from the west.

Knowing the witch and her brother were on the hunt as well, Black at first didn't expect to sense what he felt coming in his direction. Concern gripped at his heart, but he reined his worry in and focused on what the best course of action was to do. When he made his decision, he started southern just as the children had finally left the village and started back east. He would catch up with them later.

For now, he had to get the other Hunters off their tail and deal with them before they could get to the kids first.

~ The Heartless Machine ~

Lameika

Lameika sat in the passenger seat next to Lee who had the controls of the Hellhound. His helmet was off and his eyes scanned the horizon outside the windshield over the many buttons and switches. He would regularly keep track of pressure gauges but at the same time checking the heat-signature scanners near the Overdrive. If anything alive popped up on the scanners, he would know immediately.

Lameika on the other hand sat back, muttering words of ancient power into her hands, which held a pile of seeds which glowed a faint purple. What kind of seeds they were, were unknown to the witch, for she got them from her homeland off of one of the old warlocks. But she spoke to them softly, tenderly as a mother would her children. In the Wastelands, there were many unexplainable phenomenon's; not just the mutations and radiation scourge that held the world in a strange sense of time. Ancient magic once thought to have been lost thousands of years ago were coming back; spirits wandering the lands, contracts of blood, and many more occultist practices, making the Wastelands something to be reckoned with. The seeds were of no exception, Lameika had been told and as she casted her spells upon the unknown children, she was very careful not to stumble upon any hidden secrets locked within the husks.

Behind Lameika and Lee were the other three Hunters who accompanied them. Together the five of them would find those brats. There was a sixth member of the guild, but he was currently operating in Xerxes. He would catch up with them soon; after they claimed what they needed from those kids.

In the seat *right* behind her, the one called Pyro sat reclined in his seat with his feet propped on top of his dashboard. His steel boots and armor were still on, but his helmet had been removed, revealing the disfigured face of a cyborg. The upper left half of his head was robotic, with a clear computer chip lodged in the back of the skull. The rest of his face was normal; human, but badly scarred. He had no hair, facial or otherwise. His cheeks were deeply scarred and his lips were torn. His eyelid was gone, and his forehead had a deep dent in it. His robotic eye zoomed in and out on the apple he was carving up and eating with his knife; his iron teeth grinding the pieces with each clashing bite.

In the back, Tank sat cleaning his rocket launcher, beside where the one known as Slitzar sat watching him do his cleaning. Slitzar was a Lacerta; a reptilian creature born from the sludge left by atomic wastes many years ago. Big, strong, and capable of everything a reptile was, as well as human.

She used to live in the swamps of Grog, but soon joined the crew when they happened to be hunting in her area. Her sense of smell and sheer brutality made her a valued member of the team. When she got bored of watching Tank, she passed the rest of the time watching the passing valley below as the Hellhound pushed on towards their objective. She always did that it seemed: watch, and listen. Despite being very much like a human, she as really just a monster; a beast that was intelligent as well as dangerous.

"Whatcha looking at?" the gruff voice of the Lacerta asked the cyborg peering at them from his seat.

"Chill out, Scales," Pyro said with a dismissive wave. "Just checkin' on my buddies. C'mon, don't be sucha killjoy."

Slitzar growled at him and Tank told them both to knock it off. "You both are annoying." he said.

"Oh, look what you did, Scales." Pyro teased. "You pissed off Rustbucket here."

"Knock it off, both of you." Lee said turning his head briefly to look at them. "Lameika is concentrating."

"On what?" Pyro asked now pulling out a deck of cards and shuffling them in his hand. "How to turn us into frogs? Oi, Tank, put the gun down for a bit and let's play some B.S."

"Not interested." Tank said despite placing his rocket launcher down at his feet. "I just want to sit and relax."

"Relax what? You ain't got any muscles."

Slitar growled. "Doncha ever shut up?"

"No. Not when I'm awake. You up for a round, Scales?"

"Hmmm… Fine."

Lameika knew what the three behind her were all doing despite not ever having to look at them. She could see it. She could *sense* what they were doing as she breathed her unholy powers into the seeds resting in her soft and pale palm.

Eventually, Lameika stopped casting her spell into the seeds and took a deep breath as if exhausted after a long run. She opened her eyes to see Lee looking at her from the corner of his eye- looking as though he was concerned.

"You okay?" he asked.

She nodded. "I'm fine." It was none of his concern anyway.

"The Master?"

"He's helped me."

"With?"

Lameika rolled her eyes. Did her brother really have to know every little thing? "Nothing yet. It still needs time- to ripen."

Lee nodded. "I see." he said clearly not seeing at all.

"Patience, Brother." She shoved the seeds into her pocket, ending the conversation. "What's our ETA?"

"Fifty miles out." Lee said shifting his eyes forward again. "We traveled all night, Sister."

"Too long already if you ask me." Pyro gripped shoving an apple slice into his mouth. He was staring at his sleeve of cards and around bites he said, "All we see down there are a couple of wolves and giant slugs. First you start heading like you wanna go to Xerxes and then you suddenly turn and head southward. Lee, I don't think you're in the right mind to drive."

"Why are you so annoying?" Lee demanded.

"Well, gimme a break. Where are those brats?"

"We're not looking for the children yet, my friend." Lee said between clenched teeth. For once, Lameika could agree with his impatience for the cybernetic Hunter. "We have a stop to make. Business to attend to."

"I like it already." Pyro said mockingly before he called out the three of spades.

"Not for you." Lameika said.

"Excuse me?" Pyro spat, his game forgotten.

"You heard me."

"Listen you-" he was cut short by Lee's sharp gaze. At least her brother had *some* use. Pyro mumbled to himself a bit before daring to continue. "Look, what is it we gotta deal with anyway?"

"Black." Lee said. "That slimy bastard is fast, and if the stories are true, he will find those children. He looked like he was on something, but he slowed down. This is our chance. As our 'dear' Baron had said, he will not harm them, and as you remembered the other day, the kids won't go without a fight."

"I see." Pyro said still unsatisfied.

"So one of us is going to stop him while the rest of us continue on." Lameika said finishing for her brother. "Unfortunately, Lee will not be going as well." This seemed to irritate Lee, the way he clenched his jaw but Lameika didn't care in the slightest. Let him pout, she thought bitterly.

"And who might that be, Princess?" Pyro snorted. "Instead of one of us, we should all stop. C'mon, I mean, five against one? He'd never last."

"I will *not* lose anymore time tracking those kids." Lameika said sharply. "Tank is the fastest on foot, so after he dispatches of our Hunter friend, he will catch up to us when we make camp at mid-day."

"Oh, come on." Pyro said tossing his apple core onto the floor. "Him?" He pointed a thumb at the robot who had finished cleaning his gun.

"As you wish." Tank said, and if his creator gave him a mouth, he would have been smiling. "This will be most delightful."

"Make sure that gun of yours is ready." Lee said. "Cause he's below us now as we speak. Forty degrees."

"Stay your course." Lameika ordered her brother.

"Yes, Sister."

"Tank, get ready to drop."

Tank locked on his rocket launcher to his wrist, and from his other, his broadsword shot out like a switchblade. "Ready." He stood up and waited standing in the center of the floor. Pyro buckled up, whereas Slitzar stayed seated, her dilated eyes never leaving the land that passed beneath the ship.

Lee smiled cruelly as he flicked a switch. A crosshairs logo appeared on the windshield and, using a joystick he moved the crosshairs until it hovered over Black, the Hunter still moving fast on his Hoverbike and not looking back at the Hellhound catching up to him.

"Prepare to open the hatch." Lee said.

Pyro laughed as he held an arm out, grasping the release lever near the rear of the ship.

Goodbye, Black. "Fire," Lameika said with such glee.

Lee laughed as he hit the trigger on his stirring column, and below them a missile launched and dove like a hawk after fish towards the young Hunter. As soon as the nose struck the rear of the bike it exploded in a flash of fire and smoke. At the same time Pyro had released his own switch, letting Tank drop down to the frontier below. To Lee and Lameika's astonishment however, they saw a small figure fly forward from where the bike had exploded, and land in a powdery poof in the snow.

"If he is not dead now," Lameika said with shrewd eyes. "He will be." In her heart she hoped the Hunter known as Black was dead, and if not, would hopefully be too weak to fight against Tank. She had heard stories of the Hunter, but surely no man could survive that, *and* be in good enough shape to go against a battle-bot.

"Agreed." Lee said boosting the thrusters and propelling the Hellhound forward, passing the wreckage and moving on for their hunt.

Tank
As the world's gravitational pull brought Tank closer to the ground, the air and snow collided with him, pushing back and blowing in his face but he did not flinch, for he felt no change in his core temperature.

Despite the frost accumulating on his metallic husk, his interior circuits continued to stay warm and running properly. As he neared the ground the spring locks in the calves of his legs extended, preparing to meet the ground and ease the landing. As his legs struck the ground his feet dug into the snow and the ground beneath it, spraying up dirty snow in a deep and wide radius around him. His spring locks depleted and the air pressure in his valves released, giving him more comfort in his landing. As he stood up his back-up computer did a systems-check, checking for any damage done to his body or the mechanisms within from the fall. When he saw nothing was wrong he began to trudge forward to the wreckage where he landed a good ten yards behind. The wind continued to blow, pushing him back but he kept on trudging; a minor snow storm wouldn't stop him.

Scraps of metal littered the ground and smoke trailed from the major mechanisms of the destroyed Hoverbike. Tank- his rocket-launcher extended and ready to fire -scanned the surrounding area, his heat sensors looking for the body of the Hunter. His sword retracted into his forearm and he placed his free hand on the barrel of the launcher for better aim. He kept his massive head on a swivel in the search for the body. But apart from the shattered bike, he saw nothing but snow. Far from any old city ruins or forests, snow just blanketed clear across the horizon- the foggy air making it hard to see further than half a mile. Tank could see no sign of the Hunter- his corpse or otherwise. It made no sense, and Tank was-

Tank suddenly lurched forward as he was struck with a sharp blow to his back. Nothing hurt him but the force shoved him forward violently. Growling with movement, he turned on his heels to see the Hunter standing before him, his shotgun aimed at him with the barrel smoking. The man didn't look hurt; covered in snow and dirt maybe but not hurt as far as Tank could tell. There were no traces of blood where he saw the Hunter had crawled and popped out of the snow behind Tank.

The Hunter had tunneled around him!

If Tank could smile, he would be doing so now. "You survived." Tank stated. "You are quite resilient. However, I'm afraid your tricks won't save you any longer." He took aim at Black with the rocket-launcher, wondering how Black would look like in a million pieces.

The Hunter Black reached behind him with his spare hand, and pulled his longsword from its sheathe. Tank watched as the sword glowed bright blue as it flickered in electric arcs. "Your vocabulary is a lot more advanced than most robots. But I do not have time for this." Black said, his eyes flashing coldly as they glared at the robot before them.

"Guess you better make time." Tank said and fired his weapon.

The Hunter had sprinted to the side, dodging the blast of the rocket which erupted right where he was once standing in a flash of fire and snow. The man in turn continued to fire his shotgun, the buckshot crashing into Tank's torso but only to bounce off and land into the snow as if they were gravel being thrown by a child. Tank fired again and again but the man dove from side to side like a rabbit escaping a hawk; the rockets exploding in blasts of incredible heat behind Black's darkened figure as he neared Tank. When he was about a good ten feet away the man leapt and fired at Tanks' head. At this time, Tank had extended his sword from its slot and swung at the man who somersaulted in the air, his sword spinning like a windmill right past Tanks left side. Tank turned sharply, seeing Black had landed back in a crouching position, both hands on his sword and knees bent.

Tank spun back around. "You can't dodge me forever." His voice was cut short when he saw the front half of his launcher land in the snow in front of him. He looked down at his arm to see that the gun was cut clean at the stock. Wires sparked and crackled at the ends and smoke seeped from the edges. Despite his predicament Tank was impressed.

"*Very* impressive." He lowered his sparkling stump. "Please, tell me what kind of steel that is."

Black turned his head to look at Tank, and with his back still to the massive machine he stood up. "Ebony Bronze. Tough to break, and can usually cut through many metals, aside from a few."

Tank hummed in irritation. "Interesting. I'll have to look into it. Well, despite what kind it is and how much more pressure those boots have to launch you, you won't last long." From his shoulder a slot opened and a mounted laser rifle took aim at Black. He telescoped his sword out as well, and took a stance. "However, if you agree to turn around and go back to the city, you will be spared."

"I wish I could believe you," Black said emotionlessly. He turned and took a stance facing the machine. "However your reputation is questionable under the circumstance. Especially with the company you keep."

Tank hummed and fired his rifle. With sharp reflexes Black tilted his blade, and the laser beam was deflected, crashing into the snow beside him.

"You're fast." Tank noticed still firing. "I don't see what kind of device you have to make you as fast, but no man can beat machine, and live." And with that he charged at Black, rifle firing and sword ready.

Black deflected each shot and then dove to the side as Tanks sword came down, cutting through snow and dirt. He felt a shock through his core as Black swung at his leg, merely scratching the metal but the electric shock coursing through Tanks' circuits were strong enough for him to feel it in his internal motherboard. He swung around, but Black ducked beneath the blade and made an upward cut, scratching Tanks arm and shocking him again. He punched out at Black with his stump and landed a blow to the chest. The puny human flew backwards and landed ten feet in the snow with a heavy *poof*. Immediately he fired his rifle again and again but still Black was back up and he rolled away and onto his feet as he deflected the beams with that accursed sword of his.

Tank was growing more and more irritated by the minute. "Stop running!" He fired again and Black leapt aside again, this time swinging towards Tanks face. The robot held up his sword to deflect the blow and succeeded, but the shock coursed through the blade, through his arms and down to his core. His inner alarms were blaring 'warning overload' and 'damage to the motherboard' but Tank ignored it and swung again. Black dodged and deflected again and again, he was shoved back with each blow due to Tanks immense strength in each swing. But the shocks were making him grow more tired, and his gun continued to overheat with each shot.

"Die!" the robot shouted out and swung again, hoping to cleave the Hunter in two, but the man sidestepped as the blade sunk into the snow and then to Tank's surprise, Black began to run up the blade and up the robots' arm before stabbing through the center of Tanks forehead with that blade. Everything went black for a moment, but then everything came back hazy and filled with static.

Regardless however, Tank was not done with this Hunter. The blade missed the motherboard despite the amount of electricity coursing through his metallic skeleton and burning up the circuits at his core, so Tank was able to shove Black back with a punch of his stump, launching the Hunter into the air. As he tore his sword out of the ground, Tank looked up to see Black falling towards him and his blade swinging downward to Tanks massive head.

Black landed in a crouch before Tank, his head bowed but then brought back up, looking into the eyes of Tank, which were flickering. Beneath him, droplets of oil began to fall into the snow. "You have skill, human," Tank said. "But... how...."

"Why did you join the witch and her brother?" Black said not moving from his spot and not breaking eye-contact with the robot. He didn't seem to care about what Tank's question was.

Tank hissed and moaned until he spoke. "Why… Not?..." Before he completely shuts down, Tank wanted to ask the Hunter how he was able to move in ways that no human was ever capable of. There had to be an explanation; there just had to be. But before he could even utter any words, with that the two vertical halves of Tank came apart; a clean cut from the top of his head to the split of his legs. The massive chunks of metal fell apart into the snow with a *poof*.

Tank laid there, shutting down and leaving Black alone and looking towards the direction the Hellhound had gone, and the new dangers he would now face without his Hoverbike. Tank had succeeded in at least stopping the Hunter Black for the time being, but the dissembled robot had also made the Hunter question something else aside from how he was going to catch up with the crew: why did they suddenly attack him if they were on the same side.

All this, were Tank's last thoughts as he completely shut down, and was no more.

~ The Lost World ~

Markus

Markus and the girls were once again on the move across the snowy landscape towards the vast emptiness of the Wastelands before the eastern countryside.

The snow had let up since earlier that morning, and Ruth appeared to be doing a little better since they had left the cave. They were now hovering at a constant speed to reduce any motion sickness. She had thrown up once but was now holding it down. Beside her and Markus, Ashlyn hovered alongside them, her scarf covering her cheeks and her hair continued to billow like auburn fire in the wind; the scarf itself flapped behind her like a banner. Ruth held her brother's waist tighter, their agreed code for Markus to stop. He caught Ashlyn's attention and they all stopped at an abandoned house that had long since been forgotten. All that was left of the relic was the skeletal frame of the house that had no doubt been blasted apart along with the possible farmlands beneath the snow.

"What is it?" he asked worriedly.

"Look," she said pointing with a gloved hand. He followed her finger and saw what she was referring to: A herd of Behemoth Slugs were moving across the plain, leaving a trail of slime in the snow almost ten feet wide. They squished and squirmed ahead as steam came off of their moist green bodies from the cold. There were about seven in total, the biggest one leading the herd. One turned its large eyes towards the teens, and its front opened wide in a low moan as it yawned at them.

"Wow," Ashlyn said staring. "I've never seen a herd of them before."

"Me neither." Markus said impressed. He looked away from the view to the direction they were previously following. The sensation he had was still strong in the particular direction he was looking at, and it seemed to be getting stronger and stronger as they moved further and further into the unknown Wastelands lost in time. It was strange to describe the pulling feeling inside of him. It was as if instinct itself was guiding him, telling him to keep going. "We should keep going." he eventually said.

"Shouldn't we know where we are going exactly?" Ashlyn asked, her eyes never leaving the Slugs. "I mean, we made it pretty far and there's no way the Baron would waste Guards or even time in general catching a couple of runaways, right? But we should still at least know where we are going." She looked at Markus with a peculiar glance and said, "And you've yet to explain how you know where we are going."

"It's difficult to explain," Markus replied but remained silent. He was still unsure about the whole thing about how he knew, and he took out his knife and tapped the crystal. The image came up again before his eyes. He studied the lines within his head and then pointed with a straight arm across the plains to a lump of darkness that seemed to cut into the vast snow. "We've made it about seventy, eighty miles from the city. "That there, is the Dark Forest." We need to go through there."

"Why there?" Ruth asked. "It's dangerous in there. Remember the stories?"

The Dark Forest was notorious for its legends of mutated beasts and humans lurking in the darkness, as well as the shroud of dark spirits within the mass of trees that seemed to grow from the radiation-soaked soil. Some said that even staying in there for too long would cause horrible hallucinations and visions. What they were no one said. Anyone who entered never returned-supposedly. Not only that, but it was a popular place to tell of a witch who used to live there, feeding off the bones of children and making her home out of the bones themselves. Whether this was true or not remained as a mystery, but then again, so were many things in this strange world.

Markus cleared his throat. "Maybe they are just stories? Look, on one side of the forest is Xerxes' territory, and the other is the Lake of the Moon, which is right smack inside the mountain range which is too steep to climb on the bikes. And Arachnards live up there, I'd rather avoid them. The Dark

Forest provides good cover and wood for fires. As long as we keep them lit, the wildlife should leave us alone." *And whatever spirits that actually do linger around in there.*

"Also, if we cut through the forest, then we will end up out of Xerxe territory and beyond Nineveh's reach. Then we can either head north through the Burning Plains or stop at the village of Spineshire, whichever direction we are being taken."

Ashlyn pursed her lips. "I guess that makes sense… But what if we don't end up going to Spineshire after that? What else is there beyond the forest?"

Markus took out his crumpled map and studied the eastern countryside of the Northern Wastelands. "Map ends near the Razorback Mountains… as far as I know, nothing else."

Ashlyn frowned. "So we brave the forest to lose any possible pursuers, if there are any, Xerxe or Ninevite, only to end up in the middle of nowhere? I'm all for the forest and all, just to be safe, but I think we should try and stop at Spineshire before we venture any further into no-man's land."

"Agreed. But there is also one more problem." Markus continued. "If the legends are true then the spirits of the forest might not be happy with us there. Some of them might want us to leave. That, and the waters and plants are poisonous."

"So the water we have is all we got." Ruth said.

"Aside from all the snow we can melt, yes." Markus figured they could probably refill their canteens before entering the forest.

"How far is it?" Ashlyn asked.

"About seven or eight miles through and through- at least from where we are. It's not that big of a forest, it literally just sits there like a patchy spot in the plains. We should reach the other side within a couple of hours depending on how fast you can take it, Ruth."

"I can take it," Ruth said but queasily.

"What about the forest itself?" Ashlyn asked.

"For sake of argument let's expect that it's about ten miles across from where we are at right now. If we just go without stopping, we could be out of there before the sun sets."

"Not very large, is it?"

Markus nodded. "Looks like there's a lake a mile before the forest." Markus pointed at a mass of fog some ways away from the base of the hill they have stopped at. "We should stop there and fish. We need to make what food we have last."

"Agreed." Ashlyn said. "Water should be clean as well."

"Then let's go!" Ruth said before coughing. "Let's go!" She shook Markus in excitement.

"Alright, alright." Markus laughed tucking his knife back into his belt and with it, the crystal. "Let's do it."

They rode for a good long while, not stopping and not uttering a word to one another as they continued to glide across the snow. Ashlyn zoomed past Markus on one occasion but he had managed to keep up with her despite Ruth behind him. He decided to take it easy on the bike from then on out.

Above them, flocks of Ahools and a swarm of Fireflies flew past them. The massive bat-like creatures seemed to vibrate the air below them as they screeched with echolocation, and the teens could all feel the pressure of the sound waves against their backs. The Fireflies were worse because of their fast-paced hovering, and the fact that they flew so close to the ground made the pressure intensify. Markus figured that they should still be hibernating due to the cold, but then again, Spring was supposed to be here, so they were coming back. The Ahools on the other hand never hibernated, although they do sleep long periods of time during the day and usually hunted at night. Seeing them now this late in the afternoon made him worry. Were they migrating? Or were they hunting? Either way they seemed to pay no attention to the little treats beneath them as they crossed the plains and flew towards the Razorback Mountains to the east.

Seeing them made Markus wish that the long winter would just end already. As he and the girls rode longer and longer the mist and fog got denser and denser. For some this would be bad news, for who knew if you were close to hitting something or –least likely- someone? But if Markus was right, they were closer to the lake.

And sure enough, he was. They stopped at the top of a hill overlooking the lake. Steam rose from the still waters and condensed into the fog around them. In the center of the lake a Waterbeast shot out of the waters, disturbing the glassy surface and then landing on its scaled back causing a thunderous splash. To the right of the group, the line of dark trees known as the Dark Forest stretched miles across the plains. Overhead more Ahools and even Owls flew overhead as the sun began to sink beneath the horizon and night starts to take the skies.

"Wow." Ashlyn said beneath her scarf.

"Yeah, wow." Ruth agreed.

"C'mon." Markus said and began glide down the hill to the shores of the lake, which were covered in slushy snow from the waves the Waterbeast made from his tidal splashes. They had parked their bikes a good three meters away from the water, and then shut them down.

Markus was lowering Ruth to the ground when Ashlyn went to the water's edge. She stuck a hand inside and brought it full of water to her lips. "It's cool, but not as cold as the air."

"Good," Markus said stooping down beside her and drinking from the waters himself. He filled up one of their canteens and offered it to Ruth as well.

"Why is it steaming?" Ruth asked spreading her bedroll before taking the water.

"The water is warmer than the air," Markus explained after clearing his throat with the cool clean water. "So it produces steam in the chilled air despite how cold the water may be."

"That's weird." she said.

"Yeah, it is." Ashlyn said joining her and undoing her pack from her bike. She fell to her knees and began undoing the straps. She pulled out some equipment and food and laid it out in a line before her as if making sure everything was still there when they would need it. She pulled aside a concentrated food tube and a can of beans.

"Yum," she said unconvincingly handing it to Ruth who then sat them aside for dinner. It was curious, Markus thought, how careful the street-rat really was. She really was a girl after all.

Ashlyn then looked up as Markus came to join them. He tossed his bedroll aside and then looked over towards something in the distance. On the shores of the lake a few meters away, he saw an old boat. A radio-ship used during the old war by the looks of it. It appeared to have run ashore against the rocks; the hull was torn revealing a darkened hole. Seaweed and other vegetation seemed to grow out of the cracks of the ship, and the glass windows were shattered and stained with some dark splatter. The smokestack was badly bent, and appeared to be cocked at an angle, giving it a funny look. It made Markus wonder what good use a ship would have in a lake in the middle of nowhere.

Curious to find out and wondering of the possibility of finding something useful, Markus stood and then began to walk towards it.

Ashlyn stood abruptly. "Hey where you going?"

"I'm going to get some wood, or something for a fire." Markus said stopping to turn. "I'll be back."

"Are you sure?" Ashlyn asked nervously. "Maybe we should go together?"

"I'll be fine." he assured her starting to move again. "You stay here with Ruth... and stay away from the water." He didn't know if Waterbeasts were carnivorous or not, and he wasn't about to find out.

"Okay," she said uneasily. "Be safe."

"I will." Markus said not looking back as he made his way to the ship.

As he reached the old boat, Markus stopped to take a look around it.

The bulk of the ship seemed to be embedded into the sand, which was slushy from the waves of the lake caused by the Water Beast. Some boxes were strewn around the ship; the markings on them faded and smeared. Some of them had been cracked open and was spilling many different contents that have long since been rotted.

He took off one of his gloves and touched one of the boxes furthest from the water. It was cold to the touch but it was dry. He looked inside to find it empty. He figured as much and he picked up the crate and was about to head back when something stopped him; a clanging sound, hollow and eerie was coming from inside the ship, echoing from the tear in the hull. Markus turned to look at it. Part of him wanted to see what was inside the radio-ship, and see the secrets it kept while patrolling the massive lake. But the other part wanted to dismiss it, assume that it was the wind or some creature loose inside the ship.

But then again, he was still curious as to what he would find inside. Markus dropped the crate to the ground and went over to the ship. He pulled out his blade and telescoped it into the staff. The gem began to glow, casting a dim light against the hull of the boat. He soon found a nearby chain dangling from the deck above his head, swaying lightly in the breeze. Strapping the staff against his back, Markus used his arms to climb up to the deck. His hands froze against the metal railing and he felt much relief when he finally released it when both feet were on the deck which seemed to groan beneath his weight.

He pulled back his staff and using the light to guide his footing, he carefully stepped over to a nearby door to the captains control room. It was open just a crack, so Markus used his free hand to pry it open. He then stuck his staff inside, and the glowing crystal revealed the shattered remains of a once proud Capitol cabin before the smell of musty lake condensation struck his nose.

Shattered control panels and tattered chairs surrounded the room beneath some broken glass leading to the hull of the ship. Cobwebs and moss grasped the wind and an old tapestry laid in a torn bundle on the floor. What caught Markus' attention most were the two skeletons in the room. Both wore old tattered uniforms of grey and black boots. One laid against some control panels while the other laid in a fetal position in the corner; both had holes in their heads and rusty guns laid nearby. Markus' stomach turned in he saw a Badrat crawling over the skeleton in the corner. This one was no bigger than a cat, but its twisted whiskers and raw hide was a hideous sight, along with a hiss between its dagger-like teeth made Markus slam the door to the cabin. He sighed and decided it was best to leave the ship alone in the end.

He retracted his staff and tucked the blade into his belt before climbing back down to retrieve the crate. He had to get it back to camp and get the girls warm; and push the thought of that monster of a rat out of his mind. But like an unescapable thought, something took the rats place.

Confused, Markus looked back at the deck of the ship. Upon the deck he thought he saw a man standing on board the ship. But instead, it was another rat, who sat perched on the rusted railing of the ship. It clicked its teeth as it peered down at Markus, who then turned and ran back to camp, stooping over and retrieving the crate before he left the area. As he huffed his way across the cold shoreline, Markus decided that it was unnecessary to tell the girls about what he had seen.

He hoped that the rat stayed on the old boat.

Ruth began to cough later that night. It was the same coughing fit that made Markus shudder with each break of breath, the memory of her greatest fit back home making him fear the absolute worst.

It happened so suddenly. Ashlyn had just gotten back from taking a quick bath in the lakes chilled waters and Markus was just feeding the fire again when it started. He did not even remember getting up to hold Ruth. All he remembered that she was coughing badly, and he was suddenly by her side. The thought of how many times he had done this, made him nauseous. Ashlyn stood beside him, her hair dripping cold droplets on his shoulder as Markus cradled Ruth's head and patted her back.

"Calm down," he said in an un-calmly matter. "It's gonna be okay, Ruth," he said trying his best to calm her down and ease the coughing. He was praying that she would not throw up, she needed that food and energy and they could not afford to waste it.

"It's okay baby-girl I'm here." he said again, trying to give off some sort of assurance to his sister as his father used to; to let her know that it was going to be okay. *Since when have I started calling her that?* He thought in his state of panic.

The fit continued for what felt like minutes. To Markus' relief however, no sign of blood showered from the spittle she coughed up. He was beginning to have hope when the hissing began. A wicked sound that was heard beyond the fire.

Ashlyn heard it too. She picked up a stray log from the fire and held it up, lighting up the darkness around them. Sure enough in the distance beyond the fires reach was a pair of glowing red eyes. The eyes of a Badrat- no, not one pair, but many.

A pack of the little beasts was near the camp. The coughing must have riled them up and now they were here, checking out the possibility of an easy meal. With numbers on their side, they could easily overpower the three teens, but they were keeping their distance, away from the fire. Markus told Ruth to stay calm as he sat her down and stood into a crouch not leaving her side as she curled into a fetal position. He took out his blade and telescoped it into the staff and took aim at the biggest pair of eyes. Ashlyn, hair still wet and her clothes damp, backed up to Markus' side. Immediately the eyes seemed to get closer.

"Not good…" Ashlyn said stooping down to retrieve her pistol from her pack.

"Stay cool," Markus said trying hard to keep his voice level. If he lost his head now, it would be all over. Ruth coughed into her pillow, her eyes never leaving the glowing orbs watching them. "They won't come near the fire, but you can't be too careful. Save your shots until the last possible moment."

"They're getting *closer*," Ashlyn said in a panicked tone. Sure enough, the pairs of eyes seemed to come closer to the fire, the hissing growing louder as well.

Markus was scared too, but he could not afford to appear afraid. The girls needed him. Ruth especially. "Do *not* move. And do not fire unless necessary."

They are still kittens…

"What did you say?" Markus asked Ashlyn, thinking that the shrill and quiet voice was from her.

"I didn't say anything," Ashlyn said still keeping her gun trained on the nearest oversized rodent.

Their nest isn't from here, why have they come?

"Ashlyn, that is not funny!" Markus growled not starting to get irritated.

"I'm not-"

"Shh!" Markus then hissed when another voice joined the first.

That one was on the metal boat. That's the one who entered my cave.

It wasn't Ashlyn or even Ruth that had been talking. Somehow, for some reason, it was the rats themselves. Markus didn't know how or why, but hearing the little creatures only made him all the more terrified. As other voices seemed to join, talking about the taste of fresh meat and warm blood to stay the cold, Markus tried to shut it all out. It couldn't be real; he didn't want it to be. It was scary enough as it is.

For minutes it felt like a standoff between the two packs. Niether of them took their eyes off of each other and not daring to move. Markus felt his heart slamming in his chest, the fear of them being eaten by a pack of rats seeming both ridiculous and frightening at the same time; having come all this way and something like this ended their lives. At least the voices he had been hearing had finally gone away. It had to have been imagination. It had to be…

Eventually, the eyes of the rat pack seemed to back out before disappearing into the darkness. Markus heard Ashlyn let out a sigh of relief as she plopped down onto her bag.

"That was close," she said.

"Stay alert," Markus told her. "They could come back." He then turned to Ruth, who had stopped coughing. "You okay?"

"I'll be fine…" she croaked. "I think."

"Try and get some sleep, okay?" he said, then turning to Ashlyn. "You too. They might come back so I'm going to take first watch, okay?"

"I can stay up," Ashlyn offered.

"No. You need to sleep so you can take over in a few hours. Then, I'll sleep. Okay?"

"Okay..." Ashlyn said looking at Ruth. She then crawled over to her sleeping roll and kicked off her boots. She tucked her feet and legs into the bag before zipping it up, locking out the cold and trapping her heat immediately. She then turned her body to face Markus and his sister, whom he helped lay down onto her own bedroll. He tucked Ruth in and told her to sleep well. She said goodnight and closed her eyes. Markus stood up and fed the fire a little more before taking a seat on his pack as he began his watch; the flickering flames being his only company as he listened, alert and very much afraid.

As the night grew deeper and deeper into its state of dominance over the land, the sounds of the creatures of the night made it very difficult to fall asleep to. Which for Markus was just fine. He would listen to the hoot of an owl, the screech of an Ahool, or the chatter of night bugs amongst the occasional hiss or scurrying of the Badrats who refused to wander far from their camp.

He felt so tired but he kept his staff across his lap in the mere chance something *was* to come at them. He would die before they took Ruth or Ashlyn. Markus, would sometimes on occasion look up to see the bright stars that speckled the black sky. The moon was gone tonight but the billions upon billions of twinkling lights kept him company among the horrors around him. It amazed him that thousands of years ago, it was almost impossible to see the stars. Out here, that just didn't seem possible. The world truly has changed since the fall of mankind.

The fog had long since lifted, which made the view all the better. Ruth would cough in her sleep from time to time but would eventually fall back into deep sleep, thus making Markus calm down enough to pay attention to the sounds around him and to occasionally look up at the stars. It also amazed him how many were out there, and how he could only see a few among the vast numbers of galaxies and stars here on the planet. Even though he could see billions, there was still so much more out there.

How many are out there? How many stars, planets, galaxies, or maybe even distance universes beyond ours? He alone was just a small speck of dust compared to the vastness of the entire universe; and it made Markus feel small and as insignificant as an ant.

He was startled when he felt a hand on his shoulder. It was Ashlyn, all bundled up in her coat and boots. How long had he been gazing? What had he missed? What if a monster had come by as he was dreaming? What if-

"You okay?" Ashlyn's soft voice broke through his barrier of thoughts.

"Yeah." Markus said nodding. "I'm fine. What are you doing up?"

"You should get some sleep." Ashlyn said in a softer voice, almost dreamily. She was still tired, he could tell.

"I could watch the rest of the night." he offered.

"No." Ashlyn said grabbing Markus' shoulders and gently pulling him up. "Go to bed." He wanted to argue, but his body relented to Ashlyn's will. She led him over to his mat where he shrugged off her hands and sheathed his weapon before lying down. He slithered into the sleeping bag and pulled up the zipper, wrapping his body into a cocoon. Markus then turned to face away from the fire. He listened to the shuffling as Ashlyn took a seat where he had previously sat. For a good minute, he just laid there not able to sleep.

Eventually, unable to handle the overwhelming silence between them, he sighed and said over his shoulder, "Do you miss your mom and your sister?"

Ashlyn was silent for a long time and Markus thought she hadn't heard him at first. She simply sat there, looking out into the darkness beyond as the fire flickered small shadows on her face. *Did she not hear me?*

But then before he could ask again, she finally answered. "Every day."

"Why were they…" he couldn't bring himself to ask the question entirely.

"My mother was accused of helping the army during the siege. So they came to the house and…" She shrugged as if trying to pass it off as not that big of a deal. "Anyways, I managed to get my sister and myself out of the house in time before the shooting started. But as we were running, she was shot in the back. I couldn't do anything for her, so I… I just ran. I ran and ran and ran…"

Markus stared at Ashlyn. *So she also knows what it's like, to watch your family get killed right in front of you…* The two of them really did have a lot in common. He felt there was more to the story than Ashlyn was letting on, but he didn't dare question it. It made no sense that only she was spared and no one

else wasn't before she was casted out, but he felt she wouldn't have said anything if she had a good reason.

"I'm sorry." he then said. She was silent so Markus decided to ask another question. "Where was your father?"

He turned to see Ashlyn gripping the gun with intense rage. The veins in her small hands popped out as she spoke broodingly. "My father was the commander who gave the order for my family to be killed. General Veegar- at least, that's who he is now."

Markus was so shocked at this horrific news that he bolted upright. *The General of The Guard!?* "Oh man... I'm so sorry Ashlyn..."

"It's life." But as she said it, Markus noticed a single tear drop from her smooth cheek in the firelight. "It's not like it can be changed now..." She wiped away the tear fast, acting strong- like she probably had for years and years. She sounded so heartbroken at the memory, that Markus felt ashamed for even asking such a thing.

Crap, nice one, Markus. With a sigh, he said, "You're very brave, you know that?"

Ashlyn looked at him. "How?"

"Living on your own. Fending for yourself." He shook his head. "That's... incredible."

"Didn't have much of a choice." She said with a shrug.

"Why didn't your father take you in afterwards?"

She looked at Markus with a look of pure sadness. Bitterness and agony seemed to spread in her face as she finally spoke. "I have no father anymore. As soon as he joined The Guard, he belonged to the Baron." She was silent for a moment and then she said, "It's funny. My sister and I always dreamed of leaving Nineveh. Build our very own house, somewhere out here... maybe near a lake or forest."

Markus bit his lip. "What was your sister's name?"

"Kira."

She said nothing more and not wanting to cause any more distress, Markus curled back up and shared the silence with her before falling into a pitiful sleep.

I'm such an idiot.

That was his last thought as he listened to the flickering fire, and eventually, sleep took him away from the world so cold, and to the land of Dreams.

~ Savages ~

Black

Black trudged across the snowy valley cold and miserable. His boots sunk deep in the snow with every step, and he nearly tripped again and again. His cowl and hood protected his head and face from the cruel winds, and his armor kept him warm despite the blizzard's harsh whispers.

He could not see much in the dark wilderness; however he could make out the path of the children's bikes through his aptitude to sense the little things not seen by the normal human eye. He could sense the depth of the snow where the Hoverbikes boosters melted the snow, he could smell the stench of gasoline and the aura of the sick little girl. As long as he held the crystal in his hand, Black could see exactly where the trio were going; and as he could see from the jet lines made by the Hellhound, the band of common blackguards were not far behind. He would have to hurry if he wanted to catch those children before they did.

As fate would have it, the crystal began to glow dark red, making Black stop in disquiet alertness. He turned his head to the sound of footsteps; many, moving fast and heading right towards him and in the darkness, carrying with them bright lanterns, Black saw them.

Metal Heads.

Riding upon the backs of Leaper Dragons, the men hooted and hollered at the Hunter, all four of them wielding pistols, shotguns and other weapons such as swords and pikes. Black saw on one of the beast's backs was a Gatling

Laser positioned in front of a brute man garbed in Werecat pelts and a cloak of Ahool wings. His head, as his clan's namesake, was a helmet of spiked metal obscuring any facial recognition aside from his lower jaw and mouth, revealing a smile full of sharp iron teeth. As his three clan members rode their vicious beasts around Black; completely surrounding the Hunter, the leader spurred his Dragon forward. The massive and slick lizard took a few steps towards Black who faced it with no desire to flee, which seemed to confuse the creature the way it tasted the air with its purple forked tongue. The fins on either side of its leathery head indicated it to be the alpha of the pack, and it hissed and circled around Black. The beast in front of him snorted as it came within ten feet of the Hunter before stopping, its massive claws digging small trenches in the snow. The Metal Head leader aimed the mounted Gatling at the Hunter in patient grace.

"Well, well, well," the leader said in a gruff voice behind his helmet, causing his clan members to snort and cackle as they continued to circle Black. He then clicked his iron teeth together as if he was cold. "What do we have here? A lonesome traveler, lost in the snow?"

"And who might you be?" Black said in a cool voice.

Clearly surprised by the Hunter's demeanor, the Metal Head leader let out a huff of indignation. "You speak to Raki, second-chief of the Metal Head tribe, brother of Kizuato, Captain of the Fallen Angel."

"So the dreaded pirate still lives?" Black said ignoring Raki's speech. "How interesting. He has been so quiet I thought he had moved on to the Southern Isles, and only Wastelanders patrol these lands now."

"You wish." Raki said roughly. Black carefully placed the crystal in his pocket, but the leader immediately noticed it. "What was that?" Raki demanded. "You got something for a couple of dogs of the valley?" This was met with laughter from the other men, the Dragons shook their heads in clear disapproval as their yellow eyes glowed brightly at Black, hoping for a bite of their next meal.

"I have no quarrel with you." Black said. "I *would* however like to buy one of your lizards, if you're willing to maybe barter?"

"Ha," Raki sneered. "Do you have any idea who you're dealing with?"

"I was just about to ask you the same thing."

"Oh, really?" the Metal Head sneered tilting the barrels of the Gatling at the Hunter. "Do you know this one? Surrender what was in your pocket as well as any other weapons on your person and we will let you go... and, I like that cloak of yours, I'll take that as well."

"We're wasting time." Black said impatiently. "Will you, or will you not, sell me a Dragon so I can continue my journey?"

"No." Raki said dismissively. He shook his head in wonder. "This guy... Now, are you going to comply with my demands? Or am I gonna have to blow ya full of holes?"

Black reached up and grasped the hilt of his sword, pulling it out a little bit to show off the blade to the Metal Heads. Raki's boys 'ooed' and 'awed at the weapon, their fists gripping their weapons tighter. "Attack me, and all of your men shall die." he warned.

Raki began to shake in indignation. "Lotta talk for a lonely little man," And he pulled back the lever on the Gatling which whirled to life and began to spew red bolts of energy at the Hunter. "Eat this!"

Black whipped out his sword and began to spin it before him, catching each beam with the blade and deflecting it into the snow around him. The leader's eyes went wide in both admiration and fear. Black purposely shifted his sword so a stray laser would hit one of the Metal Heads who was blown off his Dragon into the snow. The beast lurched back in surprise as the weight of its master was relieved from its massive shoulders before bounding away suddenly.

Another Metal Head spurred his beast forward, which leapt to Black with black teeth and talons bared. Black leapt out of the way and the Gatlings lasers smacked into the beast's brown torso, making it roar in pain as it leapt at the Metal Head leader. Raki gasped as he leapt off his mount and the two Dragon's collided, shredding each other's bellies in a flash of claws and teeth. Blood splattered and melted the snow and the last Metal Head riding the one that attacked fell back and into the snow. Before he could get back up his beast backed up on its hind legs, smashing him into the snow with a sickening *crunch*.

"Damn you," Raki swore as he pulled himself off the ground. He watched as his last clan member charged at the Hunter spear ready and shooting his shotgun as the beast slithered at Black at break neck speeds. The Hunter leapt away from the snapping jaws and slid his sword across the beasts head, making a gash that bled terribly. The monster shook its head and hissed as its rider stabbed at the hunter with his Shock Spear.

Black however swung upwards cutting the tip and making it fly into the air. He then charged at the monster which stood up on its hind legs ready to pounce on its prey. Black stabbed at the monster's heart and swung on the handle up to the Metal Head who watched in terror as the Hunter pulled out the blade in midair before swinging at the rider himself. The man flew off the beast into the snow in a flash of red, and as soon as Black landed on the ground the Dragon too fell on its side with a moan.

Raki seethed in anger as he whipped out his Tommy gun and fired a spray of bullets at the Hunter, who sidestepped and spun his blade, cutting each bullet in half and making them fly past either side of him into the snow. He continued to do so until Raki's gun ran out of ammo. Behind him the two lizards had stopped their fighting as the alpha rose from its fallen foe with bloody teeth. Raki whistled and the victorious beast slithered up to him. He leapt up and landed on the beasts back once more.

He took ahold of the Gatling and pulled back the lever again, bringing once again a swarm of bolts at the Hunter. As Black leapt aside and continued to run, the leader continued to shoot at him, laughing in a raving matter. Blacks right hand clenched into a fist and his gauntlet opened up with a spring lock, revealing a grappling hook. He took aim at the Metal Head and squeezed his thumb, launching the bolt at the leader and making it stick through the Gatlings barrel, making the shooting stop. Before the leader could react the claw extended, locking into the gun's barrel and then Black squeezed his index finger, retracting the line which pulled Black towards the leader who watched in terror as the Hunters blade came darting towards him like the horn of a Rock Rhino ready to gore its enemy.

The leader held up his arm, which was laced in titanium armor. But the blade pierced through the armor and through the man's arm, making him grunt as the pain shot up his arm but when the tip of the blade stopped mere inches from his face dripping crimson, he laughed.

"Got you now," he said reaching for his dagger at his belt.

"No you don't." Black said hitting a button on the hilt of his sword. The leader convulsed and sputtered as electricity shot through his body, making his cry out in pain. Black then kicked up with a single boot, launching the leader clear off the beast which reared back and roared at its new rider took up the reins and steadied the beast. Using his sword, he sliced off the Gatling

Laser, for it was damaged and rendered useless. He retracted his grapple completely and sheathed his sword, gently petting the Dragons neck which rose and fell in its rapid breathing.

Easy. he told it, and eventually, the beast calmed down, obedient to its new master.

He then looked over at the leader who was still convulsing in fits from the blades shocks. "Thank you." Black said taking up the reins and spurring the beast forward. It slithered faster than a Hoverbike into the night, leaving the wounded Metal Head and his dead partners in the snow.

There was no time to waste; it was time to get moving again.

Raki
"Bastard…"

Raki sat up, his flank covered in snow, his body still in pain from the shock, but the pain was nothing next to the shame of defeat. He looked at his arm, which was bleeding profusely through the hole in his armor and dripping into the snow, causing steam to rise. Raki had been in countless fights before and had raided many ships and tanks that passed through this area. Even last week there was an army of Xerxe soldiers training out in the Wstelands, and even those guys didn't stand a chance against him and his men! He even killed Hunters before; two of them. They were both incredibly different in skill and weaponry, but they were both very legendary Hunters of the Capitol; and even they had fallen by his hand. But that one man… that one Hunter, he was different.

"Coward!" he screamed out into the night. He winced as he clenched his arm tightly with clenched teeth. He had never been so humiliated in his life.

Four dragons, four members of the Metal Heads against a single man- and he wiped the floor with the lot of them! Looking at the broken figure of the poor bastard that got stomped on, Raki shook his head in disgust. Weaklings, all of them. Even the Dragons who had fallen were weak. There was no room for weakness in the Metal Head Tribe; none. Panting from the pain and chilling cold, Raki whistled for the Dragon who lost its rider, and after a minute it came back its tongue darting out in search for the Hunter. Seeing that he was gone, the giant lizard lumbered up to Raki, humming in its throat as Raki petted the beasts flank.

"Good boy," he sighed while looking back in the direction the Hunter had disappeared to. Through the pain in his arm and the cold in his bones, Raki really wanted to go after him. Such humiliation, could not be forgiven. He even pulled himself up into the saddle, wincing at the pain as he climbed the dragon's hind leg to get on. He looked again at the tracks that the Hunter left and debated following him, but pushed aside the foolish idea. That man was tough, *really* tough. Besides, he was hurt and his arm was useless right now. He had to get back to camp. He would rally some men and go after that punk sooner or later.

He clicked his tongue and spurred the beast in the opposite direction, heading back to Deadman's Crest as the blizzard continued to blow around him.

~ Pursuit ~

Lee

Lee was sitting up front alone as he continued to drive throughout the night. The morning was still a few hours away and the rest of the Hunters were sleeping in the bunks provided within the sides of the walls. Lameika was among them, and with the silence only accompanied by the hum of the Helhound's engine, Lee had some time for himself to think.

    Whenever he took the time for himself, he always had a smoke. On any other occasion, he would have just waited until they landed and everyone was out. He never wanted to bother them. But instead, just for tonight, he turned on the vent closest to him and upon removing a tin of tobacco he rolled up a joint and lit it with his lighter. With the smoke now filling his lungs his mind felt all clear again after blowing it out into the vent. This was a bad habit, one that he knew that he had to break eventually. But for now, like an addict consumed by Buckweed, he needed it.

    He just had too much on his mind.

    He had a very bad feeling about this contract. Lee had been on many, with his sister and then eventually the guild the two of them had built. They mostly took on contracts for Queen Lamia back in the Capitol, and occasionally some in the other kingdoms, and he never once had to worry about a job getting done. Lameika was in charge, and Lee was second in command of the guild who would follow them anywhere. All of them, while strange in their own rights, were powerfully loyal. They would all descend into hell if Lameika commanded them too. They were dangerous, loyal, and they knew not to disobey orders.

Unlike their former member, Benaiah of the Sand.

Like all other members of their little guild, Benaiah was founded as a meager Hunter camping out along the southern border. Lee and Pyro had split from the group to go hunting and found the man sleeping among the stars. The three got well-acquainted, and even shared a bottle of tequila that the man said he made himself out in the desert. After meeting the man, Lee knew immediately that he would have made a great addition to the guild and for a while, he was right.

But then, the man said he got a 'bad feeling' about going to Mt. Nudushi. Lameika had been summoned by Father, who wanted to speak to them all. Benaiah said he didn't want to go, said it was a bad idea to go to the volcano and speak to the man who rose the twins himself. Lee was a little hesitant as well, for he did not like his father because of his favoritism of Lameika. For a brief moment after Benaiah expressed his concerns, he thought of agreeing and defending the man. After all, Father never summoned them unless he wanted something. He had no such thing as 'love' in his heart anymore, especially not for his son.

But Lameika was not having it. It was cruel, deceitful, and just simply unnecessary if Lee was being honest with himself considering what his sister had done. She had approached the man, and gently grabbed the back of his head with a single hand. She looked at him with a look that appeared sincerely disappointed and sad, and asked him if he was sure that he would not come with the guild to Mt. Nudishi. The man had sealed his fate with his answer, and with that hand still on him, Lameika killed him without so much as a second thought.

No burial or form of honorable treatment was given to Benaiah as ordered by Lameika whose hands were still covered in his blood. His body wasn't even left for the Badrats or the Snow Wolves. Instead, she commanded Slitzer to devour him. The Lacerta didn't even ask twice and went upon the body, ripping his armor and clothing off and eating him right in front of the entire guild, bones and all. It was meant to be a warning; a reminder as to what happened when someone disobeyed orders from the twins.

The very image of Benaiah's face at the moment of his death was burned into Lee's memory, so in a way, it was a reminder for him as well. And every night he would be visited by the very face, as if Benaiah was haunting him from the depths of oblivion. As a result, Lee got little to no sleep anymore. In a way, it worked out because then he could continue to fly throughout the night. But it was tiring on his body, especially his mind that was always spinning with thought.

It was at that very moment when Lee began to question just who he and his sister was, and who they have brought into their little guild. They were all pawns in some sort of fashion. There was only one way for he himself to find out his true potential.

Damion Black. Someday, he'd-

His thoughts were interrupted when he saw someone coming up alongside him and sitting into Lameika's seat. He turned and saw Pyro sitting there, his armor now on and his eyes baggy and heavy with sleep.

"Got a smoke to spare?" the Hunter asked Lee. He gave him one and Pyro lit it with his own lighter. After a single drag he sighed with relief. "Thanks. How are we holdin' up here?"

"We're fine." Lee said. Though as the night went on and slowly began to turn into day, the clouds had seemed to have gotten thicker and a fog had begun to accumulate before them. It wouldn't be long before they started flying blindly in the thick mist.

"Good. Can't wait to get this over with." Pyro yawned again, his jaw popping in the process. "This is gonna be the payday of all time."

"Yeah… right." Lee paused for a moment and then around his cigarette said, "Hey, Pyro. Why did you become a Hunter in the first place?"

Pyro looked at him, confused. "Why the sudden curiosity?"

His question was valid. Lee had never asked anyone about their personal life before. All that he and Lameika ever asked of their guildmembers were who they were, where they were from, and what they could do. Anything else was strictly business. They were not supposed to care where or who the Hunters were; they were all simple tools to achieve whatever goal was set before them. Lee was even told by Lameika to never consider the others as equals, but as pawns necessary for the completion of their contracts; and for so long, he did exactly that.

But after what happened to Benaiah, everything seemed to be changing, even now.

"No reason," Lee finally answered. "Just curious. Like… surely there were other opportunities for you. So why… why bounty hunting?"

Pyro thought about it for a moment, probably still a little skeptical of the sudden question entirely; which was justifiable. "Guess you could say I was kinda 'bred' into it. Ever heard of The Hunter Darkclaw?"

"Sounds familiar."

"Yeah, well, he was a bigshot down in Seifkr."

"Ain't that kingdom supposed to be bigger than the Capitol?" Lee asked, intrigued now.

"Not sure. But I lived there with Darkclaw when he was building up his reputation to the point where he was planning to assassinate the emperor."

"Get out."

Pyro shook his head. "No sir. Got a contract from someone who wanted to climb the ranks of the monarchy. Lemme tell ya, the worst enemy of a king or queen are usually the people closest to 'em. Anyways, he got close, but he got run out of the palace and chased out of the kingdom entirely. By none other than The Hunter Black."

"No way, really?" Lee was now growing even more excited as this story progressed.

"Yep." Pyro said taking another drag of his smoke. "Anyways, while Darkclaw was out and about, he found me at the border. It was a slave caravan."

"You were a slave?"

"Nope. But would have become one if we continued south. Anyways, Darkclaw massacred the slavers and set everyone free. I stayed, and followed him. Every time I got close he would tell me to piss off and go home."

"But you didn't listen." Lee guessed.

"Nope, never had, probably never will. Eventually he just gave up and took me in. Trained me how to become a bounty hunter like him. Gave me hints and tips as we made our way all the way to Bronzeshire before we would part ways. Our hotel was lit on fire by a group of Metalheads wanting to drive us out. We managed to escape, but obviously I got marked." Pyro pointed at his burned face to emphasize. "We slaughtered the bastards and the village thanked us by giving us all we needed before we parted ways."

"That's quite the story." Lee admitted.

"Isn't it? In a way, I have that man to thank. In the end though, I survived. I found out just a couple of years ago that Darkclaw was killed."

"By who?"

"The Capitol. Group of soldiers gunned him down."

Lee glanced at the Hunter who was now looking out the window where it was getting foggier and foggier. "Wow. That's a damn shame."

"It's fine. Lucky for me," Pyro grinned. "A contract was placed on the leader of that platoon by some farmer who claimed his daughter was, eh, 'played with' by the group. I was in Miteshire at the time, same as them."

"What did you do?"

"Burned them."

Lee nodded. That was Pyro's favorite thing to do. "So, when did the whole 'burning-thing' started?"

"Burning-thing? Ha! Man, you really must be curious." Pyro took another smoke and said, "Started during my training, after the fire in Bronzeshire. Darkclaw said that a true Hunter had his own little 'mark'."

"Mark?"

"Calling card, so to speak. His was three deep cuts into the chests of his prey. Hence the name 'Darkclaw'. I thought it was cheesy, but that was his way of doing things. He said I would have to find out my own thing, my own way to strike fear into the hearts of not only my potential prey, but also my contractors so that no one could touch me. In a way, I decided that since I got burned just because I was with Darkclaw, the same fate was deserved to those I hunt. Give 'em a taste of hell so to speak before I send them there."

"That's pretty dark."

"Says the brother of a witch."

"… Right." Lee muttered. He hated being called that, especially by his own guild. This little backstory that was the first he had ever heard from Pyro only made Lee see the Hunter as more of a person than a pawn. However, like many people and humans in general, he had his own little dark quirks. He didn't stab or shoot his victims which were favored by many Hunters because of how much easier it is and less messy. However, Pyro liked to cook people and burn them in the flames of his very own suit.

He was a butcher, and a sadistic killer of a Hunter, just like Slitzar who didn't even bat an eye when she devoured Benaiah,

Lee began to truly wonder just what his guild really was, if it was full of monsters who reason their ways because of what they once were. In all of that, what about himself and his sister? What was the point really? He began to question everything even more now to the point where his own stomach started to twist and turn as if concrete was being churned inside of him.

He did not get the chance to ask the man anything else, for Lameika appeared like a wraith behind them and told the pyromaniac to get lost. The man did so with a tilt of his invisible hat. When she was back in her original spot, she told Pyro to start waking everyone up.

The new day had begun, and so Lee replaced the mask he had worn for many years, and prepared himself for whatever was to come in the hours before them.

Lameika

It was morning now and the sun was struggling to break the gray horizon and give light to the shattered world that remained. The thermal scanners were still not picking up anything due to the fog that was now blocking their view for a good couple of miles. Lee had told Lameika this but she gave no reply as she whispered the Dark Words into the seeds in her palm once again. She had to keep her focus, so that when they did find the brats, they would be ready.

Behind her, Pyro was cleaning out his machine gun; his flamethrower sitting clean as a whistle beside his chair while he worked. The quick exchange of words between the two of them seemed almost forgotten as far as Lameika was concerned. Meanwhile, Slitzar was having breakfast, biting into a hunk of meat she had stored in the Hellhound's locker. What sort of meat it was Lameika did not care, or *want* to know. She was much too focused on the task at hand.

She breathed life into the seeds, her words carrying with them a heavy burden. Her father was the one who taught her this spell, among many others unique to her elemental abilities. It took years to perfect it and even now as she whispered the spells into the seeds it seemed to take forever if not longer. She had come a long way; since being just a simple child earning her mothers' heritage as a witch, but the dark magic still took a major toll on her body. Still, she pushed herself. She had to make the seeds perfect. If she left even a single small thing out it could botch the entire mission, and she will never have a chance to free The Master.

Clenching both the crystal in one of her hands which glowed dark purple as she spoke the Dark Words of power, Lameika put all her focus into these little seeds, which would grow not into the pants they were created to become, but to be born as something… better; something the world was never meant to have. She could *feel* what the seedlings felt as she whispered the spell into their husks; feel their pain and what they say as she cursed them. She reassured them that they would be okay, despite their cries of desperation.

What was it that caused them the most pain? The pain of the spells weaving into their husks? The pain of the unknown future they were not expecting at birth? It mattered not. It was Lameika's will as well as The Masters'. They must not fail, and at the pain and expense of others, seedlings, Hunter or otherwise, the task *must* be completed.

When she stopped, Lameika had broken out in sweat. She shoved the crystal into her pouch and its eerie glow was dying slowly as well as the seedlings who ceased their chatter when she released the spell. She panted due to the effort of the casting the spell.

"You okay?" Lee said at the wheel but not looking at her.

"I'm fine." she lied. Lee didn't need to worry about her. He *shouldn't* be worrying about her. "Where are we now?"

"A few miles from the Black Forest." Lee said clearly still troubled and Lameika could see why. A dense fog had covered the valley, obscuring the hills and trees below. "This damn fog is making it difficult to track anything. The thermal scanners are not picking up anything other than Dragonflies or Ahools above us."

"Hmm." Lameika said irritated at the process and lack of results. She decided that she had no choice but to ask Lee, "So what do we do?"

"Land maybe? Get below the fog?"

"Is that safe?" Slitzar said behind them. Lameika's spine shuddered at the gruff but clearly feminine voice around the mouthful of smelly meat.

"Can't tell." Lee said. "But we ain't gonna do any better up here. We might be able to see more if we actually touch the ground. We'll have to go in slow."

"Slow," Pyro snorted still cleaning his guns. Lameika thought of asking Lee what he and the other Hunter had been talking about, but decided against it.

Slitzar cast a look of coolness at Pyro as she tossed the remainder of her meal into her maw, bone and all. She crunched it with her many dagger-like teeth and then swallowed before speaking. "Slow is better, yes?" she asked of Pyro.

"Yes." Lameika said answering for him. "No point in flying around in hopes that the fog clears soon. Land, Lee." She commanded this sternly.

"Hold on." Lee pulled down a lever slowing the Hellhound to a point of hovering. He flicked another switch and then pulled another lever, letting the craft descended at a slow but steady pace. He continued the descent as they plunged into the fog, which casted around them as thick as pea soup.

"Careful." Lameika murmured. She didn't want the idiot to smash right into the ground and wreck their ship.

"I am." Lee said focused on the radar scanners telling him how far the ground was. "And… Here we… Go." Immediately the ship shook as it struck the ground softly. "Perfect." he said with a smile as he killed the engine.

"Can't see a thing through this fog." Slitzar said.

"Where's it coming from anyway?" Pyro demanded.

"The lake nearby." Lee said. "Morning air's too chilly."

"That's a shame." Pyro said. "How long we gotta stay here?"

"We can't go out there if we can't see." Lee said

"*I* could." Slitzar snarled.

"Not alone you aren't." Lee said looking back. "And we can't leave the ship alone."

"We'll find it again." she argued.

"Yeah," Pyro piped up standing next to the lizard-woman. "These beasts have a strong sense of smell." He leaned against one of Slitzar's bulging arms as if she were a wall. "She could pick up any scent even what we leave here. We go, take a look around, and she'll lead us back if need be."

"You have two seconds to get your arm off me," Slitzar snarled. "Before I *rip* it off."

Pyro removed his arm and held his hands up as if in surrender. "Alright, alright, jeez you guys *are* cold-blooded."

Slitzar growled at the impudent Hunter so Lameika piped in. "That plan works. We'll go take a look around. The lake can't be far."

"Nevertheless." Lee said reaching under the panel and taking out earpieces. "These have trackers placed in them. I have the chip in mine which I can use to pinpoint you guys. You take a look around if you need me just let me know and I'll be able to see you guys and come to you."

Lameika took them. "Perfect." She passed two to Slitzar and Pyro who placed them into their ears. She then did likewise. Lee inserted a chip into the panel from his own earpiece and flicked a switch. In the top left corner of the windshield three screens came to life showing the backs of Lee and his sister as well as Lameika looking at Lee. "Test, test." He said pressing a finger on the piece.

"Received." Slitzar said.

"Loud and clear." Pyro chirped.

"Gotcha." Lameika said.

Lee looked at her and then looked at the others behind them. He turned back to his sister. "You be careful." he said. "I'm gonna try and pick up Tank's frequency. It's been too quiet."

"Okay."

"As soon as you need me, I'm off."

How annoying. "Got it." She stood and grabbed ahold of her pack and opened it up, revealing a black whip of Dragon leather. The tip was barbed and the handle was wrapped in cloth. She wrapped it and hooked it to her belt before following the others outside the doors of the ship and meeting the dense fog. Lameika was able to feel the cold grip of the fog as she grasped out at it. It really was indeed thick, and she was suddenly aware of how hard finding these children might be if they were close.

"They are near." Slitzar growled a few feet away. "The lake's that way." she pointed in the direction she was facing. "I can smell 'em…"

"Okay," Lameika pressed her ear piece before speaking. "We're moving out Lee. You got us?"

"Check." Lee's voice crackled on the mike.

"Good." Lameika said following Slitzar who was already on the move. Pyro was at her heels; gun ready as they disappeared into the fog.

The Hunt was on once again.

Markus

Markus awoke suddenly to find Ashlyn already packing up both bikes to head out that morning. He looked around for his own pack for a moment before seeing it on his and Ruth's bike all strapped up to go.

She must have done that for us while we slept. He thought as he yawned and stretched; his arm shooting out of the sleeping bag like two straight rods. "Morning." He managed.

"Good morning." Ashlyn said. She looked over to Ruth who was snoring softly. "She slept all night."

"Good." Markus scooted out of his bag and began to roll it up. The cold air sprouted gooseflesh on his skin and his fingers began to go numb but Markus rolled up his bag fast and tossed it to her. He then put on his coat and jammed his fingers into his armpits. "Damn…" It was terribly cold that morning without the shelter they had the night before. The crisp morning air was tinged with the smell of lake water, and the bitter fog that was caught in his breath felt like it was freezing his lungs.

"Want me to wake her?" Ashlyn asked taking a seat next to the dimming fire.

"Let's let her sleep a little longer." Markus decided scooting up to the flames and reached out as close to the heat as he could for his hands to warm up.

"How did you sleep?" He heard Ashlyn ask as she squatted across from him.

"Alright, I guess."

"I ask because you talked in your sleep."

"Oh?" he asked embarrassed. Markus never knew of this. But then again, Ruth hasn't been up enough to see him actually asleep.

"Yeah." Ashlyn said looking over at the lake which was covered by more fog. "You were muttering nonsense mostly. But I did catch a *few* words."

"Like what?" Markus asked dreading the answer.

"You were saying, 'No not her, you'll die, I can't…' stuff like that. Like you were scared or in in pain. Like I said- no offence- nonsense." Ashlyn looked at Markus with a concerned expression. "I was worried, until you eventually calmed down."

Markus nodded. "Okay," he said. He was deeply troubled by this however, His dreams *had* been nonsense. In fact, he could not understand them himself. It had been like that for the past few nights. He would see flashes; memories of his father being killed by The Hunter Black. He saw his home being ransacked and torn apart. The faces of men he had fought off to protect Ruth and his home. Ever since they had fled Nineveh, the dreams only got worse and worse.

Markus also saw things he never saw before, but troubled him to the core nonetheless. Aventis being questioned by the Barons Guard, only to get shot for refusing to answer questions. He saw the witch back in Nineveh casting a spell upon a statue of some sort. He then saw Black holding and kissing the hand of a beautiful woman cloaked in white and gold, hair as dark as night. Markus then saw Ashlyn being chased by an Ahool but then falling to the ground.

And then finally, Markus saw a grave but couldn't see the name. Among the horrors he saw, Markus also saw some things that had placed his mind at ease. Good thoughts, good dreams. He saw Ruth laughing happily in a garden, free of sickness and fear. He saw himself studying in a vast library of many scrolls and books. Markus even saw Ashlyn holding up two crystals, one of blue like the one in his staff, the other a purplish-red color. She seemed excited as she looked at him. Markus also happened to noticed that her hair was done, and she had fresh clothing on making her innocent figure appear more cute; as if it was just a boost in what was already lying underneath that cute and small smile she would give from time to time.

He then saw a large owl of tannish gold flying overhead, and then he saw another grave. A grave whose tombstone he could actually read.

And upon it, read Damion Black.

Disturbingly, nothing filled Markus with as much joy as seeing the name of the Hunter on that tombstone next to seeing his sister, safe, alive and well.

When his mind returned to reality, he saw Ashlyn staring at him with a funny look. "What?" he asked.

"Nothing." she said. "You were scowling."

"Oh." He didn't even notice.

"Was it the dreams you've been having? That whachu thinking about?"

Seeing that there was no point in hiding it, Markus nodded.

"Do you want to talk about it?"

Markus shook his head. "No, thanks though." He appreciated the thought, but talking about it would only make things worse. He didn't want to think about the dreams- any of them.

Ashlyn then nodded in understanding sympathy. "You should smile more." she commented.

Markus snorted at that. "Nothing much to smile about in this world."

"You smiled when Ruth was okay."

Markus shrugged not really having an answer to give her.

"I guess what I'm trying to say," she pressed on. "Is that you have a nice smile. It lightens the mood we usually are in."

"Well…" Markus said not really sure what to say. "Thanks."

She smiled and nodded. "Anytime." She reached into her pocket and tossed him a bag of jerky. He opened it up and ate ravenously until it was halfway empty. When he felt satisfied, he then tucked it away, wanting Ruth to have the rest.

"So," Markus said wanting to change the subject. "The Badrats?"

"Left as soon as the sun came out. Those things were *huge*."

"That's Badrats for you." Markus said.

"Yeah." She shuddered. "Good thing they don't like the sunlight. Least we got that on our side." She looked up and sure enough the sun *was* shining overhead. It was hard to see it clearly through the fog but there was no doubt about it. The sun was out and soon it will get warm. "So where to next?" Ashlyn then asked lounging onto her side. "The forest, you said?"

Markus nodded. "I don't like it, ever since the spirits took back their forests it became just as haunted as when magic returned to the world. It could be dangerous. Who knows what kind of creatures we will find out here, what kind of mutations or dark magic we will encounter."

"I thought you didn't want to believe in magic?" Ashlyn asked giving him a funny look.

Markus shrugged. "After doing some thinking, it's kind of hard to ignore it now. I still don't quite believe it, but I can't come up with a reasonable explanation. This must have been what the old prophets must have felt or something."

"Can't argue with that." Ashlyn agreed. "It's crazy how much the world can change over a course of time."

"Yeah." Markus couldn't help but agree with that as well. "Anyways, we need to try and break through the forest as soon as we can. We will know we made it by a large cliff I saw on one of my father's old maps. Wish I brought it along with the one we have with us now… There are a few camps marked around the forest, but who knows who they belong to, or if they even exist anymore."

"I guess we'll find out when we get there, right?"

"Right."

Ruth began to stir. She moaned and yawned as she stretched. She coughed as she did so but the cough soon subsided. She flinched as her brother tossed her the bag of jerky but quickly picked it up and began to eat.

He then said, "Good morning. Sleep well?"

She nodded between bites of dried meat.

"How do you feel?" Ashlyn asked.

Ruth swallowed. "As good as I look."

"So, good?" Ashlyn offered a small smile.

Ruth returned the smile. "Maybe not *exactly* how I look."

Markus chuckled half-heartedly. "You ready for today?"

"Oh yeah, sure," Ruth said swallowing the last of her breakfast and standing up. "Dangerous forest, great plan." She walked over to the lakes edge and cupped up some water to her lips. When she returned Markus had already strapped up her bag, and laid the Werecat pelt across the seat of their bike. "You're in a hurry." She said coughing slightly.

"The sooner we get there the better." Markus explained. "I don't wanna stay out here longer than we have to." Though the Badrats were gone, that didn't mean no other creature was going to leave them alone.

Ruth didn't complain in the slightest. "Okay."

When they had finally mounted their bikes and turned over the engines, the teens began at a slow and steady pace. The fog was denser as they left the lake in the direction of the forest, and the danger of hitting something was much grander than before. The thought of hitting a rock or tree- or even a monster at full speed made Markus' stomach turn.

They continued east until they saw the dim line of trees in the distance. How far away it was they could not tell because of the fog. But seeing the massive trees gave Markus himself a feeling of relief with just a small touch of fear.

"So that's the Dark Forest?" Ashlyn called over to him.

"Yep." he replied with a nod.

"It's huge…" Ruth said behind him.

"Well, better get there soon." It was then when Markus heard a chuckle that made his blood freeze. It was a laugh, cold and cruel with a slight hiss in it, as if a snake was laughing at them. On a whim he pulled out his blade and telescoped it into the staff. Ashlyn pulled her gun, and the two started looking every which way. In the fog, they couldn't see too far away; but there was no doubt about it: someone was there.

"Who's out there?" he called out in a loud voice.

The chuckle continued. "Right in front of you. Pyro, you see me? Good."

Suddenly something flew overhead, someone laughing maniacally; and through the haze of the fog above the teens was a man- the same Hunter with the flamethrower flew above them, his jetpack rockets blazing beneath him and his gun in his hands and aimed right at the three teens. His other hand went to his headset.

"Hey, Lee, we got the brats. Come to our position."

"Go, go, go!" Markus screamed and gunned the Hoverbike. Ruth and he propelled forward and before his eyes in the fog a figure materialized as if out of air. It was the lizard creature from the city, holding out her arms snarling at them with dagger-like teeth. Markus banked right while Ashlyn banked left. Together the two sped forward passing the monster beneath her extended claws as she tried to grab for them.

She spun around as they blazed passed her. "Get back here, you little shits!" she snarled and took off in a gallop on all fours. She had seemed to be catching up for a moment but as time passed the bikes picked up speed, leaving her in the fog.

"We lost her!" Ashlyn called out from her bike.

"Not me!" the man in the suit called out overhead. His arm extended out and a grapple-hook shot out from his gauntlet, grasping the ground mere inches from Ashlyn's bike. "Come 'ere!" The man shouted as he retracted his claw.

"Hurry!" Markus turned his body and fired blindly at the pursuer, the bolt of red missing him by a mile. He began to charge the crystal again when the man took aim with his grapple a second time. Ashlyn had pulled out her laser and fired at the man, clipping one of the wings of his jetpack.

"Whoo!" the Hunter whooped out as he leveled himself out. "*That* was close, but it won't save ya! Not this time!" He fired and the hook clasped on to Ashlyn's rear booster. Slowly she began to decelerate as the man retracted the claw.

"Help!" Ashlyn cried out firing again, this time hitting the Hunter square in the chest. A smoldering star appeared on his armor but seemed to only knock the wind out of him.

"Why you little…" he grasped the wire and yanked back hard, stopping the bike dead in its tracks while Ashlyn continued to fly forward. She fell face-first into the snow with a *poof*.

"Gotcha now!" The Hunter tossed the grapple aside letting it fall beside the bike which now laid in the snow. Markus dug his left heel into the brake and banked around to a U-turn and drove right for Ashlyn, the Hunter right above her now cackling.

"Oh, too bad," the one called Pyro said clicking his tongue which from within his helmet made it sound like something tapping against sheet metal. He then took aim with his gun, a small flame bursting to life at the end of the barrel. "The Baron only wants those two Johnathon-brats. Nothing personal."

Her weapon missing somewhere in the snow, Ashlyn shielded her eyes away as the Hunter pulled the trigger. Markus was screaming when he heard a deafening blast beside his left ear as he was just about to raise his staff for another shot.

A spread of buckshot sprayed out and smacked into the Hunters side, making him miss as the pillar of flame came down mere feet from Ashlyn who rolled away and ran towards Markus and Ruth who were nearly upon her. At that moment, not realizing it until later that Ruth had grabbed one of the shotguns, Markus took aim and fired another bolt just as they zoomed past the Hunter. The blast blew off the left wing, making him lose control and fly off spinning in a roll screaming into a pile of snow beyond.

"Get on!" he screamed to Ashlyn who reached out to Markus as he grabbed ahold of her hand and practically swung her onto the bike, smashing Ruth between them like a sandwich.

"What about the bike!?" she cried out.

"Forget it!" Markus shouted he gunned the engine back towards the forest. The engine hummed in defiance against the extra weight but it picked up speed slowly, *oh so slowly*. Ashlyn held on tight around Ruth and him as they dodged an uprooted tree.

That was when Ruth screamed behind them. "Mark!"

Markus looked behind them to see the lizard creature catching up to them, still galloping at break-neck speeds. "Hold on!" He called out as they got closer to the line of trees. Ruth passed the shotgun back to Ashlyn who took aim behind them and fired at the Lacerta who leapt aside and bounded after them, zipping from side to side like a rabbit avoiding a hawk. With her covering them, the three were able to keep their distance even as they disappeared into the dark forest; the lizard creature right on their tails. Darkness shrouded them, but still they fled, the monster not slowing down even as they zipped through the mass of trees.

~ The Dark Forest ~

Lameika

Lameika stood upon a hill wearing the goggles her brother had given her.

Pyro was down somewhere in the snow, the stupid fool; couldn't do anything right without having the need to slowly burn someone to the bone. Slitzar was on the brats' tails, so hopefully she would not lose them. The Dark Forest was dangerous for them all to go in, but Lameika hoped that the Lacerta would be able to keep up and was able to get out of the enchanted forest without any harm done to her. Above her head, Lameika saw their Hellhound circling overhead and flying over to where Pyro had crashed.

"Lameika, you okay?" Lee's voice came over the earpiece.

"I'm fine." *Didn't even get a chance to reach them.* She thought. "Check Pyro. Slitzar, what's your status?"

"The brats just crossed the river," the gruff voice answered. "I won't lose them. Jeez, this forest is dark... It smells wrong, and I see a coupl'a Arachnards in here as well- up in the trees."

"Be careful," Pyro said coughing. "Those things eat lizards I hear."

"Bite me."

"*Focus.*" Lee snapped, his voice causing a tremor through the radio waves.

Sensing something else was wrong, Lameika looked to her right where she saw a Leaper Dragon slithering fast across the valley before disappearing into the woods. What surprised Lameika was not the beast itself, but the rider.

Narrowing her eyes in frustration, she reached into her pocket and started palming the seeds and crystals before her.

"Slitzar be careful. You are not alone. That Hunter is back."

"What!?" Pyro's voice snapped. "That means Tank-"

"Bit the dust." Slitzar snarled sounding unsurprised. "I'll deal with him if I run into him."

"No." Lameika told her. "Those brats are the priority. Leave the Hunter to us." She swore again off the air and then called, "Lee, pick me up when you got Pyro."

"We're on our way now." Lee said and sure enough the Hellhound that had landed where Pyro had crashed was finally lifting off the ground. The slow, stupid fools…

Lameika then asked, "Pyro, how many canisters of napalm did you bring?"

"Enough to burn down a city."

"Good." Lameika said with a cold smile. "Because if Slitzar fails, we might need it."

Ashlyn

Ashlyn hung on tight to Markus's jacket with her arm wrapped around Ruth like her life depended on it. Her gun was out of ammo and she was now using her free hand to dig for more in the pack that she was now sitting on.

Her mind went back to her bike, cursing herself for leaving it behind despite the fact that it couldn't be helped. The food and water in the pack, it was all left behind. And now that monster was closing in, bouncing from tree to tree to catch up to the darting bike. As the Lacerta leapt from tree to towering tree, bark was shredded by its claws as it snarled and snapped its teeth.

Unable to find any of the ammo beneath her without falling off, Ashlyn held Ruth closer with one arm and hugged Markus tight with the other as she looked back to watch the creature still chasing them.

"She's still following us!" she cried out.

"I'm aware of that!" Markus exclaimed frantically trying to maneuver through the many trees that they sped through.

Ruth cried out. "Mark- FASTER!"

"I'm *trying*!" he snapped desperately.

The bike jumped over logs and rocks with such speed it rocked violently, especially when Mark had to turn fast to avoid hitting one of the dark trees covered in glowing mushrooms. Trees passed by them in a blur, and the darkness seemed to swallow them up as they fled the monster still close behind. All around her, over the sound of the bike and the snarling monster closing in, Ashlyn could hear the sounds of the forest. The cackling of Jackals in the trees like hyenas, the screeches of Ahools and owls, and the glowing eyes of more dragons and beasts lurking in the darkness; all of them watching the prey fleeing the predator. Above their heads, she saw massive cobwebs snaring small birds and other flying creatures, as well as cocooned figures practically human-shaped. The thought of there being *people* inside those web cocoons made Ashlyn's stomach do a backflip..

Giant Spiders… Oh no. Her overwhelming fear was taken over by confusion when Mark handed her the staff. "Charge it up; full charge!"

"But I don't-"

"Ruth, help her! I got an idea!"

Ashlyn turned to Ruth who spoke sporadically as she pointed to where Ashlyn had to hold and at the same time which button to press to get a charge going from the crystal to the staff itself. A small gauge she hadn't seen before began to fill up with a bright blue light; the crystal glowing in response. It became an eighth full when she asked Mark how full he wanted.

"I want a *full* charge." he reminded her while keeping his eyes forward and maneuvering beneath a log that was then smashed apart by the Lacerta crushing it.

Ruth leaned forward. "Are you sure that's a good idea? Father never-"

"Just do it!" Markus snapped as they dodged another log by mere inches. "Right now!"

Though worried about Ruth's own concern, Ashlyn kept her finger on the button as tight as she could. She continued watching the lizard creature bound across the forest floor with such speed; kicking up dirt and dead pine needles as she was catching up at a disturbingly fast pace.

"I will catch you!" she heard the monster snarl as it flipped around and began running along the side of a cliff they were now passing by. Like a spider charging at them from above, it kept up in speed and was eventually forced to run along the ground once again as the cliff faded away into darkness.

"Markus?" Ashlyn groaned nervously looking at the gauge. It was only half-full.

"Keep going…" he told her.

"She's catching up…"

"You honestly think I don't know that!?" he called out. "You stay focused on that staff, Ruth try and slow her down!"

Ruth picked up her shotgun again and took aim. With each shot the tree trunks where the lizard once was would shatter into splinters just as it would bound to another tree. Ruth was trying to anticipate every bounce to try and catch it but the beast was too fast. She was slowing down slightly when she saw the shots from the gun, but she was still going fast enough to keep up with the fleeing prey.

"You little shits!" the monster snarled loudly. "I'll rip ya to shreds!

It was then when all movement stopped completely and Ashlyn found herself propelled forward again, sailing through the air despite the bike being tangled in what looked like webbing that had fallen to the ground. But this time instead of landing in snow, she collided into a sticky substance that stretched and bounced with the force of the three children. As Ashlyn looked around spastically, she saw webbing all over the trees, the ground; everywhere. Animals and sacs hung from the limbs of the trees, and one large one hung between the two largest trees in a beautiful hexagonal pattern worthy of Arachne herself.

And the three of them were stuck right in it.

"Mark!" Ashlyn screamed out, her hand never letting go of the staff. Ruth was just beneath her and Markus was stuck on his back, his face stuck in the sticky residue.

"I didn't see it!" He looked over to the staff which he reached over with his only free hand. He snatched it up out of Ashlyn's hand. Ruth struggled, squirming in her blanket which kept herself from getting caught in the webbing. Her thrashing however made the web shudder, and it made Ashlyn feel more anxious than ever.

The Lacerta dropped to the ground in front of the web's captives, hissing in a sinister chuckle. "Poor little flies, caught in a web."

Markus stuck his arm back behind him and aimed the staff right at the monster. "Get back!" he shouted.

The scaly Huntress grinned a smile of fangs as she pointed up with one finger. Ashlyn looked up and to her horror, she saw an Arachnard crawling slowly down the tree trunks to see what she had caught in her web; Ruth's thrashing having awoken her from her slumber. The giant arachnid was as large as a tank and as pale as the snow beyond the forest. It's large black eyes reflected the teens horrified faces and its mandibles curled around its mouth full of needle-like teeth, the fangs dripping with green poison. As it curled its legs and drew closer, Ashlyn could swear that she could smell it's breath; rancid, and reeking of death.

Ashlyn began to thrash and scream at the sight of it, causing all of them to shake in the webbing. She had a horrible, horrible fear of spiders; and the fact that they were in a web with one coming upon them right now was the stuff of nightmares for her. Markus was yelling at her, telling her to stop shaking but she didn't seem to hear. She only cried and sobbed like a little child; terror being the only thing she felt at that very moment.

"I only need you and you sister," the monster snarled to Markus. "Shoot me, and I can't get you out. However, your little friend will be left to distract our hungry host. Can't have it chasing us, can we?"

"No!" Ashlyn screamed tears rolling down her cheeks as she looked at Markus, pleading with him. "Don't leave me, please!" she begged him.

"Mark…" Ruth said nervously as the spider took a tentative step upon its web, its spiny feet making the strands shudder at its touch. She continued to squirm, desperate to break free of the Werecat blanket.

Markus looked so conflicted as to what he could do now. He looked at Ashlyn helplessly. She didn't mean to cry, but the thought of being left to be a spider's lunch filled her with so much terror she couldn't help it. She pleaded with him with tear-rimmed eyes. He wouldn't let the monster take them and leave her, would he?

"Please…" she begged again to him.

"Wanna save your sister?" The Hunter snarled catching Markus' attention once more. "Drop your staff."

Markus looked at the Arachnard drawing closer now, then to Ruth, to Ashlyn and back to the Lacerta. He then clenched his eyes, his conflicting thoughts expressing themselves through the pain in his face. "Oh man…"

"I will enjoy watching your sister get eaten." the lizard snarled provokingly while sitting back as if she really was looking forward to it. "I was asked to capture you both, but I'm sure *one* will suffice."

"No, please!" Ashlyn cried out. She didn't want to be left at the mercy of the giant spider, but to drag Markus and Ruth into it... it just wasn't fair. "Look," she said, deciding that she couldn't let Markus choose between what he could do. "Mark, just do it and get out of here! Please!"

She could not let Ruth get eaten because of her. Markus looked at her as if it was funny how she went from 'don't leave me' to 'leave' in a moment's notice. But this was definitely not the time for humor. "Don't worry about me, just save your sister!"

"No!" Ruth cried out still struggling, her legs now free from the blanket as she slowly started to slip free. "We stick together!"

"How heroic." the monster grinned crawling across the web-covered floor towards Ruth who immediately stopped moving when she saw the Huntress coming at her. "But futile. I'll wait right here then and watch you guys get wrapped up for me."

Markus sighed. "Crap." and he pulled the trigger.

The blast shot up where he was aiming, and the Arachnard blew apart in a flash of red light and green slime. Green slime splattered the kids, making them groan and scream as chunks of hairy meat and a few remains of spiny legs crashed to the ground beneath them.

The mutant Huntress sighed as a single leg plopped down beside her. "Shoot me if you want, you ain't got long to charge it enough again." She started towards them on her two legs again, her massive scaly arms swaying at her sides; as if she had all the time in the world now. "I'll just take you both and leave that little missy here for the jackals to pick clean."

She reached up and grasped Marks foot. He cried out and kicked out, hitting the monster square in the nose with a *crack*. The lizard chuckled as her head came back forward, holding her nose which began to bleed purple.

"A little fight in you I see." she started to reach for him again.

"Let him go!" Ruth screamed now on the ground free from the blanket still stuck in the web. She started smacking the Lacerta with a branch but the monster merely glanced at her before pushing her back with a single finger.

With Ruth now on the ground, the Lacerta turned her attention from Markus who was now charging up his staff.

"Get away from her!" he shouted.

The Lacerta merely grinned at him as she raised one of her hands. The claws extended from her finger tips and she neared Ruth with a hiss. "Don't worry, it'll be just a scratch."

Ruth watched with wide eyes as the Huntress came upon her.

Suddenly something struck the creature in the side, sending her flying and smacking against a tree; her scales tearing the bark to shreds. It was a Leaper Dragon, and it roared into the Huntress' face, both claws holding her arms back.

"I don't think so." the Lacerta snarled, throwing her arms up and tossing the Dragon back on its haunches. Ashlyn noticed the saddle across the monsters back as the Huntress leapt up and landed on the beasts back. It bucked and squirmed but immediately dropped to the ground when the lizard grabbed ahold of the it's head and snapped it to the side; breaking the neck instantly with a sickening crack. She dropped beside it, and sniffed. She began to growl looking behind her. "Thought I caught your scent." She hissed angrily.

Ashlyn's eyes peered behind the monster where a man stood on a fallen tree; garbed in black, a longsword in his hands and his head obscured by a hood and cowl of shadows. The Hunter Black.

"Step aside, Slitzar." Black said in a low voice.

The monster hissed as she squared up to the Hunter, her back now exposed to the teens as Ruth stood and started to pull on Markus. The boy stared at the Hunter, his expression a mixture of both anger and relief as Black leapt down from the log he was standing on and got into a stance, ready to fight the Lacerta. "Step aside," he said again, his voice low and threatening.

"I don't think so." Slitzar said extended her black claws which reflected the light coming from the glowing mushrooms around them. She growled at the Hunter, a monster ready to feast on the bones of the hero trying to save them.

Marked whispered something to Ashlyn and turned her head to see the Ruth pulling tighter to pull Markus free from the webbing. Her brother then telescoped his staff into a dagger and began cutting into the strands of sticky thread.

"Hurry," Ashlyn whispered.

"Working on it," Ruth said pulling tighter as her brother slowly started to break away. As he became more able to move, he started to work on the strands holding Ashlyn still in the web.

And Ashlyn herself kept her eyes on the two Hunters who lunged at one another in a flash of steel and claws.

~ Evolution ~

Slitzar

Slitzar clawed at Black who sidestepped and slashed at her, forcing her to retreat to avoid the sword's bite. She leapt back at him and clawed at the ground, tearing up the earth as Black slipped underneath her arm with feline grace while slashing at her forehead and cutting a light gash in her scales. Purple blood dribbled slowly between her eyes, and retreating again she hissed at him like a rabid cat.

She sniffed the air, catching all of the Hunter's smells. The sweat on his brow, the leather from his boots, and the stench of blood on his sword both old and fresh. But she couldn't smell the scent her tongue searched for: the stench of fear; adrenaline running through the man's veins in his fight for survival.

The Hunter Black, simply didn't reek of fear like so many humans had before him.

Among the smells that were noticeable, Slitzar also caught the scent of Tank's distinct odor. *Oil, paint fumes...* "I take it that Tank is gone?" she growled holding her arms out, ready to pounce at any given moment.

"He chose his fate." Black said simply, once again in a sturdy stance with his sword tight in his grip. He still didn't look the least bit concerned given his predicament. Such a strange man.

Slitar heard the children breaking free of their web but she ignored them. Let them run. She would catch up to them as soon as she dealt with this nuisance of a Hunter.

"I see you're no more worried about them running than I am." the Hunter did not change in scent, meaning his attitude and concern towards the children was the same if not non-existent despite him clearly seeing the kids escape on their bike.

All her time with humans, all the times Slitzar had hunted them and also working alongside the other Hunters, the Lacerta had become accustomed to smelling fear emit from the humans. Looking at her, a monster in their eyes, they *always* feared her; they *reeked* of it before their fate was settled and she would feast on their bones.

Slitzar pressed a finger to her piece. "Lee, you copy?"

"I see you. And I see our 'friend'."

"I got him occupied. The brats are heading…" She paused and listened as the Hoverbike roared to life, taking off in a directly the same way they were heading before. "Northeast. Go get 'em."

"What about you?" Lameika's voice came up.

"I'll catch up." Slitzar grinned revealing her long and jagged teeth. "I'm gonna grab a quick snack." She took off her earpiece and tossed it to the moist ground. Something else was said, but she wasn't listening. She didn't want any dstractions. She needed all of her senses focused on the Hunter in order to really enjoy this hunt.

She crouched and extended her black claws again, curling her fingers and flexing them out. "I've heard a lot about you, Black."

"And I you."

"Oh really?"

"Yes. The child who became a monster, the monster who became a fugitive, the fugitive who became a Huntress- a *cannibal* Huntress I might add." Whether he was goading Slitzar or not, the Lacerta couldn't tell. The indifference in his voice and such a flat expression, it was impossible to tell.

Slitzar hissed at the insult nonetheless. "Well, when you grow up like I did, you get the munchies." She had abandoned her humanity long ago, ever since she was brought into this world kicking and screaming; a monster since birth due to some curse be it biologically or by some sick, twisted joke of some higher power unable to be understood by the living.

"I see." Black responded to her threat, unamused.

"So, what now, *Hunter*? Will you try and strike me down as well like you did that poor bucket of bolts?"

The sword tilted in hand, revealing a faint glint of sunlight peeking through the treetops. "That depends. Will you step aside and leave me to collect my bounty?"

Slitzar bared her teeth. "Fat chance."

"Then you leave me no choice."

"Oh, no," Slitzar said with a slight chuckle. "*You* leave *me* none." And with that she pounced, teeth bared and claws out to grab the Hunter. Her claws dug deep and she bit down, catching nothing but air and the snow in her claws. She peered through her peripheral vison to see the Hunter standing ten feet from where he had stood. He appeared no different than he had before, as if he had never moved at all.

She growled and stood back up. "Fast little sucker ain't you?"

"You were too focused on me." Black said still unmoving. Slitzar with confused, what could he have meant by 'too focused on him'? Shouldn't that have been a *good* thing? "You're pretty easy to deceive, I'm not going to lie."

Slitzar bared her teeth again in indignation. "Bastard. I'll make sure not to make that mistake again!" And she leapt again, but this time Black did not disappear like before.

He sidestepped again, sliding his sword across Slitzar's arm, cutting through the scales at the same time as an electric shock made her jump. She looked down at her bleeding arm and snarled and 'barked' at him with a hollow sound.

Black then leapt towards the beast and swung horizontally where her belly was. She retreated back and clawed at the Hunter, missing his head by a mere hairs-width. He then jumped straight up and swung at her head, but this time, Slitzar was ready. Knocking the sword aside with one hand, she grabbed ahold of the Hunter with the other and threw him back onto the ground. His weapon tumbled out of his hands and fell into the dirt. She then pounced on him, grabbing his shoulders and lunging forward with her neck to bite the man's head off.

But Black was full of surprises. He had managed to get his hands on her forehead and jaw, and with such strength that far exceeded a normal man's, he pushed back against her; holding her back and keeping her from digging her teeth into his face.

Shocked but undeterred, Slitzar snapped her teeth in his face and pushed harder, determined to chomp on his head. Some slimey saliva had dribbled past her lips and had speckled Black's face, but his face remained unmoved as he pushed back. This man... he was strong- too strong to be human. She had many try and keep her from biting their own heads off, but in the end, they were all the same; too weak to hold her back as she devoured them while they were still screaming.

But Black... No matter how much effort Slitzar pushed to get closer, the Hunter resisted without even struggling it seemed. His face just didn't show any strain whatsoever.

What is with this guy? Slitzar wondered in frustration as she strained her neck more and more in her attempt to bite Black's face off. Seeing that he wasn't wearing down in the slightest, Slitzar gave up on her attempt to bite, and removing one hand from Black's shoulder, she pulled her arm back, ready to instead just claw the bastard into shreds. But then something else happened that once again Slitzar wasn't expecting at all.

Black's eyes suddenly flashed dark red, almost maroon in color that completely blooted out any shred of the blue that was once there. He then grabbed ahold of Slitzar's other arm and the Lacerta thought she saw blood-red lighting coursing through his fingertips. At that moment, a flash of shadows suddenly blew into Slitzar's face like a sudden gust of wind, forcing her to retreat back and rub at her eyes.

Though she was a dangerous creature, her primal instincts were *screaming* at her now; telling her to get away. But she ignored her born-instincts and when her vision cleared, she stood her ground, ready for the Hunter Black who was already on his feet with his sword back in his hands.

His eyes were no longer maroon, but the same cold blue that they were originally. Not only that, but Slitzar couldn't smell or sense what she had felt earlier when Black had grabbed her. Maybe it was her imagination, a hallucination brought upon her by the cursed forest they fought in.

Clicking her teeth, she crouched down on all fours agin, ignoring the buzzing in the back of her head. "Come on, you bastard, let's see what you really got!"

And tearing the very ground with the force of her lunge, Slitzar closed the distance between the two of them in only one bound; her claws reaching out to Black and her teeth ready to dig into his flesh as he charged right into her attack and swung his sword.

Markus

Markus continued to push the hoverbike to go as fast as it could.

Ruth and Ashlyn held on tight in the back in complete silence; their energy spent on escaping the web and getting as far away from the Lacerta and now Black as fast as they could. They were working on getting the remaining strands of web out of their hair while continueing to be silent for what felt like hours until Markus saw a clearing near a small pond. He slowed and stopped in the meadow area.

The girls jumped off as he killed the engine and then he rolled right off the bike; falling and collapsing onto the ground with a sigh. His heart was slamming in his chest and by the way the girls looked still covered in slime and webbing all the while looking traumitized, Markus could tell they were shaken up almost as bad as he was. Now that they were here by the little pond lost in a dark forest that seemed to stretch on for miles and miles, he felt a little afer but at the same time all too exposed. He continued to keep watch while his brain worked out what has just occurred and considered what to do now.

Their encounter with the Arachnard was jarring, and the last thing he wanted was to get caught off-guard by some other horrible creature hiding in the strange bushes and trees that seemed to tower over them like sentinels. He didn't know how far they had fled, but he knew they couldn't be too far away from Black or the Lacerta. One of them would be back on their trail again at some point or another.

Markus decided that the three of them would catch their breath, rest for a few minutes, and then take off again. The further they got from Black and that monster, the better. Just had to go a little further, cover their tracks carefully, and they could probably get away with hiding overnight before leaving again in the morning. With his thoughts now calmed and organized, Markus felt comfortable with his plan.

That was when the coughing of Ruth exceeded new heights and with it, familiar horrors.

"Mark!" he heard Ashlyn scream his name.

He bolted upright and scrambled to his sister who was on her side hugging her small stomach and spewing the worst coughing-fit since they had left the city. Blood speckled the ground next to her face, and his heart sank deeper and deeper with each dreadful cough. Markus pulled Ruth close to him, patting her back as she coughed coughed up some more blood.

"Get me some water!" he told Ashlyn in a shrill tone of voice.

"They were in my bike!" Ashlyn cried in front of me on her knees. "We left it!"

"The pond then, hurry!"

"We don't know what's in there!"

"Ashlyn!" he snapped angrily and yet pleadingly as a single tear dripped from his eye. She was so startled by his sudden ferocity that she actually stumbled back, scared of him it seemed as if he was a wolf trying to protect its pup. "Do it now! We don't have time to boil it; she needs fluids *now*!" He was just as worried as Ashlyn was concerning parasites and God-knows-what floating in the pond, but that couldn't be helped now.

He turned his attention back to Ruth who was still coughing horribly as Ashlyn got up with a look of fear imprinted on her face. "It's gonna be okay, Ruth." Markus whispered. "You're gonna be okay… I promise."

His promise was responded by more coughing, and a lot more blood.

Slitzar

Slitzar slammed against a tree with enough force to splinter the bark and make it snap. The tree itself groaned and pine needles fell from its limbs as it threatened to come crashing down at any moment. Her arms and torso were crisscrossed with many cuts from the Hunter's sword, and her cheek dripped purple so she stretched her tongue out to lick the cut on her cheek clean.

She glowered at the Hunter before her with such hatred. He had a few scrapes of his own but not nearly as severe as hers. Slitzar was *angry*; she wanted to rip Black's arms off and beat him into the ground with them; to rip off his head and tear at his guts as he stood! Though her survival instincts were still telling her to flee, that this prey had teeth to fight back with, she stood her ground; unwilling to back down from this fight.

"I have to admit," she hissed. "You're a tough little bastard. But it won't be enough to stop me, I killed worse than some punk with a sword."

"I wish I could believe you." Black said in that irritating voice of emotionless indifference. "But your predicament is not in your favor." He flicked his wrist and whatever purple gore was still on his sword immediately slid off and speckled the webbing on the ground.

"Oh?" Slitzar growled smiling. "Then I guess I better get a little more serious. Do you know *this* one? Now you see me…" It then appeared as if her scales were flipping inside out, shimmering until she was no longer visibly there, just the shattered stump behind her and the dark forest beyond. "Now, you don't."

"Intriguing." Black said his eyes darting to and fro, now searching for the seeming-invisible Lacerta through his surroundings. "Camouflage, and at the strength of a true Lacerta. Though, I'm a little intrigued that you only now thought of using it. Could it be that you just didn't think of it; that you had forgotten about such an ability? Or were you just too simple-minded to recall?"

Despite his goading her, Slitzar remained silent and watchful. Black scanned the surrounding trees and plants beyond the webbing, trying to see any movement at all; looking for the slightest disturbance. A leaf moving, a rock shifting, anything that could give Slitzar away. Just like a rabbit searching for a wolf that had suddenly hidden from view, Black was cautiously keeing his head on a swivel.

The sight amused Slitzar and only fueled her desire to stay despite her instincts still screaming at her to just leave and go after the kids under the cover of the shadows. But instead she stayed, determined to feast on Black's bones.

"You look a little nervous, Hunter." Slitzar said her voice sounding just above him which drew his attention to the limbs above. She wasn't there, of course. She was just circling around him, throwing her voice to throw him off so that she could strike at safer opening. She could merely smell something different in her prey, but he did not give the slightest hint of being afraid.

Black retorted in bored defiance, "You *sound* nervous if you're thinking of trying to get the drop on me."

"Who says I'm above you?"

Black started to turn but Slitzar was already lunging for his exposed back. The sword came in fast and she had to resort to ducking low and with the little bit of opening she had left, she clawed at the back of his head with enough force to shred even stone into ribbons. She felt her claws drag against his skull and Black flew forward and tumbled in the dirt before steadying his tumble to land on his feet, now facing the spot where he had been hit.

He held his blade up, still smelling of ozone and the creature's blood. To Slitzar's surprise, the man's head was still intact. She knew she felt her her claws against bone, but he looked as though he was merely thrown off-balance rather than getting swiped at with claws, even as his hood fluttered with obvious tears in the cloth.

"Tell me," he said behind clenched teeth from his jarring head, still keeping alert for Slitzar who was once again stalking towards him invisible and still hunting. "Who taught you how to throw your voice like that?"

"Don't like it huh?" Slitzar casted her voice to his left. "Too bad." This time towards the right. "I learned from a coupl'a Metal Heads I met in the south. Interesting people, and I must say, quite tasty too."

"So it is true then." Black said his voice more controlled now seeing a leaf twitch to his right but made no movement to show that he had seen anything. "You're far from human now; You've become the monster everyone says you are."

Slitzar hissed in agitation, now circling to Black's left where his attention was diverted. "I am *nothing* like you weak humans. Fragile, weak, pathetic little creatures. When I gave in to what I truly am- who my family was, I was given true power; true *freedom*. The true strength of a hunter, unlike yourself; a human, so fragile and too weak to keep up. You've no idea what it was like, living like I did. But, it has made me stronger; evolved more than any human in history. However, you've lasted longer than any of your kind I've ever faced, so I tip my hat to you. You're the toughest warrior I've ever had the pleasure of facing. I will enjoy tasting the meat on that pretty little face of yours." At this point, she was right behind him, claws ready to tear him limb from limb.

Black spun on his heel and swung upward and both he and Slitzar both saw purple blood splash upwards, and through the cut that sliced through her scales, Slitzar screamed and immediately lost the focus of keeping her camofloge aligned with her surroundings, leaving her now exposed. She was clutching her left hand which was now missing two fingers, the cuts aligned with a deep cut across her chest.

"Aagh! Damn you!" Slitzar roared and clawed out at Black who ducked, making her rake the tree he had been standing next to. He sliced at her leg and she drove her fist downward, making him sidestep and get out of range of the attack. With himself now at a safe distance, Black acknowledged her with a brooding expression.

"You are right," he said. "We humans *are* weak creatures. We are easily knocked down, and we get beaten back down as we try to get back up. But, that is what makes us special. No matter how many times monsters like you knock us down, we always come back up. We might lose a lot; we might even die, but we'll always give you a fight to remember."

Slitzar hissed. "I'll be sure to remember that, when I'm shitting you out somewhere in these woods!" She then lunged forward and accepted the blade that sunk into her arm. With her other hand, she backhanded him with all her might, sending him flying into the same tree he threw *her* at with a sickening *crunch*. He groaned as he laid against the trunk, shaking in jarring pain.

Slitzar began to giggle as she wrenched the sword out that was stuck in her arm. Tossing it aside, she growled, "What's the matter, Black? Met your match?" She lunged forward but once again, Black leapt out of the way just mere seconds before she dug her claws into the bark. Now that he was behind her, Slitzar saw that his eyes were glowing maroon now, his scent changing drastically.

But he was right where she wanted him, and she wrenched her claws free from the tree, ripping out a good chunk of the trunk itself. It's weight now lingering more to one side, the tree groaned as it began to tip and fall towards Black, smashing him with a thundering *crash*.

When the dust settled, Slitzar allowed herself to relax. She walked over to the Hunter, whose lower torso had been crushed by the tree, pinning him to the ground. He was coughing up blood and his hood and cowl had come off from the claw marks she scratched into the back of his head. It was a miracle the man was still alive, but Slitzar crouched down beside the pinned Hunter and hooked her fingers through his long black hair, holding his head up and exposing his throat.

With brute strength and a victorious gleam in her eyes, she grabbed Black beneath the chin and ripped the head clean off his shoulders. She then held the severed head in front of her face and she chuckled disturbingly into his face.

"Gotcha," she muttered to the dead Hunter Black, opening her mouth wider for that first bite.

"No, you didn't." she heard the voice from just behind her that was unmistakably Black's.

Impossible! she thought and then turned just in time to see Black's sword swinging towards her exposed neck.

~ Man in Wolf's Clothing ~

Ruth

Ruth watched in horror as her own blood speckled onto the ground like dew caught in the rising sun. Her body ached with each crippling cough that shattered her lungs, and it felt like her little eyes would pop out of their sockets.

This is what dying feels like… she decided. She began to spill tears as she cried and coughed all at once.

The pain was just *excruciating*. She felt as if glass was bouncing around inside of her. She looked back up at Mark who was patting her back and rubbing it, trying to soothe the misery shattering her poor weak body. The look of distraught and fear flashed through his eyes, and Ruth felt so horrible for putting him through this. He had yelled at Ashlyn, who had returned with a large leaf.

She held it out to Ruth. Ruth could not understand the words coming from Ashlyn's lips; they all sounded muffled as her head pounded horribly. But she let Ashlyn tip the leaf towards her lips. Cold and slimy water seemed to slow the cough down for a bit, washing down the painful bile and blood trying to escape her body. She cleared her throat and sipped some more. She thought she felt something thick and slimy go down her throat with the water, but she pushed the thought from her mind. She had drunk worse than pond water before.

The growling was what made her stop drinking and forget her terrible coughing altogether.

Mark immediately rose to his feet, setting her down gently before unsheathing his weapon and telescoping it out. He got a charge buzzing while taking aim at the source, and Ruth followed his gaze to see a large wolf standing at the edge of the pond, staring at them with orbs of purple. The wolf did not seem eager to move from his spot; in fact, he just stood there, staring at the youths while standing a monstrous eight feet tall at the shoulder. Its fur was as black as coal, and its paws as large as solar disks.

"Mark…" Ruth coughed.

"Ruth, stay down," Mark said sounding very afraid. Ashlyn had backed up to join them, her lips quivering at the sight of the monstrosity.

The wolf, however, did not advance. It tilted its head slightly, as if in curiosity. Other than that however, it remained where it was. It sniffed as if it could tell that something was wrong. It then looked past the youths.

Ashlyn turned to look behind them. Her eyes widened. "Mark?"

Mark looked back not turning his back to the wolf. Ruth looked as well, for behind them were more glowing orbs in the darkness of the forest. Pairs of cat-like eyes watched them, and ice clawed at the hearts of the group as they all heard the cackling laughter of Ice Jackals.

Try as she might, Ruth could not stop coughing, and the sound drew the eyes closer until one of the creatures came into view from the light. It was a small and vicious-looking creature, no bigger than Ruth herself. It had smooth black fur and a rat-like tail. The snout was flat and snarling with jagged scissor-like teeth. The eyes glowed bright and yellow in the light of the reflected pond.

Mark instantly spun on his heel and fired a shot, blowing the creature back who yelped in terrible pain. As he was charging another round however, the pack moved in, closing in on them.

Ruth began to huddle close to Mark, hugging his leg while Ashlyn stood beside him, a hand on his arm with another holding her knife. He had looked at her, and then looked down at Ruth helplessly.

So this is it. Ruth thought as tears began to form in her eyes. The coughing had finally ceased. There was no point in coughing anymore; her sickness wouldn't haunt her for much longer.

That was when the wolf suddenly appeared beside them.

It made them all jump at the sight of it; it didn't even make a sound of movement. Yet here it was standing beside them like a ghost, not looking at them but at the pack of Jackals which slowed to a stop before the beast before them. The wolf did not growl, the only sound coming from it was its heavy breathing. Ruth could see its massive chest rising and falling as it peered at the creatures before it. Some barked and snapped at the wolf, but the beast did not seem to care. In fact, it stood its ground beside the terrified group of youths. Mark had crouched down and placed a hand on Ruth with Ashlyn at his back.

The wolf then took one step towards the Jackals, and they, in turn, stepped back. The creatures then appeared to have taken a sudden interest in the ground before them, tucking their tails between their legs and slowly retreating back into the darkness from which where they came.

Soon they were all out of sight, and Ruth, still terrified, looked up at the wolf to see it looking down at them; those purple eyes studying them with such curiosity. Mark seemed to forget all about his staff, staring wide-eyed and slack-jawed before this magnificent beast that stood mere inches away from them.

Some compulsive desire built up within her, and Ruth then reached out slightly towards the wolf. Mark started to say something, but he wilted as the wolf turned to look at him. Ruth's hand continued its ascent until her fingers were soon caught in the locks of the wolfs lower shoulder. She could feel the muscles in its powerful leg, and the fur warmed her hand like no fire ever could. Not only that, but it was soft. Soft as a newborn's head of hair, pure and clean. The wolf snorted slightly with its snout, letting out a puff of air visible like steam in the cold.

That tickles.

Ruth pulled her hand back in astonishment. "What was that?" she asked.

"What?" Ashlyn said still staring in wonder.

"I heard a voice..." Ruth said.

"What voice?" Mark asked, his voice cracked slightly.

The wolf then turned and began walking toward the line of trees away from the youths. Ruth stood up and began forward, but Mark held her back at the last second.

"Wait!" she called out. The wolf then stopped at the sudden command and turned its head, its body still planted, so its back was to them despite looking at the girl. "Thank you," Ruth said coughing slightly.

The wolf, giving no indication that he even understood the child turned his head forward and continued to walk away before disappearing in the darkness.

Mark let out a huge sigh of relief. "What was that?"

"That," Ashlyn said her voice still shaking as she dropped down to the ground behind them. "Was one giant wolf… I have never seen one that close before…"

"It was amazing," Ruth said dreamily. She hadn't even noticed that her coughing had all but stopped- almost instantly.

"What did you mean?" Mark said sitting down and retracting his staff. "Earlier, what did you hear?"

"It's hard to say…" Ruth said still not quite sure whether she really heard something or not. "But it sounded deep. Like father's, but, older… A voice I mean."

"A voice?" Ashlyn said giving Ruth a peculiar look. Mark gave her a similar look of doubt.

"Yeah," Ruth said looking back at where the wolf had disappeared. "It said, 'that tickles'…"

"Lovely," Mark said sighing as if that was obvious. It was obvious that he didn't believe her; Ruth couldn't believe it herself.

"Now I'm kinda like you," she said with a slight grin.

"I don't talk to animals." Though as he said this, Markus looked a little uneasy.

"No, but in a way, given how you see things that we don't…"

Markus snorted. He looked out back towards the direction they had come from and said, "We should keep going."

"We can't," Ashlyn said shaking her head.

"We need to."

"I know, but we can't. Ruth just had a fit, and we're all scared. We need to rest, gather our strength."

"Here?" Mark sighed, and Ruth could understand his hesitation. Out here in the middle of the Dark Forest, without any knowledge of whether those Jackals or something much worse was watching them in the darkness behind the circle of trees around the pond, made her worry as well. Still, she had a feeling; a sense that she was being watched over, and she looked back in the direction where the wolf had disappeared to.

Mark eventually gave in, having lost to Ashlyn's piercing gaze telling him to listen. "Okay, okay, you're right." He pulled out his knife. "We need to get a fire going. Keep whatever other monsters are out here at bay. But we are only staying for a few hours. As soon as trouble comes, we go."

"Right..." Ruth said looking back down at the blood in the snow. "Monsters."

"I'll stay near the bike," Ashlyn said standing up.

"We're only staying for a little while," Mark repeated himself. "Okay?"

Ashlyn nodded, having already gotten the message but didn't argue nonetheless. "Okay."

Ruth looked up at the forest canopy. The many limbs and branches made like a ceiling above their heads, obscuring any light that would otherwise reach them this far below at the ground. It was a surreal feeling, seeing so much darkness in a place so big. But in the little bit of light they had with the glowing mushrooms and soon Mark's fire, Ruth thought of just how beautiful the forest really was. It was dangerous, and cursed, yes. But the Dark Forest was still full of life; a different kind of ecosystem and a world within its own. The sounds of the birds and creatures lingering in the darkness, the smell of pine and other plants, it was truly wonderful. All her life, Ruth had only known the smell of oil and smoke, having been born in the city of Nineveh. Never would she had thought that she would be able to smell a forest in her life.

She wondered just what else she would experience on this trip- if she would last that long. *The world really is so much bigger, outside the walls.*

Markus

Markus sat near the large fire he and Ashlyn had put together in the middle of a bunch of small spot-fires. Ashlyn had placed them all around the pond area, so they could better see their surroundings. Ruth laid propped against their single pack across from Markus; looking up at nothingness while Ashlyn had gone to filter some water from the pond. He dreaded thinking about what kind of parasites Ruth had swallowed.

Looking over at his sister, Markus couldn't help but think of what she was like as a baby. How innocent and vulnerable she was to the world. Yet here they are now, running away and on their own, and she's *still* so fragile and weak. The sickness was getting worse, and it was making Markus dread the *absolute* worst. Not only that, but their other pack was *gone*. All of their food, fuel, everything that was in that pack. Now it was lost, and there was no way they could go back.

The fires were probably a bad idea, considering the Hunters that were still out there somewhere in the dark forest, and the monsters that Markus saw staring at them from afar were like demons creeping at their door, ready to pounce. But he was afraid. He didn't know what else to do, and the darkness was not going to help them. He wanted to go hunting soon, maybe catch something small, but then again, he could not risk leaving Ruth alone.

And what about Ashlyn? Without her gun, she would be defenseless against any monster attacks. *And what about the Hunters?* She wouldn't stand a chance against them either. Not that any of them would, but Markus couldn't just abandon the two like that.

He took a deep breath and shuddered a sigh. They were on their own, and things were only getting worse. The bike was nearly out of fuel, and soon they might end up walking on foot. Water would not be a problem to come by, but what about food? If they don't freeze to death they will starve, if they didn't starve, they could freeze. Markus began to clench his eyes in frustration and fear.

What are we going to do?

It was like every scenario he played in his head only resulted as the worst-case. Every thought was a dreadful one, and he was consumed with worry.

He had never felt so helpless as he did now.

He heard the chortle of a Jackal, and Markus immediately felt his spine tingle at the sound. The little beasts were still there, watching the group in the comfort of the darkness, away from the fires. It was like they were laughing at him specifically; enjoying his torment as he struggled to find a solution to an unsolvable problem. Time was running, out, and soon-

"Hey," Markus opened his eyes and turned to see Ashlyn taking a seat next to him. The mist of her breath was visible in the late afternoon cold.

It had gotten darker, and Markus wondered if the sun had hidden behind a cloud. Not only that, but a few stray snowflakes had managed to slip through the limbs high above and make it to the freezing ground; giving the forest a darker, but slightly beautiful look to it despite the terror still grasping onto their hearts. In the firelight, Ashlyn seemed more afraid than outside of the forest in the sunlight, as if in this special kind of light all of her fears were drawn in little shadows across her face. All of her worries and thoughts; visible to all. And right now, all of those thoughts were looking right at Markus with those worrying eyes of hers.

"How are you doing?" she asked after a while.

He turned away to look at Ruth again, who was still resting. "I'm alright," he said.

"Are you?"

He sighed. "No."

"What's on your mind? Tell me."

Markus looked down at his boots. "I thought she was going to die... I'm *scared*, Ashlyn. I can't lose her. But also, I'm worried about all of us in general. Will we even make it? We have no more fuel or food. We will run out of fuel before or even by the time we reach the end of this cursed forest. Then we need to cross the Fiery Plains, which isn't as hot this deep in the winter, but it will still be hard to cross. Then the mountains, just finding the city in those behemoths, I don't know I…"

Markus wanted to say that he felt hopeless; that he did not think they were going to make it. That… Ruth would die, Ashlyn would die, and even he would eventually die out here in this cold, harsh wilderness, if the Hunters don't get ahold of them first. All alone, without anyone else knowing who they were. He just… didn't know what to do.

They were doomed.

Markus started when he felt Ashlyn's cool fingers wipe his cheek, for he realized that he had begun to cry. Markus wiped his face angrily, not letting her touch him. He was embarrassed to be seen like this; he shouldn't behave so pitiful. She looked hurt at this, but then nodded understandably.

"It's okay to cry once in a while, Markus," she said.

"No, it's not," he said bitterly. "I need to be strong. I gotta keep a level head, to keep you two alive. I can't… I can't give in now. I can't go weak on you two."

Ashlyn raised an eyebrow at him. "You are *not* weak, Mark. You never were."

"Yeah, right."

"No, you're not!" she insisted as she bit her lip in thought. "Look, in that house when you told me to get out, I knew you were scared. You were scared for Ruth, but you were ready to fight back and do whatever it took to keep her safe. You saved me, twice already. We broke out of Ninevah, we evaded those Hunters again, and we escaped…" She shuddered. "The web. All through that you kept strong for Ruth and me. You stayed brave for us, took care of us, and made sure everything would be okay. It's just now starting to get at you. Crying is just one of many things we do to let out the pain we feel, and the fact that you're doing it now only means that there is something that's gotta come out. That's not weakness, Markus. That just means you're human. You *are* brave. Just like your dad."

Markus looked up at her but remained silent.

Ashlyn averted her gaze from his. "You really are." She said again. "And, I'm sure he was scared too. Having to fight Black, knowing he was going to die protecting you and Ruth. And here you are, not knowing what we are going to find in this 'City of Angels'; and yet here we are. All because of you, because Ruth and I believe in you."

Markus let that sink in for a bit. He looked down at his boots again, with Ashlyn's right next to them.

He heard her speak again. "It really is okay to cry, Mark. Because you care. You took care of Ruth for so long, and now you're taking care of us. Other people would be terrified to deal with what we did, but you remained brave for our sake. You put yourself before others. Not a lot of people do that anymore."

He looked at her again. "How do you know I have not already given up?"

"'Cause if you did, you would go back to that giant lizard with open arms. Or even Black."

Markus chuckled. "I'd die before I surrendered us to Black."

Ashlyn smiled. "Good. Wait… not good I… I would rather you stay alive." She looked away again, embarrassed.

Markus cleared his throat, feeling the heat rise into his own cheeks. "Um, you should rest for a bit. I plan to ride and not stop until we have to."

"You sure? I can watch if you want?"

"I'd rather not." Markus looked over at Ruth, to see that her eyes were closed. How could she sleep, even after everything that has happened thus far?

Ashlyn nodded understandably, and then to Markus' surprise, she crawled over and placed her head into his lap. Before Markus could even say anything, she closed her eyes, and began to try and sleep.

Markus then looked over to Ruth and saw that she was still asleep, and then looked back down at Ashlyn. Her hair parted slightly so he could see the left side of her face. Her smooth cheeks; clean of the filth of the city, her button nose and angelic eyes inside a moon-shaped face. When her breathing became slow, and she hadn't stirred for a long while, Markus relented a sigh that had built up in his chest.

"Truth is," Markus said in a whisper so she could not actually hear in case she was still awake. "I've always felt alone. My whole life. Even though… even though I had Ruth. After my father was killed, I felt like I alone had to protect Ruth and keep her safe. It did not matter what I felt, what demons tortured me or what nightmares I had. I had to keep strong for her. And… despite having so many try and help in our desperate times, I still felt all alone. Like the whole world was and still is on my shoulders… Like a drug coursing through my veins, just getting heavier and heavier until I break down like a baby. I hate myself for it; for feeling that way. For feeling so alone. Still today, I can't help it, because now I have you to watch over as well." He then chuckled at himself, wondering just what Ashlyn would think if she could hear this.

"But, you know what? I can't help but think, maybe I don't feel so alone now despite our situation- how hopeless it may seem." Markus closed his eyes as he lowered a hand, touching Ashlyn's cheek with his scraped knuckle. "So why do I feel so worried? Why do I still feel so alone despite having you two to give me strength?"

His eyes soon began to grow heavy, and his body soon drifted into an unwelcome sleep. As he unwilfully drifted away, he was unaware that Ashlyn had been awake the whole time, a single eye having being opened when he fell silent to check up on him. As he slept, it was there, in the darkness behind closed eyes when he heard a deep voice, warm and familiar resonating in the back of his head as the crystal in his staff started to glow just a little brighter.

Like a heartbeat, reacting to a dream.

You're not alone.

~ Forest Fire ~

Lameika

By the time it was morning, Lameika was still standing outside the ship staring at the legendary Dark Forest before her. She had waited all night for Slitzar's signal, and now that the sun has come up, she was getting agitated. She had not gotten a wink of sleep, which was noticeable around her eyes which were circled in dark bags. Lee was working on something concerning the Hellhound behind her as she whispered the Ancient Words coolly into the seeds she held in her palm. Her frustration was transferred into the seedlings, and she could hear them scream. Let them scream; let them suffer.

Her concentration was broken when Pyro walked up beside her. "What's up?" He asked.

"Slitzar hasn't responded still," Lameika answered shoving her seeds into her pocket. "I think she might be dead."

Pyro snorted in his helmet. "Black?"

"No doubt. He rode in after her."

"She's probably dead then," Lee commented behind them. "I mean, Black is one tough son of a-"

"So is Slitzar." Pyro said this almost sternly. It made Lameika raise an eyebrow at the sudden outburst. He then looked to her, his eyes set and determined; the look of a warrior awaiting orders before a battle. "What's the plan then? Go after them in there? They hadn't come out yet. I've circled the place all night."

Lameika nodded. "Lee went out earlier as well to the other side and circled around. Those brats haven't come out yet."

"Not only that," Lee said coming up behind them and wiping his hands clean with a rag. "But something is wrong with the scanners. Can't pick up any specific heat signatures inside the forest. It's like the whole place is on fire there is too much activity."

Lameika scowled. "Not to mention, Black's still in there as well. Probably even close by." She then turned and looked at Pyro through his visors and dead in his eyes. "Burn it down," she commanded.

Behind his helmet, Pyro's cheeks stretched out into a large and hideous grin. "It would be my pleasure."

"We'll flush them out," Lameika said as she got down onto her knees. She pulled out the seedlings and began to whisper the last of her spell. Normally, she would make sure no one else could hear the ancient words, but it didn't matter now; not if they lost those children.

"And if Slitzar is still alive?" Lee said watching her with annoyingly keen eyes. "Then what?"

"If she doesn't get out she is no use to us anyways," Lameika said to her comrades as she then shoved the seeds into the cold dirt beneath the snow. The frost bit at her skin but she ignored the pain. "She failed us." She stood up as the earth began to shake beneath her. Pyro steadied himself with his pack.

"Get what you need," she told him, staring down at the spot her palm had punctured the snow. "Burn the entire forest down."

Pyro nodded and ran back to the ship to get what he needed; and after a minute Lameika watched as he flew overhead, his flame-thrower in hand. Beneath him, a rippling rift in the earth followed the Hunter towards the forest as if something was tunneling beneath the surface. Lameika then smiled as Lee stood beside her, watching the two devastating forces head for the Dark Forest.

"There will be no escape this time," she said to no one in particular, smiling in excitement to watch the cursed forest go up in brilliant flames- and drawing out those children who had evaded them for far too long.

There would be nowhere left to hide.

"Come on," she told her brother. "Let's watch from the skies."

Lee turned to follow, though seemingly disgruntled. "Agreed."

Ashlyn

They had packed up and left at the break of dawn. Markus had let them sleep throughout the night despite the urgency to leave immediately. The monsters, for some reason, kept their distance, and there was no sign of the Hunters anywhere in the forest. Though Markus seemed worried about what happened with the Lacerta as well as Black, Ashlyn didn't press the matter and simply helped Ruth prepare for their departure. Now they were riding fast through the unnaturally quiet forest, ready to leave it entirely.

"Think we'll make it without anything stopping us?" Ruth called behind her up to Markus.

"Let's hope," Markus said flooring the bike. "Let's hope we break the line before we run out of fuel."

"Yeah," Ashlyn said hugging his torso tight from behind. Partly because she didn't want to fall, partly because she *wanted* to hold on tight. Markus' body felt warm, and it gave her reassurance that he was still there, just as he was when she woke up to see him still awake watching over her and Ruth. The fact that he was really here, and this wasn't some twisted dream gave her the reassurance that all of this was real, and that they were still alive together.

She felt safe with him. There was no doubt in Ashlyn's mind right now.

A muffled *boom* suddenly sounded from behind, and both she and Ruth looked back while Markus drove on, but still looked back as worried as they were.

"What was that?" he asked.

Ashlyn didn't have the words to give an answer, for the whole forest ceiling was suddenly lit up with the flames that then trickled down to engulf the entire area behind them. She felt heat rush across her body as the flames snaked around the giant trunks of the trees, licking the bark away from their trunks.

Following the explosion of flames, both her and Ruth watched as many animals suddenly erupted from the foliage, screaming and shrieking as they hurried to get away from the fires that were quickly devouring their home. She saw Jackals getting trampled underfoot by giant stags, and she saw many birds and flying creatures zipping past the trees above their heads.

What caught her attention the most was what was behind them; for as Ashlyn looked back again, she saw three creatures fleeing the fast-approaching flames while their bodies were slowly being consumed by fire. She saw an

Arachnard soon crumble and crinkle like paper, as well as an Ahool who crashed right into a tree, the flames on its massive wings burning the grass and bushes around it. She also saw a six-legged horse, screaming wildly as it followed the Hoverbike close behind, its hide consumed with flames. It had stuck close by for a long while until its legs eventually slowed down, its screams for help soon overpowered by the flames as it suddenly dropped to the ground and burned.

"My God…" Ruth whispered behind her. The wall of fire was quickly catching up to them as well, and everything that it passed through was immediately devoured by the inferno.

"Mark!" Ashlyn said shaking her friend's shoulders.

"On it!" He banked around and passing over a small river as he changed courses and started towards another direction. "Hold on!"

They passed by a Slug who moaned as its slime suddenly caught a stray ember and was immediately engulfed in flames as if it was covered in gasoline. Smoke hung in the forest canopy like a thick ceiling, and embers falling like colorful leaves of autumn floated around the teens as they made their way through the forest faster; the forest fire itself being slowed down by the river they had crossed. Though the heat of the inferno was finally off their backs, both Ruth and Ashlyn hung on for dear life, fearing for what will happen should they not escape these woods alive.

"Don't worry," Markus called back to them as if he had read their thoughts. "I'll get us out- I promise."

Ashlyn hugged his torso tighter, relieved to hear such words. Though the words she had heard last night still resonated in her mind, she knew that Markus meant what he now said. Though he was scared, though he was worried about them, he was still willing to keep on going for their sake. He was willing to burn through all their fuel if it meant getting out of the burning forest alive. Despite feeling defeated and on his own, he was still willing to fight for them and protect them both. It was his words that brought her comfort and reassurance; and made Ashlyn want to support him even more once they were out of harm's way.

"The forest…" Rush whispered behind her. "It's…"

"Don't look back," Ashlyn told her reaching back and hugging her close to her body. Without the Werecat blanket to cover her, she could feel Ruth's body now; and it was trembling. "Don't look back, Ruth."

"The animals… the trees… they are all screaming." Though Ashlyn believed that Ruth meant literally, because of their desperate cries for escape as well as the crackle and roar of the flames that were now across the river and devouring the land even more so, she could have sworn that she too heard screaming within the forest engulfed in smoke and flame.

She heard people; men, women, and even children, all screaming in terrible, terrible pain.

Pyro
Pyro laughed as he dropped a second napalm bomb onto the trees, which were soon stripped of their pine needles and were reduced to burning skeletons. For each bomblet he dropped, the flames converged into one another, creating a bigger blast of fire that spread out like a nuke; incinerating all in its path.

"Ha!" he laughed as he saw a twelve-horned stag bound through the forest, its flank burning before it fell squirming like a pathetic worm in the snow. "Run little doggies, *run*!" He grinned madly as he let loose with the flamethrower, burning more of the canopy that had not been touched yet by the fires. He then hit a switch on his wrist. "Come on out, little kiddies! How 'bout a clusta-bomb?"

Immediately, rockets shot out of the top of his pack, only to explode in the air, dropping smaller bomblets which detonated on impact of anything, incinerating all life around it. He fired his machine gun at an Ahool which tried to take flight. The creature screamed as it turned and fell into the burning forest in a flash of crimson.

"Gotcha." He then let loose some more bombs onto more trees; soon the whole forest would be consumed by the flames.

He loved this job. He loved the feeling of the heat on his skin, the smell of smoke and cooking meat in his nostrils; the ecstasy of the sound of crackling flame like paper.

There had been a time, when Pyro once feared the fire. The burnt scars all over his body were constant reminders of his past, and what happened when you played with fire- be that literally or figuratively. But through the years of his work, and developing his 'calling card', he had learned to control the hungry flames. Like a god created in hellfire, he had learned to make those he was to hunt fear him and feel his wrath

He would make them all feel the flame; all the living creatures within the forest taste the fires of hell that Pyro himself had felt firsthand. As soon as he got those kids, he would have a little fun with them before handing them over to the Twins, he had decided. If he can survive the flame, so could they. He wanted nothing more than to make them scream for what happened to Tank and Slitzar. He wanted them all, to taste the hellfire that had consumed his own soul, long ago.

The key was to burn in controlled bursts. If he were to just unleash his flames willy-nilly, then he would lose the children immediately. He had to guide them; herd them as if they were sheep and he the dog. The fires were the gates of hell, seeming to guide the children towards what they believe to be safety. Then he would catch them and-

In the corner of his eye, Pyro suddenly caught movement. He turned his head to see a Hoverbike breaking from the tree-line and fleeing the burning forest; heading towards the canyon leading to the Fiery Plains. He grinned behind his helmet while then reaching for a rocket strapped to his pack and shoved it into his gun. He took aim at the fleeing brats and bored down the heat-seeking sights. As soon as he had a lock-on, he chuckled.

They were heading towards safety, now it was time to cripple them and catch them before the flames became overzealous and consumed them without so much as a second thought. That was what fire was after all; a force to handle carefully. Otherwise it would destroy everything.

"Boom," he said and pulled the trigger. Just as the rocket was launched at the youths something struck the left wing of his rocket pack.

He turned to see a grapple claw sticking right through it, sending out sparks. "What the-" His eyes trailed the wire connected to it and saw what was zipping up towards him with a cloak flapping like the wings of an Ahool as he came at Pyro, his sword swinging at him.

Black!?

Panic spread across Pyros face as his enemy seemed to fly straight for him. He turned his flamethrower towards Black and let loose a spray of flames, but even if he had gotten the now empty rocket-launcher off the main mechanism, it was too late. Black had already swung upward, slicing the front half of the gun into the air and then catching the *right* wing of the jet pack. Pyro then felt the world spin around him as the single rocket began to spin him around and then suddenly dive down into the sea of fiery trees. Black followed close behind; his arm still attached to the wire of his grapple claw. He soon removed the gauntlet from his wrists, and using his cloak as a type of parachute he slowed his decent, watching Pyro who crashed into the trees and clouds of smoke below him.

Pyro had smacked right into a trunk and then spun off to strike another, this one burning and tumbling down from the force of his body. It fell down with a *crash* just as he had struck the ground, his pack falling apart with the pieces scattering across the forest floor as he came to a stop near some burning bushes.

He groaned and spat out blood, which stuck to his helmet. He tore off his helmet and breathed the smoky air around him. His actual arm felt broken, but his robotic arm seemed to be functioning properly. He looked down at his broken arm and groaned at the sight of the angle it was in. He was then startled as he heard something land behind him. He turned fast to see Black crouched before him, slowly standing up his face still covered by that black cowl of his. With the flames all around him, he looked like the Reaper himself, ready to collect Pyro's soul.

Pyro grinned as he hoisted himself up, careful not to damage himself anymore than he already was. As he rose, he reached for his boot, where his laser pistol was strapped. He brought it up as he stood to full height, clicking the safety off and making it hum to life.

"So, you are still alive huh?" he asked blood seeping from his lips. Black took a step forward, and he seemed to have stumbled slightly. Pyro saw why through his cybernetic eye.

"I see," he said. "She got ya good still. Grazed the ribs I see, sliced a chunk off yer leg as well. That looks bad."

"Just a scratch," Black said as annoyingly carefree as ever.

"Hmm." Pyro sounded. "You're as stubborn as my brother."

"I remember him," Black said stopping after a few steps. "Met him in Seifkr, and then once more in Pieta, after hunting some pirates from the sea. Brought the bounty to the sheriff of the village and got paid- with his blood."

"A good man he was," Pyro said bringing up his weapon, ready to fire. He wasn't about to be goaded by this bastard. "Darkclaw was always good at closing his contracts."

"You learned everything from him I imagine?"

"No. I taught myself. And as ya could see, I like watching things burn. Better than cutting people up."

"Is that why he has the same burns on his body as you?"

Angry at the mention of such a thing, Pyro fired his weapon and Black raised his blade just as the bolt flew straight for him. The laser bounced off his blade and landed in some bushes. The dead leaves immediately caught on fire like the rest of the trees around them. Pyro watched in amazement to see that his robotic hand was gone as was the gun it gripped. Black stood closer this time he had noticed.

When did he...? Pyro saw his severed hand land in the dirt beside the two of them; still squeezing the trigger of his gun and sending out shots into the inferno still closing in around them.

"Dammit," Pyro said to Black trying hard to sound more confident than he was. The Hunter was fast- too fast to be human. "You indeed are an incredible Hunter." He grinned as he lowered his stump which sparkled at its frayed wiring.

"So what now?" he asked taking a step back. For some reason, Black didn't follow and stayed where he was; intimidating, and cold. "You gonna kill me like Slitzar? Or leave me to burn with the rest of the spirits in this forest?" At this point, Pyro saw no sense in fighting anymore. If it was time for him to go to hell, he would accept the flames with open-arms.

"Slitzar is alive," Black said. "We had a little trouble and got separated. Where she is, I do not know."

"I see..." Pyro then wondered if she made it out of the forest alive. If not, then it would be him that killed her. Normally, he thought he would have felt bad; after all, he and the giant lizard got along so well. But as he stood before Black as the world around him seemed to be consumed by flames like his own world was long ago, he just didn't seem to care anymore.

"The spirits have left." Black continued. "The animals, or whatever's left has fled. Most of them anyway." Black said sheathing his sword. Did he not intend to attack Pyro any longer? It confused the cybernetic Hunter as Black continued to drawl out his words. "So I am not worried about them."

"Oh?" Pyro said feeling his head spin from all the smoke he had inhaled since he crashed.

"But there is one problem, however: You." Black waved his hand over his head, motioning towards the forest around them. Was it just Pyro's imagination, or were the Hunters' eyes now glowing dark and maroon? "You have destroyed this sacred forest which took thousands of years to regrow from the ashes of mankind's destruction, and you must pay."

"Then get it over with, you piece of filth," Pyro said indigenously. He raised his arms, surrendering himself to be killed by the Hunter Black. "Go ahead. I ain't afraid of you. Let's go right here and now, ya hardass."

Black lowered his hand. "Where you are mistaken is, *I'm* not going to kill you. But our friend behind you is."

Confused, Pyro turned his head, and his nose was now nearly three inches from the snout of a large black wolf. The massive creature stood above him, its nose letting out puffs of hot breath that blasted into his face; its glowing purple eyes bearing through the cyborg's soul. The jet-black fur seemed to deflect the hot embers which rained down from above, and the relentless growling made Pyro shake in his boots.

He looked to the side, not moving as Black walked past them like the Angel of Death as if he had all the time in the world.

"He says you destroyed his forest," Black said as he passed the wolf. Was it just Pyro, or were the wolf's eyes now glowing maroon like red wine, just like Blacks? "Now you will suffer."

And Pyro, brother of Darkclaw the Butcher, and who loved to burn, met his fate in a flash of bloody teeth before the fires of his own creation seared the flesh from his bones like the fires of hell itself.

~ The Inferno ~

Black

As Black left the gruesome scene, he picked up his pace into a sprint towards the direction the kids had gone as the cries of Pyro and the snarling of the wolf was drowned by the roar of the flames all around him. The man died too quick, but he appreciated the help of Fethawit and hoped that Pyro would make up with his brother in the next world- whichever one they both went to.

This was really starting to get out of hand. Slitzar had every chance to ignore him and take off after the children, and yet she allowed them to escape in order to fight him. Tank was the same way. He had killed Pyro only to stop the Hunter from throwing any more fire onto the forest which would soon no longer stand on this world. As he watched the burning embers dance and tumble around him like falling leaves of autumn, Black felt the grief the forest felt and all that lived within.

As he ran across the river that separated the flames, he noticed something- a feeling of something following him. He felt a disturbance in the earth beneath him, and shifting his eyes towards the ground he saw the rippling in the earth beside him, passing him with such speed. The rift that stretched like a tear in a once great tapestry cut through the forest and disappeared somewhere within the inferno up ahead. Whatever was beneath the earth, it was not of this world. He felt darkness; a cold intelligence that seemed to rake their claws upon his mind; telling him to stay away.

Despite their threats, Black's eyes narrowed in determination as he quickened his pace. He had to hurry. That witch must have another trick up her sleeve for those children. He eventually caught up with the rippling earth and the strange and alien conscience reaching out to him screeched like that of a demon; telling him to turn back. He did not allow their words to deter him, however, and both he and whatever was tunneling beneath the ground continued on until they both made it out of the line of trees.

The forest continued to burn behind them. However the rift suddenly banked around and started towards Black who leaped away from the rippling just as a dark hand shot out from the earth and tried to claw at him. It was inhuman, the owner hissing with rage as it continued on its way and sink deeper beneath the surface.

Stay away, Oathbreaker! the voices hummed in unison within his head again, buzzing like a swarm of mosquitos. *Stay away, or you will die!* It then continued to turn and circle around the burning forest, leaving Black behind as it seemed to be now hunting something; and Black knew exactly who they were looking for.

They, not *it*, as he realized. With a groan from the burning pain in his lungs and the ache in his leg, Black took off running again. He had to hurry- and fast. As he ran, he kept an ear open for the hum of the Hellhound. If he ran into the Twins or if they caught up to those kids first, then there would be trouble.

Damion Black was losing time; he had to hurry.

Markus

When he was able, Markus looked back to see the black smoke rise up from the burning forest. They had just broken through the tree line, and though they were safe from the inferno that continued to devour the once immense forest, dread still clenched his heart as the smoke continued to rise into the clouds to the point where it was almost impossible to tell where the sky began and ended.

Ashlyn and Ruth were looking as well with horror-stricken faces. Now that they were all free, all they could do was watch as whatever wildlife remained escaped the woods and fled into the snowy hills. Many were terribly hurt, having been trampled by bigger beasts, and some were even on fire; rolling in the snow in a desperate attempt to quench the flames that ate at their hides. One of the fullest grown forests in the Northern Wastelands that took thousands of years to regrow would soon be reduced to a smoldering scar on the earth; the entire ecosystem that lived within driven from their homes without any warning. All the horrors around them… it felt all too much closer than it did when the whole forest was teeming with life.

Markus sighed and kept forward. "We can't stop," he said regretting the words as soon as they passed his lips.

The Hoverbike began to sputter, and cough and they were starting to decelerate at an alarming pace. "Oh no…" he whispered, looking at the fuel gauge which read 'empty'. "No! Dammit not now- no!"

"Mark!" Ruth's voice screamed, and he turned just in time to see something heading their way; coming fast and belching smoke and fire behind it as it followed close behind. Realizing what it was, Markus grabbed ahold of the girls.

"Get off!" he shouted as he shoved them to the side and once they both fell into the snow he grabbed their bag and then bailed just as the rocket struck the rear of his Hoverbike. The blast propelled him forward and made him tumble across the snow as smoking pieces of shrapnel rained down around him. Though he was unhurt as he dug himself back out of the snow, Markus did not want to look at the wreck. He kept his back to it as he trudged back to the girls who were just trying to get out of the snow. As if being low on gas wasn't bad enough, now they had absolutely zero transportation to take them across the Wastelands.

"Dammit…" he swore under his breath as he helped Ruth to her feet. After making sure she was okay, he checked on Ashlyn. She was a little roughed up for she took most of the fall when she and Ruth fell together, but there was nothing serious that he needed to worry about. With them all out of the snow, Markus plopped down onto his butt and rested his head in his hands deep in frustrated thought.

I need to pull myself together… "Okay," he said finally after minutes of tense silence. He looked at Ashlyn and Ruth, who had huddled together in order to give him the space he needed. He was grateful for that; he felt that if he had tried to speak any sooner, he would have snapped at them- which was the last thing they needed as of now. "Sorry about that. We have no bike now. So we're gonna have to continue on foot."

There was no point in turning back, not now. Their priority would have to be to just get as far away from the fires as possible, and find some shelter before nightfall- or better yet, make it to the Fiery Plains where they could hide from the Hunters and God-knows-what out here in the Wastelands. He turned to Ruth with a somber gaze. "Think you could make it, Sis?"

His sister shrugged. "I'll have to."

While still worried about her last coughing fit as well as what they could possibly encounter next without their bike, Markus nodded. "Okay." He turned, so he was facing both her and Ashlyn again. "We'll take it easy, but we'll have to move soon. If we follow the canyon…" He fished out his blade and lit the crystal again, bringing up the map in his mind. Reassurance washed over him like a flood, telling him the way.

"Yes, if we follow the canyon there will be a break in the gap that we can cross, from there we can head straight for The Plains. I wanted to just fly the bike over there, but the break is the only way across now." All of this that Markus saw, the girls did not. But they did not question him, even when he began pointing at nothingness in the air. He felt silly when he realized it, though he couldn't blame them if they thought it was strange. It was bizarre, even for him.

"Do we need to worry about anything when we cross the canyon?" Ashlyn asked while shouldering their last pack.

"Other than the heat? There shouldn't be anything in The Plains." Markus said putting away his dagger. *Hopefully.* "It's all just the heated crust that's been exposed. Nothing can live there- even the trees that used to grow there wilt under the intense heat. It's not as bad this time of year 'cause of the cold, but it is still a desolate place. I don't think we'll run into trouble."

"Heat…" Ashlyn said almost dreamily.

"I hope we don't run into trouble," Ruth said tightening her coat around her shoulders. She coughed into it before looking back towards the black smoke that continued to rise above the Dark Forest. "I'm sad about the animals…"

Markus looked back towards the burning inferno. Despite having almost been killed by a majority of the wildlife they have seen thus far, he did feel a little bad about the forest.

"Nothing we can do now." he eventually said while standing up. "Let's go. If we can make it to the breaking point within the next hour, we can rest, and then keep going for a few more. We'll keep taking breaks until we make it out of The Plains. Sound like a plan, guys?"

"We'll follow you anywhere," Ashlyn said smiling.

"Right," Ruth said standing with them weakly but determined.

That made Markus smile. "Let's move."

The three continued to walk for what felt like hours.

Ruth had two coughing fits but not bad enough to spill blood. They all drank from their canteen scarcely, so that they wouldn't run out before they made camp and boil some snow down. The fact that the weather seemed to be on a stand-still made it easier to transverse through the snow; with Markus leading Ruth while Ashlyn led the way. Markus had heard the hum of a Hellhound engine, but every time he looked up into the sky he couldn't see anything. If the Hunters were nearby, they weren't too close. It was all the more reason to keep on going.

Eventually, they had reached the beginning of The Scar; a deep canyon that stretched a good couple of miles further to the north. The canyon that now separated them from the Fiery Plains on the other side was a thing of immense beauty. Being told to be three miles deep and home to many Ahools and Dragons living within the canyon walls. Further north was the village of Miteshire who lived *inside* The Scar within the walls as well. They had built a massive mining system that produced many of the iron ore for the Capitol, as well as have made bridges that crisscrossed across the abyss far below.

Markus sometimes wondered what it would be like to live there. But he couldn't think about such things at a time like this. If he and the girls could make it to The Plains by nightfall they wouldn't be followed. In fact, Markus didn't even think the Hunters would even consider looking. If The Fiery Plains was as desolate as travelers say, then no one, man or beast would venture in there. What was the point? With any luck, the Hunters may just give up.

At least, he hoped so.

A Jackalope bounded past them as they were walking past an old car which seemed to have been *melted* into a large tree just alongside The Scar. After The Fall, many cars were scattered across cities and other areas, now burned or reduced to scraps. After the fallout, the human race was able to rebuild some of the cars and hovercraft they once used. Mankind had come so much further in technology at that point in history, only to be reduced straight to poverty and starvation caused by corrupt leaders caring for one thing only: control.

A world of complete control and surrender under their watchful eyes. Baron Ovid being one of many who seeks to take control over the continent was not the most ruthless in history. But he was definitely just the kind of scum no different than those who led mankind to the condition it was in now. The sheer thought of it sickened Markus. He turned his head to look at Ruth who offered a smile when she saw him. People like her should never have to struggle like this. He smiled back and looked at Ashlyn who was watching her feet as she took each step in the snow.

Amazing, all that has happened to us in this awful world of ours, and we still made it out. We are still breathing and surviving. Would we have been able to do this under better circumstances?

Probably not, he decided. Because if life was good and easy, Markus believed that they wouldn't have strived for a better life; a better future, a better chance. And even now as they crossed an entire region looking for the ancient City of Angels, they still pushed on. *Maybe we don't know exactly what we are getting into still. Maybe we're not going to find anything. Even then, here they were, still pushing on. And to be honest, it's a good chance to take, all in all, I'd like to think. The chance to be at peace, the chance of Ashlyn being safe, and the chance for a cure for Ruth, is worth more than anything we had dealt with so far.*

Ashlyn had pulled back and began walking alongside Markus. She then spoke up after a few steps of silence, breaking him out of his thoughts. "Hey."

"Hey." He looked back to Ruth who followed behind them, but a little further than he had seen earlier. That, and she was *smiling*. "What's up?" Markus asked skeptically, curious as to what was going on.

"Just thinking." She looked down at her boots again. She was quiet until she spoke again. "I never thanked you."

Markus looked at her. "For what?"

"For not leaving me. With the spider, I mean. *And* for taking care of it before it came down on us."

He blinked at her. "Well, I couldn't leave you and Ruth up there." He rubbed the back of his head nervously. "It was either let the Lacerta catch us, or let that giant spider get you or Ruth first."

Ashlyn chuckled humorlessly at that. "Either way, thank you."

He smiled at her. "You're welcome."

"I hate spiders…" she said frowning.

Markus chuckled. She really was a normal girl after all. "I'm sorry."

"It's a dumb thing to be scared about, I know."

"Hey, I was scared too," Markus said offering some words of comfort. "I mean, that thing was freaking *huge*."

"That's what made it worse. I never liked spiders. I have always been afraid of them since I was a little kid. And the fact that the one we saw back in the forest was as big as a freaking *truck*, it made me so much more scared."

"Yes, you told us to not leave you, and then *to* leave you." Markus pointed out. "You wanted that Huntress to take Ruth and I and leave you up there with that spider?"

"…Yeah…"

He looked at her with a softer expression. "Why would you sacrifice yourself like that? Especially with the thing you are most afraid of? Not that we would even allow you to make that kind of choice even for our safety anyway, but still, why?"

Ashlyn bit her lip in thought. Then, "Ruth means a lot to you. The world it seems. I wish I had a brother like you." She paused for a moment leaving Markus in deep thought. She continued. "If Ruth were to be killed by that monster, you would be hurt. I couldn't bear it if either of you got hurt… or worse."

Her words gladdened Markus but at the same time made him sad. She cares that much for us? Two strangers, she hardly knew and went along with them on this crazy suicide journey. "Why?"

"'Cause you care. And you would have done the same for me, Mark."

"I almost *shot* you though," he reminded her.

"But you didn't. Did you?"

They walked in silence after that. Markus didn't shoot her, that was true, and he had told her he *would* have if Ruth hadn't stopped him. But why would she think she'd owed them something in return for helping her? Is that what human nature is? Give and take and give in return?

No. It was given because you cared. *Take when necessary, yes, but you gave and helped others because you can. Because you care. That's what makes us human. That was why Ashlyn is now unofficially mine and Ruth's family now. She is now with us, and she seemed intent on staying.*

But for how long? He wondered this as they continued their journey; The Scar seeming to never once change in length despite how long they had already walked alongside it.

When they had finally arrived at the breaking point; which was a thin crevice breaking The Scar in the earth almost like a bridge of stone, Markus and the girls stopped to rest and drink some water. Seeing this one spot in the canyon after seeing what felt like miles of an endless pit of darkness made Markus curious as to how the canyon was made.

But he pushed the thought from his head. The important thing was they had made it, and after they were rested they soon would cross, and after a few minutes of walking they would be in the Fiery Plains safe from danger for the time being. They would cross the Plains, and then from there, cross the valley beyond to the mountains.

And hidden among them; the City of Angels- hopefully.

Markus was studying the bridge-like break when Ruth began to cough again. Once again spitting blood. Ashlyn had quickly jumped up with the canteen and made her drink. The water seemed to soothe her throat, but it did not by any means stop the coughing, and she ended up hacking all of the water out, and Markus immediately began to panic.

"Hey," he said scooting over to her. "Sis?"

Coughing was her only response.

Why now of all times? "We'll wait then, okay? We'll leave later. Just, relax and try to-"

"But we should get there soon," Ruth argued trying to hold her cough in. Her face looked so strained it looked like it might erupt if she held it in for too long. "So that we don't get caught out here at night."

"It's not worth you getting worse." Ashlyn insisted. Markus shot her a glance of thanks. "We'll wait for you, Ruth."

"Okay..." she said unconvinced. She coughed once more, this time without any blood spilling.

"Take your time," Markus said pushing her gently back down to sit. *Please.*

"Time's up." the voice said behind him before Markus turned he felt something strong clock him right across the face.

He felt himself sail through the air only to stop a sheer foot from the canyon's edge; a mere twelve inches from falling to his death. Dazed and bleeding from a cut in his cheek, Markus raised his head to see Ashlyn floating up by her arm. She was kicking and screaming as she reached for her knife and plunged it into nothingness. A snarl sounded as she too seemed to be 'thrown' aside, leaving ruth cowering into a ball. And then suddenly, materializing from the very air, Markus watched as something began to shimmer into a form of the Lacerta from earlier. Scales flipped and shifted to reveal the dark green skin covered in bruises and multiple cuts. The monstrous lizard was soon visible before the three, grinning from ear to ear with jagged teeth.

"You…" Markus groaned as he attempted to push himself back up and reach for his weapon.

"Well, most of me anyway." the lizard growled showing off her left hand, which was a mere stump covered in dirt and twigs to stop the purple blood from spilling any more than it already was. "That Hunter took off a couple fingers first, but nothing that I'll miss too much. He put up one hell of a fight though." She then looked down at Ruth and chuckled. "However, this little game of tag ends here. She reached down and grabbed Ruth by the scruff of her coat, making her squeal.

"You and your brother are coming with me." she snarled. At that moment, Markus' staff was extended and aimed right at the beast.

"Put her down," he said in a low voice while getting up on one knee. "Now."

"Or what?" the lizard hissed with laughter. "You ain't got enough juice in there to hurt me, kid." She then turned so that Ruth's small body was in front of her chest. "But just enough should be enough to cook your sister. Do you really want that?"

Anger seemed to flow through Markus' blood like adrenaline. Seeing that monster taunting him with his sister in her claws made him so angry he wanted to blow a hole right through that ugly face of hers.

"Don't you dare hurt her," Markus said between clenched teeth. "I'll kill you."

The lizard hissed again with laughter; amused at his threat. "Go ahead. Show me that you can." And then raising her thumb in the same hand she held Ruth in she pressed an extended claw against her throat. Ruth gasped as blood began to seep slowly from the puncture. The lizard removed her thumb, and with a long purple tongue, she licked the blood from Ruth's neck.

"Tasty. Maybe I can have a taste of her once in a while on our way back to the ship. Do you want that, boy?"

Markus began to scream and what happened next was too unbelievable to explain completely.

A bolt of bright blue lightning seemed to shoot through Markus' body as if he was being stuck in a storm. He felt all of his hair suddenly stand up from the energy flowing through his cells. It did not hurt in the slightest; in fact, he didn't feel anything but rage. As this newfound energy coursed through his body, Markus soon became aware of everything; the energy auras of the Ahools in the canyon, the poisonous aura of the Lacerta…

No.

Slitzar.

He knew her name. Markus could see inside her; like she was an opened book and he the reader. He was suddenly capable of reading her history which was dark, cloudy, and most disturbing. Same went for Ashlyn and Ruth, who were overwhelmed by fear, except for Ruth's was also slightly clouded by the sickness eating the very breath in her lungs.

Markus' eyes burned bright with the new sense of life, knowing all living things around him. *What is this?*

His eyes lingered to his staff, which was suddenly at full power. He then cried out as he released the energy at Slitzar's face; instead of shooting out a beam of light, her face suddenly went up in a brilliant flame of sapphire. It was as if someone had dumped gasoline on her head and lit a match. Markus watched as Slitzar screamed and reared back, dropping Ruth into the ground beneath her. The Lacerta clawed her face, desperate to extinguish the flames on her head. As she did so, Markus found himself charging at the creature; closing the distance between the two of them and then leaping up he kicked her in the chest with both feet, sending her sprawling across the snow and away from Ruth. Such a feat would have been impossible for a normal human being, and yet Slitzar went *flying*.

Immediately upon landing, Markus felt the overpowering energy disappear from his body; as if the lights were shut down in heaven, and he was left alone on solid ground. He collapsed at the sudden tide of exhaustion. He felt as if he had just run a thousand miles; and as he fell into the snow, steam seemed to seep from his pores. He managed to catch himself on his hands and knees, panting like crazy.

Far ahead of him Ashlyn and Ruth were half-crawling half-running back to him, calling his name as they eventually reached him. Far beyond them, Slitzar was sitting up, her face smoking and covered in soot from the scales eaten away by the strange flames. She was shaking her head in pain. Markus could see it even from this distance that she was hurt very badly. Her ribs were cracked, and her arm had broken during impact.

But she was alive; and *very* angry.

"What was that?" she growled as she got up hugging her side and trudging towards the three. Ashlyn and Ruth were now crouched beside Markus as Slitzar cleared the distance between them wincing at each step she took. "That was interesting. I've never seen someone use a Crystal with such power."

"What?" Markus croaked.

"Doesn't matter," Slitzar growled. "I'm not letting you brats get away again. I'm gonna make you pay for that…"

But then something awful happened.

They all saw it. There was a large ripple in the ground, coming for them as if something was tunneling beneath the surface of the earth. Slitzar turned at the sound and began to ask what was happening. The rippling came right for her suddenly, and her feet disappeared into the cracks. Crooked hands shot up from the ground and seized her, making her scream in terror as they began to drag her under.

She flayed out with her claws, raking the ground around her for something sturdy to grab onto, but she kept on sinking- and fast. She roared as she clawed at the dirt now around her thighs but then her good hand was caught by another inhuman hand and sinking rapidly. She screamed out holding a hand out to the sky as if beckoning the angels to save her as her body sank up to her shoulders. Soon her chest went beneath the crust as did her neck. She still screamed out holding that hand up as her head went under, then her arm, and then finally her hand which opened and closed before it disappeared into the soil.

The girls and Markus were gaping at the mound in horror. Slitzar was gone, Markus could tell because the aura he felt surrounding the Lacerta had gone out; like the flame of a candle, it was no longer there. It was like a pair of fingers simply snuffed it out. But what frightened him more was the life essence that he could now *sense* coming up through the snow.

A hand shot out of the earth like a flower. However this hand was unlike any normal hand; human, mutant or android. It was human shaped, but it was roped and knobbed with what looked like bark... No. Not bark. Roots. The fingertips were sharpened to points, and small green vines wrapped around the wrists like veins. Following the hand was an arm of thicker roots, then a gnarled shoulder like a branch, and then the bulk creature crawled out of the ground.

It was hideously humanoid and completely made of roots and bark. Its face was covered in a veil of thin moss, but a single slit was open where a mouth was screaming with sharpened teeth of stone. Behind it, five more of the monsters shot out of the ground, crying a similar shriek. Markus soon saw two red orbs glow behind the veil which had to be its eyes and his heart stopped dead in his chest even as he gripped his staff tighter in his hand.

What are those things?

The creatures began to move forward, their fingers curling as they chuckled; the sound being like twigs tapping against rocks.

Little ones, he then suddenly heard, hearing the hissing voices that seemed to be engulfed in pain and hatred. It was like an overwhelming cloud had shrouded his head; becoming worse as the creatures moved in closer. *Come here, little ones. We won't hurt you.*

Markus tightened his grip on the staff. Whatever he was hearing, he didn't believe the inhuman voices and was ready to fight for his and his family's life. Despite his bravado, however, he couldn't quench the fear he felt in his heart, nor the doubt that thundered in his brain as the voices continued to speak to him.

Come to us, or we will bury you alive!

~ Freak of Nature ~

Lameika

In the air riding in the Hellhound once again, Lameika's eyes began to glow blood red, and she jerked back in her seat gasping for breath.

They had been flying around the hills beyond the Dark Forest, searching for any sign of the children who had escaped- again. They had found the wreckage of their Hoverbike, but their whereabouts now were unknown. Without anything left behind for them to track down their elusive prey, the Twins simply flew around close to the ground, trying to find some sort of trail that they could follow.

It was a little later when Lameika suddenly let out a spine-tingling scream like the cries of the damned; her jugular was strained and bulging, and her teeth appeared to have sharpened into fangs. This startled her brother, and normally Lameika would laugh at his face, but the fire she felt scorching her very soul burned every cell in her body; taking over all form of thought. It felt as if she was being possessed, and in a way, she was. Her spell was now taking hold of her, and she was now seeing through the eyes of her monstrous minions.

Through her eyes like a veil overlapping what she saw right in front of her, she saw the three children, huddled close together and looking terrified as the eyes she was now looking through seemed to move in closer. Her eyes widened with excitement; they had found them! Her eyes soon shrank back to normal size as she took another deep breath before crying out again as her eyes felt to be burning in their sockets. Her teeth returned to normal, and she noticed that even her nails had changed during the connection with her marvelous creations. She then started to giggle, which turned into a curt fit of laughter as she cackled in her seat.

"Hey!" Lee said stopping the ship and placing a hand on his sister's shoulder. "You okay?"

"They found them." she gasped in a fit of ecstasy. She then smacked Lee's hand away- the nasty thing should never have touched her, but she didn't care; not now. "We got them! I can see them!" She snapped back to Lee who jumped as her sudden ferocity. "Head northwest to the Fiery Plains! They're close there!"

"Okay," Lee said taking hold of the steering column again and punching the boosters. "Okay, we're heading there now." His voice was shaky; he was scared of her. He *should* be. Their prizes were finally within her grasp, and if anything were to get in their way- even him… well, Lameika had her ways.

She slumped back into her seat laughing and crying at the pain and joy of finally seeing those brats. The fire still licked at her skin, but she was beyond the point of feeling such frustrating impatience.

"We got them now," she whispered not only to Lee, but to herself as if trying to reassure whatever doubt she foolishly allowed to seep into her mind.

"We got them now…"

Ruth

The coughing started up again when the monsters began to advance towards them.

Ruth was frightened, she clung to Mark in pure fear as the tree-like creatures began to walk towards them with outstretched branches and glowing red eyes. But then the coughing began, it felt as if rocks were bouncing around in her lungs it hurt so bad that she forgot the creatures were even there for a moment. Then she saw the speckled droplets of blood on Mark's shoulder, and she began to panic even more so than before.

"Mark!" she cried out as she collapsed to the ground.

"Ruth, sit back and stay back." Mark gasped as he stood up. Ashlyn did likewise. "Ashlyn I need you to stay back. Get Ruth across the breakage and into The Plains!"

"What about you?" Ashlyn cried out.

"Just *go!*" Mark snapped. He looked pained to make them go, but he was about to make his stand to protect them. He had already made up his mind; Ruth could see it in his sapphire eyes.

She just couldn't bear the thought of him facing the monsters alone. "Mark, no!" she cried out as Ashlyn took her arm and began to drag her away from her brother. She began to cough some more. "No, Mark, please!"

"Go, *now!*" Mark shouted almost angrily, not taking his eyes off of the six creatures before him who began to chuckle and hiss. He started toward them without waiting, and Ruth slowly got her feet to move from under her so Ashlyn could help her run for the breakage across The Scar.

Come back, little ones! that inhuman voice hissed and chuckled inside her head; taunting her.

The little sick one needs help… come back!

We won't hurt you!

Come to us!

We'll bury you!

All of the voices she heard, there was no kindness in their words. They were cold; menacing, seeming to have saturated in hatred and anger. She could feel the negative energy seeming to pulsate through the creatures as they converged on Markus while at the same time looking at the girls who fled across the bridge.

"What is that!" Ruth screamed out as Ashlyn continued to pull her across the bridge, the vast mouth of The Scar gaping beneath them; threatening to swallow them in darkness should they fall over.

"Don't listen!" Ashlyn told her looking back. "Keep moving!" Though she listened to Ashlyn, Ruth could not help but look back at Markus once again.

That was when she noticed two of the monsters disappear into the ground; and before she knew it, she was violently grabbed and was hanging in the air by the scruff of her coat, the face of the plant-like monster suddenly right in hers. A horrible rancid smell blew into her face as the creature hissed at her, something like rotting meat and soaked wood after a rainfall.

Got you! She heard the horrible voice again that threatened to split her skull in two. Ashlyn was caught likewise by the other one who was chuckling menacingly.

Thought you could get away? the other one said to Ashlyn who had pulled her dagger again and started stabbing the creature ineffectively in the chest.

"Mark!" Ruth cried out spitting out blood in the process. Markus looked back and cried out before firing a shot from the staff. It was a light beam, but it struck the creature in the side, making it stumble aside from the blast but otherwise kept its balance, its right arm now a burning stump. It chuckled as the roots began to grow back before Ruth's very eyes. It continued to laugh at her, as it held her up high like a trophy.

Hold still... it hissed at her as it extended a finger towards her. Before her eyes Ruth saw a small flower suddenly bulb out and open before her; the stigma seeming to reach out towards her face like tentacles. *It will all be over soon, just don't fight it.*

A similar flower was opened up to Ashlyn, who sliced the flower off despite another growing out towards her. The creature holding her then struck her across the face, creating some bloody cuts across her cheeks as the tentacles of the flower began to circle around her neck. Ruth struggled as well, pummeling the creatures face with her weak fists. The creature seemed to just laugh menacingly at her as it shook her violently, giving her whiplash and making her almost go limp in its hand.

Do that again, and I'll wear your skin like a coat!

"Markus!" Ruth screamed again, blood now dribbling down her chin. Looking past the monsters head, she watched in horror as the remaining monsters lunged at Mark, claws of sharpened thorns extended and ready to tear him apart where he stood.

Markus

It was like they always say: your life really does flash before your eyes. It is like the human brain somehow knows when its time is almost up, and the adrenaline that floods the veins of its vessel causes it to remember everything it had witnessed in its entire lifetime. The human being itself, being left with the last memories of their life before their string is cut; and they travel to the judgment beyond.

Markus realized this to be true, as the monsters came at him. They circled him like wolves, hissing and clicking their stone teeth. Vines stretched out from their limbs, ready to snare him like tentacles. Behind him, he could hear the screams of Ruth but to turn around would mean death. But it mattered little, as the creatures screamed menacingly and lunged for their prey.

He sliced one stretching limb aside and stabbed another through its torso. That same one, however, stretched out its spiny fingers, and the branches ran right through Markus' left shoulder. A vine stretched out and snared his right leg, pinning him in place as another came right in from the front, and raised a clawed hand, laughing as it prepared to cut him down. It was at this point when Markus saw his very life in Nineveh flash through his mind in a blur of thoughts. The branch in his shoulder, the vine crushing his leg, it all should have all been painful; but surprisingly, he wasn't thinking of the pain. Instead, all that was on Markus' mind was... everything else.

He saw his father, Johnathon the Adventurer, slain by the Hunter Black.

He saw Aventis throwing him a party for his seventh birthday- his *only* memory of a birthday at all.

He saw Ruth first getting sick.

He saw Ashlyn coming into his home, begging for protection from The Guard.

He saw himself making his first battle-bot to gamble with at the Winking Badrat.

He heard the announcement of The Baron beginning the genocide in the city; the purging of the 'parasites' and teachings that spoke against him.

He saw the effect of the war with Xerxes, that one kid who crawled out of the sewer, begging for help...

He saw the night the Crystal in the staff came to life and told him about The City of Angels.

He saw Ruth's sickness continuing to get worse, and worse.

He saw a blur, a hazy image of a woman singing to him.

He then finally saw his first time flying. His first time, using his father's Eagles Wings to fly above the city and-

Markus mentally kicked himself as he screamed out loud, the pain in his shoulder and leg coming in like a raging current. *I am so stupid! I forgot about my wings which were concealed in my pack!* Now it was lost in the woods. Not only was all their food gone, but their only chance of making it out in time was gone. Markus thought if they had that with them, they wouldn't be here now.

But that hardly mattered now. He had left it behind; them being chased made them lose too much, and in the end, it just didn't matter. They had all run from Nineveh and managed to escape. They have all lasted a few days out in the Wastelands; braving the blizzards, the threats of pirates and other monstrous abominations, and worse. They had all managed to evade the Hunters for longer than Markus first thought possible.

But it didn't matter anymore. They couldn't run anymore, and this would be where the journey ended. Right here, at the edge of the canyon; The Scar that broke through the earth at the hands of whatever god wished to make their mark. This was where their journey to find the city in the sky ended.

This is where I'm going to die.

Markus raised his weakened arm holding his staff one last time, for a final effort to fight, before he fell.

Jim... Kaltrina... Aventis... Father... Ashlyn...

...I'm sorry...

The blade of the staff cut through the snarling face of the wooden creature who screamed as the claws came down upon him. Markus didn't even care anymore as he thought of only reality starting to shatter like glass. Everything he had feared was coming true; and worst off, he had allowed it to happen because of Ruth.

Ruth, I'm sorry I couldn't do it. I'm sorry I brought you out here; a desolate place where safety is an illusion. I'm sorry for believing that I could save you and get you to the city. I'm sorry, that in the end, I failed.

But suddenly, like a jagged knife slicing through every memory in his embrace, Markus watched as the branches and vines that had grabbed him were suddenly severed off the creatures arms. With the branch in his shoulder and the tangled vine at his leg, Markus fell into the snow as something brushed in front of his vision and forced the creatures back away from him. His electric sword hummed in one hand, the tip of Markus' staff in the other. If he had not grabbed it, Markus would have impaled *him* instead of the monsters. Markus sat there, aghast at the speed it took for Black to stop everything all at once as Markus was coming back to the broken reality. The pain in his shoulder was slowly creeping back, but even that was nothing compared to the shock he was in. The Hunter did not turn to look at him as he released the staff; the cut on his palm bleeding slightly. But without looking back, he uttered but one word to the boy; a command, and a plea.

"Run."

He then suddenly spun around, and from his wrist, the grapple-gun went off. The wire zipped over Markus' head, and the hook speared the wooden creature that had grabbed Ruth, and with a mighty tug, Black pulled the creature right off its feet, making it drop Ruth in the process. He then spun his body as the creature came barreling back screaming and he knocked some of the others aside before he swung his sword and sliced off the arm of the one who tried to intercept him; slicing off the vines that had ensnared Markus in the process.

"Run!" he commanded again.

This time, Markus listened.

Black

The child had turned and ran to help his friends from the last remaining Woodie. Meanwhile, Black kept his focus on the five in front of him, who hissed at his interference.

Oathbreaker! he heard the words of Lameika the Witch pass through their twisted and monstrous conscious.

Murderer!

Nuisance! This one lunged at Black who sidestepped the creature and sliced it from the right shoulder down to its left hip. It tried to grab him again, but upon grabbing the creature by its head, it erupted into brilliant maroon and blood-red flames. The Woodie was then tossed aside screaming as its wooden body burnt up like kindle.

Black then whirled back around, keeping his sword at the ready as the remaining crouched and began to try and circle him. One disappeared beneath the ground, but Black caught where it was and stabbed downward into the dirt just before it could jump out at him. An inhuman high-pitch cry emitted like nails scraping against rusted metal. He looked up to see another coming at him; its branch-arm shifted into a mass of vines that reached out to him like tentacles.

He sidestepped the downward strike and swung upwards. The appendages flew off at the elbow and wriggled like dying worms. The creature growled in frustration as it tried to grow it back. However, the electric current flowing through the sword had burnt the ends of the roots, preventing growth. The Woodie hissed angrily as Black beheaded it in one solid slash of his sword.

"I will put an end to your pitiful existence," he told them all both in voice and in mind.

The other two Woodies hissed vulgarly as they both rushed at him, extending all fingers and lashing out at him like quills. Black had cut through them all and managed to slice one Woodie in half right down the middle. Another one came around behind Black while the one he had stabbed in the ground had gotten up out of the ground with a burning hole in the center of its chest. He was surrounded now, but Black wasn't worried about himself.

Out of the corner of his eye, he saw that Markus had shot the last Woodie holding onto his friend. It had released her as its arm caught fire and she kicked it at the knee, making it drop before Markus proceeded to run it through the head with the blade of Johnathon's staff. He spun on his heel and cast the Woodie right off the bridge, and it fell into the chasm screaming that unholy cry.

Little Ruth was now pulling herself off the ground coughing horribly as Markus snatched her up and tried to help her. Through his eyes, Black saw the flame of their lives burning bright with the excited fear of the chase.

What *did* worry him, however, was Ruth's own essence, which was flickering like a candle going out at the end of its wick.

But Black couldn't do anything for them as of now. He ducked beneath the claws of the Woodie who had come up behind him, and he proceeded to slice the legs off of it before beheading it while it hung in the air. His ears then caught the distinct sound of a Hellhound engine, and he proceeded to hurry with the last Woodie. He dodged its last attack of spiked claws and sliced the hand off right at the wrist. The Woodie snarled and slashed at him, but it could not land a single blow on its enemy. Black soon found an opening, and after deflecting the creatures attack yet again, he reached up with his free hand, grabbed ahold of the Woodie's head and 'pulsed'. The creature gave out one final cry as its head suddenly ripped open and twisted as flames erupted from its skull. It fell to the ground headless before the Hunter, who sighed at the sudden use of energy.

From the clouds above the Hellhound of the Twins emerged as a monster from the darkest pits of the void. He turned to the youths who were still on the bridge, gawking at the ship.

"Go!" he bellowed.

Markus grabbed ahold of his coughing sister and with his friend the three turned and fled across the chasm into the Fiery Plains. Satisfied Black turned his attention back to the Hellhound hovering overhead as the Woodies began to pick themselves back up, trying to put their heads back on with intertwining roots at the neck that just couldn't grow anymore. He listened to them cursing him as they stitched themselves back up. Black magic really was the worst kind.

He placed his hand upon the ground, and 'pulsed' once more. A deep crack rippled through the earth right to the bridge in the canyon. The entire thing shattered and crumbled into the abyss below. Now the Woodies could not chase after the kids. That was one less thing for them to deal with, aside from the Hunters who hovered overhead staring down at him. He stared back, seeing them through the windshield as the few Woodie's he had not destroyed yet started to move in on him again. The Hellhound then changed in pitch and hovered across The Scar, disappearing into the acidic fumes of the Fiery Plains. They wouldn't be able to see the children, not with all the smog coming up from the smoldering earth.

However, Black noticed a flame of life dangling along the chasm walls on the other side. It then tunneled into the wall and disappeared without a trace. Black cursed, furious that one had survived the fall.

He turned his attention back to the surrounding Woodies, and considered his options.

~ The Keeper ~

Markus

Markus couldn't believe it.

As they trudged the broken landscape known as the Fiery Plains, the heat he could feel seeping from the very soil beneath his feet wore him down and he was forced to set Ruth down on a flat bed of rock near a shriveled tree. The pain in his shoulder was excruciating, and he could feel his entire arm soaked with blood. The toxic fumes didn't help his case either; it felt as if something was sitting right on top of his chest making it near impossible to breathe. There were scorched skeletons of mighty beasts every few feet when they first entered the Plains, but as they dwelled deeper within, there were some bigger ones- a rib cage alone looked about as big as The Winking Badrat.

Hearing Ruth cough again, he crouched down beside her and held her head against his own, trying to calm her down while rubbing her back. Ashlyn stood beside him, panting heavily. He was just replaying all that had just happened when his sister began to cough once again- this time so violently that there was no time for her to turn before her blood speckled his face.

"Ruth!" he gasped aloud as he pulled her close and burying her face in his good shoulder. "You're going to be okay. You hear me?" He started to look around; the steamy air thick as fog and hiding the shattered and dying Plains. This air… it wasn't good for her, not with her coughing so much now.

Why… oh why did we come here at all? "You're gonna be okay…"

This was met with more coughing; and that was when Markus heard the snap of a branch. He snapped his head around and Ashlyn followed his gaze. The steam made it difficult to see anything further than a couple of feet away, but there was no doubt in Markus' mind: something was out there, watching them.

"Mark..." Ruth croaked as she coughed into her hand. This time, the blood came out like a waterfall; seeping through her fingers and dripping into the smoldering dirt and hissing upon contact.

"Ashlyn," Markus said gently standing and releasing his sister. "Watch Ruth." He then stood up and extended his staff. "No matter what happens, stay there."

Ashlyn went to Ruth and cradled her. "We'll be fine." she said. Ruth nodded and coughed some more. She placed a hand over her mouth and blood *spilled* down her front. Desperate and afraid, Markus turned and stepped away from the tree. The fumes made him feel lightheaded, like he was drunk and about to fall over. But he kept his eyes sharp and focused on his surroundings. If he were to allow himself to fall now, then this would be where Ashlyn and Ruth would die.

He couldn't allow that- he *wouldn't*.

What happened next was nearly as bizarre as when Markus caused a shimmering blast of energy against the wooden creatures. Out of the corner of his eye, Markus saw the crystal in his staff begin to glow bright blue again. Immediately everything became clear as the world engulfed in sunlight.

He could see everything.

It was like, he was in a dream. Markus felt no hunger, no pain, and no worry. The pain in his shoulder was gone, and his vision was no longer hazy. He could see the bacteria floating among the very fumes he was breathing along with the clusters of poisonous toxins, and he was even aware of all of their side effects. He could see the life essence of the trees that stood dead and dying among the soil of heated particles. There was little life in them but not enough to grow or produce seeds. He could hear their agony as they slowly rot and burn from the inside out. He could sense the Ahools far in the depths of The Scar, and Markus could even sense the Hellhound circling somewhere above them where the steam was at its thickest. He could see the very aura of Ashlyn, which was a bluish haze. She was worried and afraid for Ruth who laid in her lap; her aura, a flickering red with every violent cough that shattered her lungs.

What Markus could lastly see, was directly beneath him. Underneath the miles of decomposed trees and insects was something else; something heading right for him.

"Below!" he shouted to no one in particular.

He saw the strange aura shimmering over his arms immediately flashed blue and Markus leapt up into the air just as the ground beneath him broke to reveal sharp wooden spears jutting out of the crust. As he fell back down he realized that he had jumped ten feet into the air when gravity finally brought him down, but the blade of his staff swung faster; slicing off the points before Markus landed nimbly on one of the spikes. He leapt sideways as an arm shot out of the ground and tried to grab him. His surprise was visible across his face as he landed.

How did I do that? Soon the entire creature clawed out of the earth, its branches slightly dried from the soil's concentrated heat.

It was the same Woodie Markus had shot into the canyon. It took a step towards him, and hissed in rage.

You little… It's alien thoughts broke through Markus' like a needle piercing skin.

Markus took aim and fired a bolt at the creature. It fell back in a flash of sparks but it steadied itself despite the gaping hole through it chest. It hissed at Markus and tunneled back underground and out of sight. But not completely, for Markus saw its aura, hazy, dark, angry, and savage tunneling deep and shooting up right towards him again. He leapt back just as it broke the surface with its arms above its head. It screeched in frustration, seeing that its prey had evaded its grasp but it turned to a scream of pain when Markus stabbed the blade-end down into its forehead. It cried out and clawed at Markus and grazing his shirt. He ripped the blade out and kept it at the ready in case it came after him again. The creature pulled itself out of the ground and two began to circle one another; turning every way the other turned. It was as if the monster was waiting for a way to trick Markus and attack him when he least expected it.

Poor little boy, lost in the haze, it hissed. *Cooking in the kettle, the air choking his breath.*

Markus lunged forward, his staff swinging at its neck. The creature ducked and clawed at Markus again, but it realized too late that the boy was no longer where it had thought he was and turned just in time for Markus' blade to slice through its wooden neck and lop its ugly head off. It rolled through the soil and came to a stop a few feet away the body. Even Markus himself was amazed with how fast he had moved at that moment.

He then felt *electricity* flow through his veins and he ducked as the arm of the headless monster swung over his head. He stabbed with his blade and gasped as he felt energy seep through body into the staff and through the Woodie which screamed chillingly as it burst into brilliant blue flames. The monster fell back thrashing and writhing in the ground until it went still. Finally, the head of Woodie came at Markus, crawling on roots like a spider as it leapt at him, its roots grabbing for his head. Markus knocked it aside with his staff but the force of the attack made him fall back onto the ground. It felt hotter, being so close to the smoldering dirt.

Before Markus could recover he was knocked onto his back as the Woodie tackled him and wrapped its roots around his neck. It then grew two large legs that made it grow and still having ahold of Markus it lifted him up into the air as it screamed into the boys face, spraying dirt and an ugly stench that made Markus' head spin. He then reached out for its face and when his palm pressed against it Markus screamed as he felt his arm began to burn up. He felt the creature shake beneath his fingers as Markus looked, its eyes began to spill black smoke. For a brief moment, Markus saw that he wasn't looking at some plant-creature from hell, but the witch that he had seen in Nineveh. She screamed out furiously at him and then just like that in a flash of blue, the Woodie reappeared, this time the flame of life extinguished from its gnarled body. It dropped him before falling on its side, and then like water it collapsed down into a smoldering pile of burning ash.

Markus was panting as he turned to look at the girls. He sheathed his weapon as he sprinted towards them; the task being complete, he just wanted to return to them. Ruth's coughing had still not gone down, and Ashlyn was flagging him down with a scared expression on her face. When he finally came to them he gently pried his sister from Ashlyn's arms and held her as she continued to cough, but little by little, not as violently.

He was beginning to have hope. He pressed two fingers against Ruth's jugular and sighed. Ruth coughed once and began to shake again.

She coughed again, her eyes staring at Markus. Tears were spilling down either side of her face, she was in so much pain. He reached out for her, touching her face. She whispered something barely audible but he managed to catch every single word.

"Markus…"

"I'm here." he said trying to keep his voice from cracking.

"Does Taiyou make it to the princess?" she then asked, raspy and weak. "Does he… defeat the Orks, and save her?"

Markus looked at Ashlyn, then turned back to his sister, nodding softly. "Yes, yes he does. He… he makes the pirates pretend to fly the kingdoms' colors, to scare the Orks, thinking that they were reinforcements. The monsters flee, and the kingdom is saved."

Ruth coughed out again. "And he finds, Tsuki?"

"That's right. He finds her, and shows her the pendant she gave her."

"Markus…" he heard Ashlyn whisper but he ignored her.

"Do they marry?" Ruth asked.

"Yes."

"And they live… Happily, ever after?"

Markus couldn't help but laugh as he nodded to his sister. Why… why was he crying now? "That's right. They lived happily ever after."

Ruth smiled and sighed. "Good…" She then reached up to Markus, and pulled his head towards her own so that she could whisper in his ear. She told him what she wanted.

She's gonna be alright… he thought, realizing he was lying to himself. Nevertheless, he nodded to his sister. "Okay… okay."

But then, with a sad smile on her face, Ruth went still. Her eyes stared up blankly at the skies above, as if she was imagining ships in the sky, flying far, far away beyond the toxic steam of the Fiery Plains.

"Ruth?" Markus asked as if trying to look past the illusion he had just witnessed. "Ruth?"

No reply. Her eyes stared upward still, never moving, never blinking. It seemed as if the very light in them had gone out like a lantern. And her aura, was now gone. Those pale green eyes, were glazed, never to see again. This wasn't an illusion.

This was very much real.

"Ruth!" Markus cried out. He pulled Ruth close, hugging her tightly, as if afraid that she would now just vanish into nothingness if he even loosened his grip even a little bit. Sorrow and agony seeped into his heart, as he began to cry. "Ruth!" *No, no, no!*

He felt hands grab him and he fought. He had hit Ashlyn in the cheek but Markus did not care at the moment. All that mattered was Ruth. He held her tight, her face pressed against his chest as he began to scream. *First Mom, then father, and now my sister. I'm all alone. My family, is all dead...* His reality; the one thing he held onto to keep going in a world so cold and cruel, was shattered like glass.

Markus screamed once more; angrily, desperately. "Ruth! Dammit Ruth, NO! PLEASE!"

"Mark! Stop it!" Ashlyn cried out behind him, hugging him tight around his shoulders. She had stopped pulling and merely held her friend in place, hugging Markus so tight he thought that he would choke by her hand instead of his own sobs. The two of them stayed there, holding Ruth who had left this world, the sickness finally winning the long battle.

It was then when Markus felt a presence and looked up to notice that Black was a few feet from them watching solemnly, his hand at his side which was bleeding profusely. He looked to Ruth and lowered his head. He pulled out a black box from his pocket and pressed a red button as he began to walk towards the two who remained.

"Get back!" Markus screamed reaching for his staff. "Stay away from us!" the Hunter stopped now, keeping a clear distance. Markus wanted to shoot the man, but found that he couldn't. He just didn't have the strength to fight anymore; the whole world was churning into a haze around him. He felt defeated, broken beyond repair. He felt like he was in a nightmare that had come to life.

Markus heard nothing but the echo of his cries, and saw only his dear sister laying in the smoldering dirt. The girl he helped raise after Father died; the one he had protected and cared for as her sickness took place; the one who mattered most on this venture, was now dead. The disease had finally caught up to her, and choked the very breath out of her and all Markus could do was watch.

We had come all this way, for nothing.

Markus gave up fighting and merely sat there defeated. Tears streaked his face and he felt more on the back of his neck where Ashlyn's own cheek was pressed. Black was waving downwards as if he was summoning something. Markus ignored him, and continued to cry, never taking his eyes off of Ruth even as a man in black leather came down and scooped her up in a flash of black and gold, followed by another who took Black.

Markus then felt the pressure of Ashlyn's hug suddenly release him and he was left to fall into the dirt, only to be grabbed by someone else. He kicked and howled like a wild animal and then suddenly felt all desire to fight stop as a rag was pressed over his mouth and nose; and then Markus knew nothing but darkness.

Darkness and despair.

Sorrow for his little sister, whom he had failed in the end, choked him even in sleep.

Ruth…

Lameika

Lameika smiled as she and Lee watched the Firefly take off to the East, its long wings vibrating like an insect's as it hovered its large black body across the Wastelands; its destination a mystery, for now. Someone had found Black and the children in the fumes drifting over the Plains. They were now taking them away.

And Lameika knew where.

She turned to her brother. "Follow them."

"I'm turning on Cloaking." He flicked a switch and outside the panels of the Hellhound shifted until they matched the color of the sky above them. No one would be able to see the siblings following them.

"It has to be *them*." Lameika whispered. "The Angels."

"Let's hope." Lee said softly indifferent. "Is He ready?"

"Oh, He will be. He still calls to us. We'll find Him."

Lee nodded. "We got 'em now, sis."

She nodded. "We got 'em." It had taken three lives of their own crew, but Lameika and Lee almost had their prey. Soon the children would be theirs, and hopefully, the Eldest. Soon, unimaginable power would return to them; and no one, not even The Capitol itself could stand up to them. She was still concerned about Cath's tactics, but it didn't matter as of now. She was pure in blood and magic; who was better to lead the new world than her? With Lee, serving her, Lameika would know true happiness; the entire world at her fingertips.

Unbeknownst to the siblings however, the Spider tracking device below the left wing of the Hellhound was watching the departing Firefly as well; and the viewer on the other end was also having a fit of ecstasy from the excitement of soon finding the City of Angels.

Ovid

Ovid watched on the screen in front of his throne with a large grin beneath his black beard. He rubbed his hands together like he was washing his hands; the buzzing feeling of excitement coursing through his very palms.

The Firefly the Wasteland Siblings were following had the ancient markings etched onto its side; a pair of wings on either side of a simply-drawn owls face. And Black... The traitor was alive and well on that ship with those children. He was leading the group there the whole time!

No matter. The City would soon be in view and then Baron Ovid will finally have a lead to capture the most powerful city besides the Capitol. Vast amounts of treasure and weapons, and best of all, technology beyond the worlds' own understanding. His excitement was well hidden behind his mask of calm demeanor. Soon he would have it all. First the City of Angels, then the entire Region.

He turned to General Veegar who was watching with him, grinning like a fox. "It's time, General." The Baron said rising from his throne. "Will you be prepared to lead this city in the defense when the Capitol comes to claim its land?"

"It will be my pleasure." Veegar said still smiling. He turned to his master however, the smile having been a mask of his own this whole time. "But sir, how do we know it is really them? How do we know it really is the Angels, and not just a separate group?"

"Then we will find out." Ovid said simply. "Those markings... they match the ancient markings within Johnathon's notes. It cannot be a coincidence. Even if it isn't them, we will find out where they acquired that chopper. Look at the structure even... have you ever seen a Firefly made like that?"

"Not with that big of a body, no."

Ovid nodded. Veegar was still unsure, that much was certain. But his general didn't need to worry himself with such specifics. This was to be Ovid's endeavor; his rise to ultimate power. Veegar only needed to concern himself with Nineveh, until he received word from Ovid. Besides, there was no better opportunity after this. They were running out of time, and they had to hurry.

Ovid breathed deeply, and rose from his throne; his heavy body shrouding the stone floor before him in darkness. "As soon as we take the Forbidden City, I will return and we will act on full force and move forward with the plan. Prepare The Leviathan and all our Hellhounds. I want to move out by dawn at the latest."

Veegar bowed. "Yes, my dear Baron. Would you like me to inform the Dark Twins?"

"No. First rule of control, Captain: never turn your back on your enemy, and never tell them you are behind theirs."

"Yes, sir."

"I'm counting on you, Captain," Ovid said as he walked heavily past Veegar, his boots echoing throughout the room. "You must lead this city and keep control until I return. As your former commander can tell you, I don't take disappointments well."

"Yes, sir," Veegar said almost immediately. He knew all too well how his master took disappointments. "I shall not fail."

Ovid chuckled as he exited his hall and began to ascend up the stairs into his quarters to prepare for war. Those twins have been useful, but their usefulness was quickly coming to an end. As soon as they reach The City, the tracker will blare like a frantic alarm, and The Leviathan will track it down in only a matter of hours. Ovid himself would personally deal with Black and those Drifters who bore Levitika's colors with extreme prejudice. His glory and victory cannot and *would not* be shared with anyone, and the traitor Black will hang after the City is taken and all of its power became Ovid's. He would make the indifferent Hunter squeal like the swine he and all who were beneath the great Baron Ovid was.

Soon the power of Angels would be all his. Soon, the entire Region- and maybe one day, the world -would be his. Magic, weapons, technology beyond the world's capabilities will be enough to crush all of his enemies. The very city who defied The Capitol, and started the revolution that divided the many kingdoms would lead him to a glorious victory. He was nearly there. It was now time to assemble his army. War was coming, but he was going to start it by plucking the wings off the Angels and bring their heaven crashing down to earth. Long had he searched for The City of Angels; and now it was within his grasp.

War never ends in this world. After each one, a new power grows, and with it another war will develop. And this one will be the new beginning of a new, more perfect world order. A river of blood would cut through the Wastelands and reshape the country; and from there beyond the borders he would stretch out to the unknown and claim his right as supreme ruler of the new world order.

His, world order.

~ Agony ~

Markus
Drowning.

    Markus felt as if he was swimming in the deepest ocean. Surrounded by unseen fish and sea monsters. The crushing weight choked the breath right out of him. As the water filled up his lungs and his legs having no effect despite how hard he kicked to the surface, he simply continued to sink into the darkness. Without any sound but the roaring in his ears, the dream of what happened to Ruth blazed right through his eyes. Every time he saw the dream he would cry out, the words muffled by the sounds of the water flooding his lungs; and little by little, his legs began to give up on struggling. Markus heard his name called out again and again, and he kicked out desperate to reach the surface. But, he also wondered if it would even matter. It would be so much easier, just to… stop kicking.

    And so, he sank.

Mark…
Dad…
Mark…
…Mom?...
Mark.
Mark.
Mark!
"MARK!"

Markus gasped as he shot up reaching for his blade only to feel cool hands push him back down. He was shirtless and was sitting in a white cot of linen in a circular room of stone. His shoulder was bandaged up and his torso was slick with cold sweat. He took some deep breaths, his body refusing to settle back down as he took in where he was.

A yellow crystal hung above his head, giving out bright light into the room which was filled with cots and tables. Some white sheets covered some of the other cots around the room, his sitting on one of them. A tube and an IV bag stood by his side, as well as a heart monitor that bleeped rapidly with his pounding heart. His head was spinning the more he tried to figure out where he was.

How did I get here? Where am I? Where-

A face flashed before his eyes which then immediately snapped open. "Ruth!" Markus shot up again only to be held down again by the same soft hands. Ashlyn's face came into his view, her expression concerned but at the same time annoyed. She had a bandage on her cheek from where she had been cut, and she looked like she hadn't slept in weeks her eyes were so dark.

"Mark!" she said in a low but stern voice as if to not upset him. "Relax! You're safe. We're safe!"

"What?" He demanded looking past her at the man who stood behind her. He started to struggle again, but Ashlyn held him firmly.

"Mark, it's okay." Ashlyn said keeping her hand over his pounding heart. He struggled still but not as rough as before, and still his friend never took her hands off him.

"We're safe." she said again panting heavily. The dark circles under her eyes made their pleading all the more painful.

"Ruth?" Markus asked grabbing Ashlyn's wrists, startling her. "Where's Ruth?" A sapphire fire burned in his eyes, his expression demanding answers. "Where is she?" he asked again.

Ashlyn looked down as if she developed a sudden interest in the covers he was laying under. The man behind her cleared his throat and Markus could finally recognize that it was the Hunter Black, now standing right beside her.

"What are you doing here!?" Markus demanded with such hostility.

"Markus, hold on." Ashlyn said placing her hands on his shoulders and forcing him to face her. "He saved us. But…

Black cleared his throat again before he spoke blunt and heartless. "Markus, I'm afraid… that Ruth is dead."

All strength in Markus' body quickly diminished in an instant. He fell back into the cot, surrendering to Ashlyn's hands as he felt his spirit just give up entirely. He just couldn't kick anymore, and allowed himself to sink.

So it was true. Ruth was gone. Markus thought he knew for sure, but it felt as if once again the world was pulled out from under him, and the air he was suspended in was replaced with waves of agony, ready to crush him beneath its watery tides of sorrow. He could not believe it, and yet Markus knew it was true. No matter how much he wished it was a dream… he was awake; stuck in reality.

That's right, I was there. Ruth is… gone.

"Oh…" he moaned as he felt his very heart shatter like glass and sprinkle throughout the rest of his insides. All will and strength were gone at that moment and Markus allowed himself to surrender against the cruel tide washing over him and he just laid back against the cot staring at the ceiling. "Ruth…" He said as tears trickled down his cheek. He threw a hand up and covered his face as he wept bitterly. Ashlyn sniffed and wiped her eyes as she crouched to the floor so she was eye-level with him.

"Markus, I-"

"Leave me alone." he said turning so that his back was to her. He did not mean to hurt her but right now Markus just wanted to be left alone in his misery. "Just… go away." He wanted to take the world and throttle it. He wanted to just sink into the cot and disappear. He felt anger, hatred, pain, and sorrow all tearing him apart. He wanted to be left in his own despair; and let agony carry him away with the tide.

He just… wanted to be alone.

Ruth…

Black

Black sighed as Ashlyn began to softly cry at Markus' back. It pained him to see them like this, but he had no way to express such feelings. He had wondered how they were doing all this time, especially young Ruth whose illness had finally claimed her. Now the two survivors were here, stricken with grief. They had managed to escape the city of Nineveh, and cross the Wastelands knowing what dangers and risks they were taking. And in the end, there was still pain. They had taken the road unfollowed, and there was literally hell to pay. Markus had lost so much all these years, and his one anchor holding him onto this world was gone.

But Black knew that with any trial that you come across, you are able to grow should you wish to just try. You just had to have the will to pick yourself back up no matter how hard you had fallen,.

He leaned down and touched a hand to Ashlyn's shoulder, startling her and making her look back towards him. "Leave him be, for now. You can come back in when I'm done."

The girl took one last look at Markus, and then without looking at back at Black, Ashlyn stood up and walked away. After he helped them escape the Fiery Plains, she seemed to trust him now. Or maybe she was just so brokenhearted that she simply did not have the energy to argue any longer. She truly was a strong girl, aiding Markus in his time of need- to the best of her abilities. It would take time with Markus, but that was fine. They were safe now. Now it was only a matter of time.

When Black heard the door shut behind him, he grabbed one of the chairs along the wall and pulled it alongside Markus' cot. He sat there watching the youth for a moment, taking the time to think of what was needed to say as well as give Markus the time he needed to be with himself. He didn't hear the youth crying, but he could definitely feel the boys' pain emit like a fog within the room. The aura around Markus was not bright blue as it was before in Black's eyes. In fact, it was now a darker shade of violet, the shade of brokenness.

And Markus is indeed, broken. Black thought as he could feel the boy's sorrow in his heart. "I'm sorry." he finally said after minutes of prolonged silence. He was impressed by Markus' strength to hold back his sobs despite the horrible tragedy. "Truly, I am."

"Why do you care?" Markus demanded not moving from where he laid. His voice was cold, defensive.

Black sighed and considered his options. "I had a sister once too, you know."

"Bite me."

Ignoring the retort, Black continued. "She died from cancer. She died in my father's arms."

"I don't care what happened." Markus suddenly snapped. He fell silent for a moment and then sighed with a tinge of regret in his voice. "I'm sorry for your sister, but not you."

Black stared at him. "Do you really hate me that much?"

That got to him. Markus sat up fast and pivoted, his eyes red and dripping with tears, his teeth lashing out as he snapped, "Just get the hell out of here! You killed my father, and I will *never* forgive you for that! And now my sister is dead, and *now* you wanna talk about family!? You don't care about me, *or* my family! You just wanted to bring us to the Baron! Well congratulations, *Hunter*!" Markus held his hands up in mock praise. "You sure do live up to your reputation! I don't care anymore, so just leave me alone. Just, get out."

With that, he slammed himself against his cot and pulled up the sheets until his face was completely covered. Black heard silent sobbing beneath it; the sobs finally breaking free of their cage. He sat there for a good minute taking in what he had just heard.

He is still, just a child. he thought somberly.

Finally, he spoke again, and his voice didn't change in pitch or emotion. "I *tried* to save her, Markus," he said while standing up. "And that is the truth. There was nothing we could do, and I am truly sorry for that. And you are not at the Baron's castle. I never intended to take you there. I saved you and your friend. Ruth, I am sorry for. Terribly. But there was nothing I could do."

Markus said nothing but remained hidden beneath the sheets, where only he himself could experience his agony.

"I have asked the men to store her in the containment units." Black then told him. "When you are ready, I will be outside to take you to her. Ashlyn will be here soon. If you want to hide under the sheets, then very well. But if you really do respect your sister and love her as much as you claim, you won't just stay there and give up."

He then reached down and picked up a small pack containing Markus' Eagle-Wings. The metal gleamed in the crystals light as he sat it down beside Markus on the cot. "I found this in the woods by the way." And with a turn of his cloak, he turned and walked for the door. He stepped outside and told Ashlyn she should wait.

"I have to go see him…" Ashlyn protested.

"Go ahead then," Black answered. "But let him rest. Let him grieve." After she went back inside, Black took a seat in the chair Ashlyn was originally waiting in by the door. He kept watch down the hall, never moving, never fidgeting. But deep inside him, he did feel something.

Hurt.

He truly does hate me, and rightfully so.

But then again, he did lose his entire family now. No one can ever truly get over such pain like that. Even Black himself, still could not be completely over it. He *did* know Markus' pain, and he truly hoped that the boy would be alright. If his words had not reached him, he hoped his friend would be able to convince Markus to stand back up. There would be time for grieving soon, but it should be in the presence of his little sister. Markus didn't deserve such a fate to be brought upon him, but he was here, and there was no going back. He would be exposed to so much before he even comes close to having time to hide beneath the sheets in his misery. It wasn't fair, but that was how it was meant to be. It had already been predicted.

And it was Black's job to ensure that the boy was prepared for his future.

Ashlyn

Ashlyn said nothing as she took a seat in Black's chair, looking back at Markus.

She sat there for what felt like hours. Hours went by, and by nightfall, Ashlyn was suggested by Black to get some rest. But she refused, saying that she would stay with her friend. The Hunter responded by having food brought to them, bread and some chicken. She had asked Markus if he wanted any, but he didn't answer. For two straight days, he never answered even as women clad in white came in to change his IV and check his pulse. After they were done, they always left them alone.

All of Markus' pain reminded Ashlyn of her own when her family had been killed. Understanding the fate of her mother who sacrificed herself in order for her and Kira to escape, and then Kira was shot while running away. And all Ashlyn could do was run. Run, and scream, and run some more. There was no time for her to grieve, and then her father, Veegar who gave the command for the death of her family, sent out the Guard after her. The manhunt for the last member of his family who had gone into hiding. She escaped, and she ran. She ran, and spent the rest of her days since, running and hiding from the horrible memory that haunted her very dreams.

She since then hated herself for being the only survivor, for running. Still to this day she does, but she had to fight through it all. It was the only way she could have survived for as long as she did. *The pain never goes away. You just learn to get used to it.* However, that was not what Markus needed to hear.

By the mid-afternoon of the second day, Ashlyn crawled up off the floor where she had been sleeping by Markus' side, and taking the chair that she had sat in for what felt like forever, she decided to try and speak to Markus again.

"She was lucky, you know?" she said, hoping to finally coast him into coming out from under the sheets.

Thankfully, Markus lowered the sheets to reveal his red face streaked with his sorrowful tears. He hadn't eaten or had anything to drink in the last few days, and he looked horrible. "What?" he croaked.

She cleared her throat, swallowing the lump that had formed in it. "Ruth. She was lucky to have you as a brother."

He frowned. "Yeah, right," Markus said looking up at the ceiling his hands on his chest. "Lotta good it did her…" He sniffed.

"No, she was." Ashlyn insisted. "Look, I would give *anything* to have someone care about me when I was her age as much as you care about her."

"But I *failed* her. I took her out of the city on a suicide mission in hopes that she could be cured by some flying city." He shook his head broodingly. "I'm an idiot. I'm an idiot for believing that it was a good idea. I'm an idiot for believing we even stood a chance…"

"But we *did* make it," Ashlyn said. When Markus gave her a peculiar look, she continued. "We made it to the city, Mark. We're here in Levitika."

"We made it…?" Markus whispered not quite in disbelief but in only acknowledgment.

Ashlyn nodded. "They took us away after Ruth… They *tried* Markus. They really did… and so did Black."

Markus frowned and lowered his eyes. "We made it… But… but she didn't."

Ashlyn didn't say anything. There wasn't much to say, considering the cold hard truth. They *had* made it, but Ruth, Markus' reason for leaving Nineveh in hopes of finding a cure, she didn't. She would never see the floating city that Markus promised to take her to. Ashlyn couldn't imagine the horrible, horrible guilt he must have felt. He was probably beating himself up about it right now.

Markus then sniffed. "He really tried to help?" He asked, referring to the Hunter Black.

Ashlyn nodded. "He was with the doctors while you were still sleeping in here…" She looked down at her feet. "I heard you two talking…"

"Oh?"

"Yeah."

"So what?"

Ashlyn brought her eyes back to Markus, who was staring right at her. Those bright pools of liquid sapphire seemed to burn right into her own eyes. "He *tried* to, Markus. I saw the desperation in his eyes as he tried to help her. But…" *Nothing could be done.* Is what they had said.

"He doesn't care," Markus said shaking his head. "There was nothing he could do anyway. Ruth was already dead. I knew she was dead out there before he or anyone could even get to her. He knew it too. He doesn't care."

"You don't mean that."

Markus scoffed. "How do you figure, Ashlyn?"

Ashlyn licked her lips as she thought of what to say next. She truly didn't know exactly *what* to tell her friend. She could tell by the tone of his voice that there was nothing she could really do to convince him.

So, she tried a different approach. "At least he brought your wings back." She offered pathetically.

"I guess," Markus said indifferently. "It doesn't matter still. Ruth is gone. It doesn't matter if we made it to Levitika or wherever we really are. It doesn't matter if Black tried or not. Nothing; none of it matters anymore."

Ashlyn frowned, her brow furrowing at this attitude Markus now had. The boy she met in that cruddy shack, she wondered, where was he now? Who was this one, laying in the cot before her?

"Mark, you can't blame him for what happened to Ruth. And you can't blame yourself."

"It *is* my fault though," Markus said turning back to her. "Don't you get it? I screwed up. I shouldn't have taken her out of Nineveh… I shouldn't have… Shouldn't…"

Ashlyn pursed her lips sadly and then said, "When my family died, I blamed myself. Convinced myself that it was my fault they died. I was the only one who managed to get away, only because I ran away. The Guard didn't even *try* to catch me. I ran away, to save myself. And it only made the pain so much worse. But what happened to them, it wasn't really my fault my family died. There was nothing I could do. And Ruth… what happened was *not* your fault, Mark. You did what you believed needed to be done, and you were determined to do it. And you *did* get her here at least."

"A lot of good it did her though," Mark said sarcastically. "She's never going to know, Ashlyn. And now my whole family's gone. What do I got to live for now?"

Ashlyn pursed her lips. "Me?"

Markus looked Ashlyn dead in the eyes, surprise catching him almost as much as it did her. Neither spoke as if they were both trying to read each other's minds. Without the staff, Markus seemed to be having trouble reading Ashlyn. Which was all right with her. She had heard some whispers about his staff from the men who were helping Black, how it 'had to be him'. She didn't pay a lot of attention at the time; she simply just wanted Markus and Ruth to be alright.

"What do you know?" he suddenly demanded and turned away, hurting Ashlyn. "You have *no* idea how I feel."

"Yes, I do." she insisted coolly, almost angrily and yet at the same time as patiently as she could. "I lost my family too, I know *exactly* how you feel. Whether you want to admit it or not, I do know how you feel. I'm just saying, you don't have to carry that burden alone. You are *not* alone, Mark. Even if you feel that way, you have me. And we are here, in the City of Angels. And I don't plan to go anywhere in this place without you."

"Then ask Black maybe, if you trust him so much."

Ashlyn didn't take the comment to heart. She knew Markus was hurt, and didn't mean it. "I'd rather have you by my side." She reached for his hand, and upon taking it and feeling his hardened and scarred fingers, she squeezed them. "You're my best friend."

Markus looked at her, and Ashlyn saw another tear break free from his eyes and slip down his cheek. She reached out and caught it before flicking it away. Then with a small smile, Markus wiped his face, chuckling slightly as he did so.

He then looked away and sighed. "Well… thanks." He looked back at her. "I'm sorry I snapped at you…"

Ashlyn smiled back. "It's okay."

"No, it's not. Thank you."

"I just don't want you to give up," Ashlyn told him. "If I gave up when my family... you know. If I gave up then, I would never have gotten to meet you or Ruth. You guys... you're my family now."

Markus looked truly touched at this, and he looked down, and Ashlyn realized that he was looking at their hands which were still together.

Ashlyn quickly released him and cleared her throat. "Come on." She nudged his arm, gently so that she didn't disturb his injured shoulder. "If you are feeling alright... Let's go see Ruth, together."

Mark closed his eyes in thought. "I don't know if I can..." He was quiet for so long Ashlyn thought he might have fallen asleep. "I still want to believe that this is just a bad dream... and maybe I'll wake up."

"Maybe." Ashlyn agreed. She sometimes wished that as well, but at the same time, she didn't want to wake up if it was, not yet. "Well, at least you don't have to go alone."

He opened his eyes, looked at her, and sighed. "Okay," he said. He sat up and sighed. His scarred torso was so pale he was almost white as paper. Ashlyn caught herself staring, and she looked away. "Least I have my pants still." she heard Markus say. "Do you know where my shirt and coat is?"

Ashlyn reached under the cot and pulled up his clothes. He sat on the bed putting them on. She stole but one glance at the dirtied thing covered his body. When he was ready, he turned and stepped onto the floor before he stood up. He wavered slightly, but after a few steps, he appeared ready. He then went for his pack and his staff which was on the floor. He shortened it into a dagger and slipped it into his belt. All this time, Ashlyn watched him, ready to spring for him should he slip and fall.

He's so strong. Ashlyn thought to herself. *Stronger than he realizes.*

"Lead the way." he then said to her.

And with a nod, Ashlyn stood and together the two of them started for the door, where Black was waiting.

~ Loss ~

Markus

When the Markus and Ashlyn stepped outside, Black was still waiting for them in a chair. He stood up without looking at either of the two as he spoke. "You ready?"

"I guess," Markus said shoving his hands into his pockets. The Hunter nodded and began to lead them down the stone hallway lit by torches of bright green fire fed through a gas line. All the while, Markus kept one eye on the Hunter, and the other taking in his surroundings.

The hall had an old-fashion-castle look to it, like in one of father's stories. The walls and floor were layered with stone filled with granite which smelled faintly of a forest. There were some posts where the torches rested which were of a dark brown color, with thin pipes of similar color lined alongside the posts. Markus had only seen this much of the new place they were in, and he was already impressed. He remembered being young and was once taken to the Baron's dungeons for some misunderstanding that he was 'captured and detained' for. And those halls had nothing on the halls they were walking through right now. But then again, no hallways leading to dungeons have ever looked great, Markus supposed.

When they exited the hallway, Black led them into a large circular room with many doors lining the walls. A large metallic statue of an owl stood in the center on a block of bronze. Its wings were folded against its back in shining iron, and its hooded face was curved with bronze platings. Its eyes were glowing red with rubies the size of a pair of fists. At most this thing looked to be almost as tall as halfway towards the glass dome ceiling which was about fifty feet high above their heads. Beyond the glass, Markus could see a pale blue sky shining down upon them.

"Wow," he said, impressed.

"The Levitikans are influenced by The Great Owl here," Black said. "A spirit of the wind and wisdom. And also, the symbol of the rebellion that took place long ago, when the city became disconnected with The Capitol and the rest of the world."

"That's incredible," Ashlyn said still staring in awe.

"Didn't know people believed in such things," Markus said while distastefully glaring at Black as he walked in front of them. He didn't truly know if he was in Levitika or not, and if they weren't, Black was doing a good job of trying to convince him otherwise.

"Well, there is no actual spirit, per se," Black said. "There is actually a legend of someone who donned a mask, respectfully appearing like that of an owl. This person aided the rebellion against The Capitol, back when the kingdoms who dot the landscape today were merely holds, and the Northern Wastelands was actually a massive empire. Since the Great Owl represents wisdom and wind, I assume that The Owl as the locals named the hero, used the symbol as a way to lead Levitika to freedom. Whether it was an actual spirit or not remains a mystery however. But, some say it really was an actual person who once defeated The Mad King a long time ago."

"Oh." was all Markus could say. He had heard of The Mad King; he was a horrible tyrant who ruled the entirety of the Northern Wastelands from The Capitol, before the kingdoms were made and separated across the land.

That was over a hundred years ago, Markus thought. Is this city we are in now really that old?... If this is actually The City of Angels at all.

"Come." Black turned to his left where an iron door stood, the sign above it written in a language Markus did not understand. He pushed it open and stepped aside. He held out his hand to the room which was darkened except for the table which was sat in the back. Surrounding the table were a great many crates and vases including burial urns of gold and bronze.

And on the table itself, was a glass coffin where inside Markus saw a familiar figure within. He felt a lump immediately form in his throat and he felt like his heart had suddenly been punched with an iron fist.

"I'll wait outside," Black said. "Take your time."

"Thank you," Ashlyn said as Markus uneasily stepped inside with her by his side. The door then closed behind them, locking the two inside the dark; the only light coming from the table area. Another illuminating crystal sat beside the coffin on the table, and its glow was brighter than any torch or lantern, reflecting against the glass and Ruth's pale face within.

Markus felt drawn to the light and closer to Ruth who laid there as if asleep. A bundle of white roses rested against the glass. Markus couldn't smell them; in fact, he wasn't quite seeing them to begin with. His heart grew heavier and heavier with each step towards Ruth; and when he finally came close enough to press his hand against the glass, he felt tears filling the brims of his eyes once again.

"Ruth…" he whispered as one finally broke free and trailed down his cheek. He hung his head against the glass, crying for his sister who slept soundly. Ashlyn remained by his side, but she did not try to speak to him. She was simply letting her friend know that she was here; that she was staying. Markus did not look up or even attempt to wipe the tears off his face as he cried in silence for Ruth.

Ruth had been properly cared for by the looks of it. Her soft cheeks laid still and pale, her hair which was no longer a rat's nest of blonde streams but now neatly combed. She was also no longer wearing her torn up pants and coat. She was now clothed in a white linen gown reaching down to her knees. Her hands overlapped each other across her still chest. No longer would they shake and shatter from that dreadful cough. In fact, it looked as if she would rest for eternity in a peace she never knew in life.

"I'm sorry." he heard Ashlyn said beside him.

"Don't be," he said wiping his tears away with his free hand. He was grateful for her company. He took a deep breath and turned to her. "At least… she is in peace now." *Never again will her body be shattered by that dreadful disease...*

"I suppose," Ashlyn said breaking into his thoughts.

"Yeah." Markus nodded, letting his head rest against the glass again. He resisted the urge to beat his fist against the glass.

"So, now what?" she then asked. "What will we do now?"

"I don't know," he said while turning to face her but he still didn't look at her. "All I know is there's nothing much left for us here. If we really did make it to The City, regardless of how or why, what good is it us being here? What is even the point now?"

"What about what the Crystal said?" she asked. "The prophecy? Or what about even starting a new life here?"

"We don't even know where 'here' is," Markus said. "And frankly, I don't give a crap about the prophecy anymore. It was all a bunch of mumbo-jumbo and we both know it. All I wanted was to find a cure for Ruth, no matter what. And the new life? How can I do that without her?"

"She would want that. Remember what we talked about earlier?

That stunned Markus. But he knew she was right. They were here now, there had to be *some* purpose to it. Markus still didn't really care about the prophecy in the crystal or whatever these 'Levtikans' wanted with him. In fact, the thought of it all only made him angry.

"That's bullshit." he suddenly said.

"What?" Ashlyn said, shocked at this sudden outburst.

"Is that really all I can do now?" he demanded while clenching his fists. "Move on? Live my life when she is gone? How can I do that? Why should I?"

Ashlyn frowned. "You never know unless you try and find out."

"What kind of answer is that!?" he demanded, glaring at her with blood-shot eyes.

Ashlyn looked at him and said, "You still have her memory when she was alive. Even if you lost one precious thing in your life, it doesn't mean your life is over. You can have another thing, or a thousand things that can give you a reason to keep living. I was struggling to find something to live for, and then I found you two. I'm sad that we lost Ruth too, but it was because of both her and you that I found another reason to keep breathing. If I can do it, so can you."

Markus sighed after thinking over Ashlyn's words. "Must you have an answer for everything?"

Ashlyn smiled at that. "You want me to answer that?"

Markus looked back at Ruth who laid still in her eternal slumber. "No. I already know the answer." He turned back. "I'm sorry. I guess we just go back to Black, for now." He didn't want to though. He just wanted to curl up somewhere and sleep away the pain eating his chest from the inside out. But at the same time, he didn't know what else he could do. He was doing no good here, and he didn't know where else to go from there.

He wanted to find out more, before making his final decision.

"You hate him a lot, don't you?" Ashlyn asked him.

He stared at her. "How many times am I gonna be asked that?"

"Do you?"

Without missing a beat, Markus replied, "Yes."

"Even though he brought us here?" Ashlyn asked this while giving him a peculiar look.

Now that *really* hurt. "What do you want me to say?"

"Someday, you're going to have to forgive him, Markus. You can't hold it against him forever. I know I hurts, but maybe he's changed since then. Besides, holding a grudge is just dead weight. You don't need any more weight upon your shoulders; you can't bear everything forever."

"Would you forgive Veegar for killing your family?"

She looked down at her feet in silence.

"Didn't think so." He ran a hand through his hair with a sigh. "Ashlyn, you just don't understand... My family is all gone, and one of those members was killed by Black. *Right* in front of me, dead. And Ruth, she died right in my arms. Even if the doctors- even if Black 'tried' to save her, there was still nothing they could do. Nothing. My whole family is dead, and yes, I can't blame Black for what happened to Ruth. But I sure as hell can blame him for killing my father. You really expect me to see all that, and then think that he actually cares about Ruth or even me? You just don't understand; I can't accept that. No matter how much-"

Smack!

Markus' left cheek stung, and there was a ringing in his ear from the sound of Ashlyn's palm making contact with his face. He looked back at her and Markus saw that she didn't look sad, but rather angry. In fact, if he didn't know any better, Ashlyn looked *furious*. It shocked Markus into silence as she spoke.

"I don't understand, huh?" she said in a dangerously low tone. "You say I don't understand having your family killed right in front of you; that I wouldn't be able to forgive the man who did. I told you already, I *do* understand. Think about my father and I. He left me for *dead*. He tried to kill me just as he killed my mother and sister. And you say I don't understand? Shame on you. Shame on you and your pity-party. I'm sorry, but that's all you are doing now, not just grieving. No, don't say anything. Just let me talk so you can figure out what you can do from this point on. Nothing will ever make me forget the pain he caused me. Having to live on my own, escape The Guard and simply *survive*. Sleeping wherever I could and eating whatever I could find, all the while hating my father for what he had done. But hating him doesn't make anything better. Hating him never made me *feel* better. It only made me miserable. Has hating Black done you any good? And what about now? What about after he saved us and tried his best to help Ruth?"

Markus was stunned into silence. He didn't know what to say to her.

Ashlyn looked down and then looked back up. "If you really hate someone, you have to do something about it. If there is nothing you can do about it then what's the point in carrying all that baggage!?" Her raised voice echoed in the dark room, and all Markus could do was stare at her as she glared back at him. Ashlyn sighed and took a deep breath before continuing. "He really tried to save her, Mark. Whether you believe it or not."

Markus' jaw twitched, still in pain from the slap. "Okay, okay, I'm sorry. I should have listened to you the first time. I get it. You do understand; probably are the only one I know who does. But… I don't know, why did Black kill my only parent, only to go out of his way to save Ruth and I?"

Ashlyn pursed her lips. "I don't know. I really don't. Why did Veegar kill my family to earn Ovid's trust? Why do men… why does anyone do the things they do to win the praise others?"

Markus nodded understandably. "I guess we'll never know for sure…"

"You should ask."

Markus scoffed at that, the thought of it humored him slightly. "Right. I don't think that will go well."

"What's the harm in trying?"

The truth was, he didn't have the answer to that. And as much as it irritated him, Markus knew she was right. What harm could there be? He would never know until he found out for sure; he'd be able to find out the truth behind it all. He was owed that much at least.

Besides, they were here; here in Levitika, apparently. Why now, Markus did not know for sure. Would they be able to start fresh here? Would he be dragged into this so-called prophecy? Did anyone here even know about it? Since waking up, the only people he's seen were Ashlyn and the Hunter. Markus himself was still left in the dark; ignorant by what the people he would soon meet would want with him.

All he knew was that it was him and Ashlyn against the world now, and they had to stick together until the end.

"I'm not asking you to forgive him, yet," Ashlyn said. "But I *am* saying, stop letting your hatred just pull you down. You're better than that. What good has it done to you since that day? Don't forgive him for his sake, do it because you deserve peace… Besides, with what has happened, the last thing you need is more pain. You deserve to be at peace."

"Deserve peace…" Markus mumbled looking back at Ruth. "In this world, is there really such a thing?"

"Only if we look," Ashlyn said, and for a long while, Markus stared at her, taking her words and running them through his brain which was still going a million miles an hour.

"Come on." Markus eventually said. "Let's get back to Black."

"Are you sure?"

"You're the one who said…" He shrugged.

"But you have to *want* to," Ashlyn said. She looked over at Ruth who still slept peacefully. "Ruth would want you to feel peace, Markus. And sometimes, being at peace is to forgive and at least hear someone's reasons for the things they do."

"Easier said than done," Markus said.

Ashlyn chuckled humorlessly. "Can't blame you there. But you've been hurt for too long because of this. Don't you want to feel that weight lift finally?"

Markus looked down at Ruth. "How can I, now that she is gone? This is…"

Ashlyn grabbed Markus' hand again and gave it a squeeze to get his attention. "There is no rush to things like this. Best part is, you don't have to deal with any of it alone."

He smiled at her sadly. "Thanks…"

"Come on," Ashlyn said releasing his hand. "Let's go find out where we are at now."

"Right."

And with that the two left Ruth in that room in her case of glass, sleeping away the pain and sorrow left behind in this world.

~ The Queen of the Sky ~

Markus

Markus and Ashlyn followed Black down the halls once again in silence. Shadows danced across the walls; cast by the green light of the torches. Their three bodies were shrouded in the shadows as they ventured further down the many halls that to Markus felt like a labyrinth.

They soon came upon a tall set of double-doors of bronze and steel. Electronic hinges and massive cogs and gears held the doors in place, and a palm-scanner rested on a little generator to the left. Black stalked towards it like a fluid shadow and stopped; his hand hovering just over the scanner. He then turned to look at Markus and Ashlyn with a serious expression.

"Before we enter the Throne Room, I need you two to understand some things: The Queen is busy. However she will greet us when she is done. So be patient, and we will figure out what to do then."

The Queen? "What's with the 'we' stuff?" Markus muttered. Ashlyn jabbed him in the ribs at that comment. Before he could even say anything to her, Black had pressed his palm onto the scanner, which lit up and beeped as the generators began to hum, and the gears around the door slowly began to turn with a mighty hiss.

"You are here now," Black explained as he stepped back to avoid getting hit by the slowly moving doors. "So there's no point in waiting now."

"Waiting for what?" Ashlyn asked.

"Queen Elizabetha will explain." The large doors swung open with a mighty groan to reveal an elaborate room that Markus would later learn was the Throne Room of the castle they were in. Markus heard Ashlyn gasp beside him at the view, and he had to admit, he too was blown away by the sight that beheld them as well.

It was a circular room with a dome roof of stainless glass which opened up to the heavens above; although it now had some gray clouds coming in with threatening storms. The walls were of stacked stone, laminated with bronze and iron. The floor was covered with red satin carpet, and at the very end of the hall the carpet broke off into bronze steps leading up to two thrones.

The largest was the one on the right, with wings of gold on either side with the face of an owl on the head. The second was of the same detail however it looked to be made of silver and was just a little smaller in size. Sitting in the larger throne was a beautiful woman with black hair and olive-colored skin. Her lips were red as cherries, and her hair was tied into a braid beneath a tiara of gold and sapphire. Her gown which was as white as snow was also laced along the edges with a lighter color of blue. Her boots were of simple leather, and her eyes… As blue as the Sea of Monsters; bluer than the sky on the brightest day. It was a beautiful shade of blue, bluer than Markus' own. The comparison left him feeling slack-jawed in awe.

She was listening to a man garbed in gray robes, his face obscured by a hood laced in red. He seemed to be arguing with the queen about something. Another man stood by with leather-gray skin and a nose that seemed to have been *melted* in his face. He looked about as strong as an ox, with shoulders as wide as one. As the lady looked over the man to see the visitors she held up her hand, yielding his tongue.

"I am aware, Slagar." the lady said in a voice as light as the songbirds of spring. "I will deal with it presently. For now, I must speak with our guests. They are important." She pointed towards the doors Markus and Ashlyn had been led through. "You may go."

"Look," the man in the robes said, clearly irritated. "Your Highness. Forgive me for being so bold, but this cannot wait. You know what would happen if-"

"*I*," the lady said in a stern voice which grew softer as she spoke. "Will mind The Vault."

The leathery man turned to the man in robes. "C'mon." The one called Slagar bowed stiffly to the queen and turned with a huff as the two stalked towards Black and the teens. As Slagar walked by Markus, he locked eyes with the man; whose eyes were suddenly blood-red. He felt as if something was pricking the back of his head and Markus went to scratch it. The man smiled as if amused and he stormed out the doors which boomed shut behind him and his colleague, closing the three of them in with the lady in white. Black began to walk forward, and Markus followed with Ashlyn as such, and they came up to the steps of the Throne Room.

Black then got down on one knee and bowed before the queen. Now that they were closer, there was no doubt about it now; this lady was indeed of royal blood.

"My Lady, Elizabetha," he said. Not knowing entirely what to do, Markus bowed likewise, his eyes directed straight into the crimson carpet beneath his feet. Ashlyn bowed beside him, her hair dangling in front of her face. He dared to take a peek back up to see the queen smiling brightly.

"Damion Black." Queen Elizabetha said, standing up and looking over the man with a soft expression. "It has been too long."

"Indeed," Black said standing straight up. "I would have come to see you sooner, but I had something to attend to."

The queen looked past him. "And these two... the boy. It really is him...?"

"Yes, milady."

Elizabetha's eyes sparkled at Black's words. "Stand." She commanded, and both Markus and Ashlyn stood at attention as she descended the stairs, looking directly at Markus. "Come here." She beckoned for him to approach.

Markus swallowed as he took some tentative steps towards her. He stopped within a yard of her as she looked him up and down with an observant expression. "Markus, son of Johnathon," she said finally. "You've really grown..."

He gulped. "You know me? Um... Your Majesty?"

She smiled as if amused. "You must be surprised."

"Uh... I don't even know what is going on uh, your highness. So... yes."

The queen chuckled sweetly. "Please. Call me Elizabetha." It seemed silly to Markus to speak with someone of her status so casually, but he nodded nonetheless. "Slagar was right, you *are* interesting."

"That guy?" Ashlyn asked pointing back towards the doors they came in through.

"Yes, my Court Mage. He sent me a message through telepathy- one of his many traits... He didn't try anything to you, did he? He being a master of the human mind, makes him very… irritable at times. Especially when he hypnotizes my servants into acting like complete fools."

Hypnotism? Telepathy? Now I've heard it all. "Sounds like a charming guy…" Markus muttered sarcastically.

"Oh, he is. But, he has his uses. For example, he was right. You do have power."

"Yes," Black said. "Also, milady, he has received the message. They have awakened."

Markus blinked. Message? "You mean…"

"Yes, Markus," Black said turning to the boy. "We called for you. Your crystal, it spoke to us. He, told us that you were on your way here."

Markus was now even more confused. "What?"

"Damion," Elizabetha then stepped in, looking at Black. "You mean to say that the others have possibly awakened?"

"Yes. Both for the prophecy, and so that he could save his sister." With the clarification from Black, Elizabetha gave Markus a look of condolence.

Markus stiffened at the mention of 'the prophecy', which he wondered if it was the same that Abner spoke of before they left Nineveh.

"I am, truly sorry for Ruth, Markus," she said. Markus hung his head low, not knowing what to say. He felt tears threatening to fall, but he held them back. That was when Markus felt soft fingers touch his chin and raise his head to face Elizabetha who smiled softly. "You were very brave to venture here."

Markus gulped. "Where is 'here?" he asked. "Are we…?"

Elizabetha smiled and released his chin. "Why, you are in Levitika," she said. "The City of Angels."

Mixed feelings of surprise and relief flushed through Markus' head as he shook it. "This is crazy…" He mentally kicked himself for that comment. "I'm sorry."

Elizabetha smiled even more now, amused with his words. "No need. I am not surprised by your disbelief. That just means we have done a good job protecting our city and its citizens."

She held a hand out to a second pair of doors which were obscured behind a pillar. They shifted on gears out of the way to reveal the glass opening. "We have kept the city hidden for over a hundred years, ever since my grandfather, King Pilate, and eventually his son, took the throne." She then started for the opening that Markus noticed had been activated by some lever that Black had pulled near one of the pillars.

He and Ashlyn followed the queen, the Hunter close behind them. Meanwhile, Queen Elizabetha continued saying, "Our city has grown since then, and thus its legends. And now, hopefully," She said as they all stepped outside into the cold day. "We will be able to join the world once again." Very little sun escaped the building clouds above, and so everything beyond the stone parapet was revealed to Markus and Ashlyn.

And what Markus saw before him, simply took his breath away.

Turns out, the castle they were in stood tall in stone layered with white marble; the shingles on the tower roofing and spires shined of stainless bronze, and the castle itself appeared to be taller than all of the surrounding buildings beside the enormous wall that surrounded it. They were not as high up as they would be in Baron Ovid's castle, but it looked so much better and cheerful; like the castles you would read about in a fairy tale.

The buildings that stretched beyond the castle grounds were also made of marble, with flat roofs where Markus saw people walking around on them cooking, gardening, or just enjoying the crisp cool air. The streets were made of cobblestone, but unlike the streets of Nineveh, which were cracked and littered with garbage and bodies, these were clean, well aligned and beautifully crafted. Markus could have sworn there were images and pictures etched in the streets themselves; all spreading out like roots throughout the vast city.

The people of this strange place appeared to be wearing heavy leather clothing and robes made of animal skins to keep warm. No one appeared poor or scared, but Markus noticed they all had guns and swords on their belts, even the children. Despite the beauty of the city, there was a tension in the air; as if all the people he could see were preparing for the worst. Along the massive walls of stone that surrounded the city were many towers and barracks, and between each one and on the roof of the buildings were massive cannons and cross-bolts. It reminded him of Nineveh to see walls so high, and so prepped for war. On top of the towers themselves and even on various spots along the wall, were giant statues of owls carved of what looked like bronze; the dim sunlight caught in their blazing feathers.

But what caught Markus' attention more than all of this, was what was flying above and around the city. There were no Hellhounds, no Firefly

Choppers, and no drones. Instead, what flew across the skies, were men. Men and women, with wings that blazed gold in the sunlight, like the angels of old. When one flew by, Markus' trained eye was able to see that the Eagles Wings on the soldier's back were identical to his own; confirming that this was either where Johnathon got the idea to build his own, or he got the Wings here himself.

This was why Levitika had its fabled nickname. This was what every explorer including Markus' own father saw and described the city as. Angels watched over the floating city and beyond. It was utterly breathtaking, to say the least.

"Wow," Ashlyn said breaking the silence in awe beside him now.

Markus nodded, still *gaping* at the sight. "Yeah, but everyone seems… scared," he said.

"That is because they are," Elizabetha said sadly. "We have hidden in secret high above the world, hiding in the clouds, preparing for war."

"War?" Markus asked looking back towards her.

"How are you able to make the city high in the clouds?" Ashlyn asked. "Are we really floating?"

The queen nodded. "We are, but I don't have time to show you, not yet. I'll explain everything soon."

"But… why?" Markus asked again. "About the war, I mean."

She looked down in deep thought before she raised her head. "I don't know if I should say, yet. You've been through a lot as it is."

"No, please," Markus said. "We've come this far, we have to know. I mean, are we really in the sky right now?"

"All in good time." Black intervened. "Right now, you two have not had a good bath in a long while, and it is only morning. If you would like, you can be given a tour of the city. The castle here will be your home, but you might as well visit the city."

"Really?" Ashlyn asked seeming practically ecstatic.

"Is that really okay?" Markus asked the queen.

"Of course! Please, do not worry about anything Markus. I will explain everything later tonight. Damion, will you take Markus and Ashlyn down into the city?"

"Actually, I'd rather someone else does." the Hunter said. "There are things I have to discuss with you which I should have during the time the boy has been here. Things that cannot be held off any longer."

Elizabetha considered this and nodded to the teens. "Very well. Then my daughter will give you both a tour."

"The princess?" Ashlyn asked. "Are you sure that is safe?"

"There is no safer place in the world for a princess to roam," Black said confidently. "Though, that might be an exaggeration, Levitika is well-guarded and perfectly safe. Our community here is the result of years of hardships and teamwork. The people love our queen, and our princess. Besides, I think you both would like her very much."

"That's very nice of you," Markus said, meaning it. "But... I still have so many questions to ask."

"You may ask tonight." the queen said. "For now, why don't you both go bathe and get fitted into some fresh clothes. My daughter will come for you and show you around the city. I hope you like it and will consider this place home, given all that you have risked coming here."

Markus felt sad once again and hung his head slowly. "Your majesty... about my sister..."

"If it would please you," Elizabetha said. "It would be an honor to give her a proper memorial. We will also follow whatever your heart desires concerning her current state. We do not have burials in Levitika, we usually cremate our dead for we believe it more honorable to become a part of the sky. But if you'd rather we do not do anything or you have something else in mind, please, be sure to let us know."

"That's very kind of you, thank you," Markus said, relieved that Ruth would be taken care of here in this strange place, but he was still weary. "But... with all due respect... can we trust you guys?"

"You can," Elizabetha said. "You have my solemn word."

Markus didn't know if the word of a queen was any different than the word of any common man, but he felt reassured somehow and nodded in thanks and satisfaction.

The queen smiled. "Go, both of you. Bathe and rest for a bit. Your escorts will be outside past those doors. My daughter will take you, and then we will call you again later tonight." she pointed out to where Black had brought the teens. "They will show you the rest of the castle and offer any assistance you need."

"Yes, ma'am." Markus nodded. He was still nervous as to what expect in this place that is apparently in the sky. He hoped that the tour of the city would prove his doubts wrong. But also, he wondered what would come after. There had to be a reason why Black had brought them here, and why the queen was so insistent in waiting to tell him until later.

"Black," the queen then said to the Hunter. "Stay. And come with me."

Black nodded. "As you wish." He rose ready to follow.

"And Markus, Ashlyn?" Elizabetha said before turning her back to Ashlyn and him as he led Black towards the thrones. "Welcome to my home, and my kingdom. I pray that you would find comfort and relief within these walls and rest from the long journey you have begun. I am glad you made it. And as I said, for Ruth, we will have a memorial tonight if you wish."

Markus felt relieved to hear this news. Funerals were uncommon for him, in fact he had never been to one. It was never a thing that truly mattered in the world today. His father being taken away at the time of his death didn't have one either. It was truly a respectable gift from the queen. He wondered if it was her way of apologizing, but pushed the thought from his mind.

"C'mon," Ashlyn said gently nudging Markus' ribs. "We better go bathe. I could certainly use one."

Markus agreed which earned a rougher nudge and the two turned and headed for the exit. As they walked, he leaned in close to his friend. "We better be careful though. They only brought us here for a reason. Whether we are really in Levitika or not, there is a reason why we are here."

"I agree," Ashlyn said thankfully. "But we better not make rash decisions. For now, let's just play along and wait to see how it plays out."

In the depths of his conscious, Markus heard something. It wasn't Abner, but someone closer. Hearing it sent a chill down his spine but he did not react. He did not know if it was just his imagination for what has happened or something that has really come to him. But somewhere in both his mind and heart, he heard Ruth's voice.

You are safe.

Black

After watching Markus and Ashlyn leave the room and now being escorted by their guards, Black turned and continued to follow Elizabetha who was already on the move back towards the thrones. It was when they reached the bottom steps of the two thrones when Elizabetha finally turned to face him.

They looked at each other for the longest of time. Ever since his return to Levitika, he had not gone to see Elizabetha having been kept busy with the two children he had managed to bring here. There was still so much to do, and he could afford to waste no time. Elizabetha knew that too, and was now expecting an excuse for his ignoring her.

Black held everything inside, not showing one hint of emotion for fear of making a mistake. It had been so long since he had seen her, and Elizabetha was just as beautiful as he remembered. He studied the way the queen looked at him as she backtracked towards him, only to slow down and then pick up her pace again. It was as if she was hesitant on deciding what to do; whether to rush for the man or prolong his wait. She finally stopped a good foot in front of Black, who stood a head taller than her, forcing her to look up into his eyes. She bit her lip and raised a petite and pale hand. She gently touched Black's chin, the touch of her fingers sending tendrils of cold sensations through his skin.

They were still as soft as he remembered, and Black exhaled at her touch with the smell of lavender in his nostrils.

"Damion…" the queen lowered her hand, and then all of a sudden came to him. She rested her head against his broad chest, her hands on his shoulders. For now, she wasn't the queen of Levitika, but the frightened child who took up the self-made crown her grandfather made long ago. The same child who looked to Black not as a Hunter, but as Damion for comfort as they both went their separate ways for the good of their country; and the future to which it held.

Black sighed again and wrapped his arms around Elizabetha, pulling her closer to his body. How long had it been since he held her like this? It felt like a lifetime ago. He felt a tear soak through the plates of his armor, so he began to rub her back in comfort. She purred at his touch. For too long, these hands committed nothing but terrible sins for the good of many. It was nice, to use them the way he always wanted them to; to comfort his friend, the only one remaining.

"I've missed you, Damion," she then whispered.

"And I you," Black said closing his eyes as he rested his lower cheek upon Elizabetha's brow. It felt wonderful, being here. Just breathing; being allowed to just, *breathe* with her. It was a relief that no words could ever describe.

"When you could not answer us for months, I began to worry..." Elizabetha could not continue.

Black cleared his throat. "I'm sorry. The Baron was smart. I could not risk compromising you all, or revealing what Markus is. He suspected too much, especially after Johnathon died. The things I had to do to get him off my trail, even for a little while... it was too risky to even attempt to approach Markus, especially with what I had done."

"No one blames you, Damion. John, he... he knew the risks."

"No. The boy blames me." Black corrected the queen. A fatal mistake if done to any other royalty, but Elizabetha was different. So much different than anyone in her family. "Still... it was fate itself that Markus decided to flee Nineveh in search for the kingdom. The Seven have finally awakened... I'm just glad we got here when we could."

"Me too." Elizabetha moved her head back, forcing him to raise his head. Elizabetha then raised her hands and grasped the hood. She gently pulled it back revealing the rest of Black's features. His entire face, not covered by the cowl, and his long black hair which hung down his back nearly as long as hers. She then cupped his cheeks in her soft, soft hands, and raised herself on her toes to kiss him.

With her mouth on his, the whole world began to disappear around Black. The taste of her mouth was as intoxicating as any wine, removing the cold reality of the world leaving only him and her. The memories of the horrible things he had done were washed away with the scent of her perfume and the taste of the kiss. Everything he had become, it didn't matter anymore. When they parted, Black sighed with a small smile, the first sign of happiness he had given for nearly ten years.

"I'm sorry," he said lowering his eyes. "I'm sorry."

"You did what you had to," Elizabetha said letting her hands drop back to his shoulders. "Will you be able to help Markus?"

"Not as much as I would like," he said honestly. "However, with the basics he already discovered, he still might be useful. I think we should move with the plan."

"It is too soon though..."

"I know. But Baron Ovid will be searching for us. He had sent Hunters after us, they might even know where we are now."

Elizabetha's expression turned grave. "We have even less time than I thought…"

"What will we tell the boy?"

"The truth. What else can we do?"

"Nothing. It has to be done. I don't want it to be so, he has been through too much. But… it cannot be helped."

"Do you think it will work? Do you think… that it is time?"

"It has to be."

"Okay." she looked down as if studying his armor before looking back up. "Be honest with me, Damion."

"Yes, milady?"

"Do you think we are ready? Do we have a chance against Ovid? And The Capitol?"

"I think so." he lied. The truth was, he did not know for sure.

"Okay. And the Hunters?"

"We will deal with them. One of them is a witch. I cannot sense her, however, so I believe we are safe. Don't worry. I will handle her. I won't let her get to you, *or* Markus. We *will* make it out of here alive." That was the truth. He planned to see this through until his last breath. "Then maybe, just maybe, Markus will feel ready to fulfill his role."

"Okay." Elizabetha nodded before resting her head back into Black's chest. "I'm so scared. Only you bring me comfort."

"And you for me," Black said which was also the truth. "Every day that passed I thought of you. Sending you all the message about Johnathon scared me. Every night The Eldest haunted me while The Baron watched. But I had to endure it, for Markus' safety; as well as yours."

Elizabetha smiled. "I understand… You always keep your promises."

Feeling guilty at that, Black rested his head upon hers, holding her tight in hopes that all of his fear would run as her overwhelming love swam through him. "Always." He then looked at her. "Why did you want me to lie to him? About calling him, I mean. I heard what you were thinking."

Elizabetha pursed her lips as if she was ashamed. "What else can we really tell him? The truth? There is so much he doesn't know, so much he still won't understand even if we try to tell him everything. Besides…" She trailed off, thinking about the past that has defined the present.

Black understood. But that didn't mean he agreed with it.

"Soon, we'll tell him everything, and the whole truth." Elizabeth continued. "But not now. It is best that he is given the simple answer first. I am sure what he has heard already is more than enough, considering all that he's gone through already."

"I understand," he said. "I will not question you then." She was in charge of all of this; she was the queen, and the one who had to use Markus as much as Markus had to use her. Black was just a Bounty Hunter, made to work in the shadows as he always had.

"Thank you," Elizabetha said. She fell silent for a moment, and then she said, "Tonight." she said and then a second time. "Tonight."

"Is that an order, Your Highness?"

"Yes."

Black allowed himself another smile. "I will be there."

"Now," Elizabetha said back to business. "Tell me what you know. What have you learned, my Hunter?"

~ The Princess of the Sky ~

Ashlyn

It occurred to Ashlyn when she and Mark had parted for their bathing just how early it really was.

It was nearly ten in the morning and she now laid in a large porcelain tub full of the warmest water she ever bathed in, as well as being surrounded by mountains of bubbles. She had never seen a tub this large, let alone full of such warm water that seemed to soak all the chills from her body. All of her life she struggled to find clean water just to drink, even when her family was around; before her father joined The Guard promising a better life. Even now as she soaked in the suds and looking around the large tiled bathroom, she thought of what her little sister would have given to see a place like this.

She laid her head back against the little headrest. This was supposedly the princess' bathroom, and she was to use it until her own room was finished being prepared. Markus' was prepared already, and he was already being cared for while Ashlyn sat alone in the princess' tub whom she had not yet met. The girl had a nice place. The tiled floor and walls were a hexagonal pattern of white and gold. The large marble countertop with a basin and mirror was nearly as large as herself, and another Guardian Owl was perched on top of the mirror. The princess truly was lucky to have been born into royalty.

Ashlyn wondered where the princess was anyway.

It was funny, Ashlyn thought; feeling relaxed and easy. Not having to worry who's here or who's watching. Just yesterday, she woke up from her sleep in the sickroom where Markus was still asleep from his terrible injuries. She had stayed by his side the entire time, with Black occasionally in the room. At first she was wary of the Hunter, but eventually, when he talked to her, she felt more at ease around him. The fact that he told her that he had brought them to Levitika made it a little easier to trust him as well, despite all they had gone through. It especially made it tougher when Markus finally awakened, and he had to be reminded as to what had happened.

But they really were here now. She was in a warm bath, in a magnificent castle in the legendary City of Angels. Here, Ashlyn felt safe; and knowing that Markus was doing what she was doing in another bathroom not far from her put her more at ease. They had both made it. They were safe.

…Almost all of them.

What was going through her friend's mind? Was Markus really going to be okay? Knowing the feeling of loss herself, Ashlyn knew that it would be a long time for Markus to even get close to the term 'used to it'. You never truly got over the death of someone you loved. You just… dealt with it.

What a terrible thing to think about… Ashlyn slid down and let her whole head submerge beneath the waters as she ran her fingers through her hair. The roaring of her blood and the beating of her heart passed through the waters, drowning the depressing thoughts in her head.

Was he okay? What would she say next time she saw him? She replayed different scenarios in her head, making sure if Markus was to ask and say anything remotely close to what she thought she could answer or comfort him if need be without too much hesitation. She had to be there for him, just as she had once needed someone to be there for her.

She had no one to talk to when she lost her family to her father… to Veegar. Then there was Markus who lost everything just as they made it to the Forbidden City. But she wanted to be there for him nonetheless. He saved her life many times already; the very least she could do was be there for him.

… I want to be there for him.

When she broke the surface, she ran the water out of her hair before stepping out of the tub. The cold tiles felt nice against her feet. It was strange and unreal, but it felt nice. She reached for a towel that hung on the wall rack and began to dry herself off.

It was then when she noticed her clothes on the counter- or what looked like her clothes. She walked over with the towel wrapped around her and studied the pile before her. They *were* her clothes, but something was different about them.

All the holes and tears in her faded jeans had been sewed up with elegant stitching. Her shirt was cleaned and stainless despite years of constant use. Her shoes were gone and replaced with a new pair of fresh black boots. All that was missing was her coat, which was nowhere to be found. She looked at the pile questionably.

Did someone come in here? How long was I under the water? She looked towards the bathroom door. The thought that someone had slipped in without her knowing disturbed her. She eventually shrugged and proceeded to dry herself off. As she did so, she saw just how skinny she was; just how pitiful she looked beneath the many clothes she wore just to keep warm back in Nineveh. Looking at her stomach, her legs, her breasts, she wondered just what exactly was holding herself together.

I look so thin... Shrugging off her thoughts, Ashlyn tied her hair into a ponytail and slipped on her clean clothes. The boots fit snuggly, and she was content after walking around in them for a bit.

The only thing she would complain about if she could was that her pockets were empty. The contents she had inside had been removed, probably because it was forbidden or whatever reason. Regardless, Ashlyn knew she wasn't going to get her things back. She was slightly disappointed, especially with all that has happened, but there was nothing she could do now.

She'd just have to live without it for the time being.

She then exited the bathroom, towel in hand only to stop in the realization that someone was waiting for her outside.

Her visitor was a young girl about her age. She wore a skirt of white and blue, and her hair tied into a braid which ran down her back to her waist. Her feet were bare and were just as pale as her face and arms. She looked like a small doll, with a small nose and almond eyes etched with very little makeup. Her smile was warm and welcoming but at the same time nervous as if she was shy. In her hands, she held a small brown burlap as she sat waiting on a chair against the wall.

"Hello," she said in a pleasantly soft voice.

"Hi," Ashlyn replied nervously.

The girl nodded, standing up in place. "I'm sorry if I surprised you. I'm Esmerelda. Daughter of Elizabetha."

With widening eyes Ashlyn realized who this girl was and quickly made a stiff attempt to bow, practically falling over in the process. "Your majesty," she said.

Esmerelda chuckled at that. Her voice was as soft as a songbird. "Oh please, the 'majesty' is my mother. You can just call me Esmerelda." She stopped laughing, but the smile of amusement remained. "I don't really like being called princess or anything like that either, to be honest with you."

"Oh," Ashlyn said after standing back up again. "Okay..."

"I hope my boots fit you okay?"

"These are yours?"

The princess nodded. "They didn't fit me, so I wanted to give them to you. I also stitched up your clothes." She turned red. "Sorry, I didn't knock."

"I didn't even know you came in." Ashlyn chuckled while at the same time feeling nervous that the princess had snuck in. *She sure doesn't act like one...*

Esmerelda shrugged. "I'm told I'm quiet." She held out the small bag she held in her hands towards Ashlyn who looked at it with a cocked eyebrow. "These are your pajamas and a robe," the princess explained. "I also snuck some candy treats inside," she added in a whisper.

"Oh," Ashlyn said taking the bag. "Thank you. For, er, letting me use your tub as well."

"You are welcome." Esmerelda seemed to relax as her small smile grew a little bit brighter. "We didn't have time to prepare the second room, so I offered. I figured it was the least I could do since I haven't gotten to visit you earlier. I was busy with something. If you want, I'll show you to your room if you would like? It's all ready, and I sent your guard to just wait by your door."

"What should I do with this?" Ashlyn asked gesturing her soaking towel.

"Leave it on the floor back in there." She pointed back toward the bathroom. "I'll take care of it when I bathe."

Ashlyn blinked. "You sure?"

"Yes," Esmerelda reassured.

"Okay," Ashlyn said uneasily throwing the towel over her shoulder. The princess began to walk out of the room, so Ashlyn followed close behind.

Definitely not like they are described in the stories... "You have a wonderful place here," she said.

"Thank you." The princess smiled. "I like it here, but I prefer to be in my room where my studies are. I like to read and paint."

"You read?" Ashlyn asked as they entered the empty hallway, the torches of green fire lighting up their faces in a ghoulish glow.

"I *love* reading," Esmerelda said brightening up a little more. "It's amazing how much history and stories have disappeared beneath the rubble after the Great War. It took people *years* to find even a small fraction of it. Some of the stories go back nearly as early as the planets first thousand years. Fairy tales, unlike anything told today- they are incredible! It's funny, the combination of words to make such beautiful sentences and create worlds beyond our imagination. 'An author is just a painter who uses words instead of paint to give us a picture'. That's what I always say!"

Ashlyn could not help but stare in fascination of the excitement and passion beaming from this girl. "That's well put," she said thinking of just how different their worlds really were.

"Do you like to read?" Esmerelda said looking at her.

For a few seconds the only sound was the two girls' feet striking the stone floor with each step, their steps echoing throughout the chambers. Eventually, Ashlyn muttered, "I can't read."

"What?" Esmerelda said clearly shocked. "No way!"

"Well... I can pick up a few words but... I can't read. In fact, I never read a book before."

The princess' jaw dropped so low that Ashlyn thought it might fall right off. "Oh, wow," Esmerelda said falling back into silence. Then, "*That* is unacceptable. It's something we need to remedy. Well then, I can teach you." She said with a big grin on her face.

"Really?"

"Yeah," she said, nodding with an enthusiastic smile. "It'll be fun."

"Great," Ashlyn smiled. The thought of learning to read... felt exhilarating. "Thank you."

"I just, I can't *believe* your mother never taught you," Esmerelda said stopping at a large door where Ashlyn's guard now stood.

"My mother never really had the chance back in Nineveh," Ashlyn said.

"Is she still there?"

"No." Ashlyn shook her head.

Esmerelda pursed her lips in understanding before speaking again. "I'm sorry."

"Not your fault."

"Still. Can you tell me what happened?"

"It's kind of a long story..."

"We got time." Esmerelda reasoned. "If you don't want to you don't have to."

Ashlyn nodded after thinking for a moment. "Alright."

When it became clear Ashlyn had no intention of talking just yet, Esmerelda said, "Come on," while pushing open a door to a bedroom. "Let me show you your room, and then you can tell me all about it before I go to see Markus." She led Ashlyn inside still talking. "My mother would be furious if I didn't visit all the guests."

"Can't forget Markus," Ashlyn chuckled pulling the door closed behind her. It was strange she thought, that the princess knew who Markus was as well. *Though not surprising, since everyone seems to know who he is.* She then turned and then gasped aloud as she took in what was now her bedroom.

For a good chunk of her life, Ashlyn had been living on the streets; lucky enough to find an empty dumpster to sleep in. Every once in a while she'd stumble upon a bar or restaurant; whatever would allow her to stay for a single night, or she'd find a stable and sleep in the straw with the horses. After she left Nineveh with Markus and Ruth, she slept in a thermal bag out in the cold. In truth, she had never slept in a real bed before, and the one before her nearly brought her to tears of joy.

The bed sat against the back wall; nearly ten feet wide and twice as long. It looked to be meant for a king rather than some street rat. The sheets were white as snow, with a thick blanket of fur tucked at the end. Pillows of red were piled high against the headboard of oak, the ends carved into owl heads. A nightstand stood on either side of the massive bed; white wood shelving with a little drawer near the top and an elegant lamp sat on each.

The floors were of glazed wood, the same material as the walls which were windowless. Bookcases lined the walls, filled to the very top with so much literature it would probably make a librarian jealous. A wooden desk sat between two shelves to Ashlyn's right, the chair in front made of gold and red upholstery. In the mirror above the desk where a small terminal sat upon it, Ashlyn was able to see her reflection once again.

It occurred to Ashlyn that she really hadn't looked at herself. Back in the bathroom, all she saw was how thin and frail her body appeared. The Ashlyn she was able to see now, appeared more than just that. The Ashlyn looking back at her was obviously terribly thin, but at the same time appearing almost brand-new since her cleaning. The ragged mess of hair was gone, replaced with shiny clean strands. Her skin was no longer dark from dirt and soot, but now laid pale; white as snow. Her eyes were the same, however; sharp, alert, ready for danger.

The Ashlyn in the mirror was… pretty. Not beautiful like the noblewomen or the ladies in the Baron's castle, but cute. She looked like a normal teenager depicted in the old stories and posters of the world before the fallout. She looked… She could not describe the word.

Different was close, but the word simply didn't do justice for what Ashlyn saw.

She sighed and turned to Esmerelda who sat on the foot of the bed. "I look like a young lady, almost like a kid," she said.

"Well, you are," Esmerelda said with a smile. "And a pretty one to boot."

"Never really cared for that," Ashlyn explained blushing suddenly. "Never had much reason to. It's… surreal really."

Esmerelda smiled. "Well, the girls in the city would definitely be jealous of you."

Ashlyn looked at the princess. "Jealous?"

"Of course."

That made her laugh. "No way…." Ashlyn said walking towards the bed. A moment ago, she had thought she looked pretty now, but, "I don't think I'd go far enough to think *that* at least."

"Well, there are some things I can teach you. Then maybe you can see what I am seeing." When Ashlyn inquired what she meant, Esmerelda said, "You'll see some other day. Right now, I'm more interested in your story."

Ashlyn grinned uneasily. "Oookay."

"Great." Esmerelda turned her body, so she faced Ashlyn. "So, tell me your life story. And then we'll go see Markus."

"Well, what's your story?" Ashlyn said feeling she might already know what it is.

"Not nearly as exciting as your story obviously." Esmerelda chuckled. "Besides, I asked you first."

Markus

While he was in the bath during the time that the guards were preparing 'his bedroom,' Markus had a lot of time to think and mull over on what he had heard earlier.

Everything that has happened prior and during their arrival in Levitika, seemed shrouded almost. The prophecy the voice- Abner -had mentioned concerning him, the fate of Ruth, and what has happened in meeting the queen which would undoubtedly reveal more; it all began to feel overwhelming. Like a massive wave accumulating in the sea before it crashes into the shore. Markus felt as if what he would learn tonight would be so much more than he could afford to bargain for.

They aren't telling me anything yet for a reason…

When he was done washing and was able to get dry, he dressed into his old clothes that had been washed and prepped. As he did so, he went over everything that had happened all over into something along the lines of 'conclusions'.

Keeper of the Gate…

He froze. *Abner?*

He studied his dagger that sat on the bathroom countertop where the voice of Abner had infiltrated Markus' mind as well as his reflection in the gem as he reached for it and upon grabbing it, turned it over.

"Are you there, still?" he asked, but the voice had fallen silent. "Please, if you have any wisdom at all, I need it now. You were there in the Wastelands, you have to be here now. Am I… Are we safe here?"

Nothing. Not even a hint.

Angry, Markus smacked the dagger back onto the counter and began to vigorously dry himself. "Fine. Whatever."

He carried his boots and used a towel as he walked alongside his guard, Mel, who said nothing as he led him to a set of doors at the end of the castle hallway. It was similar to the door across from it, and Mel nodded as he stood at attention beside it.

"If you need anything, I will be out here," he said in a bored tone.

"Thanks," Markus muttered as he pushed the doors open and stepped inside, closing away Mel and leaving him alone inside to take in the bedroom they had prepared for him.

It was an elegant and beautiful room with a massive bed and walls that seemed to be made entirely of bookcases filled with mountains of books and scrolls. Markus sat his boots down near the door and hung his towel on a little hook by the small desk to his left. He walked over to the bed and stared at it before he turned around and plopped down on the edge before letting himself collapse onto his back. He practically *sunk* into the fur blankets. It felt like he had landed upon a soft cloud. He stared at the ceiling a good long while his head continued to swim deep in thought.

How was he going to do this?

A knock on his door broke Markus from his thoughts. Grateful for some sort of distraction and hoping that it was Ashlyn, he sat up and groaned as his resting back protested in doing so. "Come in."

The door opened, and Markus was shocked to see not Ashlyn, but a beautiful young girl stepping inside. Her raven hair was tied in a braid, her skirt of white and blue flashed in the dim lamplight, and her face was pale like the moon. Her almond-shaped eyes were what gave her away, for the deep green of them reminded Markus of someone else.

He immediately stood up and did a lousy-attempt to bow. "Your majesty."

The girl laughed. "I already told Ashlyn, and so I'll tell you," she said in a sweet songbird-tone of a voice. "You don't have to call me that. The 'majesty' is my mother."

Markus stood straight up, embarrassed. "I'm sorry."

"Don't be, it happens." the princess walked over to Markus and bowed her head. "I'm Esmerelda. Queen Elizabetha's daughter, but you obviously already guessed that."

Markus nodded. "I could… I could see the resemblance."

"I sure hope not." Esmerelda smiled letting him know she was joking. "But, thank you."

"Uh, yeah, you're welcome."

"So," she peered at Markus as if he was the most interesting specimen she has yet come across. She eyed him up and down, her eyes taking everything in and leaving him feeling exposed and uncomfortable. "You are Markus, the son of Johnathon?"

"Uh… yes?" Markus finally said mentally kicking himself for how stupid the answer sounded. "You knew my father?"

"I've *heard* of him," she answered. "I've never met him before, but I know a lot about him. I have also heard about you, and of your travels to get here. All that you and your group had been through. That was all very brave of you to go out into the Wastelands." She shifted one foot over the other. "I heard about your sister, Ruth... In fact, I was the one who left the flowers by her coffin. I'm really sorry."

Markus felt his heart grow heavy again and he swallowed the lump that had formed in his throat as he replied, "Thank you. The flowers were kind."

She nodded back. "I know what it's like to lose a sibling. My brother was lost at childbirth."

"Oh... I'm sorry." *The commonalities never seem to cease...*

"Me too." she looked over at the desk in thought. "Sometimes I think it was better than growing up in a world like this, but at the same time, what I would give to have a little brother, you know?"

Markus *did* know. In fact, he understood completely now. He always wondered if Ruth was enjoying herself, far away from this world up in the heavens. He had even thought if it would have been easier on her, having she never being born in the first place. But such a thought was depressing and made him terribly guilty. He really didn't know what he truly had, until she was gone.

He finally answered, "I know."

The princess returned her attention back to his eyes. She looked like she was thinking hard about what to say next. Not wanting it to become awkward, Markus decided to pick back up the conversation.

"So... uh... What can I do for you?" he hoped it did not sound rude when he asked.

"Actually, it is what *I* could do for *you*," Esmerelda said looking away suddenly. "I'm sorry for just staring, I just heard so much about you. Almost my entire life."

"You did?" Markus thought it was a little strange, and his suspicions began to rise again.

"Oh yes. Since I knew you were coming. And... sorry, that makes you uncomfortable, doesn't it?"

"No, no... not at all." he lied.

"Okay," Esmerelda said this as if she could see right through him but didn't want to put him on the spot. "Anyways, I wanted to welcome you here to the city, and if you need anything that you don't want the guards to help with, I'm not far from where you and Ashlyn are."

"Thank you." Markus nodded gratefully.

"So, I am giving you and Ashlyn a tour of the city, yes?"

"You've met Ashlyn already?"

Esmerelda blinked. "Yeah, already did. She's a very nice girl."

"Yeah, she is." Markus agreed.

"I'm excited to show you around. And… I hope that we become the best of friends."

"Aren't… princesses supposed to be only friends with… y'know, royalty?"

Esmerelda laughed at that. The rich and soft laughter made Markus' heart skip a beat a bit and was relieved and yet also disappointed when the laughter stopped. "I can be friends with whoever I please. Besides, I think you and Ashlyn are very cool people, and I want to learn more about you. I'm sure everything here is so overwhelming, and I hope to somehow relieve some of that."

Markus smiled, genuinely appreciated of what this strange princess was offering. "Thank you very much."

She smiled a simple, shy, but cute smile. "Anytime." she began to play with her skirt before she spoke again. "I should probably go. Ashlyn wants to talk to you before we go." She reached into her pocket and pulled out a small radio with a dial that fit snugly into her crafted palm. "These radios are linked to the entire castle. You and Ashlyn are on channel two. The queen on one." She handed it to Markus while she continued. "Four is the guards, five is the emergency siren. And six is me if you ever need anything you don't want anyone else to know." She gave him a wink at that.

"Thank you," Markus said meaning it. "I'll make good use of this." He wondered what three was for, but he figured she would have told him if he was supposed to know.

"Good." she nodded. "Well," She did a small courtesy bow to him. "It's an honor to meet you, at last, Markus."

At last?... "You too, Esmerelda."

Esmerelda smiled. "Like I said, if you need anything, I'm just a call away."

I nodded. "Thank you, again."

She smiled as she turned to leave. She said something to someone outside the door before exiting and in her place came in Ashlyn who Markus did not recognize at first.

"You're clean." he finally said.

She stuck her tongue out at him. "I feel like a new girl," Ashlyn said with a grin. Her hair was straightened and gone were the dirt stains on her neck and hands.

"Me too. Oh! Uh, I mean," *Well that was dumb of me.* "But a new *man*."

Ashlyn laughed as she took a seat beside him. She studied the room with a curious eye. "Looks like my room... except for the window."

"No kidding?"

"Yeah." she nodded. She then looked at him, those dark eyes watching him closely.

"What?" he asked.

"What do you think?"

"About what?"

Ashlyn waved her hand. "Everything. This place so far, the people, the queen, and princess, Black... You know, *everything*." She shrugged.

"That's a big list," he muttered.

"We got a little time."

Despite the princess waiting for us outside, Markus thought while saying, "It seems alright, I guess."

"Really?" Ashlyn asked this with a raised eyebrow.

Markus scratched his head in the careful thought of how to explain. "Well, I feel like we are safe here, for now."

"Are you worried about the queen and how close Black seems to be to her?"

"Well that, and I don't know what to think just yet. I'm hoping some fresh air will clear my head and that we can get some answers later tonight."

"What do you mean?"

"The way the queen was *studying* me. And that princess? I mean, she seemed okay, reasonable, but... like everyone else thus far, I don't trust them."

Ashlyn nodded. "I see. Well, we'll just have to be careful. I kind of agree with you. To be honest, I feel safe here, like I don't have to look over my shoulder anymore."

"And the actual bed."

Ashlyn smiled. "That too. But seriously. I meant what I said when I said I'd follow you anywhere and believed in you. No matter how bizarre it all sounds, considering your suspicion that we are just being used. We don't wanna tread too deep in unknown waters."

Markus shrugged. "Well, we already seem kinda neck-deep as it is. We're already here."

"I guess we better learn to start swimming."

He smiled. "Alright."

Ashlyn nodded, twiddling her thumbs as she glanced towards the small clock sitting on the desktop. "We should probably go. Come on." She grabbed his hand and pulled him up off the bed. "I got your back."

Markus didn't even need to ask if she meant it or not. "And I got yours."

She nodded. "Let's do it."

~ The City of Angels ~

Markus

Markus had to admit: he was impressed.

Upon leading him and Ashlyn downstairs and out the main entrance to the castle, Esmerelda took them into a large clearing which spider-webbed into the streets of Levitika which were full of life and amazing effulgence. Esmerelda led them down a central path through the forest of marble buildings, and now that they were in a more populated area, the two newcomers of the city got to see the entire culture unseen by the rest of the world.

People flocked the streets dressed in many varieties of clothing that both Markus and Ashlyn never thought possible. The crisp cold air kept everyone in winter attire, but the varieties of fur, wool, polyester, and leather showed just how unique everyone can present themselves. The roads of polished cobblestone were lined with numerous shops, bakeries, bustling trading carts, and among them either above or in-between, homes of the owners. The buildings of marble stood tall over the three despite being overshadowed by the great wall surrounding them and the castle behind them. Around the buildings themselves were planted trees of pine and birch, bringing forth the wonderful scent of bark and sap amidst baked and grilled goods and other aromas.

What intrigued Markus was how the people around them behaved. They did not appear afraid as Markus had originally thought back in the castle, just cautious, and many were visibly armed. Men and women, both human and mutant or otherwise, many kept different varieties of weapons close and visible.

If they were in Nineveh, anyone caught with open-carry be it gun or sword, they would be shot on the spot. Which also pointed out to Markus the lack of foot soldiers or guards in the streets of Nineveh, and he asked the princess about that.

"Most of the 'royal' guard or soldiers man the castle and the walls," Esmerelda explained. "Everyone here is trained in weaponry. In other words, the whole kingdom is practically a large military base with everyone encouraged to train with weaponry- save for the children and those unable to fight."

"Are people *required* to train?" Ashlyn asked.

"No, though they are recommended to do so. Those who'd rather not train and fight are usually trained to become nurses or work as scavengers; taking hovercraft down to the surface in order to obtain different minerals and necessities. Since we are always so high up in the sky, we still need basic necessities from the rest of the region."

"Isn't that risky?" Markus asked.

"It is," Esmerelda admitted. "But that is why we have many brave men and women willing to do what is necessary for the good of their community."

"Everyone works together, huh?" Ashlyn asked as they passed by a tavern where some men were looking over and pointing towards Esmerelda.

"We try our best, anyway," Esmerelda said with a smile.

The princess turned out to be very popular among the people of Levitika. She was kind to every person the trio would come across; always asking many personal questions and calling them by name. She got along so well with everyone that Markus was impressed by how kind she was and how the people, in turn, seemed to respect her. It made it even more difficult to believe that Esmerelda was like a real princess. Though everyone called her 'your highness' or 'princess,' they all spoke to one another like a good neighbor.

It amazed him more that there was no one really *guarding* Esmerelda. In fact, there didn't appear to be any concern of anyone coming to try and attack her or anything. The princess just didn't seem to be worried at all. Without a care in the world, she greeted every single person with a smile, and in turn, she received even more.

He asked her how she knew so many people and she simply answered, "I just like talking to people."

I never would have guessed. Markus thought, remembering how shy Esmerelda was at first. But then again, she and Ashlyn seemed to have hit it off exceedingly well. By watching the girls point out different outfits within the windows of shops and laughing together, he knew they had become really good friends.

He was happy for Ashlyn. He was glad that in the end, she was able to come here.

The thought made him wonder if Esmerelda and Ruth would have gotten along well together.

Some kids younger than the group were playing next to an old bakery. All were boys except for one girl, throwing a frisbee between one another and wrestling one another to get the toy. It was amusing to watch the girl overpower one of the boys in a struggle to take the frisbee away.

Unlike the kids in Nineveh, they were clean and looked very healthy. Not one of them looked to be scrawny or had any sign of malnutrition in the slightest; and when they smiled, Markus could clearly see all of their teeth, shiny and white. It made him worry about his own teeth, and he began to run his tongue across them as if to make sure they were still there. He only brushed as often as he could with baking soda but never quite enough considering the living conditions back home.

He looked at Ashlyn who had gone to meet the girl who had the same color hair like her. Ashlyn's smile wasn't perfect by any means with some crooked bits and gaps, but they appeared clean. Markus kept his mouth closed subconsciously in fear that they weren't completely healthy. He would have to start a habit of brushing as long as he was here in Levitika.

The girl said something to Ashlyn, and she laughed while patting the girl's head. The girl responded by grabbing ahold of Ashlyn's hair and pulling on it. Esmerelda freaked out and started trying to help Ashlyn pry the little girl off, but Markus merely laughed at the sight.

"I am so sorry!" Esmerelda said as she led them away.

"It's fine!" Ashlyn said with a hearty laugh. "Reminded me of when I had a little sister to play with each other's hair."

"That's so sweet," Esmerelda said with relief. They passed by a stand serving some sort of meat and vegetable on a stick, and Markus' stomach growled loud enough for the girls to hear. After laughing at him, Esmerelda suggested they stopped for lunch and something to warm them up.

Markus, who was red in the cheeks, said that it sounded like a great idea.

They eventually stopped at a makeshift coffee stand where Esmerelda got her friends a chocolaty hot drink with a hint of mint that Markus was able to taste after his first sip. Esmerelda also asked for a few small loaves of black bread and butter to go with it.

"We don't want to eat too much," she said. "I don't want to spoil dinner for you two."

"Don't worry about me," Ashlyn said sipping at her chocolate drink. Markus who was hungry and yet not, picked at his bread while staring at the vendor.

The man was large and husky, with pale white skin and sausage-shaped fingers. He was bald which was covered under a flat leather cap. He looked the three over with his three eyes with the one in the middle of his forehead focusing on Markus entirely as he asked he and Ashlyn where they were from.

"Nineveh," Ashlyn said licking her lips that had the residue of her drink upon them.

"Ah, Nineveh." The vendor said resting his chin on his hand. His two normal eyes closed as if he remembered something, while his third eye continued to blink at Markus creepily. "That's where Johnathon went, eh?"

"That's right," Esmerelda said almost stiffly.

"You knew my father?" Markus asked suddenly interested. He was eager to know how his father had a connection here. If he was really an adventurer, one that even Esmerelda remembered, maybe he could learn a little after all.

"Your father?" the vendor said scratching his bald head. His middle eye suddenly went wide as if he realized something. "Oh yeah! You're that Markus boy."

"You know me?"

"Half the city does."

That didn't sit well with Markus at all. He looked to Esmerelda who told the three-eyed mutant that Markus 'was not who he thought he was.'

"Whatever ya say." the man said with a dismissive wave that was absolutely rude. He then turned back to Markus. "But yeah, I knew your father, Johnny-Boy I called him. Would come down here once in a while for a beer or two, eh." He stuck his fat hand towards Markus. "Name's Vic. I own half the shops in this part o' town."

Markus shook his hand, which was sweaty and big enough to swallow his own. He caught the distinct and familiar stench of Buckweed off the man's person. The last time he had smelled such a thing was back in Nineveh with the bums outside the Drunken Badrat.

… No, much sooner than that, he thought. He couldn't place the time of last time he smelt the drug, but it was thick on the man who finally released his hand.

"Charmed," he answered. He then caught a warning look from Esmerelda and caught the message. "Sir." he corrected himself. "Were you two buddies?"

"Somethin' like that," the man said giggling. Markus couldn't help but noticed each of his teeth had a gap between each one. "Good man, he was. A punk at times, but a good man. Used to race in the skies, we did. Build weapons and go hunting as well. I own the bakery over yonder, as well as my own shop."

"What are you doing here then?" Ashlyn asked.

"Helping a buddy who is… out of town." the man said with a grin. A clear message even without words: none of their business.

"Was my father good?" Markus asked. "At flying I mean."

"Oh yeah, lost a lot of money to him, I did. Had to pay him back by fixing some of his toys. He was a good pilot, shame the punk is gone."

"Thank you, sir," Markus grumbled as he raised his cup to him. "And for the hot chocolate."

"Anytime." the man said giving Markus an almost hungry grin. "You ever need somthin', you come to see ol' Uncle V. The queen loves me services, just like yer daddy. It'd be an honor to help his son. Wonder if you'll end up just like him in the future." He said it as if he was simply rubbing something into Markus' face and wasn't willing to explain his subtext.

Needless to say, Markus was relieved when Esmerelda suggested they continue the tour of the city. The three walked for a bit, and once they were out of earshot, Markus spoke.

"What the hell is his problem?"

The princess pursed her lips. "Vic is a kind of guy who gets in deep with the wrong kind of people," Esmerelda replied drinking the last of her drink before tossing it in the nearest trash. "He gets into other peoples' business and such."

"What kinda people?" Ashlyn said still babying her cup.

"I have a better question," Markus said stopping and forcing the girls to stop with him. "What Vic said, about me."

"Oh," Esmerelda said scratching the back of her neck. *"That."*

"Esmerelda," Ashlyn said intervening before Markus could even get a word in. "Does Levitika know about Markus?"

Esmerelda hesitated and looked away distractedly.

"Your Highness?" Markus attempted, succeeding in grabbing the princess's attention.

"I'm not supposed to say," she said. "My mom was supposed to explain."

"Explain what exactly?" Markus asked. "Did my father… do something here?"

"He did, yes, but nothing bad. Far from that… in most cases or so I've been told. All I know is… that you're pretty important."

"How so?"

Esmerelda thought about it for a moment and then shook her head. "Not here. Come on. I want to show you my favorite part of the city, where we might have a chance to talk. I can only say so much, however, so don't quote me on anything, okay?"

But it was too late for that. Markus was already quoting. A lot. Nevertheless, he and Ashlyn followed Esmerelda who appeared to be heading for the city walls, where a large break in it stood a large tower. At the base of it was a doorway with a spiraled staircase. After getting permission from the guard on duty, Esmerelda led the two up the staircase. They climbed what felt like forever until they made it to the top where Markus started to feel even more light-headed than he did before.

His discomfort was immediately quelled by the sight before him.

Beyond the wall, was just a vast landscape miles beneath them. Clouds floated between the island and the world below. Hidden in said clouds, the island of Levitika revealed the entire region to the north of the Northern Wastelands where the Razorback Mountains curled and contained The Capitol beyond. He saw thin frozen streams and hills, and to the east, he saw where the mountains curled and deteriorated before reaching the Southern Sands south of the region.

"Wow…" Ashlyn said peering over the parapet of the wall to look straight down. We're so high up…"

"How is this possible?" Markus asked out of breath both in terms of oxygen and in awe.

"That, I can show you later," Esmerelda said, turning so that her back was against the parapet with her arms crossed. She looked at Markus more seriously, and he could see a little of Queen Elizabetha in her. "So."

"So…" Markus said uneasily. The view alone took the wind right out of his sails, and he didn't know where to start.

"Esmerelda," Ashlyn said stepping up and taking over. "What do you know about Markus?"

"Aside from what I have heard?"

"That and if there is more, then yes."

Esmerelda thought about it for a second. "I heard that the patrols got summoned. That they had found Damion Black, one of our own."

"Wait," Markus spoke up. "Black was with you guys? This whole time?"

"Have been since the beginning. Our own… personal Hunter, as it were."

"Why was he in Nineveh then?"

"Not sure. Probably to keep an eye on your father, Johnathon, the one who found us first." Even as she said it, it didn't sound like Esmerelda was telling the whole truth. The way she kept averting her eyes and looking at the clouds that passed by gave Markus and Ashlyn both the hint.

"He was hired to hunt us down after we fled the city," Markus told her.

"Ashlyn told me a little about that," Esmerelda said. "It all sounded terrifying."

"It was. But the point is, he was hired by the Baron along with a few others to track us down. In the end, though, he brought us here. Why?"

"You were in need," Esmerelda said uneasily simply. "We help those in need. Those who scavenge around the surface look for many who are in need. Many of the citizens here are from the surface and have been here ever since."

"So why do Ashlyn and I get the special treatment?" Markus inquired shrewdly. "With all due respect and though we are thankful for your mother's hospitality, I doubt that any of your other rescues were welcomed just as kindly."

"Maybe it was because the Hunter was with you." Esmerelda shrugged.

"Esmerelda," Ashlyn said cautiously. "Are you sure that is why?"

"Why would there be any other reason?"

"Because you practically told Vic to shut up," Markus said. "Told him about I am not who he thought I was. Everyone looks at me like I'm something special at the castle, your own mother included, but then when we get recognized like with Vic, who knew my own father, you were quick to shut it down. Then when we ask, you are avoiding the question. No one is telling us the whole truth, not even you."

Esmerelda looked pained at this, but she didn't say anything. Not even Ashlyn, who looked at Markus as if he was being harsh, and maybe he was. But he wanted answers and not be looked at like he was some ancient artifact.

"There's something else too," he said a little more carefully. "Something I've been wanting to ask since I met your mother. Do you… do you know about a prophecy of some sort?"

Markus removed his dagger from his belt and showed her the Crystal attached. Her eyes had widened at the sight, and he told her about what the spirit known as Abner had said before they had left Nineveh.

"He mentioned a prophecy in the end, and only have been guiding us here ever since," Markus said once he was finished. "I can't help but think that if we were brought here because of Abner's warning, to the very place where the queen said something similar, it couldn't be a coincidence."

Esmerelda now looked even more uncomfortable. "I cannot say."

"Please, Esmerelda," Ashlyn said. "If you know something, can't you tell us?"

"I've already told you too much as it is," Esmerelda said almost desperately though as calmly as possible. "You were to just stay, rest, and recover from your journey. After what happened to your little sister… it would be cruel to tell you anything now."

"And yet here I am, talking to you now," Markus said.

"My mother said she would be the one to talk to you when the time came," Esmerelda said unaltered by his words. "You must understand, we wish you no harm. Far from that, please believe that. I'm only trying to make it easier on you, so that you don't receive unwanted attention or stress."

"Then why are we here?" Markus demanded now growing more impatient than ever. "Why does the queen have us in her home? Why are you here talking to us now? C'mon, if you know something-"

"Mark," Ashlyn said placing a firm hand on his shoulder. When he took a deep breath to calm down, she addressed the princess in a different matter. "Why can't we know now? Can you at least tell us that?"

Esmerelda pursed her lips. It took a long time for her to answer, and when she did, it brought only more questions in Markus' head. But he kept his mouth shut even afterward when it came time to follow the princess again. Besides, he was also curious about the last bit.

"It would be better if you would follow me first," she said. "It'll show you just what I know, and how this city is floating in the sky.

Esmerelda

Esmerelda had taken the two back to the castle and led them into the chambers where The Great Owl statue was kept. On the far wall to the left before they started for the way to the Throne Room was an elevator hidden behind one of the support pillars. She told the guard to let them in, and the man in black and white power armor did as he was told.

The elevator seemed to go so far down that anyone not used to it would have thought that you would fall right out the bottom of the island. But Esmerelda was not worried. She was excited and also nervous to show Markus and Ashlyn the true power of Levitika, and when the doors finally opened, she led them down a torch-lit corridor to a steel door. Upon placing her hand on the palm scanner, she got the door opened, and the three of them stepped inside.

There was so much she couldn't tell him, not yet. But the very least she could do was show him just what makes the kingdom float in the clouds which in turn, would bring her to tell him at least the first part of the truth.

"What I am about to show you will explain how our kingdom is the way it is," Esmerelda told him. "Hopefully it will also answer some questions about your own Crystal, and from there, kind of see where my people and I are coming from."

Markus didn't look convinced as she continued to lead him and Ashlyn down the corridor, but he didn't stop or slow down.

She took her two friends by the hand and led them inside what looked to be a giant cave inside the floating island; as if the land itself had been hollowed out at some point in its life. Pipes and power generators as large as Great Behemoths lined the walls, leading to a central platform guarded by security cameras linked to energy turrets. By the looks on their faces, Ashlyn and Markus appeared to be in a trance by all the beauty around them.

There were four engines on opposite sides of the caves, with thin wires leading up the walls and across the ceiling where they met in the middle right above the platform. On the platform itself, held in place by a power converter beneath a pane of glass, was a bright green Crystal the size of a basketball; shining rays of light in every direction and bouncing off the walls and casting many more colors like a rainbow.

Markus and Ashlyn stared in awe at the beautiful sight, and they had every reason to. It took Esmerelda's breath away every time she looked at it, and she lived here her whole life. She felt the warm presence emitting from the Crystal as if it was saying, 'hello.'

"Behold," she said pointing to the Crystal dramatically. "The Crystal of Levitika: the source of power that created the legend of the floating island, and The City of Angels."

"It's so big…" Markus murmured. "Bigger than the one in my staff."

"Beautiful," Ashlyn muttered. "Princess… you're telling us that… *this* makes the island float?"

"Yes, ma'am," Esmerelda said smiling sadly, turning back to look at it. "This Crystal is constantly putting off a spell that had been cast years ago, keeping this entire plot of land that contains the whole city floating safely among the clouds. All these machines and more are what helps us control the flow of its power."

"So this island… is held up by magic…" Markus said now looking at his hip where his staff had been returned. As if influenced by the Great Crystal, his was glowing just a little bit brighter. "That's… unbelievable."

"So are a lot of things in life," Esmerelda said.

You've come back… Esmerelda heard a faint voice travel through the air, and her two friends stared aghast at the Crystal. He had revealed himself already, and even The Keeper had heard it.

"Don't tell me," Markus then asked looking back at the princess. "This is like this one here?"

"In a way, it is," Esmerelda said. "You must have heard mentioning's of the Great Owl since you got here, right?"

"Black mentioned it, yes."

"Good, good. Well, The Great Owl is the one who managed to obtain this Crystal, the first of many more that had been created. It was she who cast the spell to protect our city from The Capitol back when it was once the powerhouse of the Northern Wastelands."

Ashlyn glanced at her, and Markus merely looked somberly at the Crystal. Levitika's greatest source of power happened to be just another trapped spirit just like all the others. Doomed to be used like parts in a machine until the war is over and The Dreaming can finally be closed forever. It was both a blessing, and also a burden, that even Esmerelda herself longed to end.

Growing up, she used to always come down here and try to speak to the son trapped in the Crystal. Sometimes she would get no response at all, but sometimes… sometimes he would speak. It always filled her with such joy and hope; to hear the words of one who longed for the Dreaming to close, and for his father's terrible legacy to end forever. And so he had agreed with The Owl in order to-

"So what does this have to do with me?" Markus asked.

"I don't know for absolute certain." Esmerelda lied shaking her head. "Only a very few people do. But… according to our history, someone important was to come. The spirit within that Crystal up there mentioned someone was coming. That someone, my mother believes, is you."

"Me?" Markus asked bewildered as he stared at her. "Why me?"

"I cannot say," Esmerelda said. "My mother will explain everything later, I promise."

"You can't just expect us to drop this like that," Ashlyn told her. "We've been through too much, and what you are telling us confirms that we were only brought here because you believe Markus is necessary for something."

"I know, I know, it isn't fair." Esmerelda told them both. "But I promise, we do not intend to force or do anything to you. That is not who we are. What comes first is your guys' needs especially concerning your sister, Markus. I promise you, everything will be explained later. But for now, please, just trust us."

"Why in the world would I trust you?" Markus asked. "For all I know, you only saved me because you want to use me for something. Do you really believe that whatever is in that Crystal told your family that someone like me was important?"

Now it was Esmerelda's turn to ask a question. "Do you believe that the spirit Abner would have guided you if you weren't?"

"I did it for Ruth," Markus said pointing a finger at her. "I did it for her, and no one else. Now she's gone. I haven't heard from Abner since. As far as I'm concerned, I was just a fooled who got played."

"I know you feel like a normal person," Esmerelda said bitterly. "When my mother tells you everything, you are free to remain as such. But whatever happens next whether you stay with us in the castle or not, I promise you nothing will be expected of you. Like I said, we are not like that. You are just as much of a person as anyone else in this city and more. Our first priority is your and Ashlyn's care. Second, is your sister's remains. Once your needs are met, then you will be told what is happening to Levitika."

"You make it sound like you guys are in trouble," Ashlyn said nervously.

"That's because we are," Esmerelda said hating herself for even allowing it to slip out. "It's hard to explain, and it will be with everything else that my mother has to say. But what I can say is, Levitika may not be safe for much longer."

She paused, allowing Markus and Ashlyn to think about her words before she spoke up again. "Will you at least wait, and hear what my mother has to say before you make any more assumptions about us?"

"That's easier said than done," Markus said though he didn't sound as irritated as he had before. "And... you *did* help us. What do you think, Ashlyn?"

Ashlyn pursed her lips in thought. "A lot has happened for us to ignore the fact that we were brought here," she said. "So... I think we should at least wait and talk about it later. After all, it's not like we can leave Levitika now, right?"

"You aren't prisoners," Esmerelda spoke up. "You can come and go as you please. It's just... there isn't a lot of places for you to go."

"Other than home," Markus said. "But that... that isn't an option right now. So, yes. We will wait. And... I am sorry I yelled at you, Esmerelda. I just... I just want to know why I am here. I wanna know what my father did here, what he has to do with you guys and what it has to do with me. What Vic said, only gives me more questions. I just don't want to be in the dark anymore."

Esmerelda smiled softly, hoping to reassure him even just a little. "I understand. You won't be, not for long, I promise. How about we go back outside? There is one more place in the city I'd like to show you before we are summoned back to the castle."

"That's fine," Ashlyn said. "It would be nice to get going. This place... it gives me the creeps. No offense."

Esmerelda said she didn't take any. As she led the two out of the great room, she felt something like cold hands reaching out and touching her back. By the way, Markus had shuddered on their way back to the elevator, it became apparent to her that he too had felt the spirit's presence.

It had to be Markus. It *had* to be.

Markus

Markus had a lot to think about as Esmerelda led them out of the castle once again as the sun was passing to the east and was now out of sight behind the wall. It was still daytime by how bright the sky was, but so much time had passed since the tour began and it seemed to go by faster with what was on his mind. As Esmerelda and Ashlyn talked a bit, he focused his attention on what he knows as of now.

They were brought here for a reason, that was apparent. Why exactly, he would know tonight he was told. What he would do afterward, that was another mystery entirely. The whole thing was insane; the fact that the island was *actually* in the sky was insane. What Esmerelda told them before a Crystal that his own had a reaction to… that was insane too. Everything about this was insane in this kingdom. His whole world was altered completely ever since the moment he had that dream and has continued to change upon his arrival in this city.

It truly was a completely different world than the one Markus and Ashlyn left behind.

"There." Markus heard Esmerelda say as she stopped. He looked forward and stopped as his mind became addled by what was registered before him.

It was a fountain. That much was clear, but the massive architect of marble and gold was too much to be an ordinary fountain. It stood nearly ten meters tall, each spout carved into the shape of a fish and multiplying in numbers as they went lower and lower to the basin filled with water. The basin itself was about fifty feet in diameter, and about five feet deep, and beneath the rippling surface Markus saw giant catfish swimming in a circle around the fountain.

It was a magnificent thing of beauty that he could not help but stare at it for what felt like hours. Beneath the fish, the bottom of the fountain was glistening with many coins of all sorts, adding to the beauty along with the scales of the fish.

Ashlyn seemed transfixed on the beautiful fountain as well by the look of her eyes as Markus stole a glance at her.

"That's…" she said in awe.

"Beautiful." Markus finished for her.

"Crafted by my grandfather," Esmerelda explained. "This was supposedly where a massacre took place, and The Great Owl wished to create this fountain in a way to make sure that the lives lost would never be forgotten."

"There was a massacre?" Ashlyn asked.

"Long ago, before Levitika broke free from The Capitol and was led by The Owl to become its own kingdom once again."

"That's incredible," Markus said. Little by little, he got to learn more and more about Levitika's history which although was still bloody, rose from the ashes of war to become the floating City of Angels it was known as today.

Esmerelda nodded. "I come here often to listen to the water and read. Especially in the summer. The waters never stop circulating, so it never freezes over, and the water remains at a perfect temperature due to some heating pipes beneath the marble; it keeps the catfish alive and healthy year-round."

"Wow," Ashlyn said, her drink long forgotten. "It's so beautiful."

Markus laughed at the repetition. "Indeed."

They all sat on the edge of the fountain watching the fish play tag beneath the water. Markus tried to count the small glimmering coins that Esmerelda explained were tossed when people made wishes here. He dug into his pockets, forgetting that he never carried money. However, Esmerelda removed three coppers from her pocket and passed one to Markus and another to Ashlyn.

After thinking about it, Markus made his wish, blew onto the coin and flicked it into the water, making the fish scatter at the break of their current. Ashlyn and Esmerelda's coins soon followed.

"What did you wish for?" Esmerelda asked him and Ashlyn.

"Not telling," Ashlyn said.

"Nice try." Markus grinned though his smile was forced just for the benefit of the moment.

Esmerelda smiled at them. "Didn't want to tell you guys mine anyway." They all broke into laughter in their own blissful childishness. But even as they did so, Markus felt like an adult, only pretending to laugh for the benefit of the doubt. He still had too much on his mind in order to enjoy himself again.

"Thank you for taking us out." Markus finally said. "This city, it's all beautiful."

"Thank you both for coming," Esmerelda said looking back at the fountain. "It's been a while since I had actual friends to do this kind of stuff with."

"What are you talking about?" Ashlyn asked. "You got the whole city."

"No one I can actually *talk* to. Not about what I feel or think." She started to kick her feet where she sat. "It gets lonely in the castle sometimes."

"Oh, I see," Markus said wondering what a normal day in the castle might be like for the princess. Though she was nice to the people and they, in turn, were nice to her, how much could she really talk to them about?

"Well, you got us now," Ashlyn said smiling.

Considering Markus knew so little of Esmerelda despite how much time they had spent with her today. Already they have known her longer than anyone else in the kingdom. And… she seemed trustworthy in some strange way. *We all need friends. And if* anyone *in this city seems trustworthy, it was Esmerelda.*

"Thank you," she said blushing slightly. She looked behind her friends, and Markus turned to see a massive clock standing on a pole past next to what looked like a bar. The blinking sign read 'The Winking Ahool'. The clock read 'five-thirty-nine.'

"It's time to go," Esmerelda said standing up. "Dinner will be ready really soon." Markus looked down to see that she was tightening her shoes. "I bet I can beat you both in a race back up to the castle."

"Oh, you're on," Ashlyn said zipping her coat up tighter.

"Let's do it," Markus said standing up.

"Okay," the princess said standing and then, "Ready-set-go!" She shouted as she broke off into a sprint.

"Hey!" Ashlyn protested as they chased after her.

"You took a head start!" Markus called up while fake-laughing as the three of them raced to the castle, receiving glances of both displeasure and glee from all who witnessed them racing like little kids.

Markus' thoughts went back to Ruth, in thinking of how she would do if she was better.

If she was still alive, oh how she would have loved to run again.

~ Revelation ~

Markus

When they arrived at the castle, the guard from earlier, Mel, was there to meet them.

"Queen Elizabetha would like to see you both now," he said to Markus and Ashlyn. "Thank you, Princess Esmerelda. I'll take them from here."

"I'd rather come as well," Esmerelda told him. "That okay?"

"Of course," Mel said with a tip of his head. He turned and led the rest of the way, back through the castle and into the Throne Room where both the queen and the Hunter Black was waiting for them. At the sight of them, Markus felt bile rise in his throat. All that he had learned so far, he wanted to demand answers right then and there.

What Esmerelda had shown him mostly scratched only the surface of Levitika's history and only gave a minimum explanation as to how the City of Angels worked. He admitted mostly to himself that he was impressed and honestly excited for what beheld him in this place. But his search for answers was only met with more questions, especially about his father and himself and how he supposedly fit into the strange history as well as the present and future. He wanted desperately to demand answers of the queen right then and there.

But instead, he kept his promise and remained patient as Mel excused himself and left the five of them alone in the great room. With Esmerelda joining them, Markus felt more at ease now than he did earlier when it was just him and Ashlyn here.

"Welcome back," Elizabetha said warmly while beckoning her daughter to join her by her side. Esmerelda did so quietly, giving her mother a quick hug before stepping aside and taking a seat on the steps leading to the thrones of silver and gold.

"How did you like the city?" Black asked sitting in a folded chair that had not been there before. "Did Princess Esmerelda show you a lot?"

"Definitely," Markus answered. "Your city, it's beautiful, your majesty."

Elizabetha smiled brightly. "I am glad you liked it. We do try our best to make it beautiful and just a place where many can call it home. I certainly hope that you would consider it as well. Your father certainly did."

"Your majesty," Markus said. "If my father was here, why did he return to Nineveh? And why... why was Black there? I guess the real question is... why are *we* here?"

Elizabetha was silent for a long moment, and then she sighed. "Straight to the point. You really are like... like Johnathon. It can't be helped now, not with what I know now. It is a long tale, but if you must insist... I'll have to tell you where it all began first so that you can understand where your father comes into place."

"And me," Markus said. He almost ratted Esmerelda out, but one look at the princess made him change his words. "I have the feeling that I was brought here for a reason. Is that true?"

Elizabetha's lips tightened, and it was Black who managed to break her from whatever spell she was under. "There's no point in hiding anything anymore. Go ahead, my lady. It is time."

The queen nodded and took a deep breath. "Very well. It all began when the Capitol controlled the entire Northern Wastelands, many years ago."

"Long ago, many years after the Fallout and war for control over the lands, the five kingdoms of the region you know of today belonged together as one. They worked, they built, and through the scavenging of lost technology and their will to grow from the ground up, their economy erupted as well as the population. Just like many countries or regions in the world, the Northern Wastelands became a strong nation second only to the Southern Sands. But then, everything changed when the Northern Governor died, and his son took his place. The son began making new decrees, new laws, and new taxes.

Anyone who would not comply with them were marked as traitors, and the districts they lived in would pay the ultimate price.

"Through this, he brought the whole country together, but he had far too much control over the land… It turned the nation into a prison more than a home. Eventually, the people rebelled, tired of being ruled by a single king, and the war over the Northern Wasteland began. This in turn created the kingdoms you know of today: The Capitol, (where the country was first created), Nineveh, Xerxes, the Kaiken Isles, and Levitika, all broke apart and even helped in the creation of the smaller villages in the Wastelands. War continued to brew, until finally, the leaders came into a pact, that the five kingdoms would forever be separated and left alone to follow their own traditions and laws.

"However, the leader of the Capitol did not want to let his world go, so on his dying wish, one hundred and fifty years after the war he called upon his seven sons and daughters, and with them plotted to take back the Wastelands by force. Kings and leaders were assassinated, governments were toppled over, and the kingdoms were once again brought under the control of the King's reign. However, when he died, his legacy was short-lived.

"The children divided the kingdoms again, for they thought that it was a perfect opportunity to have their own laws, their own order. And for years, the separated kingdoms lived in peace. But that would also be short-lived, for the eldest son who was against the division, killed the youngest daughter of the King and took over the Capitol. Eventually, he took it upon himself to invade the entire North and take back the entire Nation. Xerxes, seeing that there was no hope in fighting, gave in to the new order. Nineveh was less than compliant, and rebelled, as well as the pirates of the Kaiken Isles. Eventually, through unfortunate circumstances, Levitika also joined The Capitol, without putting up any more of a fight."

Queen Elizabetha looked up at the ceiling as if the memories were flooding her, and she would have to swim out before continuing. She then pressed on after a moment of silence.

"Eventually, a new rebellion began in Levitika. One that crippled The Capitol's control over the kingdom and a new government was brought up, thanks to a certain freedom fighter, known as The Owl. It was because of her will to fight that Levitika became ours again, but in the process, fueled The Eldest's desire to take us back, and war for our home begun once again.

"It was there we realized what had truly happened to the Capitol and all who was ruled under it. They were not just taken by armies, or artillery, but by a different force altogether. A power which had not been used for thousands of years, and thought only to be used by shaman and witches in the Wastelands. In fact, it completely obliterated whatever was left of our old home."

"Magic." Markus guessed. Ashlyn stared at him, and then looked back towards Queen Elizabetha. It was far too obvious for that not to be the case, given all that the two have witnessed and experienced first-hand.

"That is right." the queen nodded. "The Eldest son had found a new form of magic. One that had not been used since the early years of the world's life. With it, he was able to conjure his being into a Crystal, and with it, transported his life force into a robot. With it, he was capable of crushing all who opposed him and his rule. Thankfully, however, The Great Owl had gained a similar form of magic and helped the rebellion push back The Eldest and his armies.

"Knowing the son and his legion of androids and magicians were coming to take Levitika back, our ancestors took it upon themselves and with the help of the Great Owl among other spirits, to fight back with equal strength and liberate the control of The Capitol. The Owl explained that the Crystals that The Eldest had created were the cause of this new form of magic, and was eventually able to steal another one; but, at a terrible price…

"The Owl used that same Crystal to create this floating island, and helped us take the entire city and flee towards the mountains. As we fled further south we built up our walls, our weapons, and prepared for war another attack. We soon outfitted our troops with what you yourself have, Markus: Eagle-Wings. With them, our men were able to fly concealed in the clouds, and with that, confident that we were ready, we fought back. When The Eldest and his Legion came for us, our ancestors put up a valiant fight. We lost many men in the battle with his army, but soon we were able to defeat them with our most powerful weapon obtained; the Shi Ray. It was a gift to us from The Owl, before she sacrificed herself to help us get away. With the weapon of terrible power, we obliterated the Master Ship, and within, The Eldest along with whatever Crystals he had in his possession.

"After scrounging the wreckage, we found many interesting things. Weapons capable of annihilating entire Firefly choppers to dust. Crystals capable of keeping power in our city for years to come, and then books and scrolls about more Crystals The Eldest had created before his own, as well as the one we took to power up our own island. We found that the Crystals, if fused together can possibly create life itself. It was then we found where The Eldest had gotten the gems, which were formed out of the igneous rock made by the Nudushi Volcano in the Northern Mountains; The Well of Souls, as it is nicknamed, where the blackguard trapped the spirits of great warriors in the Crystals where he used to create many more.

"It was discovered that these Crystals opened a gateway to a magic unlike anything mankind has ever seen; more than what The Eldest or The Owl had in their own possession. A power hidden, in the unseen realms around us. However, in the blast of the Shi Ray, the Crystals were scattered across the entire Wastelands. The one you have, happens to be one of the seven Spirit Crystals created by The Well. Unlike the one The Owl stole to control floating islands, these were made using the most powerful of spirits that The Eldest had by his side. We found that Seven were created- nine if you counted The Eldest crystal and the first he created among them. All of different souls and with them, different gateways into The Dreaming."

Pausing, the queen then turned to Black who stood idly while listening to the story with the two teens who were mesmerized by the tale. "The one that Black has, is one of the such Crystals."

Markus turned to Black who moved his hand out from under his cloak to reveal a Crystal similar to that of Markus' except that it was red, almost like it was made of frozen blood.

Everything about Elizabetha's story was absolutely fascinating, absolutely nothing like what he had been taught his entire life. Magic in general, conducted by these Crystals including the one Markus had in his possession that led him here, was incredible. The fact that it wasn't some mystical calling but the Angels themselves calling to him, bringing him here to a kingdom that was raised to the skies with such magic… it was almost like one of the fantasy stories of old, and yet… this was supposed to be real.

"But, how did my father get his hands on this one?" Markus asked reaching for his dagger and showing Elizabetha the Crystal embedded within.

Elizabetha's eyes softened at the sight of it, as if she recognized it like an old friend. "We gave it to him." she said simply.

"What?"

"I will explain in a moment." The queen said patiently before continuing the amazing tale.

"Among the wreckage, in the mangled and burnt husk The Eldest was in, we found The Eldest Crystal still with him despite all the others being lost in the explosion that sent them across the continent. We took The Eldest with us, and managed to find that within, he was still alive despite being trapped like all the others.

"Incapable of reaching out into the world he tried to create, he remained dormant inside the Crystal. Like all Crystals, only those who have a bond with it can use it. If the Crystal does not conform to your own spirit, it is as useless as a rock. Which is why I am not surprised that your Crystal will carry out its own powers through you. You *are* your father's son after all. When we finally deciphered what we found from The Eldest, we locked his Crystal up in a secure vault within the center of this castle, where only two people can access it; myself being one of them. We couldn't risk The Eldest escaping again and influencing the minds of any who drew too close, so for the past hundred years, my father and all who now rule under me, have been doing what we can to locate the remaining Crystals. We've spent a long time preparing to return to the world, and now we are ready to strike. We cannot allow the powers of the Crystal's to fall into the terrible hands of the Capitol; where The Eldest had left his youngest son in charge of the dreadful city. Queen Lamia, daughter of that son, rules The Capitol today.

"Even as we speak, she too is looking for the Crystals. In fact, she may have one of them in her possession right now. With it, she wishes to create more advanced weapons almost as superior as our own and cast a shroud of fear across the land. Her army is settling to attack Xerxes as we speak, and one day Nineveh and The Kaiken Isles; in order to reclaim the Wasteland and finish what her grandfather had started. If she gets her hands on any more- if she hasn't already -she could unleash a magic that could completely destroy and enslave the Northern Wastelands. Everyone in these lands, would be subject to the Dark Queen's slavery, just as they were with the Mad King, long ago."

Markus felt as if concrete had formed in his stomach the idea made it curdle so much.

"Oh no…" Ashlyn whispered.

"That still doesn't explain why my father got the Crystal from you." Markus said when he managed to find his voice. "Or what exactly these things do."

"He was my brother." the queen said sadly.

Markus' eyes grew wide, and his whole world seemed to be turned upside down. "What? My father was… royalty?"

"No. Your father… well, he was a bastard. He was not born of the same mother as I was, but that is beside the point. He volunteered to go to Nineveh, the Capitol's second target. One to gather information about Ovid and the rebels, and one, to protect you and your sister."

Markus couldn't believe what he was hearing. "What? Ruth and I?"

Elizabetha enlightened him. "Yes, Markus. You were born here, in Levitika. The Eldest cannot reach out and exploit his powers upon us, however he does have *some* influence on the world, even from within our vault. He reaches out to our dreams, our nightmares, trying to frighten us and control us through such fears. Your father struggled to keep his wits about him, and also struggled to keep you from hurting yourself. The Eldest knew you are capable of finding the Crystals, should you receive Johnathon's own, and use their power. He tried everything he could to break you both down, and have you in his clutches.

"So for your safety, your father fled and kept you and the Crystal a secret as he lived in Nineveh and shared with us information about Baron Ovid and the city in general. From within the city walls, you both were safe, and we were able to gather information."

The queen then glanced over at Black. "But sadly, your father was caught by the cruel Baron, and had Black, our spy and your father's partner, execute him."

"What?" Markus stared at Black. *Black was a spy as well? Yet he was ordered by Ovid to kill Father? But that means…*

Black merely nodded, as if he had just read Markus' mind. "I'm sorry, Markus. But I had to. Elizabetha knew it was inevitable, despite how much we did not want that to happen. But the mission to gather more information and keep you and Ruth safe were the top priorities. Your father understood that." He looked off into the distance. "So he willingly gave his life, and we made sure you both were kept safe. The plan was that I was to take you, but obviously, you wouldn't have come. Besides, it was too risky, especially with Baron Ovid keeping a close eye on me. I had planned to wait and eventually sneak you and Ruth out, but then, you both decided to escape."

"By Abner's wishes." the queen said to Black. "Xerxes was already planning another attack on Nineveh. In fact, they left in the nick of time. They are within a siege of the city now."

It made Markus worry about the people they had left behind on this crazy journey. Nineveh was about to go to war with Xerxes, and he left everyone behind there. He felt guilty, and worried about Jim and the others.

"Agreed." Black said in a low tone. "Those fools... if they keep this up, there will be no strength left to hold back against The Capitol."

"I'm sure that is what Lamia was hoping for all along." Elizabetha agreed sadly.

Markus spoke up. "So my father, he was working with you guys the whole time?" He asked still grasping the concept of how little of his father he really knew. "To protect the city?"

"*And* to protect you." Black said looking at the boy with a soft gaze. "You are necessary for our very survival." He looked to the queen. There was something about his gaze, almost like he was pleading with the queen.

"Markus," Elizabetha sighed. "It's time you know the truth as to why you are necessary for Levitika's survival."

Markus swallowed hard and said, "I don't understand..."

"You are the only one capable of bringing the kingdoms together, and destroying the Eldest Crystal." the queen explained. "The Eldest cannot be destroyed. Even with the most powerful magicians and tools, we still could not crack it. However, The Great Owl sent us one last message before she disappeared forever. This was when she managed to steal the very crystal we now use to keep this city afloat. she spoke of an ancient prophecy that she had found out while fighting The Eldest within The Dreaming, where the Crystals obtain their energy. Long story short, it says that the Eldest Son of the Bastard of Pilate of Levitika, with the power of the Seven can destroy the Eldest Crystal, and bring peace to the North, and prevent an evil from escaping beyond its borders. You, Markus, are the Child of Prophecy; The Keeper of the Gate."

Markus gulped. He was still trying to wrap his head around what he had just heard and then asked the queen, "The Keeper... But... why me?"

"You can use the Crystals." Black explained stepping in. "All of them. The Keeper is said to be able to... sync with all of the Crystals created by the power of The Dreaming. They are merely gateways to a new realm of magic, and only the spirits inside can choose who can use them or not. With this new kind of sorcery, you can sense the auras of all living things as you noticed in The Plains. You are also capable of giving your own body newfound energy to make you stronger. With this new power, you are the only one who can find these Crystals, and destroy the Eldest and his sinister darkness."

"Why not you?" Markus asked.

"Because I am not The Keeper." Black said simply. "I was not chosen like you have long ago. The spirits have made it perfectly clear. They have chosen you, the moment your father gave you that staff and his Crystal within. While other people like myself are capable of using them, only you can use them all."

Markus looked down at his feet. "This is crazy, I mean… I'm just me. I'm just a mechanic… I'm no one special."

"Yes," the queen said almost bluntly. "But you will not be alone. We Levitikans have hidden ourselves for hundreds of years, preparing for the purge of all evil in the world. We will take care of the battles, and escort you to the many areas where the Crystals are possibly being used. The closest, happens to be in Nineveh."

"Nineveh?" Markus asked.

"Baron Ovid knows about the Crystals." Black said. "In fact, he has one in his possession right now. It was another reason why Johnathon and I infiltrated the city. He knows that the Eldest's granddaughter plans to use them for global domination; and he knew the minute your father came into his city what he had in his possession. He tried to break Johnathon to try and get to Levitika. I could only do so much to protect you and your sister. That was why he sent the other Hunters after you. He doesn't want *you*, he wants the Crystal you have in your staff. It would give him the leverage he needs in the war, and he might have even used it to find the City of Angels and through force take all of our research and weapons. And then all hope would have been lost."

"So he is on his way here?" Ashlyn asked.

"Yes." Black nodded. "Among the other Hunters chasing you, Ovid had also sent a witch after Markus. A follower of a cult dedicated to the study of the Dreaming, and, I am disturbed to mention, she is influenced by The Eldest. I could sense it within her while she was in The Baron's courts."

Esmerelda cleared her throat and with permission from her mother, spoke up. "Okay. So we know they are coming. Knowing Ovid, he has probably sent his army after the witch so he would find us."

"Most likely." Black agreed.

"And so we need to prepare ourselves." Elizabetha told Markus and Ashlyn. "We cannot allow the witch to enter the premises, and if Ovid *does* find us, we need to fight back."

"Then he'll have the Crystal, right?" Markus asked. "We can just take it from him, right?"

"The Baron never takes the Crystal with him." Black said. "But if he is determined to seize this city he *might* bring it. So by then, we *might* be able to claim it. If he doesn't use it to destroy us first."

How powerful are these things? Markus wondered looking at the dagger in his hands, his reflection glistening in the Crystal within. *What sort of... terrible magic is stored in these, and what could someone like Ovid do with them?*

"So we will be preparing for his arrival." Elizabetha said. "We need to prepare the people for battle. You as well, Markus and Ashlyn. As Markus' duty, we can-"

"No." Markus suddenly said to everyone's surprise. No one said anything as they stared at him while Markus spoke his mind. "No. I'm not doing that. I did not come all the way here to fight your wars. I came here to save Ruth, nothing more."

The queen tried to speak. "Markus, you don't under-"

"No!" Markus suddenly snapped. "I've been through *hell* with these damn things. This whole prophecy thing... No. You really expect me to just accept that role? Well you can forget it! This is not my fight!"

Silence enveloped the room like a shroud. Eventually however, Elizabetha spoke up with a low and cold tone. "So you will condemn all those people you saw out there, to die?"

Markus said nothing, startled by the memory of all those people in the city. The guilt that was now placed on him, ate its way into his heart, and he hated both Black and Elizabetha for placing it in there. "It's not-"

"Elizabetha," Black said cautiously. "It isn't fair to him."

"Oh don't go trying to defend me." Markus said angrily at him. "You're the one who brought us here in the first place!"

"Mark..." Ashlyn started.

Elizabetha sighed audibly. "I'm sorry, forgive me. I understand. I do not expect you to accept all of it, or do everything. In all honesty, I wish we had more time so we didn't have to bring this all upon you now, so you could heal and get used to living here like your father wanted. But we don't have that option now. We *will* help you, and Black will train you."

"I'm not doing it." Markus said immediately.

"Markus, please. We will raise you up little by little, until you are ready. The prophecy"-

"I don't care!" Markus bellowed loudly. "I don't care! I'm not your savior, and I'm not listening to this anymore. I just gone through hell, my sister is dead, and now you wanna just drop it on me that I'm now supposed to fight your war? Screw that!"

He had figured that Elizabetha would have been outraged and send him and Ashlyn to the dungeons. In fact, he kind of hoped that she would. But instead she simply said, "Whether you want to believe it or not, you have been chosen by The Seven who wish to ensure that The Eldest is destroyed, and no one else follows his destructive path."

"I didn't ask for that." Markus said shaking his head. "I didn't ask for any of this!"

"And yet here you are." Black piped in. "Your father once told me that if anything ever happened to him, I had to make sure you came back here so you can fulfill your destiny. I don't expect you to understand anything of which my Queen has said, but even so… Even so, you have your own free will. Will cannot force you to fulfill your destiny.

"Destiny? Don't talk to me about that! I mean…" Markus suddenly remembered Aventis and the others at the Drunken Badrat. He wondered about all the people in The Narrows, as well as the witch Zerona. Would they be killed as well? If this war was indeed inevitable, how many would die? Can Markus really do anything about it?

"I can't do it," he said shaking his head. "I can't save your city, I couldn't even save my sister…"

"Markus, we need your help." Black insisted calmly. "You are right, it isn't fair that this is expected of you, and we will not expect anything. But, if we lose this war, and The Capitol obtains the necessary power it needs, they will take over the Wastelands and try to spread it beyond its borders. They will create a world of our darkest nightmares. If you wish for that to happen, then by all means, let it happen."

"What if I don't care?" Markus demanded and then suddenly frowned, feeling ashamed with himself. This was all really too much too soon. He had just come here, and he already had such a heavy burden to bear. On top of the weight of Ruth's death, he was given the responsibility of this strange city's 'savior'.

"Markus…" Elizabetha said. "Surely you don't mean that."

"No, your Majesty, I do." Markus continued. "I don't know who you people think you are, but I'm not doing it. I appreciate your hospitality, but I am not going to stay here any longer if my only reason for being here at all is to fight your war. C'mon, Ashlyn, let's go." He then turned and started for the door.

"Markus," Ashlyn started for him. "Wait!"

"You two are able to stay with us in my home." Elizabetha said which was what made Markus stop. If you wait for but a few moments, we can have someone take you to your rooms."

"So, we're prisoners now?" Markus asked turning to look at the queen and Black who had not moved from his spot.

"No." Elizabetha answered. "You're free to go anywhere you want. I only suggest you don't leave the castle just yet, until you are healed and we know what to do with your sister."

"… Fine."

A few moments later, some men took Markus and Ashlyn from the throne room and they were escorted down the hall. He noticed Ashlyn looking at him the entire time, but he didn't look back at her.

He just didn't know what to think at the moment.

~ A Choice ~

Ashlyn

They were both taken into separate bedrooms that thankfully were right across the hall of each other. However, they both insisted to the men in black and white power armor that they were in the same room, and the men obliged.

The bedroom they were in if it was indeed meant to be a prison was by far the nicest prison Ashlyn had ever been in.

But Ashlyn wasn't focused on the bedroom as much as she was on Markus.

Her friend took his knife and hurled it onto the desk without a second look. The Crystal glowed dimly against the glass of the window above it which was blocked off by more walls in the distance. He then threw himself on his bed and crossed his arms over his face. Like a child throwing a tantrum, he grumbled profanity underneath his arms.

"Was all of that really necessary?" Ashlyn asked sitting on the edge of the bed with her friend but with her back to him. Outside their door she heard mumbling and what sounded like a chair being drug across the floor towards it.

"I don't wanna talk about it." Markus said lowering his arms and letting them rest on his chest. A moment passed and then he said, "Though I was pretty rude to the queen, wasn't I?"

"Yes, you were."

Her blunt response made Markus squeeze his eyes shut.

"Mark," Ashlyn said. "I know you're upset. But…"

"I don't want to talk about it." Markus said again till staring up at the maple ceiling. Not really wanting to argue about it, Ashlyn just sat there staring blankly at the wall. She was upset with how Markus had behaved, but at the same time it wasn't as if his reaction wasn't entirely unjustifiable. So all she did was sit there and shared the silence with him. He would have to figure out what he wanted on his own.

"Won't you say something?" he eventually demanded after minutes of prolonged quietness.

"Are you going to say you're gonna apologize to the queen?" Ashlyn asked.

"No."

"Then I'm just going to sit here as quiet as a mouse."

Markus grumbled and turned so that he faced the opposite wall. "Now you're on their side? What was that in there then?"

"To give you time. Mark… you can't just talk to a queen like that."

"I don't care. It isn't fair for us to be asked that. Whatever they are talking about with this prophecy and this war, it isn't our problem."

"You're right, it isn't our fight." Ashlyn said. "But I still think we should help them. They really sound like they could use some help, even if there wasn't some prophecy about you."

"Ashlyn, we're just kids. What can we do?"

"You thought the same thing before we left Nineveh. Look where it got us."

"Yeah, look where it got *us*. Where is Ruth?" Markus paused as if to let the words sink in and then said, "Look, we got our own problems."

"Then what do you plan to do?" Ashlyn asked.

"… I don't know."

"What if it was Nineveh that needed our help, and not Levitika?" Ashlyn posed this other question in a softer tone. "Obviously, you wouldn't help for Ovid's sake. You'd help for the others, right?"

"They aren't here right now."

"No, they aren't. But those people we saw out there… they are here. And they're just as real as your friends, and the rest of The Narrows."

Markus turned onto his back, still staring up at the ceiling and not meeting Ashlyn's eyes. "The Narrows didn't care when Ruth was having her coughing fit. Only you did, and Jim and Kaltrina. But still, I can't do it."

"Can't, or won't?"

"Pick one." Markus said now glaring at Ashlyn who glared right back. "I don't understand why you seem so keen on defending those people. They saved us only because they are delusional enough to believe that I am important."

"Whoever said you *weren't* important?" Ashlyn demanded.

"That's not the point-"

"It *is* the point, Mark. I understand why you were upset. It was too much as it was to be asked of all of that as soon as you finally got up and out of bed and got to see Ruth. But at the same time, whether you like it or not, Black and the queen has helped us. I think we owe it to them to help however we can. Prophecy or not. And I still go by my gut by saying your behavior was not only childish, but stupid."

"What are you, my mom now?" Markus grumbled.

"I might as well be. Look, all I'm saying is, if this place is in trouble, then I want to help. Not only because we're alive because of them, but because of all those people we saw out there. Someone has to help, and I'm willing to. In fact, I plan to help whether you're here or not."

"Ashlyn, no matter how many times you say it, you don't owe those people anything. The queen, I admit, I can understand. But you don't even know those people."

"No, I don't. But I do know what is right. And I know without a doubt, that you are being foolish to behave so rash. You and I both know that Black did his best for Ruth. The queen was able to do her best to help the three of us. She even let you walk away when you deserve to be imprisoned for your words. I sure as hell know that Baron Ovid would have done far worse if that was him instead of her."

Markus sighed and sat up rubbing his eyes. "Do you trust them, really?"

"No, I don't. But at the same time, what else can I do? After all that we were just told... I can't just *not* do something. Those people... if what the queen said is true, then I feel like I have to do something to help."

"What if she asks too much?" Markus asked. "You ever thought of that? Remember, she thinks I'm some 'savior' some dead person told her and her family about for years. They are insane."

"So were we for leaving Nineveh." Ashlyn argued. "What if all of this is true, Markus? What if The Capitol is coming back? What if they go for Nineveh?

What then? Like I said before: What if it was Jim and the others here in Levitika instead? Would you have done something to help them?"

Markus thought about it for a moment. He then pulled his knees up to his chest and rested his chin on them. "I can't do it." he said again. "I'm not strong enough. We're just kids and… I'm nobody."

This time, Ashlyn moved. She moved over to him and gently slugged his chin just to get his attention. "You're somebody to me. And I know that together, you and I can do anything. We couldn't save Ruth, and I will never forgive myself for what has happened."

"It wasn't your-"

"Let me finish. We couldn't save Ruth, but I'm always here for you still. And I'm telling you, we should hear the queen out. We should listen, and then make a decision later. I plan to help however I can, and I suggest you do the same. Just hear her out, and then make your decision. Not for me or for her, but for yourself and the people we saw out there."

"Myself?" Markus asked with Ashlyn's fist still against his chin.

"What else are you gonna do?" Ashlyn asked now letting her fist drop. "You're just gonna sit in here forever? You're just gonna stop living or even helping others? Ruth wouldn't want that. She'd want you to live. She'd… she'd want you to do the best you can for the people around you. She wouldn't want you to be like this anymore."

Markus frowned. "I'm not strong enough…"

"No one ever is." Ashlyn said. "But… that's what makes us human. That's why… we try to stand even when we don't have the strength. I promise, Markus, I'm never going to leave you. But I'm going to help them. And I hope that you are willing to as well."

Markus remained silent. He sat thinking in silence for a long time but even still, Ashlyn never stirred. She was going to hear his answer, one way or another.

Eventually, Markus sighed and rubbed his face. Appearing to have made his decision, he looked at her. "Fine. I'll listen."

Ashlyn smiled and held out her hand. "C'mon. Let's go together."

Markus looked at her hand, and then took it as they both crawled off the soft bed. "Yeah. Okay. Just… let me pick up my knife real quick."

Markus

It was strange, that few minutes of silence Markus had before he had made his decision. He had been thinking about Ashlyn's words but they weren't the only reason why he agreed to at least hear the queen out completely.

He doubted that if he were to tell her what he heard she would believe him.

While he was on the bed with Ashlyn just sitting beside him and giving him all of the reasons why he should be willing to help, he noticed that on the table the Crystal in his dagger was glowing just a little brighter. Not bright enough for anyone to notice it, but enough to grab his attention. It felt like the thing was reaching out to him like a ghost again, this time with a more powerful essence that cannot be explained by mere words. The best that he could ever describe it if he ever had to, was that it felt like someone was standing right next to the desk with their hand on the gem and looking right at him.

Given all that has happened since the departure from Nineveh as well as the loss he had experienced, Markus wasn't at all surprised and didn't even show it as he just laid there staring at the wall as Ashlyn continued to speak. He had expected the eerie spirit, Abner to reach out to him. To apologize for his loss and then to explain how he really was the 'chosen one' and must overcome his grief for the good of the city and those around him. He would have told Abner to stick it, and to just leave him alone. That the whole world and everyone in it, should just leave him alone.

But it wasn't Abner who he heard.

It was Ruth, and she was telling him to get up and help them.

Help them.

That was all he could hear, and though Ashlyn couldn't see it, Markus' arms were now riddled with gooseflesh. He almost said Ruth's name out loud, but was too afraid to even dare to. He didn't even know if he really did hear it, or if his mind was just paying a cruel trick on him.

Help them.

That was all she said, three times in fact. At this point, Ashlyn wasn't talking anymore. She was just sitting, waiting patiently for a response. Markus took the time to really think, and listen for Ruth's voice. She said the same thing again only two more times before he finally decided to agree and go talk to the queen. Whether it was Ruth or some guilt on his conscious, Markus was still angry and upset. But at the same time… he didn't want anyone else to die. Deep in his gut, he knew that was his only desire. He was still just a kid, and believed that the whole prophecy was a bunch of crap.

But at the same time... what else could he do, especially if Ruth's memory might actually haunt him if he doesn't get up and do something with himself now that he was here in Levitika.

Our father's old home... he thought still bewildered.

When they exited the bedroom they both were surprised to see only Black waiting for them outside, sitting on a chair just outside the door. Markus had demanded if he had been listening in and the Hunter stood up slowly and straight with the grace of a lord, and just as silent as ever.

"Are you ready to go back and listen now?" he asked them.

"So you *were* listening." Markus grumbled distastefully.

Black said nothing but led the way back to the throne room. He remained silent the entire way until they came back to the door and he stopped to turn and look at Markus in particular.

"Ashlyn, go inside." he told her.

"But-"

"I need to talk to Markus. Just he and I. Go on. It's okay."

Ashlyn looked at Markus helplessly and though he hoped she wouldn't, she passed through the doors just as Black opened it with the palm scanner. When the doors were closed again, the Hunter turned back to Markus with a softer expression that the boy didn't believe possible.

"I want to apologize." Black said. "I want to apologize for what went on in there. It wasn't at all our intention to bring this up upon you, especially after such a terrible loss. We cannot expect you to do anything, let alone come to any agreement that what we say is true. It is unbelievable, I know. But your father believed it, and he was willing to take you away from this place if it meant protecting you from the Dark Master. You *and* Ruth."

Markus bit his lip. "I don't want to believe it at all. I can't."

"And you don't have to. But what my queen said was true, we *do* need your help. We need all able-bodied men and women to help us in this fight for the good of the North. And with your abilities with your own Crystal, I believe you will be a powerful edition. That is also your choice however, and neither I, Queen Elizabetha, or anyone else in this castle will force you to do anything.

"But, if you *do* fight with us," Black continued but in a softer tone. "I can promise you one thing: you won't ever be alone. There are many men and women your age, and older, all willing to put their life on the line for the hopes of a better future. I will teach you more about the power contained in that Crystal of yours or at least what I know, and I will tell you everything you wish to know about your father and what he has done for us here in Levitika. If you fight with us, not *for* us, Markus, we can create a better future. One that no one will ever have to live their lives in fear or sickness again."

Markus was afraid. He had come all his way, lost so much, only to be told all of this. He was sure the queen and Black meant well, telling him that he didn't have to bear the weight of this 'prophecy' alone, but it still didn't pacify his troubled mind and heart.

Deciding it was best to play it off for now, Markus turned back to him. "Okay. I'll hear her out, at least."

Black nodded as if he expected it, and then after opening the door the two of them entered to find Ashlyn and the queen talking to each other. They both fell silent as the two men joined them.

Markus shuffled a foot nervously as he thought of what to say. "Look, uh… I'm sorry I snapped at you, your majesty. I…"

Elizabetha raised her hand. "Do not worry. I take no offence. I am sorry as well. I do hope you understand we mean no illness towards you and what you have gone through. As a queen and a leader, it is my job to serve my people and protect them to the best of my ability. With what we have been told all our lives, belief is the only true powerful weapon we have. It was wrong of me to dump that all on you, and I hope you can forgive me."

"I do." Markus said, meaning it. "I still stand by what I said though, I don't believe I am anything special. But… I am still human I guess, and I want to try to find another reason to keep on breathing. If that means helping… well…" He looked at Ashlyn, and then back to the queen. "I'm willing to do my part, for the family I have left."

Ashlyn smiled softly and a soft pink tinge collected in her cheeks. The queen smiled as well and nodded her head slowly. "Very well then. Will you stand by me, and those who serve Levitika?"

"Even though you said we might fail should Ovid really come?" Markus asked.

The queen pursed her lips. "Like I said: I don't think we are fully prepared for a preemptive strike and I believe it's too early to throw all of this upon you so suddenly. I wish we had more time, but we don't. And that makes me nervous."

Markus shifted his foot not really knowing what to say. What *could* he say? The truth? A lie? He was stuck, but he had to tell them. "Look, I would like to help you guys." They all looked at him as he continued. "But I just don't know. What can a kid like me do?"

"You escaped Nineveh with us." Ashlyn piped up. "You fought off those Woodies… You saved us from the spider. And you never gave up on us." She looked away as if embarrassed that she spoke out. "I mean… That's reason enough, for me anyway." She turned back to him and said, "Whatever you do, or wherever you go, I go."

Though gladdened by her words, Markus was still unconvinced. "But…"

"We know you can do it, Markus." Black said holding out the blood-red Crystal in his hand. As he looked at it, Markus could feel as if someone, or something else was staring back at him through the glassy gem. "I promised to protect you and Ruth, and I have failed. You are now all that's left. I promise, I *will* help you. I *will* show you how to use the Crystal's power even better than you can now… If you allow me to."

Looking at the crimson gem, the very aura which emitted from it, part of Markus wanted to fight this. He wanted to tell Black off and say he would handle it on his own. But what choice did he have? Besides, all that had happened out in the Wasteland, he was a *little* curious. He wanted answers as to what exactly happened to him out there.

"Why would you put your hopes on me?" he asked turning to Elizabetha. "You don't even know me personally, or what I've been through. I know hardly anything about you and this war. All of this is just… Why would you place your hope on a kid like me who doesn't believe in himself?"

"It's *hope* that's gotten us this far." Elizabetha answered simply.

"And what if I still say no?" Markus asked.

Elizabetha turned to Black who nodded. She then said, "That is your choice. We all have different purposes in life, Markus. The people believe that The Keeper would come, and lead us to victory. You don't have to accept that fate. No one should ever have to accept the burdens placed upon them.

However, when it comes to doing what is best for the good of many, that is when our choice really has impact. You can choose whatever you want, we will not force you. We do ask that you stay with us, and live with us. But if you choose not to fight, that is your choice. You are still welcome to stay in my castle for as long as you must. You just need to ask yourself, what is the right thing to do? Not just for the greater good of others, but for yourself. If your home, Nineveh, was in danger, would you choose to fight for it, or would you choose not to?"

"What if I don't believe that it is worth fighting anymore?" Markus asked. "What if I've already given up?"

"That's why you lean on others." Elizabetha said smiling now at Ashlyn. "When the world turns its back on you, you can't turn your back on those who care for you. If you have truly given up, then ask yourself this: what would you do, if those you love were in danger? Would you fight, or flee?"

Though Markus knew what he should say and what he would say anyway, he didn't want to answer.

"Whatever you decide, we will respect it." Black said, backing up what Elizabetha had said earlier. "But then you must deal with the consequences of your choices, whether they are in our favor or not. You cannot run from your destiny, but you *can* choose your fate. If you decide to stay out of this, we will still care for you and treat you as our own. But if you choose to fight with us, save us all, then we will always be by your side. You'll never be alone."

Never be alone… Such a thing was unknown to Markus. He knew he wasn't alone, but now with such a greater burden being expected of him, he felt like he would have to handle the weight alone. He looked at Ashlyn who smiled softly at him, as if saying that wherever he went, she would go with him. Even now, she stuck by his side.

This city and all those people need our help. Was he really meant to save them? Either way, it would be good to get back on Ovid's lawless actions and rule against the very people of Nineveh. It would be nice to save Aventis, Jim and Kaltrina from such a horrible dictator. But would Markus even make it? Was he really meant to save this city and possibly the entire region? He truly didn't know. But he did know that he *did* need help. And they only had a little bit of time to do so. He didn't want anyone to die, that much had to be reason enough for him to at least try.

Besides, He thought. *What else am I going to do? I don't have Ruth, and if there was a war, there is a chance I might die...*

"I'll think about it." Markus answered finally. "But just in case... What do I have to do?"

~ The Spies and the Hypnotist ~

Lee
Lameika watched over Lee's shoulder as he controlled his Spider-Cam.

Unable to get too close to the floating city without popping up on the radar, he launched the bot which had attached to the tail of the Firefly taking Black and the children. When it had landed, the remote-controlled spider scoured the city. It studied the inhabitants of the city; the people, the mutants, androids, all seeming to be prepped for war.

Lameika had remained silent since the launch of the Spider-Cam, her eyes set on the screen and unwavering while Lee worked.

The walls that surrounded the city were huge and armed with the highest concentration of Cannon Blasters. The castle; massive in size with thick marble and armed in each tower with scanners and Gatling Lasers. The entire place looked to Lee like a fortress; like that of one of the prisons in The Capitol.

Getting into the castle with the Spider-Cam was easy, and Lee maneuvered it down the vast halls that seemed to go on forever until the metallic arachnid scuttled into a great hall where the statue of the 'legendary' Owl stood. It was there when Lee started following the group who were with Black and who had to have been the queen.

Where was he going, and what she was discussing? A war? Well, that was not surprising. It was no secret throughout the country that war was brewing. To Lee, the world was just a giant matchbox, and all it took was for one person to light a single match. It was only a matter of time, and will. When Black and the queen talked to the boy, they already mentioned everything the twins knew. Especially the fact that Ovid was coming. Trust was never easily obtained in the world, and the same went especially for leaders such as the Baron. But it didn't matter all that much.

What Lameika needed, was the location of The Eldest Crystal, and now the queen had given it to them. The Vault was in the center of the city, probably in the castle itself. After scouring the castle again, dodging patrols and avoiding cameras, Lee finally found it. An eight-by-eight door of steel with electromagnetic locking rods, palm scanner, and four guards armed with rifles guarding it. Getting in was not going to be easy. But with Lee now knowing the layout of the castle, and Lameika's convincing witchcraft, he soon had a plan to get his sister in.

"Okay, so we know where it is." he said after a careful analysis and calling the Spider-Cam to leave the area, where it would then dispose of itself right off the edge of the closest wall; making it seem like it was never there. He cut the feed, and then turned to his sister. "Now it's a matter of getting you in, and getting a crack at that safe. The lock won't be difficult to break, but the palm scanner is what we need."

"That won't be a problem either." Lameika said in an eager tone, almost hungry it seemed. "I'll just cut my way through." Lee had a feeling she wasn't talking about the safe in general.

"Well we can't move you in now. The scanners would catch us even in cloaking. However…"

"Yes?" Lameika said with an impatient tone.

"If Ovid is indeed coming, then we can use that as an advantage. The idiot will most likely attack on sight, and we can use the distraction as a way in. Chances are they'll just be looking for how many are invading the island; they won't be too concerned with *who* it is exactly. By then, we can swoop in, and I can drop you onto the roof."

"And if the Gatlings fire?"

"Then we ditch."

"Alright." Lameika stood up and started for the back of the Hellhound. "Do you really believe Ovid is coming? You seem so sure, Brother."

With an eager smile to prove his sister just how valuable he really was, Lee reached into his pocket and pulled out a small camera; the back end being burned off and the glass cracked. "I found this just this morning before we went after 'em. Ovid's been watching us the whole time. The snake probably knows where we are now, even without the camera."

"I was wondering why you went outside while we were still in the air." Lameika said coming back with her attention still on the city in the far-off distance. With the clouds moving in, it almost blended in perfectly. It was no wonder that Levitika managed to evade the world for so long.

"Right," Lee said now setting the tracker onto the console. His sister must have sensed his discomfort and uneasy thoughts, for she returned to his side and looked at him.

"What is troubling you?" she asked him.

"Nothing."

"Do not lie to me."

Lee sighed. "I'm just thinking…"

"It is good that you are thinking. However, *what* are you thinking about exactly? Spit it out."

Lee sighed. "I've just been thinking about all of this."

"What about it?"

"Is it really worth it?"

Lameika looked at her brother with a dangerous gleam in her eye. "What do you mean by that? And why now?"

"I mean… we're here with the city in view. We're closer to our mission than ever before. But with what we have lost along the way… the others-"

"Were weak." Lameika cut her brother off with her hand slicing the air before her. "In this world, only the strong survive. You and I know that better than anyone. Slitzar, Tank, Pyro, they were all too weak in the end. They served their purpose as best as they could, and now they are gone. We are still here. It doesn't matter if they didn't make it with us."

Lee looked at his sister bitterly. "Lameika, they were our guildmates."

"They were pawns and nothing more. I thought I told you that was all that they were; pieces of a large game board. Since when did you start caring for them anyway?"

Lee's mmouth tightened in rebellion against his tongue. When he found it safe to loosen it again he said, "It was because of them we were able to remain on those brat's tails and keep the Hunter Black off our asses."

"And they did just that. Just like when we drop and get split up in the city, I expect you to join me in the end. Otherwise, you have served your purpose to the end." Lameika turned and started to go.

Leaving the ship in autopilot, Lee stood and slammed his fist onto the chair, stopping her with the sound. "That's not good enough!"

Lameika turned her head, giving her brother another cold glare. Her lips slowly parted, revealing to him a hideous smile. For a moment, just a brief moment, Lee thought he saw Lameika's skin go transparent, revealing her skull which was still grinning all the while. It was so brief that Lee could have said it was a trick of his eyes, but he knew better. It was getting worse. Much worse.

"Just do your part, Lee." Lameika told him. "Do whatever you feel you have to do, just make sure to be there to help me return to Father. Otherwise, I will leave you behind. Remember that it was me who made sure you were even allowed to leave The Well. Father would have just kept you locked away where you could no longer embarrass him if it wasn't for me. Know your place, and know your worth. Because if you do not, then someone else will show you how much you are worth surviving. Only the strong survive, so make sure you are strong and not fall by the hands of some Levitikan, or even your current target."

Lee clenched his fists tightly. "I know my worth."

"Then prove it." Lameika told him. "Prove to me just how strong you are; show *Father* just how useful you really are." She then returned to whatever it was she had to do and said, "So now we wait, until the battle commences."

"Right..." Lee said seeing more of Father in Lameika than ever before, and knowing exactly what he had to do when everything was said and done. "We wait."

Elizabetha

"Let's get some food in you." Elizabetha said leading the group down the hall towards the dining room. "My council will want to meet you all. We will then discuss any and all training the both of you will be receiving while under our care."

"Both?" Ashlyn asked.

"My daughter will need someone close to keep her company, yes, but I would like you to train using a rifle. Just in case. Besides, if war does come to Levitika, any and all able-bodied men and women will need to help fight."

"I know how to shoot."

"Perhaps. But practice makes perfect."

"Can't argue with that." Markus muttered.

"What are you saying?" Ashlyn said half-jokingly.

"Nothing." Markus said simply. "Nothing at all."

Elizabetha smiled. These two really were something else. Though she had waited for the son of Johnathon to finally come back, she was not prepared for just how similar the two were; a decent sense of humor but obviously very protective. At least he had gained those attributes, and not everything else... "When time permits we will show you the rest of the castle." Elizabetha then said. "And eventually, if we feel ready enough, we will show you The Eldest, Markus."

"Like I said," he said defiantly. "I'm only helping you because I don't want anyone else to die. I want nothing to do with this prophecy of yours." Ashlyn glared at him but Elizabetha just looked at the boy understandably.

Just like his father, She thought. *Stubborn as an ox. But still, so innocent in the ways of the world. How little does he know, that in war, many die.* "Come." She then said placing her hand on a palm-scanner next to a large set of wooden doors. "My cooks have prepared a magnificent supper, I hear." She said opening the doors to a large dining room with many elegant tables.

Chairs of beautifully carved patterns and cuts circled each table, and a glass chandelier hung over each one; the biggest one shining bright over the largest table in the middle. The youths began to stare at the many people sitting at the large table, who suddenly fell into silence upon their arrival.

"They have waited patiently for us." The queen murmured. "Come." She led them to the table where the chatter started up again, growing progressively louder and louder.

After she had seated Ashlyn and Markus to her left and Black to her right- save the open seat between them -Elizabetha took her own seat. As soon as she sat down the whole table took their seat again. All of her alchemists, scientists, friends, and her Court Mage Slagar- who sat right across from her at foot of the table -all smiled at her guests. They all sat in silence as they awaited her introduction.

"Friends," she said holding out her hand, gesturing to Markus beside her. "I would like to introduce to you, Markus son of Johnathon." This was met with some looks of wonder, and some of disdain, as to be expected. "He is here, and he shall be our guest of honor during the war against The Dark Queen."

Markus squirmed in his seat and Elizabetha felt bad for putting him on the spot like that. But she had no choice. It was no secret who he was and what was expected of him here at this table. For so long she had kept up what her father had taught her, in order to preserve hope in the prophecy and the future it would bring about Levitika and the rest of the world.

Nevertheless, she continued. "But I asked you all to join us today because we have current pressing matters to discuss. Though The Keeper is here, this cannot wait: The Baron of Nineveh, our original target, has been following us, and it is possible that he and his army might be on their way here right now."

Unsurprisingly, the accusations came flying across the table like sharp daggers.

"It's the boy!"

"Black!"

"That girl- who is she!?"

"We can't trust them!"

"Is that really The Keeper? What took him so long!?"

Looking at the teens, Elizabetha could see the strain come upon their faces. Markus' especially. It would be no wonder if they were now dreading attending such a dinner.

Just about as good as expected, Elizabetha thought. *After being told of what his role is, he now has to deal with this riff-raff. Maybe I should have just let it be Black, Esmerelda, and I.*

"Enough!" She shouted. When the chatter died down she continued. "How Ovid is finding us we already know, and our guests have nothing to do with it." Markus knew she was lying for them, but it didn't make him feel any better. She took a deep breath, allowing herself to relax before speaking again. "As I was saying, not only is Markus here a lot earlier than expected, but Ovid's on his way. We have the manpower to fight back, but without the original plan regarding to Markus, we but have little choice."

Thankfully, everyone remained silent as she continued.

"In the little time that we have, Black will teach the boy as much as he can so that it will be enough to hold off against The Baron, while the rest of us prepare the defenses. I want all Angels on standby. We will pause our advance towards Nineveh and wait for Ovid here. He may have one of The Seven, and we cannot risk to tuck tail and run. We have been running for too long, my friends. Now is the perfect time for the world to know that The City of Angels is very much real, and the good people of this city will fight to bring the kingdoms together. And then, finally bring peace to a world sought with ruin and war its entire life. And it will all begin, with the fall of such a dreadful dictator. We do not know how much power The Baron has. But it is nothing compared to the strength we carry, or the strength we will soon have as we take back our region, one fallen city at a time. Our hearts beat as one, and silences even the thunder. We will bring peace and prosperity to all we save, and they in turn will help us. Our force will become stronger through the hearts of the brave and bold; and with Markus' help, we will find The Seven, and with them, liberate The North from The Dark Queen and the darkness she seeks."

Little by little, the hope seemed to spark once again in the eyes of Elizabetha's council. Some even looked apologetically at Markus, who appeared relieved that the negative attention was finally off of him and Ashlyn.

Elizabetha continued. "Think my friends, the lives we have led, the struggle of it all, and we will be the ones to show the world just what we as human beings are capable of. Whether you are black, white, man, woman, mutant, cyborg, or android; we are all one, and we must *unite* as one. We must start the ascension from the darkness, and together we can save this world, and bring it to light."

Elizabetha waited a few seconds for her words to sink into the minds of all who sat before her. She saw the looks on their faces, concern, hope, dread, everything. They wanted to believe her, but they were afraid. That was okay. It meant they believed in their righteous cause.

When they seemed ready once more, she continued once again. "I know we all carry different views on Markus, this war, the politics, religion, separation, and government. All are important to discuss, I agree. But we cannot play the game without *all* the pieces; and our first piece is either with The Baron himself, or in Nineveh. The Baron is coming now, so he will be the first piece we face in this start of the long game. We must work together, help Markus to fulfill his destiny the Great Owl has prophesized, and hopefully the spirits will be on our side as we push on and take back our land, and our home. Agreed?"

After seconds of silence, the table slowly lit up with agreements, disgruntled and otherwise. Satisfied, The queen of Levitika said, "Good. Until then, I want no word against Markus or his friend. I want all talk of the prophecy from this point on quelled. Anyone who tries to strain him, will have to personally deal with Damion Black. And be warned, friends, Black is not as forgiving as I am."

Everyone, excluding Slagar, nodded in understanding. One by one, they began to apologize to Markus and Ashlyn. Markus tried to wave them off, saying that it was okay, but he appeared relieved. At least he wouldn't have to feel any more pressure from the council at least; from The Keeper's perspective.

And so with that, Queen Elizabetha clapped her hands, indicating that the time had come for the cooks to bring the food. "Now, let us eat while we talk further about our future."

Markus
I sincerely hate this…

As the queen began discussing the plans for the city defenses concerning Ovid and his army, the food came at a flow Markus had never witnessed before in his entire life. He had played his part, and now he was glad to have some sort of distraction. He didn't even pay attention to what the queen was saying to the council who listened attentively. He was simply too mesmerized by all the food that came his way.

The cooks, who were garbed in white came in with platefuls of many cuisines and meals. Mountains of rolls, steamed vegetables, potatoes, and two large plates carrying whole roasted hogs with apples in their mouths. Many different bottles of wine were also passed around, and Markus didn't decline a glass as his plate was piled high with a mountain of food of all sorts.

He was amazed beyond words, and looking at Ashlyn beside him, she was just as astounded. She probably had never seen so much food in her life, even when she lived with her family; back when Veeger was just a simple member of The Guard back in Nineveh. The two of them tasted everything; with Markus not remembering when the last time he tasted food this good. Especially considering these were not in a can, or roasted on a spit or even from a trash can.

However, Markus wasn't really that hungry. Ashlyn was eating, not ravenously but still quite a bit more than he. Markus however was merely tasting his food, taking small bites and hardly putting a dent in the mountain on his plate. It just didn't feel right to try and enjoy himself after everything that had happened, thus his appetite was almost nonexistent. He felt the eyes of the councilmen upon him as they continued to speak to the queen, and he wanted nothing more than to just disappear. Even when he wasn't the center of attention, even though he didn't have to say or pretend anymore, they were all... watching him.

Just rubbing it in my face it seems, he thought to himself. *They really aren't going to let me go, are they?*

Looking away, Markus then found himself thinking about Ruth. *What would she think of all this food, and all these people? Would she be surprised? Would she zone out of the conversation and stuff her face like she deserved? Never hungry, never looking over her shoulder? Would she... would she be as nervous or afraid as I am right now?*

What am I thinking? I'm still *nervous of all these people. I don't trust them in the slightest. Ashlyn is the only one I can at the moment, even if Ruth was here eating her heart out like we all dreamed of when we were kids, she would still have to be as nervous as I am. Maybe not as* nervous *but nervous nonetheless. Elizabetha's plan, will it really work? Or am I building false hope upon myself like I did when I believed I could save Ruth? What would she be doing now? What would be going through her mind? What would she even say?*

So much went through Markus' head it began to weigh down his heart once again. Not even the intoxicating wine seemed tempting enough to try.

He soon came aware that someone had spoken his name and Markus looked up all of a sudden. "I'm sorry, what was that?"

The Court Mage, Slagar was staring at him with squinted eyes, his elbows on the table and his fingers intertwined. The other councilmen developed a sudden interest in their own meals, as if afraid to get in the way. He sighed as if he was talking to a small child who could hardly pay attention.

"I said, you appear to be thinking of something else *other* than the plan. What can be that important, other than the matters at hand?"

Markus felt heat rising to his cheeks. He was embarrassed to even look at the man before him. Ashlyn looked at him worriedly, while everyone else seemed to only pity him.

"Slagar," Elizabetha said. "He already knows of the plan. You are being rude. He probably has a lot on his mind, and what is to come is probably the last thing he wants to think about at the moment. I'm sure he wasn't expecting to be having dinner with such a large crowd after all he had gone through."

"Yeah," One of the scientists said while swirling her goblet of wine. "Not to mention how rude we were earlier to him."

Slagar smirked and then waved his hand dismissively. "My apologies. Then might I ask, what he thinks of it then? Surely he must have *some* thought on the present eh, situation."

What is this? Markus pursed his lips in thought. "I think it might work." He answered simply, although unconvincingly even to him. He figured if he gave the man what he probably wanted to hear, he would then be left alone. "I… I think it's a start."

Slagar raised an eyebrow and Markus was able to see the pale red eyes without pupil's glare at him. It wasn't some sudden thing Markus thought he saw; the man legitimately had *inhuman* eyes. "Yet you seem unconvinced, and have limited training on the Crystal's capabilities as well as your own in regards to how to actually use it?"

"Slagar…" the person sitting next to him warned.

"Black will teach me." Markus said thinking fast. "He knows more about it than I do." He noticed Black steal a glance at him but the Hunter said nothing. For some reason, as he looked into the Mage's eyes, Markus felt very sleepy. He looked away again, which seemed to only please the strange magician.

"Indeed he does." Slagar nodded. "In fact, he knows quite a lot about all of this, doesn't he?" Slagar's eyes were now squinting at Black. It felt like the room had suddenly dropped ten degrees. "After all, he has to train The Keeper after all."

"I thought I said we weren't going to discuss about that." Elizabetha warned the magician.

Slagar bowed his head while taking a sip of his wine. "Only a speculation, your majesty."

"What are you suggesting, Slagar?" One of the scientists asked rubbing his bald head nervously despite the glare he received from Black himself.

"Oh, nothing." Slagar said with a wave of his hand yet his dark eyes never lingered from Black's. "Just a simple… analysis."

Elizabetha's brow furrowed at this. "At any rate," she said. "It should still give us time to better prepare him and ourselves for the inescapable attack as well as the future. There will be time to worry about such things later. Right now, Markus is just like any of us; as well as my guest."

"Indeed." Slagar said while taking a silver fork and stabbing at his meat before dropping a juicy morsel into his mouth. He talked while he chewed. "Forgive my table manners, but I do have something you all might like to know as well. Something *other* than The Keeper who appears unprepared."

Markus decided that he hated the man.

"Yes?" One of the noblewomen asked as she played with the braid in her hair.

Slagar swallowed before he spoke. "My scanners picked a massive spike in energy emitting from The Eldest. It's been on and off for years, but all of a sudden it's been regular, steady, and almost unchanged. Any idea why?" He looked at Black as if expecting the answer from him.

Black spoke softly, not intimidated in the slightest. "We all know how The Eldest can manipulate us, scare us in our nightmares as we sleep. Sometimes he can even convince others to do things out of the ordinary. This sort of thing happened before, long ago. It had pushed Johnathon to the point of insanity until he got out of the city and away from it all. But even then, he suffered from slight headaches and even once mentioned some… communication, with The Eldest. He said he would hear him speak sometimes. It's obvious that The Eldest has gotten stronger during his time trapped within The Dreaming. He's reaching out to someone. To whom I don't know for sure, though it is most likely someone who has a Crystal." His eyes lingered to Markus for a moment; a warning sort of look almost.

"How do we know it's not you or the kid?" Slagar asked. "You both got Crystal's, correct me if I'm wrong." His statement was met with combined looks of worry towards the Hunter.

"Are you accusing me?" Black asked emotionlessly but the threat was as plain as the writing on the wall. As he looked at him, Markus felt as if the atmosphere had just gotten even colder than before. "We are not the only ones with Crystals, you know."

Slagar smirked at him. "No, I'm not accusing you… Not really. But I don't quite understand why you know so much about The Eldest and won't share *all* the information with me. Are we not all on the same side?"

This confused Markus as well. Why would Black keep secrets from the man? Were the Crystals really that dangerous, or was he hiding something?

"I will not lie," the Hunter said crossing his arms. "The Eldest has spoken to me from time to time, but he has no control as long as I keep my Crystal with me, and keep control of my own thoughts. The spirit within my own has provided much in service regarding my own protection. That is how it has been easy for him to get to me through the Crystal, but it also gives me a chance to set up wards and barriers; anything to keep him at bay. I might be just as vulnerable as any other person who carries a Crystal, but I only remain vulnerable if I allow such thoughts to slip into my head; anything that The Eldest can use against me."

"Intriguing." Slagar said sitting back. "And I suppose it won't work if we put it on a broadcaster and send a signal throughout the city so that none of *us* gets influenced?"

Elizabetha sighed audibly. Markus deducted that this sort of question had already been brought up once before.

"No." Black said simply. "It wouldn't work like that. As I have already told you before, if I recall. Besides," He then added with a chilling smirk. "Even if it would work, I doubt the spirits within The Dreaming would want to work with you. The spirits, they don't like you."

Everyone turned to the magician, who smiled at the remark. "You don't say?" Slagar demanded just as coolly. "You said, 'spirits', as in plural. May I ask, *which* spirits exactly don't want you to talk to me?"

"Enough." The queen said planting her hand down hard on the table and snapping everyone to attention. "Enough of this. Black has always been faithful to Levitika- to all of us. He has a bond with his own Crystal, and I believe he's managed to control it. He won't give in to that demon. He has his reasons to keep information that our own minds cannot fathom, Slagar." Everyone turned back to the magician, afraid to break the terrible silence that has settled over the table.

"Perhaps not." Slagar eventually said leaning back in his chair. "Just being careful, you understand."

"Understood." Black said ending the conversation.

"I want no more discussion of this." Elizabetha said again. "That is final."

Slagar raised his hands in surrender. "Apologies. I won't speak of The Keeper or the Crystals anymore."

Markus began to pick at his food once again uneasily. He noticed that Ashlyn had stopped eating and was looking at him for comfort. This was bad news seeing it before their eyes. They haven't even started yet, and the council was already at each other's throats. Not only that, but the discussion that Black and Slagar were having… spirits, The Dreaming, this Eldest Spirit who was trying to reach out to someone who had a Crystal… it truly was unsettling news for everyone; including Markus himself who might very well be at the center of it all.

Guess I'm not the only one with doubts.

"Very well then." Elizabetha then said. "If Black says that the boy is safe for now, then I believe him. As should you all. He hasn't done anything for us to suspect him of anything." Elizabetha then looked every single person in the eye as she asked, "Does anyone else have any more questions? Concerns? Comments?" At the last word, her eyes settled on Slagar who didn't meet her gaze. When no one spoke up, she nodded contently. "When you are finished with your food, return to your duties."

One by one they all left, all welcoming Markus and Ashlyn into the city-'properly this time'. Eventually, only Slagar was left finishing his pie. He licked up the sweet apple caramel from his fingers and then wiped his mouth with his napkin. He then rose, thanked everyone for the meal and then left without another word. Leaving only the queen, Markus, Black, and Ashlyn.

Eventually Elizabetha rose from her seat as the butlers began to clear the table. "I am sorry," she said. "I shouldn't have had you eat with those men just yet. They just really wanted to see if the rumors were true and-"

"It's because I'm 'The Keeper'." Markus cut her off. "I understand… sorry for interrupting you, Elizabetha."

Elizabetha smiled, sadly, and understandably. "We should go. I'm sure you both would like to actually rest?"

"That's kind of you, ma'am." Markus said with a last-second bow of his head. Rest was he needed. Not any more talk of useless politics or prophecies or magic of any sort. He just wanted to sleep and forget about everything that had happened tonight.

He just wanted to be alone with his thoughts.

"Yeah, and thank you again." Ashlyn said nodding. She then tilted her head. "About what was said-"

"Don't worry about it." Black said suddenly. "I'm sorry you both were placed in such an unpleasant situation. Most of the people in charge here are resting on blind hope towards a prophecy they have been waiting many years to come true- before their own fathers' even heard such words. Slagar, though a powerful ally, is still just another man found wandering in the Wastelands. He only shares with us his hatred for The Capitol, and he only trusts us as far as we trust him. Don't let him get to you, Markus. He is only just as much afraid as any of us are."

"It's not that." Markus said. "It's just… everything."

Black nodded his head. "I understand. Rest assured, you've done nothing wrong. Don't worry, everything will be alright. It will all make sense, hopefully sooner rather than later."

Markus, still uneasy about everything that has happened within the last couple hours, was also grateful that the nightmare has finally ended- for now. "Thank you, thank you all."

The queen smiled. "Go, both of you. Bathe and rest for a bit. Your escorts will be outside past those doors. My daughter will take you, and then we will call you again later tonight." she pointed where Black had brought the teens. "They will show you the rest of the castle and offer any assistance you need."

Back to business it seems. "Yes ma'am." Markus nodded. He was still nervous as to what kind of training he would have to do with Black, but he supposed he had no choice in the matter. After all… he was the supposed 'Keeper'. But more importantly, if training meant that he would soon have to fight Baron Ovid at least, that was just fine with him.

"Black," She said. "Stay. And come with me."

Black nodded. "As you wish." He rose ready to follow.

"And Markus?" Elizabetha said before turning her back to Ashlyn and him who rose from their own seats. "Thank you. I'm glad you made it. For Ruth, we will have a funeral tonight if you would like."

Markus felt relieved to hear this news. Funerals were uncommon for him, in fact he had never been to one. It was never a thing that truly mattered in the world today. His father being taken away at the time of his death, didn't have one either. It was truly a respectable gift from the queen. He wondered if it was her way of apologizing, but pushed the thought from his mind.

"That would be amazing. I'm honored to receive such a gift." He said this despite the pain returning to his heart.

Elizabetha nodded. "An hour then." She looked at Black and with a nod, began to walk, with him in close pursuit. Markus watched them for a bit, wondering just what Ruth would think of her, when they paid their respects to her.

Ashlyn shook his arm. "C'mon." she said. "I got your back."

Markus nodded, ready to push everything to the back of his mind, and just take some time just to rest. He stared at his plate of unfinished food, wondering where it would go. "Okay."

Esmerelda appeared and with a small smile, offered her hand to Markus. "Are you ready?"

"No." he said honestly.

Esmerelda chuckled uneasily. "I understand. But if it makes you feel any better, I'm happy you decided to stay at least. Both of you." She immediately corrected herself for Ashlyn.

Ashlyn said she was happy too, and then the princess led the two from the dining room to prepare for the funeral, where they would all say their final goodbyes to Ruth.

Markus thought he would be prepared for it, but he would soon really feel the gravity of his loss in remembrance of the little girl who once started a stupid snowball fight on their way home before their father returned from work.

~ Departure ~

Markus

The funeral wasn't too bad, considering.

Ruth's glass coffin rested upon a bed of roses on the balcony of the castle while some men played a lament on violins. It seemed like queen Elizabetha had pulled all the stops and asked everyone in the castle to mourn Markus' sister's death, for it looked like a good group of people had gathered inside the Great Hall, all carrying single candles that glowed like many orange stars. All for someone they never knew.

Far below beyond the balcony, the citizens of Levitika didn't seem to notice the fires of farewell that burned beside Ruth's coffin. That was fine with Markus. He didn't want Ruth's death to be put on display for everyone to see, and the queen and princess appeared to be very understanding of that.

It made Markus feel honored, but at the same time kind of offended by the people who stood behind him with their candles and prayers. *They don't even know* who *they are mourning.*

The queen began speaking the final goodbyes while Markus stood beside Ashlyn who kept her hand intertwined with his as he struggled to keep himself from crying. Markus had to be strong for Ruth; and breaking down would not be considered strong or brave, let alone around these people who sat among them; including Esmerelda, Slagar, and the rest of the court.

Black was there as well, but rather than standing with the rest of the group, he stood in the back with his back pressed against the wall. His arms were crossed as he watched in silence. When the music and speech stopped the mob moved about their business as they left for home or their other duties, leaving Markus alone with the royal family as well as Black who remained where he was. In the sky, the moon casted its eerie glow upon the city, and reflected off of Ruth's coffin. She looked like an angel sleeping beneath its pale light.

Markus was so focused on the coffin he did not realize Elizabetha had come in front of him until Ashlyn shook him back to reality.

The queen nodded towards him respectfully. "Are you okay?" she asked.

"I'll be fine." Markus answered. He did not know if he was indeed going to be *fine* let alone *okay*. But he knew that someday, he would. It would be a long time, but for now, he wasn't going to be fine. Not for good long while. But someday, he would. He knew he would.

Elizabetha nodded as if she could see right through his lie. Just like her daughter. "I wanted to remind you that it is customary for cremation here in Levitika. But, we will try to make an exception for you. If there is a place you would rather we bury Ruth, please, say so. The coffin will leave her untouched by decay."

Markus nodded, honestly impressed that such a thing was possible. "I'll keep that in mind, thank you." Where would he have her be buried? He'd have to think about that after the supposed battle that was approaching is over.

"Your guards will take you to your rooms as soon as you are ready." Elizabetha said just as Esmerelda came at her mother's side. The princess, though sad at the event, nodded in encouragement to Markus and Ashlyn.

"Thank you. For everything." Markus said meaning it from the bottom of his heart.

The queen smiled. "You are welcome."

Ashlyn

Later that night as she laid in her bed, Ashlyn was having trouble falling asleep.

The bed was comfortable; in fact, it was the most comfortable thing she had ever felt, and the dark quiet room with the reassurance that there was a guard watching over her outside left her at ease. She felt safe, like she could sleep with both eyes closed instead of waking at every sound she heard.

But it still felt wrong. She felt… alone. More alone than she had ever felt in her life. After her family was killed she had always slept alone until she met

Ruth and Mark. And now, sleeping in her own bed made her somewhat restless and uneasy. The clock on the dresser in the corner ticked away, taunting her with the time and adding to the feeling desolation.

I wonder how Mark is doing… After the funeral and Ruth's body was sent back into the room Ashlyn took him to earlier, Markus really didn't say much. Not about Ruth, or anything that was expected to happen while in Levitika. She expected him to cry actually, but instead he said nothing and expressed nothing. It was as if her friend had gone numb; something was far too broken inside for him to even register the will to cry. He was holding it in, that much she could tell, but it was effortless and even afterwards he moved about like a drone without a purpose.

Even when she had finally released his hand he only looked at her sadly when she said goodnight. After the door was closed between then, Ashlyn found herself staring at her hand for a good chunk of time before finally deciding to retire.

Even now she was staring at that same hand that had released him when she said goodnight.

"What a pain…" she muttered to herself as she clenched her fist and allowed it to rest upon her breast.

After some careful thinking, she got out of bed and padded silently to her door. She stepped out and the guard stood immediately at attention, his helmet humming to life as he turned to her. She wondered if it turned on automatically or if he just turned it on when she came out.

"Is everything okay?" he asked.

"I'm fine." Ashlyn told him. "I need you to take me to Markus."

"It is an hour past two, miss."

She looked at the man. The clock hadn't been lying after all. "Please?"

The guard nodded and pressed the earpiece of his helmet. "I am taking Ashlyn to Markus' room."

"Roger," a voice said loud enough for Ashlyn to hear.

"Go right ahead." The guard gestured across the hall to Markus' door where his guard nodded approval.

"Thank you both," she said as she walked to the door and pushed it open.

She stepped inside the dark room dimly lit by a small lamp on the night stand. The covers lumped up like a small hill in the middle of the gigantic bed, and it rose and fell with long and steady breathing.

"Mark?" She called softly to the lump beneath the sheets. She walked forward and sat on the edge of the bed beside the lump. "Mark?"

"What are you doing up?" Markus said stiffly and muffled. He sounded like he was ill, or had even just got done crying. His head was covered, and he didn't come up.

Like a turtle in a shell... "Are you okay?"

"I'm fine."

"You're crying, aren't you?" When Markus didn't respond, she continued in a softer tone. "I came because I didn't want to sleep alone tonight. Would you... like some company?"

Minutes passed in silence but Ashlyn had no plans to leave anytime soon. Finally, Markus replied in almost a whisper. "Please." The covers came down and Mark sat up in his bed. His shirt was rumpled and his blonde hair was a flattened mess. His face and eyes were red from crying. He wiped them quickly. "I feel so stupid, crying so much."

"Why?" Ashlyn said scooting onto the sheets and pulling the comforter over her waist. The sheets separated her from Markus but she could still feel his warmth.

"I just do. I feel weak. I have to keep acting strong... Not only for the people here, but for Ruth. I already failed her once, I can't appear weak again." Markus shook his head. "I feel like I gotta keep playing the part of a play I never wanted to act in..."

Ashlyn frowned in thought. Seeing Markus like this, was almost as if looking at a small child crying, and asking why the world was so cruel. She rested her back against the headboard and opened her arms. "Come here."

Markus looked at her skeptically.

"Come here," she insisted.

After a minute of some silent struggle, he relented and scooted closer. He leaned into her, his head softly settling into her shoulder and she hugged him tight. She felt his forehead and cheek through her shirt, damp, and warm. His hair smelled of shampoo, and his body heat was like a furnace.

He's so warm... "It *is* okay for men to cry, Mark," she said to him, running her hands up and down his back. "I told you already. A real man cries because he cares. He cares about others, and he holds it all in for those around him. But sometimes those tears need to fall. Even if it does seem silly or weak to them. No man is made of stone, and anyone who says otherwise is a fool."

She felt her shoulder get warmer and wetter as she felt his tears. He didn't say anything, and he felt like he was swallowing his choked sobs in order to keep it all together; one last barrier before it all came out like a flood.

"It's okay. I'm here." She held him tighter as he silently sobbed. She ran her fingers through his hair and held him close like a sister comforting a brother; trying to help hold him together as he fell apart tonight. Being with him again like before made her feel more at ease, and try as she may she could not stop her own eyes from getting heavy. He and Ruth, brought new light into her life, and made everything better. Because of them, they made her feel confident, and brave.

Now it was her turn to return the favor.

"Ashlyn?" Mark eventually said.

"Yeah?"

"What do you want in life?"

Such a strange question, one that hardly anyone can truly answer.

She thought long and hard after that. Then she replied softly. "To be happy. To live in a home away from all of the fear and pain, no one to tell me what to do. Be somewhere, where I can truly be free and not suffer being alone." That's what she wanted: to never be alone again. But for some reason, she could not bring herself to say it. "What about you?"

"Fairness."

"What do you mean?"

"If you do something bad, something bad will happen to you. Do good, and good will come of it- at least, that is what is said. My family only did what we had to, just to survive. I understand that my father's doings got him killed by the Baron. But what about Ruth? Why did she have to die? What did she ever do? Where's the reasoning of her death?"

Ashlyn sighed sadly. "I don't know Mark. I don't know. Sometimes… there is no good reason for the things that happen, at least, none that we can see as of now."

Markus sniffed. "All I wanted for the past few years was for her to be safe and alive. So we can survive together. Now look at me… Ruth is gone, and I don't have to fight and struggle to survive in that damn city anymore. But what do I have to live for? This so-called prophecy? Pulling an act so that the queen and her city have hope? I didn't ask for this. So I guess... I want the same thing you want... Freedom."

Ashlyn nodded, her eyes slowly shutting. Try as she might, her lids refused to stay open and sleep began to take her away from this world, and into the land of dreams; and she began to nod off. She didn't want to go, not yet. She had to be here, she had to listen to Markus speak; let him get the words out that couldn't stay in his chest forever.

She wanted him to have some freedom, in the time they had together.

Just a little longer... please let me stay with him a little longer, please...

As she slowly drifted away like a piece of driftwood in the ocean, she heard Markus say two words before she fell into the dreaming, away from all worries until morning.

"Thank you."

~ The Dreaming ~

Markus
The next morning, Markus left Ashlyn to let her sleep a little longer.

It was nearing the ninth hour, and it was time to begin his 'training'. Having very little sleep and excitement for the actual training, Markus was in a foul mood and dreaded what he would be doing this morning. Having woken up still in Ashlyn's lap with her sitting up, he barely managed to slip out of her grasp and set her gently down onto her side. He didn't want her to have a sore neck upon waking up, but he supposed that it would be too late for that. She muttered in her sleep as he moved her, but other than that, she remained asleep.

Just about as tired as I am… he thought as he got dressed with his back to her. Still, he stole a glance every so often, looking upon her sleeping face so peacefully. *It's different than it was back in the Wastelands…*

At his side, Markus harnessed his staff, with the Crystal glowing brightly within. After strapping on his backpack as well, he stepped out and then crossed the hall to meet up with the guard on duty. The man took him through the Throne Room and down another hall downstairs.

After a long walk it seemed, Markus then stepped out and saw that he was in some sort of courtyard in the center of the castle. Fresh snow had fallen, yet the sun was out, bright, but not warm in the slightest. The tall walls and towers filled with the windows revealing the interior of the castle hid the yard from the rest of the world, the bright blue sky glaring down overhead. All around him, the snow looked to Markus like a blinding carpet of fire.

Hedges circled the center of the yard, and in the center of it all stood Black, garbed in his black armor with his sword stuck in the frozen ground and his cloak flapping in the wind on it like a flag. Having said thanks to his escort, Markus left the guard behind and started forward, his feet crunching in the snow.

With each step, he talked himself out of his subdued anger towards the Hunter. It did him little good to blame the man now, considering what Markus now knew about his father's role in this whole thing as well as Black's own. It was all a part to be played in a massive game comprehendible by Markus' own present standards.

For now, he simply just had to play his own part in this giant game he had been sucked into, and Markus stopped before Black and cleared his throat.

The man looked at Markus for a while, his hair billowing in the wind like black fire. Having mostly keeping his hood on, it was strange seeing his hair flowing like that again. Now that he was closer, Markus was finally able to look upon the Hunter with different eyes. The face he looked at, aged with time and having a slightly bent nose from his fight with his father, Black was a new man.

Just like Markus was.

Eventually, Black reached into his pocket, and pulled out his Crystal, which glowed red in the sunlight. Upon seeing it, Markus' own Crystal in the dagger glowed bright and blue, as if it was reacting to the Crystal in its own presence. Not only that, but Markus himself felt something as well, as if someone else was standing next to Black, watching him.

"The Seven were designed for different purposes." Black suddenly said in a tone that was clear and stern, indicating that the lesson had begun. Markus found it funny that the man didn't even bother to say 'hello' or 'good morning'. "Each one having similar but different traits like the spirits within. However, one thing they all have in common, at least due to my personal experiences and research, is that they allow the human body to work considerably better through a different source of magic. The different realms, or dimensions within the world we live in, seem to come together into the human body, making it stronger. For example, if you will it to be, you can become stronger, faster, and can probably jump higher if you wanted to. However, your body is still as fragile as the day you are born, so I'd advise against anything rash."

Rash? Like anything about this isn't *even remotely rash...* Still, Markus kept his mouth shut. He was honestly intrigued by what Black was saying, and continued to listen as his 'teacher' continued.

"Your reflexes are that of a cat, and through the realm known as The Dreaming, can sense the life aura of all living things. In fact, you found most of this out in the Fiery Plains, against the monsters created by the witch who pursued you, did you not?"

Markus felt his mouth twitch, the memory of what happened out in the Plains flashing through his mind. "How do you figure that?"

Ignoring his question, Black asked again. "Did you?"

"Yes." Markus said still trying to grasp everything he had just heard. *The Dreaming... just like what Abner said...*

Black nodded. "Basically, if you imagine the fact that your body is stronger, you can push it beyond its natural limits through the energy passed through to you by the Crystal in your possession. The multi-layer of The Dreaming condensing in the world you and I are currently in allow you to strengthen your body and mind. It is also apparent that the Crystals will affect and react not only to your body physically, but emotionally and spiritually as well. That is part of the balance of the mind within the dimensions between our world and The Dreaming."

Markus said nothing, still trying his best to take in all of this. Black said it so casually, it was strange *not* to say anything, but Markus just didn't have the words to speak.

"Please," Black then said breaking into Markus' train of thought. "Ask me anything if none of this makes sense to you."

"It makes sense." Markus answered. "It's just surreal. Basically, there is another dimension that the Crystals draw energy from and pass onto me. That's why I was able to hold my own against the Woodies."

Black's expression softened, seeming impressed before he continued. "Tell me, what did you feel out there when the Woodies attacked?"

Markus looked down at his feet. Ashamed to say but he felt that he had no choice. Markus had to know what had happened and if he could manage it again. "I was afraid that me and the girls would die." *That Ruth would die...*

"Fear." Black nodded. "A powerful influence not only causing your body to react, but the Crystal as well. The traditional 'fight or flight' reaction, as it were."

Markus subconsciously reached up with his hands, rubbing his arms as if they suddenly got colder.

"In fact, you witnessed it first-hand when you released all of your emotion into energy, kind of like your laser bolts. But instead of energy being passed through a small generator your father installed into the spear, it passed through your very life aura; the sheer will of your human nature; thus, releasing it as a powerful expansion and eliminating the Woodies around you using the very force which is not only in the Crystals, but now inside you: Magic."

Markus looked over to his right where the nearest hedge was as he took all of this in. Markus could see the plants own life aura. Faint, dormant beneath the snow, but still very much alive.

"That's a lot to take in." he said raising his eyes back up to the Hunter. "Is this really magic?"

Black nodded. "It is a *type* of magic, yes. Ancient or new, I'm afraid I cannot tell for certain. I understand that it is a lot to take in. Which is why I am not going to teach any magic at the moment. That isn't the point of you and I meeting this morning."

Markus looked at Black, confused. "I don't understand. Then what *is* the point?"

"The best way to learn is small steps. I once read a book when I was very young. It was an old book, nearly four thousand years old, but still in good condition. I found it in a small compound beneath a building with my own father, back when I was a child."

Markus thought it was strange: thinking of Black as once being a child.

"One of the lines read, 'Life is like crossing a river. Take too big of a step and you will lose balance, and the current will sweep you away.'"

"So, with small steps, you have more control." Markus gathered.

"That's right," Black said seemingly pleased. "So, I'm going to train you to open your mind to the world around you, and so you will not be influenced by outside forces. I do not believe we will run into that problem, should Baron Ovid actually have a Crystal in his possession. In fact, if we *are* attacked, I plan to keep you as far away from the action as possible. I plan to only use you as a greater pair of eyes, which this first lesson in using magic will help us with. But let's not worry about that now.

"For now, let's just say another master of a Crystal, or even a powerful magician is in your presence, and he is *not* friendly. He will try to break you mentally and emotionally, so that you are deemed weak physically. If you open your mind to the world and better understand it without your own emotions or unnatural forces to influence you, you will have not only better control yourself and know your limits, but also better protect yourself from such entities."

"So, finding a balance in nature?"

"Not quite. It is like finding the balance between this world and The Dreaming, which influences human emotion and imagination. If you learn to control that by seeing and hearing the *current* world around you, you will achieve perfect balance and gain an advantage over the other Crystal-bearer or magical foe."

Markus nodded, piecing what he had heard together. Black, thankfully, allowed him such time to think this over. "Will the same go for witches and warlocks?"

"No. However, there are *some* that can influence the mind through great and sometimes forbidden practices. They receive their powers from potions, spirits, and radiation mutation."

"Mutants?"

"Yes and no. A mutant is only influenced by radiation, which is a biochemical and nuclear hazard. However, in reality when in terms to the mind and soul, they are no different than you or I. Magic is a different influence on the human body all-together, as well as everything around it. It is merely energy coming from spirits, potions, or even within. It is when the energy inside you and the energy around you are shifted out of balance so that you can bend things to your will. And in concern to other wielders of a Crystal, we are talking about true power from within: the power of the human mind."

Markus began to scratch his head which started to hurt. "This is all hard to completely understand…"

"I don't expect you to understand." Black said waving his hand and gesturing to the spot in front of him. "Take a seat." After Markus sat down he continued, "I don't expect you to understand it all. I only expect you to focus on the small steps. One thing at a time."

Markus nodded. "Okay. But, can I ask one thing?"

"What's that?"

"Am I *really* going to be fighting in a war? Like... this whole prophecy you all keep speaking of... is it legitimate?"

"Nothing is 'legitimate' in the world we know of today." Black answered without any hesitation at all. "We aren't going to throw you head-first into the fray. That would be irresponsible on our part and would break our promise to you. For now, you are just another piece in a big game. A major piece, but not for now. My goal, is to make you a more powerful piece so that you can choose for yourself what is right and wrong in your own eyes. Your agreement to help our cause is admirable, but I can also tell it stresses you. Our plan isn't for you to win the war for us; that would be irrational and unfair if we were to expect that. *I* plan, to make you strong so that you can use your power as The Keeper for the greater good; and then eventually, you will be able to chart your own course and pick your own battles, prophecy or none."

Markus fell silent, lost in his own thoughts. He had agreed to help the Levitikans, yes, but he also felt like this was all just a big game and he was just another pawn the way the Hunter explained it. But at the same time, Black... he made him feel like... so much more.

Markus then said, "Be honest with me... the prophecy, about me... do you really believe in it? Do you really think that I... that I am The Keeper?"

Black didn't even hesitate. "I have no doubt I my mind."

Markus looked away, honestly wishing that Black *had* hesitated. "Alright." he muttered, still uneasy, but also somewhat ready.

The Hunter nodded. "We're going to take the first step now. This is not a spell, and it will not test your body *physically*, but it will help you defend yourself from outside forces for the time being. After this I will show you how to harness the energy to make your body stronger, so that you are better suited for battle- when the time comes for you of course. We need you at your best, and since your Crystal, Abner, chose you, then you will be a very important part of this whole ordeal. But for now: the mind. Any form of magic requires mental training, and therefore that is where we will begin.

"Can I ask one more thing first?" Markus asked hoping that he wasn't being too much of a hassle though at the same time not caring *too* much.

"You may."

"You said that the Crystal 'chose me'. What does that even mean exactly? I still don't fully understand."

Black tilted his head. He actually looked confused at the question. "Did I not explain already? There is a spirit inside that crystal, a tortured soul trapped in a prison of concentrated energy. The spirit within *chose* you. That is who Abner is, the one who revealed himself to you when the Crystal finally awakened."

"But… why?"

"Who can say? It might have known you were the prophesized Keeper, or it may have just liked you. Why did mine choose me? It's like… friends, I suppose. Sometimes, you just click with people with no explanation. I am sure there is more to it than that, but we don't have time to go over it all. Maybe someday though, you can ask *him* yourself when you are strong enough to reach out to him rather than him come to you and not show up again after so long."

Markus wanted to ask and learn more, but he figured it was better just to go with the man. "Alright. The mind then."

Black nodded with approval. "As I said, it requires a lot of mental training and focus. A cluttered mind will not be able to become more aware of the world around it. It creates unbalance not only in magic, but also critical decision-making. So, I'm going to show you a type of meditation that will help us clear the clutter in your own head."

"Alright…" Markus was confused, but eager to learn what the Hunter meant actually.

"Happiness, dread, fear, pain; everything in terms of emotion must be unleashed. If there is pain, sorrow, fear, I want you to let yourself feel it all so that all stress is relieved from your mind. Once your mind is clear, reach out until you can feel everything around you. The dirt beneath you, and the people all around you. Using the Crystal, amplify your reach- but only once your mind is clear. Sit in what weighs you down, and reach."

Reach… Markus took out his dagger, and rubbing his thumb on his Crystal, feeling foolish as he began to try and 'concentrate' But every time he focused on one thing, the 'aura haze' would disappear as he looked from one hedge to another. He just couldn't focus his 'energy' at all.

"This is difficult." he griped. "There are too many plants here, and most of them are under snow. This is hard."

"That isn't the point of this meditation." Black said patiently, almost as if he expected Markus to react as such. "You're allowing yourself to be influenced by your feelings."

How? "Well, aren't feelings supposed to make us human?" Markus countered the Hunter. "What is the point anyway? Why does it matter what I feel?"

Black sighed patiently. "Right now, you have a lot of clutter; things that bottle up in your mind. Negative feelings, for example. Fear, sorrow, anger, these things only add pressure to the mind the more you hold it all in, and I can tell that you have a lot held in. Thing is, if held in together for too long, it creates too much pressure and you lose the chance to see the bigger picture around you. All that your mind is focused on, is yourself and all that effort can and will eventually explode and you will lose control of yourself both physically, mentally, and of course, magically."

"I already know that there is a bigger world out there other than me." Markus snapped but immediately pulled the reins on his frustration. He took a deep breath before speaking again. "Look, I'm not like *you*. Unlike you, I can't just… not feel anything. I have to be either happy, content, angry… or sad. That is just how life works, right? I can't just numb it all like you."

Black's brow angled slightly as he peered at Markus. For a moment, Markus though he saw anger flash through those cold eyes of the Hunter's, but the light quickly faded away when Black breathed, "You think I don't feel pain? Guilt, or loss?"

Markus said nothing, but glared defiantly.

"The reason why I appear so calm is because I allow what is hurt to hurt, and whatever thoughts I have I think in reason. It is because doing so keeps me relax and helps me *concentrate*. It helps me to think logically and not react emotionally when the time comes to protect those I care about. I'm not saying feelings are not important, as you said, they are. But in specific situations, if you allow yourself to get emotional, you will become blinded, both in magic, and in life itself. This lesson is no different than when a commander needs to make an educated decision that will either save his soldiers, or get them killed. This is a lesson in which you learn to take back control of your thinking process, and in turn, take control of your new abilities and more."

Markus stared at the Hunter, and then sighed. "Fine." He took a deep breath and began to try and focus again.

"You're still holding in the negative energy inside you."

"I am not."

"Yes, you are." Black said. "I can see it within you. It burns bright like a candle trying to breathe life into a dying flame. Sorrow, anger, regret. All welled up inside you as if you are a bottle."

"So what?" Markus snapped and he tossed his staff into the snow in front of him. "This is stupid!"

"Explain." Black said setting his hands in his lap.

"What?"

"Explain what you feel. Not only will these relieve your tension, but it might help you to overcome it so we can continue your training."

Now that made Markus angry. *What is he now, a therapist now instead of a Hunter?* "What's it to you?" Markus said in a low voice. "You don't need to know what I am feeling; it's not like you can understand anyway."

Black peered at him with a colder expression. "I'm trying to help you, Mark."

"Don't call me that." Black didn't have the right to call him that.

"Markus, then." Black said in a seemingly bored tone. The man obviously couldn't care less. "What is it you are feeling?"

"What if I don't want to tell you?" Markus demanded. "What if I say this whole thing is a bunch of crap and I don't want your help with *anything*?"

"Then we will remain sitting here until we freeze or the Baron comes to slaughter us all. Whichever comes first." Black sounded so indifferent that it was impossible to tell whether he was being serious or not. But the cold look in the man's eye, told Markus that it wasn't a threat, but a promise. A dare to try to stand and walk away.

Markus' brow furrowed as he glared at Black. "Like you care."

"Try me."

He sighed. *This guy...* "Look, it doesn't matter *what* I feel." he said. "Even if I did, I don't know how to turn whatever I *do* feel off and-"

"I never said turn them off. I said let them out."

"I can't, I cannot even explain them if I were to try. It doesn't matter…"

"That's where you're wrong. It *does* if it affects how you react to everything around you and affect your energy." Black paused. "And if it affects those around you."

"Excuse me?"

"How you feel not only influences your actions or energy. But those around you. Just look at Ashlyn. Or better, think about Ruth."

Markus felt his blood boil beneath his skin. The feeling of the cold was gone despite how chilly it was. "Shut up." he said in almost a whisper. "Don't *ever* talk about Ruth. You have no right to."

Black shrugged as if he did not care in the slightest. "Then listen to me carefully. I'm not going to sugar-coat if for you: You are mentally and emotionally unstable."

For some reason, the words stuck into Markus like a knife between the ribs.

"The mind is like your body. When you place your hand on a hot plate, it burns; it hurts. It's your brain telling you that something is wrong and you need to act. Your feelings work the same way, but instead of letting the pain register, you bottle it up. You allow your guilt, your gut feelings to surpass your common sense. You value others too much to do anything reckless; and that is good, it proves that you are an honorable young man who cares. But you allow the burden of others to affect you more than you should, and you worry so much and keep it all inside. That makes you fearful of failure and the fact that you feel that you failed your sister; it causes you to dwell on it like a child with a broken toy instead of learning from it. No matter how much you wish you could try again, it won't happen. Yet you keep dwelling nonetheless which makes you not only open to attacks on your subconscious, but a nuisance to all and whatever matters."

"Shut up!" Markus snapped and he felt his hair spike up as he heard a snap and crackle along with the smell of ozone. Black merely chuckled as if he was amused by Markus' abnormal reaction.

"You see?" Black said as if he expected this to happen. "That is a manifestation of all the pain you kept inside yourself. If you were to allow yourself to feel that sort of pain, it wouldn't have built up in such an epic proportion. Instead, you held it all in and you let me get at you when I brought up your sister and taunted you with her."

"How could I not? You can't expect me to just accept the fact that she is gone in less than a day. How can I *ever* get over the fact that she is gone!?"

"Maybe you won't, ever." Black reasoned. "But at the same time, why do you blame yourself for what happened when you couldn't have done anything to prevent it from happening?"

Markus was struck-dumb. He couldn't say anything despite how much he desperately wanted to argue.

"You blame yourself, and as a result you cannot accept that what has happened has happened. Sometimes, you can't stop terrible things from happening. Sometimes you have to pick the better of worse scenarios, or sometimes you don't even get a chance. Life just happens, and there's nothing you can do about it, other than grow from it in order to be better for yourself. Ruth would want you to grow, to become a better person for yourself and others around you, like Ashlyn. She would want you to live your life instead of letting her departure anchor you in the same spot forever. Don't you want that?"

Markus looked down at the snow, trying desperately not to cry in front of Black. He *was* right. Markus *was* afraid to fail. *And the fact that I've failed Ruth… Oh Ruth…*

"Do not ever forget your pain, Markus." Black said. "But, you can't let it control your life, not just in this training of magic, but in your entire life as a whole. Don't hold it all in Markus." Black said this a little more softly now. "Talk to me. Open yourself, and tell the plants around you. They are listening. Let it all out. What is it that you feel?"

Markus took a shuddered breath as if Death's hand was grasping his very spine, making his skin tingle and upset his stomach. He thought long and hard as to how he was going to put it all into words while Black sat there patiently; not moving a single muscle in his body as he awaited what his pupil before him would say. Still as a statue, he waited.

Finally, Markus looked up at Black, and opened his mouth. "I don't think I can do it."

Black eyes wavered, an subconscious signal for the boy to clarify.

"This whole prophecy thing? I think your mystical owl-thing made a mistake. If I can't even protect my own family, how am I going to be much help to an entire city? My father was killed in order to help you guys, my sister has died going on a crazy trip to find a kingdom in the clouds, and now the Baron is on his way here! And even if it takes him weeks or even months to get here, how are *you*, a man I *hate*, going to make *this*, into the warrior the people expect me to be?" Markus cried all this out while pointing at himself. "I can't let go of my pain because of Ruth. I'm afraid that I don't *want* to forget. I just… don't have the will to do anything anymore. Not this prophecy, or anything at all. Without her… everything seems like too much."

Black said nothing. He remained silent, staring, irritatingly staring at Markus as if he was studying him. All of that he had said thus far, he couldn't even bring himself to say to Ashlyn.

And though he felt ashamed, Markus continued. "There's nothing special about me. My father's Crystal, Abner, he should have picked someone better to fulfill any dead legend's wishes. *You* could do it! I'm sorry, but I think this is all a mistake, Black. I'm not the hero everyone wants me to be. I'm just a poor schmuck who can't get a break. The son of a mechanic- or who I want to believe was a mechanic and nothing more, regardless of what you or the queen says. There is *nothing* special about me. I've failed my sister and my father, and I will never forgive myself for it. I can't."

Still, even hearing all of this, brought no reaction from Black who continued to listen as Markus proceeded with a moment of effort.

"What if I fail Ashlyn? The queen? The city, everything will be devastated and all the dreams of hope and peace against a tyrant who wants nothing but complete control will be shattered. When he comes, that is all that will happen. What then?" He shook his head miserably and muttered. "I can't deal with that… It's just… too much."

After his rant, Markus awaited Black's response. For a long while the Hunter still sat there motionless in thought as he studied the boy before him. Markus had to admit expressing what he felt made it a little better, as if the weight on his heart has been lifted only slightly. But the weight still hung over it, just threatening to come all crashing down into reality. After minutes of uncomfortable silence Black stood with slow feline grace.

"Come with me," he said turning to walk towards the main doors.

Markus stood up in a hurry trying to catch up as he scooped up his staff. "Why, wait up. Where are we going?" Black did not answer, so Markus merely followed, confused and also afraid.

Black continued to move in swift silence, sometimes taking turns so fast that it left Markus falling behind, staggering as he tried to keep up with the elusive Hunter. After what felt like chasing the man for hours, Markus and he eventually ended up near the southern part of the castle where Markus saw warehouses filled with many tanks and flying machines. Machine guns and swords were being forged on anvils by the dozen, by many men and androids who were darkened with soot and grime.

Many nodded hellos as Markus and Black passed by and the two went to the main strip where a few Dragonfly choppers were stationed including the one Markus was told took them to the city. He was intrigued by the symbols on the side; the pair of wings on either side of a simply-drawn owl-like sigil. He thought of asking about the origin, but decided against it.

The Hunter continued to walk despite Markus eventually demanding to tell him what they were doing. Still however, the man said nothing to the point where it began to drive Markus crazy.

They all then came across a flight of stairs to one of the towers aligned with the massive wall. After climbing up to the top of the tower where a cannon blaster was mounted, they finally stood on the wall surrounding the city. They both stopped at the parapet, overlooking the entire Northern Wastelands below.

The sea of snow and trees stretched out as far as the eye could see. Beyond that, Markus was able to see the Razor-Back Mountains, and above them the circle of birds and Ahools making their last-morning flights before bedding down for the day. The sun shone bright in the far distance, setting the world aflame with its brilliant glare. The world looked so much bigger high in the sky, that Markus couldn't help but stare in awe. They really were floating in the sky.

They really were in the City of Angels.

"Wow," he eventually said.

"The view is beautiful." Black said not looking at him. "Isn't it?"

"I still can't believe how high up we are." He turned to Black. "All of this because of a Crystal?"

"I will show you it later if we have time." Black said. "Or someone will… It was actually the first Crystal ever created. Before yours or mine or any of the others were created, including The Eldest. It is because of it that we have been able to hide out for so long."

Remembering Elizabetha's story, Markus nodded. "Wow… incredible."

"The city's survival depended on being high above the clouds, and the movement of the island is so slow that almost no one notices that it moves until they realize the mountains are further away. To be honest, I'm surprised they never thought to take you out here yet. But under the circumstances…"

Markus understood. Black was trying his best not to tear up scabbed wounds. Still, he appreciated it. "That's amazing."

"Yes. That is why Levitika has managed to stretch the legend. People below in the villages and cities we monitor would only catch mere glimpses and blame the sun for mirages if we do not move among the clouds. Although, it *does* make it difficult in the summer when there are hardly any. So the city remained near the mountains for years in preparation for the second rebellion."

Markus nodded, still amazed by the view. It was incredible, thinking how small they really were in the world. But there *was* a reason Black brought him up here, and it wasn't for the view. "So why did you bring me up here?" He asked looking at the Hunter. "To tell me more about the whole war and prophecy and all?"

Black shook his head. "I noticed you brought your Eagles-Wings."

The backpack on Markus' shoulders suddenly felt heavier. "So?"

The Hunter turned so his back was against the parapet as he faced Markus. "I also remembered, from back in Nineveh, that you liked to fly." And as simple as ever like it was nothing short of normal, he fell back and over the parapet.

"Hey!" Markus gasped rushing over and looking down to see the man freefalling far below. His cloak flapped behind him until they seemed to stretch out and slow his decent like a hang glider. The updraft of air then launched him back skyward, and he turned his head to give Markus a mischievous grin.

He looked like a Ahool, flapping his 'wings' and flying across the sky. He dipped and rose three times as he glided across the clouds before turning back and shooting a grapple-hook towards the parapet, which stuck in the railing ten feet away from where Markus stood. Then in almost a minute the Hunter was brought back to the city walls, a small smile on his lips as he looked at Markus who was practically blanching over the parapet in shock and relief.

"Extenders." Black explained as he pulled himself up closer to Markus. "They help me to stretch the cloak out and catch me like a glider."

"Incredible," Markus said still amazed. He shook his head. "You're insane."

Amused by the remark, Black said, "They are not as good as the city's Eagle-Wings, for I cannot stay in the air for too long before I fall too low and cannot pull myself back to the city."

"You're insane."

Black nodded as he scaled the railing over to Markus, never letting go of the parapet or the grapple-gun in his hand. "Come."

"Wait- what?" Markus asked as Black suddenly lashed out towards his shirt like a python, pulling Markus over the ledge with him. He *screamed* as they both plummeted towards the ground, the air pushing against their faces and making their hair billow around their heads. "Gah! Good, God!" Markus cried out as he flailed in the air like a bird that had just been kicked out of its nest.

"Relax!" Black said falling head-first next to him as Markus tried to straighten himself out and slow down his decent. It was almost comical, seeing Black act so calm while Markus freaked the hell out. "Let the planet pull you towards it, and when I say so, open your wings."

"I'll *crash* before I fly at this rate!" Markus screamed. He was absolutely positive that the man was indeed *insane*.

"Well, good time to practice." Black grinned which only made the falling more surreal. "Now." And he opened his cloak and the draft pulled him high up above Markus like he had opened a parachute.

Markus then struggled to find his lever and release the pressure in his pack to open the Eagle-Wings. He felt something move behind him and the pressure of the air beneath him alleviated as he straightened himself out and his wings spread out with the neural-connector strapped to the back of his head.

With full control of his wings now, he began to glide over the valleys, still thousands of feet below the city; which Markus saw was indeed a massive island with a rocky bottom holding up the massive walls and city within. The castle was obscured at this angle but it was beautiful to see just how massive it really was. With the wind blowing past his face and through his hair, Markus practically *swam* through the gusts, feeling the adrenaline spread through his body and make him feel excited that he could actually fly.

It had been so long since he could do this. Flying high above the world, no desolate and ruined cities for miles, no sense of dread of ever having to land, Markus just felt *relieved*. Up here, he felt free; especially when the sunlight caught the glint of the bronze wings as he banked around and circled at high speeds like he used to back in Nineveh as a simple delivery boy.

He banked around to see that Black was grappling back up. He clicked on the boosters on the wings and flapped up towards The Hunter, circling him like a vulture hunting prey.

"Not bad." Black called out as he dangled there.

"I missed doing this." Markus shouted to him still circling. He saw Black peer at him as the glint from his wings reflected the sun.

"I know." The Hunter replied shielding his eyes with a free hand. "Clears your head, doesn't it?"

"How did you know?"

Black shrugged. "'Cause it's what I used to do when I was just a child."

Hearing that confused Markus. Did Black have a normal childhood? Then again, he didn't know much about the guy. Markus doubted anyone really did but the fact that the Hunter used to act like a child was bewildering to say the least.

"Take your time." Black then said hoisting himself up. "I will call you when it is time to come back for training."

Markus looked at him confused. "Aren't you going to stay awhile?"

"I'll stay at the tower, watching. Like I said: I can't glide too long or too far from the city. You just go out there, clear your head."

Markus nodded before diving down towards the ground again. Feeling the rush of the wind and the thrill of the fast-approaching world filled him with ecstasy. When he was just about to reach it, Markus pulled up, and looped up just in time for his feet to kick off some of the snow off the top of a little hill. He swirled and spun as he made his way back up, only to release the current and free-fall back down. He then opened up his wings again and merely glided easily across the sky. Far below, he saw another herd of giant slugs, oblivious to the flying human high above them.

It felt really good, and Markus felt all his fear slip away. His worries for the time being was gone. The pain from his loss was still great, but being up here made Markus feel closer to Ruth. As if he was flying right beside her; a figurative angel beside an actual angel. He smiled as a thought passed through his head.

"I know what you want." he said to her as he dipped up and began flapping back towards the city, back to Black to *actually* begin his training.

Once again, Markus sat across from Black in the courtyard; right in the exact same spot as they had before. With his dagger in his hands and resting in his lap, Markus felt the Crystals' glow tingle against the skin on his hands and travel up his arms. He tried once again to let his feelings go, and let them wander free as Black had said, and begin his journey. He closed his eyes, and opened his consciousness to the life around him.

Reach… A familiar voice that was not Black's whispered.

This time, he allowed himself to feel everything. The pain he felt when he thought of Ruth and his father, the fear he felt living in Nineveh, the regrets he had held since being a little boy, the guilt of all the things he had done, the moments of utter despair, Markus allowed himself to feel it all. It felt like a thousand needles were piercing his stomach, and he clenched his fists and felt foolish because it felt like he was on the verge of tears. Sitting here, in the cold with the Hunter Black and not doing anything but just sitting in his own trauma, hurt worse than any injury inflicted on Markus' own body. How much time had passed, he had no clue. It felt like hours of just sitting and feeling until little by little, the pain slowly left his body like a heavy spectral, and he all of a sudden felt lighter than ever as if a weight had been taken off his shoulders.

Immediately like a rush, Markus began to see it all.

Through closed eyes the world was shut out into complete and utter darkness. Yet everything around Markus was alit with life. Across from him, he saw the hazy shadow of red portraying the calm demeanor of Black, who twirled his own Crystal in his hands which glowed a brighter shade of dark purple.

Why does he feel… guilty? Markus found himself wondering as his mind began to stretch out a little further.

All of the dormant bushes and grass around them was a mere whisper of light gray, and the little insects and animals burrowed deep beneath the surface was a smoky light blue color. Little flames, like candles.

Beyond the courtyard, he saw the guards marching down the castle halls and along the walls, different shades revealed them to be human while the androids remained as dark as the environment around them for there was no life in their humanoid bodies.

Markus then saw Slagar in his study room, his shadow a whispery white, occasionally flickering red in frustration. He also saw Esmerelda and Ashlyn in another room. Ashlyn was sitting down while Esmerelda was hunched beside her. Ashlyn's bluish aura also flickered red in frustration, as if she was concentrating on something. Esmerelda on the other hand was a yellowish color, as if she was indifferent as she watched her new friend. The two apparently really hit it off and Markus was glad that Ashlyn had made a friend already. He began to push further into the fray of oblivion.

The queen, Markus saw was studying over something by the way her posture was hunched over pointing at nothing to his eyes. Her aura was as red as blood, darker than that of Black's. Markus continued to watch until he even saw the birds flying around them and the animals crawling across the world miles below the city. It was amazing to see this far without actually seeing the world with your own two eyes. He wanted to see further. He wanted to... *reach*, further...

Markus felt himself being pulled back into his own body as he felt a hand softly shake his right shoulder. Like a vacuum he was sucked right through the haze and he gasped as he felt himself collide with his own body. He opened his eyes to see Black squatting in front of him, the Hunter's face looked oddly concerned.

"Wow." Markus said realizing that he was sweating.

"You pushed yourself pretty far." Black said sitting back and standing up. "Seeing through the life essence of all around you can take a toll. Like running, you run too much you will grow fatigued. Some people have pushed too far and never made it back to their body."

Markus looked at him concerned as he stood up. As he stood up with the Hunter, Markus then asked, "Is that what happened?"

"Did what happen?"

"To The Eldest? He pushed himself too far so he just let himself become trapped in his own Crystal... didn't he?"

Black was silent as he stared at Markus in careful thought, as if he was afraid to tell the truth. Finally, he said, "Yes, in a way. The Crystal's allow you to draw power from The Dreaming, and because of that you are able to live in both dimensions. That is how you are able to reach out. And as for The Eldest... yes, that is what happened to him, in a way."

Markus thought of asking what Black meant by 'in a way', but decided against it for the time being.

The Hunter then reached behind him and unsheathed his sword, which glimmered before Markus' eyes as he brought it to a bracing posture with his feet spread and shoulders squared.

"There is no need to talk of such things. Not yet, but soon." Black then said. "For now, I will teach you to better use that staff, while training your body. Unsheathe your weapon."

Markus did as he was told and from dagger to staff he held out his weapon as if he was ready to skewer The Hunter. "You sure this is a good idea, like sword against staff?"

"Don't worry, I won't break it." Black said with a sudden gleam in his eye. "Now, defend yourself." and without so much as a warning, he came right at Markus, his sword swinging in a flash of steel.

~ Small Doorways ~

Ashlyn

Ashlyn sat at a small desk, studying the different sounds that letters made when put together. Esmerelda had been kind enough to teach her as soon as she was done with her firearms training she was assigned to upon waking up this morning. Having finished not too long ago, she met with Esmerelda and had been working on learning to read ever since.

She had gotten the letters down with ease, it was just combining the different sounds each letter made together that frustrated her. At the same time, it fascinated her; the combination of words, different phrases and messages that could be created with the stroke of a pen. When Esmerelda pointed out that this was just one language of many, it amazed Ashlyn. How could so many languages exist with millions of different words that could possibly mean the same thing?

It opened her eyes to just how vast the world of literature could be. Esmerelda was a good teacher. She was patient, and answered any and all questions Ashlyn had. For the last few minutes however, Esmerelda had left her be so she could study.

It was eventually the sweet laughter that broke Ashlyn's train of thought, making her look at the princess who was looking out her bedroom window to the courtyard below.

"What's so funny?" she asked curiously.

"Damion is out training with Markus." Esmerelda beckoned her to the window grinning like a fox. "Look at the poor guy."

Ashlyn got up and crossed the room to look out the window.

Sure enough outside in the snow, the Hunter Black and Markus were sparring. Markus wasn't doing too bad defending himself from Black's restrained blows but the Hunter still would knock the staff aside and point his blade at Markus' neck, or would even slap at Markus' side with the flat of his blade. At some point, Markus even took on the offensive and ended up getting tripped and getting a face full of snow.

Comically, Markus glared at the Hunter in frustration as he stood up. He must have said something snarky, because Black's blade suddenly flicked onto the ground and pulled Markus' ankle out from under him, making him fall into the snow again. Her friend cried out and while on the ground still, he swung at Black's legs, but stopped dead as Black blocked the attack again in a flash of sparks. The two were moving so fast that it was practically impossible for Ashlyn's eyes to keep up with them.

"He's got his work cut out for him." Ashlyn chuckled. *Though he definitely appears to not be holding back, whereas Black looks like he's just having fun.*

"Indeed." Esmerelda said. She turned back to Ashlyn. "Come on, let's get you back to your reading."

Ashlyn took her seat without argument. After finishing her exercises, Esmerelda came back and gave her more writing and reading exercises to do. As the hours went on she picked up on harder and longer words. She wanted to keep going but Esmerelda stopped her around three o'clock.

"You keep going like this, and your brain will fry." Esmerelda said. "Let's take a break. Black should be done with Markus soon and after he bathes we'll go down to the city together."

"Sounds great." Ashlyn said popping her back against the back of the chair. Had it really been almost three hours? No wonder she felt so tired. "Thank you again, for teaching me."

"No problem." Esmerelda said looking at herself in the mirror. She began to fix the braid in her hair. "Don't forget your pistol," she said.

"No worries." Ashlyn said feeling her belt where her new Laser Pistol hung on a small holster. She had received it from one of the guards when she woke up, having been told to head downstairs to a private room to shoot some targets. After being satisfied, the guard in charge of teaching her let her go, saying that her aim was good when it came to pistols.

He had asked if she had fired a gun before to which she replied 'once or twice'. In truth, she fired the gun Markus gave her more than any other. She shot BB guns and a pistol here and there with her family, back when her father was a simple member of the Guard and not the terrible man he was today. As a result she was *kind* of used to shooting, especially when it came to protecting herself in the streets of Nineveh. She was no professional, but she was told she was good enough; and that was just fine with her.

Though she was told that under Queen Elizabetha's orders, she would be taking more lessons at a range down in the city to prepare her with other weapons. Ashlyn didn't object to this in the slightest. If Markus was going to be a part of this, so was she.

While he's doing the best he can, I have to do the same. She told herself this as she holstered her new weapon that she was to carry with her at all times. After the quick lesson and check-up with Mel, the senior in command under a 'General Grim', she went on to read with Esmerelda who had been teaching her since.

"We can continue tonight in the library," the princess told her. "Markus can join us."

"Great," Ashlyn said standing up and strapping on her boots where she left them in the corner of Esmerelda's room right next to the desk she had been sitting at. The sun shining through the window close to Esmerelda's magnificent bed lit up the room beautifully, gleaming against the bookcases and shelving of books and various knickknacks.

"How long do you think Mark will be?" she then asked. When she had woken up to find herself alone, Ashlyn found out from Mel that Markus had been in training with Black as soon as he woke up. They had to be done sooner or later, and after that, she didn't know how long it would take for Markus to get ready to go.

"Not long." Esmerelda replied as she joined Ashlyn by her desk. "I mean, he is a guy after all."

Ashlyn looked at the princess, confused. "What does that have to do with it?"

Esmerelda looked at her friend. "He takes less time to get ready than a girl, 'cause… he's a guy. You never heard that phrase before?"

Ashlyn shook her head. "What does that mean? I've been in a house full of girls and then was by myself for a long time. I never took a normal bath let alone around a *guy*."

"I see." Esmerelda said grinning. She was enjoying Ashlyn's ignorance on the strange phrases she spoke of. "Well, guys don't put as much detail into themselves when they bathe. They don't put on makeup or do their hair or anything, so they take up less time than we do. So, the saying is making fun of how long girls take to get ready in difference to guys."

"That's kinda silly." Ashlyn said. It sounded so childish and silly. Who would mark the time of how long it took for someone to bathe? *We both come from completely different worlds it seems.*

Esmerelda shrugged with a smile. "No matter. Point is, he'll be done soon."

"Okay." Ashlyn said following Esmerelda outside her room as the princess shut and locked the door behind them. She then began leading down the hall so Ashlyn followed. "Do girls put on a lot of makeup or do their hair a lot?"

"Around here they do." Esmerelda nodded as they walked. "It's part of the fashion in Levitika. It also helps when a guy is around."

"Makeup is used to attract a guy?"

Esmerelda looked at Ashlyn. "You really *are* new to this whole thing, aren't you? Have you ever even been with a guy?"

"No." Ashlyn said almost defensively. "In Nineveh, finding someone to… you know, it isn't an everyday thing, especially given my circumstance back there. Also… isn't that just like wearing a mask? Shouldn't a guy like a girl by her own skin?"

"They should." Esmerelda nodded. "It's just… I don't know, it's hard to explain. It's just how some women here like to express themselves. I myself don't mind a little makeup and wearing some during parties or dances." She looked at Ashlyn again. "I'd think you'd look good with some blush. In a blue dress."

"Ha." Ashlyn shaking her head. "I never wore a dress in my life."

"I'm sure you'd look lovely. You look pretty now."

"Shut up." Ashlyn said with a wince, wondering if Esmerelda would be offended by this. But she acted so friendly all the time, it was hard to imagine the princess acting like a… *normal*, princess.

Instead, Esmerelda insisted. "No, I mean it. You don't meet a lot of girls who are comfortable in their own skin. And you my friend, are a looker. We might have trouble getting the guys off you when we tour the city."

"Now you're making fun of me…" Ashlyn said blushing. Before either her or Esmerelda could say anything else however, a loud rumbling pierced the silence. Ashlyn felt heat rise into her cheeks as the princess stifled a laugh.

"We'll grab a roll from the kitchen while we wait for Markus." Esmerelda said. "You sound a little hungry."

"A little." In truth her last meal was supper the previous day. She had not eaten breakfast so she could go shooting. As a result, she was *starving*.

"Well we'll eat when we go out, but we can't eat too much. My mother has dinner planned for tonight. Just her, Black, me, and you two without the interruption of the court- and Slagar."

"Oh, okay." Ahslyn said relieved to hear that. Something about the way Esmerelda mentioned the magician got her wondering. "You don't think highly of the guy I'm guessing?"

"He's a good guy," Esmerelda admitted. "But he's strange. He never smiles and he always works me too hard on my studies and gives everyone crap on their duties. In truth: *no one* really likes him. Him being a hypnotist and all gives him a bad reputation as it is. But he *is* a good man. He saved my mother from being assassinated once."

"No way!"

"Way. My mother is always targeted by spies or rebels in the city. People who think that she takes too long to launch the return of the City of Angels to the world. Slagar not only helps plan battle strategies and spells, he also watches over my mother when he's not trying to weasel his way into anything."

"So he's a schemer?"

"Always has been. I've learned it to be best never to trust him unless you end up in a fight, in battle, or you're about to be assassinated. In those cases: he's good at his job as the castle's Magician. Especially if you want to find the all the culprits responsible. That, and if he has to interrogate someone, he can slip into your head and pick out what he needs. My mother and I as well as a handful in the castle know how to protect ourselves though, so that he doesn't take anything vital. I could teach you as well, so that you don't have him picking at your brain if he hasn't already."

Ashlyn didn't quite understand how hypnotism worked, but she decided it wouldn't be any harm to learn. "Works just fine for me." She said, being glad that she and Markus were not the only ones who thought that there was something wrong with the guy. Even if he *was* a good guy, the way Slagar was looking at Markus was upsetting. The way he looked at her… made Ashlyn glad that Markus was by her side.

Esmerelda gave Ashlyn a small smile again. "You know something? I think we're going to get along just fine."

Ashlyn smiled back. Another thing both she and the princess could agree to. "Me too."

Markus

Markus rested his back against the wall of the castle and slid down so he could sit.

He was out of breath from sparring with Black who didn't look tired in the slightest. A small cut was on the Markus' right bicep but it wasn't bleeding too terribly. The Hunter had managed to nick him as he deflected one of the attacks, among the many bruises he would surely see come morning.

Black came up him as he sheathed his sword.

"Nicely done," he said. "There are still areas for improvement, but I believe you will do just fine."

"Thanks," Markus muttered his breath coming out in panting gasps of steam. "You're fast…"

"So are you. I doubt you noticed that you were maneuvering a lot faster than a normal person. Not only that, but your attacks are stronger. Did you feel anything while we were fighting?"

"Other than adrenaline?" Markus asked with a shrug. "Although, it did *kinda* feel the same as when I was peering out and seeing all the life around us. Like… like back in the Fiery Plains…"

A nod. "Your perceptions are stronger now." Black explained. "While wielding a Crystal, you are able to make yourself stronger. It is a change that you don't notice right away, and it will take time for you to get used to it and perfect it to the point where you can control what areas of your body are strengthened. Once you have a better understanding of The Dreaming and how to bring the two realities together, it will be easier. As for your swordplay… it will also get better."

Markus was impressed. To him, he didn't feel any different. But if he really was going as fast as he was, then it would also explain why Black was so quick when it came to swordplay. The man had a Crystal as well, and everyone back in Nineveh always marveled at the insane strength and speed of the Hunter.

Especially in that one major fight, against Markus' father…

"We are done for today." Black said turning around. "We will continue in the morning, and you will train every day with both staff, gun, and sword. When we reach Nineveh, then we will venture more into the world of magic. You did good for today. So now, go bathe. I believe the princess is taking you and your friend out to see the city."

"Her name's Ashlyn." Markus said pushing himself back up. "And yeah… least that's the plan."

"Well, you know how to find me, or anyone here." Black said as he walked past him and started to go.

"Hey," Markus called as he stopped without looking back. "Can I ask you one thing?"

"Sure." Black paused in step.

"My father… what you did… I understand it was necessary. But… did he have any regrets, before having to sacrifice himself for us?"

Black was silent for a moment, and then said, "Only that he regretted not telling you the truth before."

Markus nodded. It wasn't the answer he expected, but knew that it was all he was going to receive. "Thanks." He managed despite his pride speaking against him.

"You're welcome." Black said continuing his pace away from him.

Markus sighed and brushed himself off as he started back for where he had entered the courtyard. He had to hurry and clean himself up before meeting with the girls in the main hall. He took off sprinting back towards the doors leading to the castle and up to his room.

When he had finished washing and was in a cleaner set of pants and coat, Markus noticed something in the mirror. As he peered at his scrawny self with his hair no longer slathered dirtied grease, he leaned over to take a closer look.

Sure enough, there they were: small whiskers on his upper lip. Very soon he would have to start shaving. Excited about his newest discovery, Markus chuckled at himself. Would this be a big deal back in Nineveh? Probably not. Many men had beards- aside from Aventis and Jim.

Remembering the two bartenders made Markus homesick. Not a lot, because of it being Nineveh, but just enough for him to miss those he and the others left behind. He didn't miss the city, but he sure did miss the people he left behind.

Will I be able to see them again? What will they think, when I show up with all of this? And... without Ruth...

Markus pushed the thought from his mind. It wasn't healthy to think about that- not now. He turned and leaving his bedroom, he ran down the hall to meet the girl's downstairs, the guard, Mel following close behind.

When he began his decent down the main stairs Markus saw the girls talking by the front doors, their reflections mirroring them in the floor of polished tile. The chandelier above them was dimmed for a little sunlight was peeking through the tall windows. When Markus reached the bottom, Ashlyn waved at him, while Esmerelda offered another one of her shy smiles.

"Hey," he said when he reached them.

"All clean?" Ashlyn asked.

"I am now."

"Told you he was fast." Esmerelda said. Ashlyn gave her a dirty look.

"Um, what?" Markus asked confused.

"Don't worry about it." Ashlyn spouted while shaking her head. "So, where we going?" She turned to the princess very quickly. Markus was eager to hear what Esmerelda had planned for them as well.

"That will be all, Mel." Esmerelda said past the two and Markus turned to see Mel right behind him panting. "We'll be back soon."

"Okay..." the guard puffed. "Stay safe, the city Watch will be on patrol should you need anything... Man, you're fast, kid."

"Sorry." Markus said bashfully chuckling despite himself. He didn't realize how much in a hurry he was.

"Come on," Esmerelda said beckoning him and Ashlyn to follow her outside. "Let's go have some fun."

Black

Black had been watching the three teen's from the balcony overlooking the clearing in front of the castle. He had watched them leave the castle and head down into the city. Now the three were racing, laughing like the children they still were.

He couldn't help but smile at them. Despite all that they have been through, there was still a reason to smile; still a reason for them to behave like children. That was good. It was good to be a child, once in a while. Because such a stage wouldn't last forever, and already they had all been pulled into the world of adults, just as Esmerelda was. Even then, they were still children, and deserved even a little time to enjoy their youth.

And by the look on Esmerelda's face, the princess seemed genuinely happy to actually have people her age to bond with.

He smiled, and yet couldn't help but feel sad. He still felt bad for Markus and his friend, and knew that such adolescence would not last in the world they lived in. Their loss was just a small taste, compared to how the rest of their life could be. Because even if the prophecy turned out to be true, and there was a chance to live in peace, life simply didn't work that way.

People die, things change; there were times that even Black himself wished he could go back to being an ignorant child. Living in blissful adolescence while the world seemed at the time to be so much smaller. He envied them, and wished he could behave as foolishly as they did, despite the duties he held and the possible danger that they were in. He envied them, but also felt sorry for them.

For there comes a time, when children, must no longer remain children, in a world so cold, and cruel. They must become adults, and live in the world as such.

If, of course, they had not already become adults still wearing the skins of youth.

Esmerelda

Markus had beaten Esmerelda and Ashlyn in the race after all.

Esmerelda came in close second and was just as winded as Ashlyn who eventually caught up to them. Markus on the other hand did not look quite as tired as they did. Esmerelda didn't quite think that was fair given his…

specialties, but it was fun to finally make it to the Pilate Fountain in the center of the city.

"Nice..." she huffed at them.

"You too." Markus said with a thumb's up, not looking winded in the slightest.

Some bystanders were out and about going about their business. Some had slowed down to say a pleasant 'hello' to Esmerelda and her two new friends just as they had before. A pair of boys passed by and bowed their heads to Esmerelda but they were eye-balling Ashlyn who was now sitting on the fountain and touching the frigid water with her fingers.

Esmerelda also noticed that Markus had spotted them. His attention was quickly captured however as a Behemoth marched right by. It was one of the smaller models that Levitika had, standing no more than ten feet and waddled like a crab on a beach. The man piloting the mech gave the group a wave as he passed and headed in the direction of the castle and probably the hangars.

"They look so more complex than the ones in Nineveh." Markus commented.

"How can you tell?" Esmerelda asked, intrigued.

"Markus likes to tinker." Ashlyn said. "His home has a lot of projects and junk."

"Hey." Markus warned which made him look pretty cute. He was very protective of his hobby.

"Do you like machines and such like that then?" Esmerelda asked him.

"Yeah," he said wistfully. "My father taught me when I was very young. I made a few robots to take to fights back in Nineveh for a few coins.

"You made robots in order to fight and you win money for it?"

"Just like a cockfight." Ashlyn mentions. "Except, not as bloody and a little more humane in terms of life."

"Though the sentient 'droids never liked them much still." Markus reminded her.

"Hmm..." Esmerelda said in thought. Getting an idea, she tells Markus and Ashlyn to follow her once again. She took them back to the Drink Shack she took them to yesterday where instead of Vic working the stand was a young woman just a little older than they were. She asked the girl where Vic was and she told them that he was at the local Tailor. She thanked her and tossed her a silver piece which the woman thanked her for immensely.

"Where are you taking us?" Markus asked as they started to walk again.

"You'll see." Esmerelda said smiling like a Cheshire Cat.

A couple of blocks and after stopping by a home where a woman was bringing out fresh vegetables grown from her rooftop garden, the teens found the mutant at a place called Tabby's Tailor. The marble building had a glass front with a few mannequins garbing expensive-looking attire. Upon entering the place that smelled of leather and gas from shoeshine. Vic was talking to a man who Markus commented quietly as being 'pencil-necked' and when they approached the men, Vic turned and smiled bright and yellow at them.

"Well, well," he said. "What do I owe the pleasure of seeing you twice in the same week, Princess?"

"Hello, Tabby." Esmerelda said to the Tailor, completely ignoring Vic at first. "How is business?"

"Vibrant and doing well." the man said pleasantly while adjusting a button on his black and white coat. "We got a lot of people coming in for more protective clothing rather than exquisite attire, but, business is business. I'll be eating home-raised chickens for weeks at this rate."

"Good to hear." Only then did Esmerelda return her attention to Vic. "Vic, can I ask a favor?"

"Ask away." the mutant said with a wave of his hand. "Happy to oblige."

"Can we use your garage?"

Two eyebrows raised up while the third remained low as Vic gave her a peculiar look. "Might I ask what for?"

"For Markus here." she said pointing at her obviously uncomfortable friend. "He's good with his hands, and I thought maybe you could spare some scrap."

Vic rubbed his chin in thought and then shrugged. "Why not? Everyone is already armed and primed anyway. Go knock yourselves out… well, try not to, eh?"

"We won't." Esmerelda said thanking Vic and then leading her friends outside. "Now," she said as she turned the corner and led the way to Vic's private garage. "For your surprise, Markus."

"Can't wait." The Keeper said cautiously but at the same time curiously.

~ Creation ~

Markus

The 'garage' that Esmerelda had brought them to was a small bunker door dug in next to one of the homes in what the princess called the 'main residential area'.

She punched in a combination on the keypad and the lock unlatched and after throwing the door open she led them down a flight of concrete stairs illuminated by some makeshift lights that had to be turned on one at a time. When they reached the bottom of the stairs she pulled a breaker and the lights came on overhead to expose the vast concrete room that served as Vic's garage.

Markus immediately got envious upon looking at the treasures before him.

The room looked like it had been cleared out and completely made of concrete. Worktables lined the back wall and on either side there were little pockets of space that was used for storage crates and boxes. There was a ladder leading up a doorway which Markus assumed went up into Vic's home, and in the very back next to the workbench was a half-finished Behemoth still missing its arms and a few vital motor components at its hips. On one card table that had been brought in were a bunch of smaller boxes of screws and washers, and underneath were giant toolboxes all rusty and worn from use.

Any mechanic in Nineveh would kill for how many tools and parts were scattered all over the place. Hanging on the walls were vintage signs and flags and even a few mounted heads, but none of them interested Markus. Not as much as the possibilities hiding within the mass of scrap metal in this entire room.

"What a mess." Ashlyn muttered.

"This ain't a mess," Markus said hurrying over to the nearest box which upon opening it revealed the skeleton of an R.U.R model Android completely skinned and gutted for its parts. "This is a gold mine!"

"Like a kid in a candy store." Esmerelda commented as she joined him in the basement now looking over a Werecat-skin rug. The massive humanoid beast of fur and a snarling cat's head covered a good seven feet in dusty gray fur.

"You sure Vic is okay letting us in here?" Markus asked now looking at Esmerelda seriously.

"Of course. He wouldn't have said yes if he didn't."

"You sure he didn't just say yes because of who you are?" Ashlyn asked curiously while taking a peek inside another box of contents.

"No, Vic would let me know if he wasn't comfortable with it."

"Thought you didn't trust him?" Markus inquired.

"I don't. Not when it comes to business or talking to the wrong people about business. Vic just has his hand in a lot of jars, and personally, I don't like some of the things found in those jars. But, he is one of the many influential people down here when it comes to helping the rest of the citizens. It's part of how everyone gets along so well with one another- as well as making Vic richer."

"Are you worried that he might undermine your mother?" Ashlyn asked.

"Nah, I don't think he'd do that. In all honesty, my mother might even welcome it. Because Vic is living proof that someone here in Levitika can exceed in whatever they put their mind to. That is the kind of thinking the world needs again. Someone willing to take risks and succeed in something. I am still wary because of the few people he associates with, but all in all, Vic is just fine. The only reason why I want you guys to be careful, is because of Markus' dad."

Markus sat back on his haunches. "Did they really not get along?"

"Something like that." Esmerelda said. "I don't know the whole story. But from what I understand and of course what Vic had told us yesterday, he and your father were really close. Dangerously so."

"What do you mean?"

"They both dealt with some of the more dangerous people- the wrong kind of people I already mentioned. Those who have different views of Levitika but never say anything out loud."

"How do you know for certain?"

"Because they talk to Vic."

"Can't you just arrest those people then?" Ashlyn asked.

"We don't arrest anyone based on what they say." Esmerelda said. "We want to encourage free speech. If they were to ever do anything, that would be different. But until then, Vic is the connection that helps us understand our people more. He is… the *bridge* between the monarchy and the underground who believe that things would be better if we stayed up here rather than return to the surface."

"Guess that makes sense." Markus said now rummaging through another box. "Pros and cons on both sides."

"Exactly." Esmerelda joined him by his side and asked, "What are you going to make?"

Markus felt that Esmerelda just wanted to change the subject, but he was positive that it wasn't without a good reason. "Not sure… Need some more parts for an idea I have."

"How can we help?" Ashlyn asked.

"Do we have time?" Markus asked Esmerelda.

"Of course, plenty."

"Okay…" Markus looked into the box, thinking about what the key basic components he would need if he were to tackle the project he had in mind. It would be an easy job, one to maybe show just what he could do- as a thanks for the princess.

"Okay," he said after doing some thinking. "I need small pieces of metal and screws. If we can find a torch, that'd be great as well. I need to look for a Q.D.P. processor and an I-B7 A.I. chip."

"A what and a what?" Ashlyn asked already sorting through another box.

"Don't worry about it. Just help with the pieces." They all started to get to work and as they did so Markus decided to pass the time by learning a little more about what he was truly up against. "Esmerelda, The Eldest… can I ask a few questions?"

"You may." Esmerelda said hunched over another box with her back turned to him. "I might have an answer. *Might*."

"Okay. So, basically, all Crystals created by him are interconnected, right?"

"Sounds about right."

"The big one, the one that makes this island float. It was also made by him, yes?"

"Right."

"All of the Crystals... they have human souls in them, right?"

Esmerelda paused and then turned to look at him despite her back still on him. She sat back on her legs and motioned her lips before answering. The smile she usually had and what Markus had grown fond of had no trace of ever existing for the moment. "That's right. Seven unique and powerful individuals chosen for The Seven. The one that makes this island float was the first ever created by the Mad King."

Markus pursed his lips and stood and started for another box. "It must have been really important to him, even though he had plenty in his possession later on."

"Well, I suppose there is a reason for that." When the other two looked back to her, Esmerelda clarified, "The first human soul that The Eldest used to create that Crystal, was his own son."

Ashlyn gaped at her as well as Markus. He was utterly shocked. Levitika's greatest source of power, happened to be just a kid unlike all the other spirits that had been apparently powerful individuals; All of them doomed to be used like parts in a machine.

"Why would he do that?" Markus asked. "How could *anybody* do that?"

"I don't know." Esmerelda said shaking her head. "No one does. Some say because he hated his son, some say he was nothing more than an experiment for immortality. That was the whole reason why The Eldest took it upon himself to find such terrible magic: To find the means of eternal life, and in a way, in the end, he found it."

"At the cost of his son..." Markus whispered looking down at his hip where his dagger and Crystal hung. All too suddenly it felt really heavy on his body. "What a horrible man..."

"That's why we need to make sure he never comes back." The three gasped at the voice and all spun around to see Damion Black standing at the base of the staircase like a wraith in the shadows. He stepped closer to the group and looked at what they were doing before saying, "Or at least, another one like him doesn't rise to power."

"But then why continue to use the Crystals, especially the one keeping this island aloft?" Ashlyn asked her box forgotten. "Is this really any different than what The Eldest had done?"

"It isn't." the Hunter admitted. "But the spirit trapped in that Crystal, made a deal with The Owl. The Crystal here, the son of The Eldest, is the one who proclaimed the prophecy of The Keeper. He is the one to first speak of you, Markus. He knew that you would end this war, and stop anyone from ever using the power of The Dreaming ever again. In the end, all he wishes is to rest peacefully, when Levitika can finally land and be a nation of the world again. In a world, that can never access The Dreaming again, as the one who created this world intended."

Ashlyn looked at Markus who had remained quiet this whole time, lost in his thoughts. "What are your thoughts?" she asked him.

Markus looked away and sighed. "I dunno. I knew what we were doing was important, but… I can't let anyone fall under such a spell again. The poor kid…"

Esmerelda stared at Markus with the utmost respect. "I wish we could free him." she said. "But we don't know how."

"There has to be a way though." Markus said now holding onto a somewhat damaged processor of the generation he had been looking for. "And if I really am The Keeper, then there's gotta be a way I can figure out. But for now… one step at a time."

The Hunter Black dipped his head in a slow nod of approval. "That is right."

Esmerelda cleared her throat. "Bringing up the elephant in the room now, Damion, what are you doing here?"

"Just wanted to check on you. Vic said you were here. Wanted you to know that dinner will be at seven."

"Okay." Esmerelda said. "We'll be there."

Markus looked over at the wall and in between two torn flags was a clock. He still had a few hours. He still had time.

"I will see you there." And like the wraith he was, Black disappeared into the stairwell, leaving the teens to continue their search for parts.

As they continued to scrounge and search, the never again brought up The Eldest or the Crystals in general. Instead they talked of other things, but nothing that Markus was really paying attention to.

He just had too much on his mind, and his fingers were already at work with the parts he had already found.

Esmerelda

At some point in time, Ashlyn had fallen asleep, passed out on the Werecat rug and sleeping softly. They had all told stories both true and false. Markus was telling one about an Elf when eventually he stopped talking altogether, emerged in his little project he was tinkering on now. He had only mentioned that he had what he needed and no longer needed assistance.

So instead, Esmerelda just sat and watched. Hours had passed by with them just talking, and eventually Ashlyn woke up and the two of them talked instead while Markus continued to work. They then started just checking out some of the other equipment in the garage as well as the few boxes of collectibles that were also hanging on the wall. The two flags by the clock were faded and terribly torn, but Esmerelda could just make out one of them being a green flag with some man on the front with the words around him faded to black splotches, and the other having red and white stripes with a small section of blue with stars on it.

What the flags meant, Esmerelda had no clue. They were both relics; memories of a past lost during The Collapse countless years ago. That world was gone, and the one they were in now was much different. For better or for worse, they were here, and the world was theirs.

Ashlyn was more intrigued by some of the antique guns strapped to a rack next to the ladder leading up to the next doorway. They were Old-School weapons, old rifles and pistols and even one that looked more like a cannon than anything else. They were in good condition, and could probably fire better than any Old-School guns still out in the Northern Wastelands.

"Guys, come here!" Markus called them over and the girls hurried to see what he had finished. His fingers were blackened and browned with oil, and he had beads of sweat on his forehead but he was beaming like a child finally making it to the top of a great mountain and seeing the view that no one else could on a regular basis.

"Done." he said flicking a little switch on the back of the little contraption and bringing it to life.

The contraption was small, barely as large as a man's hand. Its body was smelted with compact pieces of metal courtesy of Esmerelda and Ashlyn finding and fitted together with a tension wire that would tighten and loosen with every command of its processor chip. The little worm-like machine had a pair of arms ending in little pincers that Markus made out of a hinge and bits of copper. On its back was a pair of currently folded rotating wings, and the head was about the size of a ripe tangerine. Markus had found the head in a scrap box labeled 'Torchbug Parts' in crude handwriting, and now the little head with telescopic eyes had hummed to life as the A.I. started up and regarded the three humans around it with unintelligent glances.

"It actually works." Ashlyn breathed stooping down so that she was eye-level with the little robot that was now crawling across the table, 'feeling' its way and observing its claws like an infant discovering its hands and feet for the first time.

"Don't act so surprise." Markus chuckled. "I've never made a sentient robot before, so I don't know how well it will work. But with the Q.D.P. Processor and the-"

"It looks great." Esmerelda said before Markus could say something she would not understand. The robot looked at her and she could see the little lenses zooming in and out on her as it looked at her. "It's like a baby." she said. "If a baby was a little robot made of a bunch of parts and whatever processor you said."

"You like it?" Markus smiled.

The robot 'inch-wormed' its way over to Esmerelda and when she offered her hand, it first poked at her palm and then pinched her finger. Not hard enough to draw blood but hard enough to get a firm grip on her so that it could curl up in her palm and then work on adjusting its new wings. They expanded and spun about above its head, and Markus warned her to be careful not to get cut. When the robot was finished, it looked to Esmerelda and then to the other two as if trying to ask if it was okay.

"It's a cute little thing." Esmerelda admitted.

"I'm glad you like it." Markus said. "Because it's yours."

Esmerelda looked at him. "Mine?"

He nodded. "Think of it as… a gift, as a thanks for all you've done for Ashlyn and I."

"I second that." Ashlyn agreed brightly. "Hopefully it doesn't blow up in your hand."

"Excuse you." Markus said to her and then to Esmerelda, "Will you accept it then?"

"Heck yeah." Esmerelda said beaming at the little robot. "Thank you so much…" She sat it down and coming around the table she gave Markus a big hug and a kiss on the cheek. She then moved over to Ashlyn to give her a hug while he stood there as red as a beet and seeming to forget where he was.

She turned her attention back to the robot and asked, "Does it have a name?"

"It can be whatever you want it to be." Markus said after momentarily forgetting how to speak. "Most mechanics call their robots 'she' unless it's an android, then they go specific based on the structure."

Esmerelda thought about it for a moment and then offering her hand to the robot again she said, "I think I'll name her Q-Pid. Like the Greek god of love, and for the fact that you said that it was a Q.D.P. Processor, or whatever."

Markus chuckled at this. "It's fitting."

"Can it understand us?" Ashlyn asked taking a closer look at Q-Pid.

"I'm sure it's trying to understand what we're saying." Markus said stooping over Esmerelda and offering his own hand to the contraption. It looked at him before crawling from Esmerelda's hand to his own. Then Markus pointed at it with his free finger and said, "Q-Pid."

The robot blinked, tilted its head and in a little buzzing voice coming from a tiny speaker installed in the side of its head it said, "Q… Pid."

"Oh my God…" Esmerelda gasped genuinely happy.

"Good, good." Markus said next pointing to Esmerelda. "Esmerelda."

The robot turned to its current holder and buzzed, "Esmerelda."

"Excellent!" Markus returned the robot to Esmerelda who appeared genuinely excited. Ashlyn placed a hand on his shoulder and told him he did good.

And Esmerelda full-heartedly agreed.

Behind them, a loud groan sounded and they all whirled around to see Vic coming out of the door and coming down the ladder. He stumbled over the group and after a quick greeting, he stared at Q-Pid with unblinking eyes.

"Blimey, what do we got here?"

"Markus made this." Esmerelda said turning and offering the robot to the mutant. Before Vic could grab her, Q-Pid took flight and she buzzed around his head before 'draping' herself on his right shoulder. He laughed as she stared at him with those zooming eyes of hers.

"Not bad at all. Haven't seen a bot this small in ages. Everyone else got some about the size of a cat." He peered at it some more and then turned to Markus. "Can you take a little criticism?"

"Uh… sure?" Markus said clearly uncomfortable still around the mutant.

"Wait here." The mutant turned and after checking on some boxes next to the unfinished Behemoth, he returned with two little black squares the size of a fingernail. "How are ya gonna charge the little buggar?"

"Um…" Markus scratched the back of his head, a clear sign that he hadn't thought about that.

"C'mere." Vic told him and after taking a set of pliers, he turned off Q-Pid and then opened the robot by the shoulders. He pulled some wires and smelted them to a new pair and then connected the black squares that now covered Q-Pids shoulders like a pair of shoulder pads.

"There." Vic said turning the bot on again and watching as she twitched and looked around confused as if she woke up from a nap. "Now there's no need for extra wires. So long as there is sunlight aplenty for a bit o' time, then she'll be buzzing around happy and well,"

"Wow, thanks." Esmerelda said taking Q-Pid back.

"Never even considered that." Markus muttered.

"It's a big place." Vic told him. "You did pretty damn good considering you didn't know where anything is around here." The mutant rubbed his chin and said, "Tell ya what, if ya want, yer more than welcome to come back here anytime. You can tinker around to yer heart's content."

Markus looked to Esmerelda who nodded, pleased by the news. He turned back to Vic and asked if he was sure.

"Sure, I'm sure." Vic said confidently. "No worries at all. Here, lemme give ya a key. Come and go as you please. This was after all partially your old man's own garage after all. I'm sure he'd appreciate it if I were to let ya use it."

"My father worked in here?" Markus asked now looking around the garage with newfound awe.

"Aye-aye. Asked if he could borrow it for a 'few days' if I recall. Freeloadin' bastard ended up staying and helping me with more projects. None of me other buddies liked 'im much, but I saw good things in him."

"Surely he could have just got something from the castle, right?" Markus asked him. "I heard he was… was…"

Vic seemed to understand and nodded. "Aye, he was. And sure, he probably could've. Asked him myself why come here, and he only said, 'privacy'. Before he left for Nineveh, took most of his tools and such with 'im. Dunno how much he had, couldn't tell from how this place still looks. But I hoped it served 'im well when he took ya there."

"Just how much about me do you know?" Markus asked skeptically.

"Not enough obviously. Never met ya." Vic cackled and after reaching into his pocket and handing Markus a little brown key he said, "I just know yer old man, or what he was like outside the castle. And I'm proud to say that I did. He was the only man I trusted in me garage. That was something no other business partner had the privilege of."

"I see…" Markus said pocketing the key obviously intrigued.

Esmerelda cleared her throat. Though she knew Vic was a good guy when he wasn't around any of his 'business partners', he was still someone who liked to keep people around for a reason, just like her own mother. Besides, they were going to be late. "We better get going. Dinner is in less than an hour."

"Oh, fer sure." Vic said. "Just head out the way ye came. I'm glad you like it here, Mark. Maybe you and I can work on something together, eh?"

"Yeah, maybe." Markus agreed though this time he wasn't nervous in the slightest. "And thank you sir, for letting me use your garage."

"Come back anytime. Now, run along ya little tyke. And keep yer bot greased, yer highness. Don't let it go stiff."

"Don't worry." Esmerelda said looking over to Q-Pid who had successfully crawled up to her shoulder and now sat perched like a snake in the bough of a great tree. "I'll remember."

"Remember." Q-Pid buzzed to which everyone laughed about, even Markus.

He really was a good guy. Even if he ended up not being The Keeper, he would still be a good guy.

With a sense of wonder as well as a tint of subconscious fear, Esmerelda began to grow just a little concerned if she was starting to actually *like* Markus.

~ Guests ~

Markus

They returned to the castle just as Mel met them outside. He urged them all to go get cleaned and dressed and then the queen would be waiting for them. As they rushed to get ready, Markus had plenty more to think about, this time mostly about his father and what exactly would become of himself here in Levitika.

He looked at himself in the mirror. Despite his hair and his chin structure, he still had his father's eyes. He remembered the calm and yet worn look they always had in his eyes. It now became apparent that Markus had earned that same look. Was it because of his journey? Was the reason why his father had that same look was because of his journey from here to Nineveh? He went from being a member of a royal family to becoming a mechanic in Nineveh. All for his own children.

Markus didn't fully understand what to make of it.

He had found a pair of clean jeans and a new shirt waiting for him on the bed and after changing out of them and tossing his old clothes aside, he admitted himself in the mirror. The jeans were no different than what he would find down on the surface (though they *were* notably cleaner), but they fit a lot better and with his belt they kept from sliding down his scrawny waist. The shirt he was wearing was long-sleeved and black, with a thick polo-collar and cuffs which felt snug on him. Pleased with his new dinner attire, he left his bedroom-

And ran right into Slagar who was waiting alongside one of the guards.

The hypnotist smiled smugly at Markus and told the guard to give them some space. As soon as the man left, Slagar turned his attention back to Markus. "Do your new clothes suit you?"

"They're fine." Markus said defensively. He noticed how Slagar was stealing glances down at his hip where his dagger and Crystal hung at his belt. "Can I… help you or something?" he asked.

Slagar's inhuman-like eyes turned back to him and he flashed that crooked smile again. Markus felt a light brush against the back of his mind but then the presence retreated and with it, the hypnotist's smile.

"Sir?"

Slagar rubbed his temple. "Sorry, got a little light-headed." It was a lie, Markus knew for one because it was too much of a coincidence given his experience thus far with the man, but also because he could somehow hear the man's heartbeat quicken. The organ itself sounded like a liar's. "I wanted to ask you a favor while you remain in this castle."

"A favor?" Markus said not trusting the man as far as he could throw him- which of course given what he had learned today was that it was possible that he could throw the man a long, long, way.

"Yes." Slagar continued. "A personal favor, man-to-man."

"Okay?"

"I meant every word I said last night. I think you know that, don't you?"

"I could guess."

"Good. Then there are no secrets between us, yes?"

"… Just what is your point?"

Slagar twiddled his fingers together as if he was a chef sprinkling herbs and spices upon a meal. "You are The Keeper, which if history is telling the truth, The Eldest might try to reach for you again. He never went for Damion Black, or your father. He only went for you. So I want you to report any unsightly encounters you might have. If not to me, then to anyone else *besides* Damion."

"Why would I do that?" Markus asked. "As far as I'm concerned, the best people to consult with about The Dreaming or anything that has to do with it, are people who are connected to it."

Slagar remained still, expressionless and yet not. "I wouldn't expect a *child* to understand something he doesn't fully grasp anyway."

That *really* rubbed Markus the wrong way. "I'm not a child. I've seen things that I'll bet you've never seen."

Slagar's eyes flashed bright, not with whatever power he had, but a mere reaction of whatever nerve Markus had struck. "Do you want to try me on that, child of prophecy? You know nothing, child of a bastard."

Now it was Markus' turn for his eyes to flash bright and dangerous. "Do not talk about my father like that."

"What? Cannot take the truth? Or are you too afraid to understand the truth? You know nothing about what your father or even Damion Black cannot see. How do you think it makes us who cannot see The Dreaming but know it exists feel? We fight a battle not just of steel and bullets, Markus. We also fight a battle of the unseen, and that frightens us who cannot see. So do not try and say I don't understand anything, because it is as clear to me now as it was last night, that you really do not understand what you can see."

"Then tell me." Markus challenged the man. "What can I see? If you can offer a better explanation, I'm all ears. Because you know what I see right now as I look at you? I see nothing but bitter greed, and fear."

"Fear is what separates us from beasts and demons." Slagar said with a warning finger. "And fear, is what will separate you from your own demise as well as our own. The Dreaming is a powerful realm that Man was never meant to discover aside from what we see in our sleep. And what we see bring either good news, or dreadful nightmares. I implore you, child, beware what you do know, and share what you do not understand. Because I promise you, you will lose far more than your father ever did. I've seen my own share of what you do not know. Would you like to know?"

"I know what my father has lost."

"Do you?" Slagar asked that smile returning with confidence. "Do you really?"

Now it was doubt that crept into Markus' mind. He didn't feel it like a spell from Slagar, but a message from someone else entirely. It was as if Abner was bringing forth the doubt himself, telling Markus that he really didn't know. And with his 'voice', came Ruth's as well, telling him that there was more to Father that he didn't understand.

"What is it then?" Markus dared to whisper.

Slagar clicked his tongue and wagged his finger. "That is the deal I am presenting you now. If you ever sense The Eldest, or have any unnatural experiences that The Hunter has not explained yet, you come to me or one of my peers. You tell us, and maybe, just maybe, you will be able to understand the burden your father was. There is a reason why his name is hardly ever spoke in this castle, despite being obviously very important in your life."

"You're lying." Markus said confidently. "I can tell you are."

"Maybe I am." Slagar said. "Or maybe, you just don't want to believe it. Speaking of which, your father said your mother died, yes? Did he ever explain why?"

Coldness gripped at Markus' mind. This time he knew for certain Slagar was digging in. He had been softening Markus' defenses, and was now attempting to pull something out of him. He had found the soft-spot and was near to retreating with whatever he had grabbed. However, a static shock wracked Markus' brain, forcing him to fall back against the wall and a thundering voice forced Slagar to retreat as well, seizing both of his temples and hissing in great pain.

"You sick bastard." Markus hissed when he was able to get back up. "Get away from me- now!"

Slagar glared at him but he started to stalk away just as the guard returned to see what the commotion was about. "You'll regret biting my hand, Keeper. My offer still stands, but, you will regret scorning me. That, I promise you. Be sure to watch your back, both in and out of the castle." He turned to the guard and with a flash of his eyes, the man stumbled as the hypnotist escaped down the hall.

"Wh… where's Slagar?" the guard asked obviously not understanding any longer what has happened. The hypnotist had made sure of that.

Beware who you tell. Abner's voice returned, advising Markus to wait. There would come a time to speak to someone. And that someone would have to be either Elizabetha or Damion Black and no one else.

Markus told the man not to worry, just as Esmerelda and Ashlyn emerged from his friend's room. His fear and discomfort was overtaken by who stood before him.

Ashlyn and Esmerelda both wore beautiful dresses of blue that hung down to their ankles. Esmerelda's neck was jeweled by a necklace of what looked like pearls joining a ruby in the middle, and she wore a circlet of silver on her head with emeralds and more rubies.

Ashlyn, wearing no jewelry, had her hair held back in a band of bronze and her bangs held back by a silver clip with a silver flower. She wore a similar shade of pale makeup as Esmerelda, with eyeliner and a little blush about the cheeks. Standing next to the princess, she looked like a member of royalty herself which made Markus stand slack-jawed and amazed.

"Don't stare at me like that…" Ashlyn said somewhat bashful.

"I…" Markus cleared his throat. "You both just look… wonderful."

Esmerelda clapped Ashlyn softly on a bare arm. "See? Told you he'd like it."

"I should change." Ashlyn said. "I don't feel comfortable in this…"

"You look beautiful though." When Ashlyn turned to Markus he averted his eyes in embarrassment. "I mean… yeah."

Ashlyn's expression softened and her hands lowered down to her sides. "Well… I guess it is a special occasion. Dinner with the queen, and all. Besides… you look handsome."

"I agree." Esmerelda said grinning brightly. "You look like a young lord."

Though pleased, Markus was also embarrassed.

"Well," Esmerelda clapped her hands. "Better not keep Mother waiting." As if on que, little Q-Pid hovered out of Ashlyn's bedroom and landed nimbly on her master's shoulder. Though obviously out of place in such beauty, Esmerelda greeted the robot gleefully.

Markus was happy that she liked it.

Esmerelda

After having to rush down the maze of hallways, the three teens finally made it to Queen Elizabetha's private eating quarters in the west wing of the castle. The room was very elegant, but simple and not quite as roomy as the dining hall.

A small round table covered with a cloth of white sat in the middle of the circular room with a glass dome for a ceiling, revealing the night sky where the moon had finally come out and was shining through with shades of silver and blue. Even with the glow of the moon lighting the room, a great many candles were lit in the lanterns sitting on the side tables next to sofas and bookcases. Even a candelabra sat in the center of the table, its tall candlesticks of white glowing brightly at the top.

Damion was already sitting there, his cloak and sword hung on a coat hanger in the back corner. Without his gear hiding his figure, his broad shoulders were revealed beneath his dense black armor which he kept on. His arms were crossed and his head was low with his eyes closed. He looked like he was sleeping. But he opened them up when he heard the teenagers come in and nodded a hello.

"You made it." he stated.

"Just in time." Esmeralda said leading her two friends over to the table. She sat between Markus and Ashlyn, Ashlyn sat next to Damion, leaving the final chair between him and Markus empty. They waited no more than a few seconds before the door opened again, revealing her mother in a gown of purple. Everyone stood at attention of her arrival. Even Markus looked like he couldn't help but marvel at her elegant beauty.

"Thank you for your patience." the queen said as she crossed the room and took her seat with such grace. Everyone then sat back done in unison. "I've been very busy, and I'm sorry I haven't been able to meet with you two earlier." she said to Markus and Ashlyn.

"It's okay, your majesty." Markus said.

"This whole thing, so much planning, and yet so little time...." She offered a small smile. "But enough about that." She clapped her hands and the doors opened again, revealing the butlers bringing in the pitchers of water and bottles of wine. When the filled drinks and cups were placed on the table, the group of men departed as quickly as they had arrived.

"Thank you." the queen called to the men. Then to the group she said, "We are here to enjoy each other's company. Without the courts and the worries of the upcoming predicament. And, unfortunately, Slagar won't be joining us tonight."

Her mother smiled upon the mentioning, which made Esmeralda chuckle. The queen poured some wine for herself and passed the bottle to Black. Markus poured himself and Esmeralda a glass of water before passing the pitcher to Ashlyn. Esmeralda gave Markus a nod of thanks.

Q-Pid, quickly adjusting to her new surroundings, flew over to Elizabetha, giving the queen a fright as it landed on the table and blinked up at her with those rapidly intelligent eyes of hers.

"What on earth... is this?" Elizabetha asked.

"I Q-Pid." the robot answered and Esmeralda explained that Markus had made it for her.

"Oh, I see." Elizabetha picked the bot up which wrapped it's tail around her wrist to achieve greater balance. "It's a cute little thing. How long did it take you to make this, Markus?"

"A long time, Ma'am." Markus answered. "It is a thanks, to Esmerelda for her tours."

"You might very well have to make me something someday." Elizabetha said happily. "I can tell it is decent craftmanship. Don't you think, Damion?"

"It is." the Hunter said taking a sip of wine. "I remember when your father would make trinkets back in Nineveh."

Markus looked a little uneasy about the saying to Esmerelda's surprise, but he didn't say anything other than muttering 'thanks'.

"Tell me about your day." Elizabetha said. "Tell me about your tours of the city."

Esmeralda let her friends do most of the talking while she sat quietly sipping her water. Markus told her mother about his training with Damion, with some uplifting commentary from the Hunter himself. Ashlyn spoke of her shooting lessons and her studies with Esmerelda. Her mother had complimented Esmerelda for her teaching skills, which made her blush.

She hated to be put on the spot, even if it was out of kindness. The queen then asked Markus about the tour of the city, which he was happy to talk about.

"The city is beautiful." he said. "The people, well, they're cautious, like anywhere else in these times, but they are all still kind. They all appear... happy but at the same time careful. Grateful for the peace, but prepared for the worst. And there's no discrimination between humans, mutants or droids. Not even the young and the old. They are all, just happy here. And Ashlyn and I, we've never seen anything like it. You have a wonderful kingdom, your majesty. Beautiful beyond measure."

The queen smiled brightly at this. "Thank you, Markus. That really means a lot. We try to make it the home it once was. Someday, the entire region will be just like it- no maybe even better when Esmerelda takes the throne when we succeed by then."

Esmerelda blushed again at this. Talk of her one day becoming queen made her *extremely* self-conscious, having so many standards to live up to. Thankfully, no one else pressed for the matter to continue.

"I wanna thank you, your majesty." Ashlyn said.

The queen turned to the girl. "Oh?"

"Yeah, for everything." Markus said for his friend. "You giving us a home here, you taking us in like this, and showing us the true beauty of the city. It's truly remarkable. It's everything the legends make it out to be."

"You're very welcome." Elizabetha then turned to Esmerelda again. "And thank you, my daughter, for being there for our guests when I couldn't."

"Yes, Mother." Esmerelda bowed her head.

"Elizabetha," Markus then spoke up. "Can I... ask you something?"

"Of course."

"... The Crystal that keeps your city in the sky... is it true that the spirit inside is The Eldest's son?"

Elizabetha looked towards her daughter and Esmerelda looked at her mother helplessly. The queen then sighed and she looked to Damion who then nodded in encouragement. "It is true." She confirmed.

"Why would he do such a thing?" Markus asked him. "His own son?"

"No one knows." Damion said again, answering for his queen. "When the Great Owl brought it here, Pilate and the other leaders didn't know why. All they knew was that they needed an energy source that would not deplete immediately."

"So they used him as a battery?" Markus asked. "And now you guys?"

"Unfortunately."

"And there isn't a way to set him free?"

"No one knows *how* to." Damion looked down at his wine, the maroon liquid reflecting his face from the candlelight. "It saddens us, but we must use him, as you had heard down below. It was only because of him that we were able to understand The Eldest and keep Levitika safe. He offered himself to The Owl because he believed Levitika would bring forth the new beginning and close The Dreaming forever. Someday, once we understand better, I hope that we can thank him by finally setting his soul free. In fact, I hope *you* are the one to free them all from their prisons, and ensure that it never happens again."

Markus looked down at his own glass, seeming to be thinking really hard on what he had heard. "Okay. Then where do we go after this?"

"I plan to teach you all I know just as we had planned before." Damion answered. "As well as introduce you to someone I know; someone who has a Crystal in his possession. Between the two of us, I am hoping that you can make contact with the spirits, and hopefully they will tell you the answers we need to find the other Crystal's and make sure another monster doesn't rise to power. That boy inside that Crystal spoke of you for a reason, Markus. I have no doubt in my mind when it comes to him."

Surprisingly, Markus turned to Esmerelda. "Do you believe I am… The Keeper?"

Esmerelda gulped. "I do," she said. There was no doubt in her mind. How could there be? She had heard about the boy sitting next to her all of her life, and now that he was here, she knew it without a doubt to be true.

He turned to Ashlyn. "Do you?"

Ashlyn pursed her lips. "I go wherever you go. You know that already. So, yes. I do."

Esmerelda felt a sharp pain in her heart all of a sudden. She didn't understand why, not yet.

Markus then turned to Damion and Elizabetha. "Do you guys? Do you really?"

Elizabetha hesitated for a moment, but eventually she nodded. "I believe with all my heart that you are the hope that this city needs. Black says that he was told you are The Keeper, and I trust him with my life."

When Markus turned his complete attention to Damion, he nodded. "Without a single doubt in my or Johnathon's mind. We both knew. We always knew. When your father found out that his eldest son would be The Keeper, and would be the one to end the curse that threatens our world, he was proud of you before you even came to be. And since you were his only son, and since Abner, the spirit in your own Crystal chose you as The Son proclaimed, there is no reason to doubt now. Your heart, and your bravery will take you to high places, Markus. If anyone in the world is The Keeper, it is you."

"But there is nothing special about me." Markus said shaking his head. "I'm just a normal kid."

"No one is special." Damion said which made even Esmerelda wince at the harsh reality of the man's words. "You are not The Keeper because you are extraordinary, Markus. You are just an ordinary guy, who once he puts his mind and heart into something, can achieve extraordinary things. That is what makes you special. That is why, I believe in you."

Markus looked down in silence. Esmerelda wanted to comfort him, but she knew that Damion's words were sinking in, and she should not interfere.

She knew it must be hard on her friend, hearing something as bizarre as the prophecy and who he was, along with his family ties.

But there was no doubt in her mind: He was The Keeper. He *had* to be. Because if he wasn't, then there was no hope for the world they lived in.

And hope was the only thing keeping Levitika afloat, the only thing that made her believe in a better future.

"Alright," Markus eventually said. "I... I..."

"Take your time." Elizabetha assured him. "There is no rush. We have plenty of time, and like we told you before, you are not by yourself on this. You have all of Levitika on your side. You have Black, me and my family, and, of course, you have your friend."

Ashlyn smiled to Markus. "And friends stick together until the end."

Markus smiled back at her, and Esmerelda felt a pain in her heart once again. "Thank you. Thank you…"

"The food should be here soon." Elizabetha then said wanting to move on from the conversation. Esmerelda was glad she brought that up. Markus needed time to think, and they didn't need to discuss this any further. "Have you shown them the royal library yet?" The queen then asked her daughter.

"Not yet." Esmerelda admitted.

"The royal library?" Markus asked as Ashlyn beamed at the second mentioning of the library.

"Yes," Elizabetha said. "A vast collection of books written and collected over the years. The stacks of ancient poetry and stories, as well as what has been written in former Levitika. Old legends, stories, studies, spell books, everything someone could ask for when seeking knowledge or a good story."

"You definitely need to show us." Markus said to Esmerelda. "Soon."

"Of course." Esmerelda said beaming with another one of her smiles. She was overjoyed to see Markus so excited for her to show him "I'm sure you both would love it."

"I only wish Ruth was here to see all of this." Markus said looking back at Ashlyn.

"I do as well." Elizabetha said somberly. "I'm sorry to ask again, but before the food arrives, have you decided on what you wanted to do with your sister's body, Markus?"

Esmerelda groaned mentally at what her mother just asked. Was it really wise to ask such a thing at this hour? Here and now? Especially after all that Markus had heard already…

She looked over at Markus who looked pained at the question, yet he remained strong when he answered.

"Actually," Markus said in a way that wasn't sad or upset but almost… hopeful. "Now that you mention it- your grace. I-"

A thunderous boom suddenly shook the entire castle, making dust and bits of stone fall down from the walls and a massive crack formed in the glass dome above. Esmerelda covered her head as well as everyone else until the falling stones and glass ceased.

"What was that?" Damion shouted standing up fast and placing a hand on the radio at his belt.

"We are under attack!" A voice blared from the radio. "An entire fleet of Hellhounds and zeppelins- and a massive ship heading for us! Shots have been fired! All personnel head for-"

"They're here." Damion said broodingly as he turned away fast. He grabbed his cloak and his scabbard and hooked it across his back. "We need to move, your majesty."

"Right." Elizabetha stood up fast. "Ashlyn, go with Esmerelda to the safe room."

"Yes, ma'am." Ashlyn said taking hold of Esmerelda's hand which was shaking.

"Markus come with me" Damion said. "You aren't fully ready, but we can use your help."

"Okay," Markus said standing. "I'll do what I can."

"That is all I ask. Milady, you should come to the Control Room as well." Damion told Elizabetha.

"I shall." The queen said. "Lead the way."

And with that the group broke up, taking opposite corridors. Ashlyn stopped and turned. "Hey, Mark!"

He turned to her, stopping while Damion and queen continued.

"Be careful." she said to him. Esmerelda sniffed at the look on her face when she said it.

Markus nodded. "You too," he said and with that, turned and ran.

"Come on." Ashlyn said stiffly to Esmerelda, who once again felt pain as Markus ran off with her mother and the Hunter. "Let's get to the safe room."

"This way." Esmerelda said this time pulling her friend into a run and muttering a silent prayer for her mother and the city's safety.

Especially Markus' own.

~ The Storming of Heaven ~

Markus

It had begun. The start of something that would change everything here in Levitika, and Markus' own life, forever.

As he followed Black and Elizabetha to an elevator, hopping in between them before the doors closed, Markus knew things were about to get tough. Especially since they were going up against the very monster who starved and beat his family, and even ordered his father's own execution. The devil himself was coming in with his fleet of Droids and Royal Guard, and he was going to take this city unless The Angels of Levitika stopped him.

And they need my *help.* Markus knew what kind of role was expected of him, but right now, he didn't have time to think about the prophecy or what was expected of him. Right now, Baron Ovid was coming, and Levitika needed help to stop him. Whatever it took, he was willing to help.

He didn't want the fate of Nineveh to befall anyone here in Levitika. He was *glad* to oblige, after all that Ovid has done to his family. *This will be for my father.* He decided. *Not just for the people here, but for my father, Ruth, and Ashlyn.* What would Black have him do at this crucial point in time? Whatever he could do to aid in the battle, he would do it.

"I thought we had time…" The queen fretted, picking at her nails.

"As did I." said Black indifferently. Markus saw that look on the Hunter's face before, but he couldn't place when or where. It seemed like despite it being an aperitive hour for Levitika, he remained calm, collected, and yet at the same time ready to fight.

When the elevator finally stopped, the three stepped inside of what looked to be a massive control room that seemed to sit inside one of the towers of the castle. All around them, Plexiglas windows opened up to the world outside. Beneath the windows were incredibly large control panels with radios, targeting mechanisms and a massive chair in the middle with countless buttons and switches on the armrests. None of the stuff was familiar to Markus, it was a far cry from basic hovercraft and robotics.

The guards and technicians stood at the attention for the queen who nodded in greeting as she took her seat on the 'captain's chair'. Black and Markus hung back while the men and women immediately sat back down at work. Looking past all the equipment and outside the windows with the pale moonrays shining through, Markus saw them.

They were miles away, but their cannon-fire still lit up the sky like exploding stars, their shells soaring with banner-like tails and upon colliding with the city walls, a tremor could be felt beneath Markus' feet. One even soared past the Control Room, making only Markus flinch while everyone else remained focused on their tasks. Behind the hail of falling fire, hundreds of Hellhounds and Dragonfly Choppers moved towards the island, with two gunships loaded with bombs of massive proportion close behind; both floating on either side of Baron Ovid's most prized ship.

The Leviathan.

The massive hovercraft was *huge*; almost as large as the castle itself. Turrets were embedded into the sides and large wings of the Leviathan, and Laser-Gatling's hung beneath the hull and nose of the ship. Across the humongous wingspan was the Baron's mark; the wolf skull and crossed weapons, both facing the cockpit windows which were tinted black, hiding the pilots. The boosters behind and beneath the craft glowed bright orange as it hovered miles above the valley far below and continued to advance; heading straight for Levitika and allowing the fleet surrounding it to begin the attack.

The smaller aircraft around it were faster and more agile. They would reach the floating island first. But if the Leviathan, or even the zeppelins flying alongside it managed to make it to the walls, the city would be destroyed by the mini-nukes strapped beneath them.

There would be no hope for the Levitikans, who appeared to have taken shelter within their homes down in the city. Still, some men and women were rushing out of their homes with guns in hand, ready for a fight. Along the walls of the city, thousands of soldiers were now rushing towards the front lines of the city; ready to defend it from the closest ships.

Seeing the flashes of gunfire from both the walls and the advancing Hellhounds, Markus felt a cold fist close around his heart. As he saw more balls of fire soar across the sky like falling stars, terror gripped his heart all the tighter.

Terror, that was what he felt. They *had* to stop them. They couldn't let Ovid and his army take The City of Angels.

We can't let them destroy this beautiful place... he thought. He looked to Black, hoping that the Hunter had another plan. But the Hunter remained still, seeming unnerved by the approaching warships.

"Milady," a guard said who was sitting in front of a massive monitor. "We have hundreds of blips on the radar, but I see a stray ship floating above the castle. It is not one of theirs."

Elizabetha froze. "We didn't launch any ships yet..." she whispered.

"How did it manage to get past?" Black demanded, his voice was calm but Markus could feel the hint of dangerous anger lurking in his tone.

"Is it attacking?" Elizabetha asked, ignoring the Hunter.

"It doesn't appear so, it's just hovering about. But I have sent some guards to intercept it."

"I'll take care of it." Black told him.

Elizabetha shook her head. "No, we need to go through with the plan, Damion."

"Understood."

"The plan?" Markus asked peering around the chair to look at the queen. *So they* did *have something in mind.*

"We're going to destroy those gunships before they get here." Black said coolly. "If we can eliminate them- or better yet *use* them to weaken the master ship, the rest of our forces can focus on the hovercraft coming in. With the mini-nukes and that monstrosity of a ship gone, it'll be easier to win this battle." He looked to his right where another guard sat by a second monitor. "Have you launched the Guardians and the other choppers?"

"The choppers are just now taking off into the air; they are heading for them." the female guard answered. "The Guardians are nearly ready to launch. Ninety-seven percent complete."

"The Guardians?" Markus asked.

"Another reason people call this The City of Angels." the queen said not turning to look at him. "An idea that came to mind long ago for extra security. Launch them when ready." Elizabetha commanded her men.

"Yes ma'am." the guard sounded returning to her work.

"Time to go." Black said heading for a release hatch in one of the glass panels. He turned the handle and opened it, letting in the cool air. "Come on." he told Markus.

"Wh-what?" Markus stuttered. "Out there? What exactly are we-"

"Just come." At the stern command of the Hunter, Markus felt his feet move on their own as he followed him out.

"Good luck." the queen called out to them as they slipped through the hatch.

Upon landing onto the roof, Markus stuck close to Black as the two slid down onto one of the walls closest to the castle. Markus was rattled because of the fall but he was unhurt. Black was already up on his feet, and was beckoning him to follow; and as Markus ran along the wall after him, he saw something soaring through the air above. Two things to be exact.

One was a flock of giant mechanized owls of Radio-Bronze metal. The very statues that stood along the wall were coming to life before his very eyes! Their eyes glowed bright red, their claws of sharpened diamond capable of slicing through the strongest of metal. They screeched in robotic hoots as they flew overhead towards the many ships set to destroy Levitika.

Behind the owls, the soldiers along the walls suddenly began to take flight on wings of gold. The metallic wings, many of them, all spread out with each and every feather extending across one another from small black bags strapped to their backs. Markus watched in wonder as the thousands of men, androids and mutants took flight with Eagles-Wings, just like his own. Their wings caught the moonlight so perfectly with their folded plates jutting from small straps across the flyer's backs that they seemed to sparkle with each flap.

No wonder this place is called The City of Angels, Markus realized. *Because Angels protect this city.* Seeing them made Markus have some shred of hope.

But turning his head to look back at the castle, he saw something else that sent a dagger of fear right through his very heart.

A black Hellhound was hovering over the courtyard area of the castle; a Hellhound Markus remembered very well. It was the same hovercraft used by the Hunters who had chased them in the Wastelands and nearly killed Black.

They found us, and now they are here. But they were not attacking them nor the Baron's fleet. It was obvious the Hunters could see Markus, but they weren't coming for him either. *Why are they here then? What could they have to gain here?*

Markus looked at Black who was still running despite noticing the hovercraft, and Markus once again looked back at the Hellhound. He soon understood why Black had no notion to go after them. The turrets on the castle were firing upon the ship, as well as other guards in the towers along the wall. Flashes of red tore through steel, and of the wings had caught on fire and the hovercraft began to spin in the air. Satisfied that they're going to crash Markus watched with delight as the Hellhound turned and spun about, knocking the roof tiles off of one tower before crashing right into the wall in an explosion of fire and shrapnel.

Good, one less problem to deal with at least. As Markus took off running after The Hunter Black towards the battle, he felt that they might still have a chance with those other Hunters gone.

But then again, he felt horrible, despite himself.

Death was not a stranger to Markus, especially when living in a city like Nineveh; you dealt with death all the time. He had seen innocents killed, men women and children gunned down, hung, or stoned to death. Even that one Xerxe soldier, who had crawled out of the sewer begging for help, only to get his head smashed in without mercy. Markus had seen a few Guards killed in rebellions against mutants and families who decided they've had enough of the tyranny. But never once had Markus wished someone to be dead, not like now. He had wished for Black to die, but not like this. He never believed it could really happen. The sudden gladness in seeing the Hellhound crash however, made Markus realize that this was very much real.

It made him sick to his stomach. Could he really be happy that someone had actually died?

He guessed it did not matter anymore at this point. But despite the necessity of their deaths, Markus still felt ashamed to be happy with such a thing. Whether they deserved it or not, it didn't make him feel any better. It only showed him a small taste of what was to come.

He shook the thought out of his mind as he caught up to Black, who was taking cover behind one of the towers which as shaking as the Gatling-Laser on the roof fired upon the incoming Hellhounds in rapid succession. Markus lingered beside the Hunter, not saying a word as they both took in the view before them.

Behind the shells of metal and weapons, behind the uniforms and flesh and wiring, Markus saw it again; the life essence of every single warrior both enemy and friend, lighting the battle like a thousand stars among the flashes of gunfire and cannon blasts across the skies. He saw the robotic owls slam into the largest of hovercraft, and saw the Angels of Levitika buzzing around like hornets and firing their own weapons as the sky was lit up with their weapons. It was like watching the very world ending before his eyes, and Markus couldn't bear to stomach the sight of seeing the first Angel fall from the sky with burning wings, and blood spilling as he fell to the world below.

Lee
Lee picked himself off of the street, spitting blood onto the road as he lifted himself up. He had bitten his lip when he ditched the Hellhound before the wreck. A few yards from him, the hovercraft was burning against the city walls. Shrapnel was scattered across the road, with smoke belching from a few of the larger pieces. In the far distance, Lee could hear the rumbling gunfire from the gunships and walls where the Baron was beginning his siege.

He sighed as he flicked on his helmet, obscuring his face and protecting it from the smoke that stung his eyes. One thing was for sure now; his sister and he were not getting out the same way they had come in. He would be able to handle himself for the time being, but they would eventually need another method of escape. In the meantime, he had his own hunting to do.

All he really had to do was wait for her signal for that was his 'part' in this game. Until then, he wanted to do some hunting. With a click of his boots, his rocket boots propelled him into the sky with a deafening roar. The guards who were coming to secure the crash site were taken aback by the one survivor rising from the smoke. They opened fired on him with both laser rifles and machine guns, but it mattered little. He maneuvered too fast, and with a few shots from his wrist guns, the group was riddled into swiss cheese in a matter of seconds. Their blood ran into the streets like a crimson river, trailing their defeat and failure.

Only the strong survive…

Turning to face the battle between the Baron and the Levitikans, Lee then surveyed the carnage. Massive metal owls tore choppers and Hellhounds apart in the sky, causing them to fall and disappear on the other side of the walls. The Angel soldiers shot many down with their weapons and in turn were shot down by the attackers' turrets.

It was anybody's victory at this point, and blood fell like rain among the explosions and gunfire. There was just so much destruction, all for what they were all searching for. Just how many more were going to fall for their desires?

Lee supposed it didn't matter. Just like his fallen guildmates, all the soldiers and angels were merely pawns in a greater game. He and Lameika, were to be bigger and more important pieces holding the ultimate piece to the whole thing. Then the true game could begin when Father has The Eldest in his possession.

Lee made a promise to himself that at least he would fulfill his role in order to receive his own honor and no longer remain in the shadow of his sister.

And so, the hunt was on.

Lameika

Lameika fell to the floor in a shower of broken glass, and as nimbly as a cat landed on her hands and feet. She stayed stooped over as she felt glass fall upon her. If it wasn't for her cloak, she would have been torn to shreds. When she felt the rainfall cease, she stood up, and surveyed the room.

It was a dining room, but it was small, simple, and not as luxurious as one of the halls in Baron Ovid's castle. It made her wonder if the Levitikan's really were as wealthy as the legends claimed. Some wine had been spilled on the table, and was now staining the tablecloth and dripping to the floor like blood. Someone had been here recently, but not anymore.

It didn't matter though. Lameika had other things on her mind; she was listening. She was *feeling* the castle for the life essence of The Eldest.

She caught the scent of many souls throughout the castle grounds. The guards in the towers and surrounding walls, the men and women rushing through the halls, two girls in a room on the far end, and the queen and her court in a large room high in the towers. There was another soul too, one she recognized, but could not quite tell who it was.

But that also didn't matter. She was focused on the strong speck of life in the center of the castle. A mixture of hate, anger, and seething patience ready to collapse.

The Eldest.

He was calling for her. Like a wave of an electric shock, she felt Him reaching for her like instinct driving a predator.

I shall come. With that she took off into a brisk sprint out of the room and down the hall, the glowing torches of green casting a devilishly eerie glow across her face which was grinning like a mad fox. She smashed through another door with a wave of her hand and in a flash of sparks and she nearly cackled as she rushed around one corner and down another corridor; the torches along the walls immediately going out as she rushed past.

She made another turn, the scent getting stronger when she suddenly ran into three guards standing in the hallway. They all stood at attention and aimed their weapons at her. "Hey!" the tallest one shouted. "Stop right there!"

"Insolent fools," Lameika muttered as her crooked hands rose above her head and began to hiss with frost. "Die."

She then raised one hand outstretched towards the three, her fingers aimed right at the guard on the left. A large ice shard suddenly shot from her fingers, impaling the woman and sending her clear down the hall in a flash of red and before spearing her right into the wall; her blood splashing out like a large blooming flower around her. The poor girl shuddered coughed and hissed out blood as she died a slow and painful death.

The second guard screamed out something incoherent and fired his gun, the weapon lighting up the hall with flashes of its muzzle. But with a snap of her fingers, Lameika disappeared into a flash of white frost, only to reappear in front of the man and twist the gun back towards the man's chest, the gun still going off. Blood splattered upon Lameika's face as the man fell back with many holes in his chest and face. The last guard, the tallest and in the most protected in black armor, went for his own weapon.

He shot at Lameika but she knocked the gun aside with a well-placed kick, making the bullet tear through the wall instead of her. But the soldier was trained for that kind of maneuver; obviously a high-ranking officer. He kicked out at the Lameika's ankle, making her balance unstable, before taking both ends of the gun in his hands, and slamming it against her throat, pinning the witch against the wall.

She coughed out as she felt her windpipe get crushed by the weight. She snarled at the guard, who gritted his teeth as he pressed harder.

"Got you." he hissed, growling in anger. "Those were my closest comrades, you *monster*."

Monster? Ha. Now *that* was something Lameika hadn't been called in a long time. She'd missed it. "Well then," she said with a sinister smile of victory. "Give them my best." She opened her mouth wide enough for the soldier to see her tonsils. His eyes widened as he saw what was coming out of Lameika's mouth-

And Mel, who served Queen Elizabetha as Captain of the Guard for three years, knew no more.

~ Angels and Devils ~

Ovid

Sitting in the captain's chair of his beloved Leviathan, Baron Ovid surveyed the carnage before him.

It was a battle that would have made King Ronin- the bastard pirate -jealous. All around him, his fleet of Hellhounds tore through the bronze of the massive owls that had suddenly joined in on the fight alongside the men with wings. The robotic birds sliced through his men with razor talons, destroying both ship and man in flashes of bronze light. The legendary Angels of Levitika were buzzing around like a swarm of insects, shooting their little guns and putting up a hell of a fight while avoiding the gunfire of the Leviathan itself.

However, the Angels still had one little thing that Ovid could work against: they were still human. Flesh and blood that can be destroyed with a single bullet, or better yet, many- or even, a nuclear bomb. And luckily for him, his zeppelins flying alongside his precious mothership were carrying just the things that would bring Levitika to its knees.

The bombs were not to be used if possible; they were primarily to be demonstrated only to scare the Levitikan's into surrendering. But should Ovid and his fleet fail, he would have those nukes dropped upon the floating city. He would not risk anyone else taking the city and using its precious armory of weapons and magicians. It was to all belong to him, and only him. No one else would benefit from the last floating city in the world. If he couldn't have it, no one would.

The thought of being so close to something so powerful made Ovid quiver and shake with excitement. "Engage the boosters. I want to get there- *fast*." he commanded his pilots who were lined up along a massive control panel below the large window. Having been seated in the middle of the entire flight crew, Ovid had complete control over all functions of the Leviathan. Radar and other monitors bleeped as the many piolets commanded orders to men throughout the ship as well as the fleet outside.

"Yes, sir!" the men answered his command in unison without even pausing their duties. Smart men.

"Send in the gunships ahead of us. Let's send these 'Angels' where they can meet the real ones!"

"Yes, Lord!" they said again repeating the Barons' orders to the rest of the fleet. Ovid liked being called that. 'Lord.' No other recognition served him better. He watched as the gunships pulled forward faster than the Leviathan. The ship's massive size and speed was commendable; in fact, they were now going faster with the turbines at max-power.

However, the blimps and the Hellhounds were made to be fast and far more maneuverable. So of course, the fleet was meeting battle long before the Leviathan would; including the few Hellhounds he had ordered to remain in formation around it to provide better protection. Ovid *always* had a backup plan just in case, and this one was indeed fool-proof.

But then again, that never stopped him from being too careful.

"Prepare to launch missles!" he bellowed.

"Target locked!" one pilot shouted. "Three O'clock high!"

And Ovid with a large grin beneath his back beard, shouted at the top of his lungs. "Fire!"

"Fox-Two!" the same pilot shouted as the fiery shells were launched from the Leviathan.

War has begun, and tonight, it would rain blood.

Markus

Missiles came flying in from the Leviathan like a mechanical god unleashing the power of the stars upon its enemies. They sailed through the sky past the battle only to connect with a Dragonfly's vibrating wings; making it explode into a ball of fire so hot that no shrapnel fell from the sky- they had all been disintegrated in the flame. Still, the remaining defenders of Levitika kept on the incoming swarm, and continued their dogfight across the starry skies.

Markus and Black both stood back watching the battle, the tower beside them shaking as the Gatling-Laser fired round after round. Some more Angels were shooting from the walls while more took flight to join their brothers in the sky. Among the explosions, speeding bullets, and laser-fire, Markus' eye caught something: another body of an Angel falling head-first to the valley below. His wings were badly burning, and his body seemed still as smoke and pieces of his armor seemed to float right off of him as he disappeared from sight below.

The sight made him sick to his stomach. *Another one… Is this… is this what war really looks like? Does it really… look so destructive?*

"Men," Black called into his radio. "There are some Ninevite Guards parachuting from the choppers- they are getting past the Guardians! Focus your fire on them!"

"Roger." came a garbled response. As if on-que, the Gatling above them suddenly changed positions and fired upon some parachutes passing through the fray and getting close to the walls. Fabric and flesh were torn apart, sending the soldiers all screaming into the clouds below. Still, more kept coming.

Black hooked his radio to his belt and turned to look at Markus. "They are still too many of them. I need to get out there. This is where I leave you for now."

Markus swallowed hard, fearful for what would happen now. "What do you need me to do?"

Black looked back and unsheathed his sword. "The first thing we need to do is blow those gunships. The Baron is not stupid; he won't risk nuking the city unless he was certain he would fail. He's trying to frighten us. But if we destroy them, then he has no leverage, and no hope of escape. I'm going to head over there, but I'm going to need your help."

"Am I coming with you?" Markus asked now feeling like his stomach turned inside out. The thought of going out there… it made him so sick he thought he was going to throw up.

Black shook his head, and then unhooked his radio from his belt before presenting it to Markus. "You, will stay and shoot with the men up here. You will also keep tabs on any enemy movement and report to the queen immediately. Remember your training, using your different eyes, and just keep watch."

"You'll be shot!" Markus argued. "The soldiers are going to see you and shoot you out of the sky! Besides, I'm not..." *Am I really ready to use such magic again?*

"And you have already forgotten that you are a good shot with your staff."

"It'll take forever to charge."

"Then use the *Crystal*. Use your own energy."

Markus stopped arguing, feeling completely silly being answered with answers so simple yet impossible. "I don't..."

"Use your crystal." Black repeated. "Use it so that your senses can see who is shooting and when. Use it to speed up charging rates in your laser and shoot the targets as they come. You can do this Markus, it is simply transferring energy. This is your first taste of the fate you have chosen. You are the final defense along with all the men and women on this wall. Do *not* let Ovid take the walls. I will be back soon. I promise. Are you ready?"

Markus looked over at the soldiers still shooting along the walls, as well as those using the Gatlings in the towers. Markus then looked back towards the dogfight in the skies beyond and sighed.

This is the fate I have chosen... I have chosen to fight... "Alright," he said. "I'm ready."

"I shall return." Black said jumping off the wall, plunging into the darkness. Markus watched the man opened up his cloak which expanded and allowed him to glide for a bit before grappling over to a nearby Dragonfly, ready to fight. A Ninevite soldier was parachuting by, and as Black took flight from the chopper again, he removed his shotgun and shot the man dead in the chest. The body dangled on the parachute that continued to float downward until it was out of sight below the walls of Levitika. The Hunter then continued to glide and use his grapple-gun to transverse through the battle, before he was concealed by the smoke of another falling hovercraft.

Go.

Markus gasped, startled at the sudden thought that was not his own.

Go. it came again.

Markus looked down at the Crystal in his dagger. He telescoped it into a staff, and peered into the blue gem. He saw his reflection within the glossy surface, but for a moment, just for a moment, he thought he saw someone else in his place, staring *right* back at him.

Go, fly. he heard it say again.

Markus looked up to see Black now flying deeper into the fray, and shook his head in self-conflict. He wanted to help, but he was just too afraid. He didn't want to go out there; he was no warrior. It was too soon.

But still, he could not help but think of all the faces he had seen here in Levitika. If they didn't stop the Baron out there and now, they would all die.

He just couldn't let them down, not like that despite how terrified he was; how *afraid* he was. But still… Black couldn't do it by himself…

Go. Abner said again. *I will guide you- you both will make it out of there alive. You will not die, while this battle rages on.*

… *But*…

Go…

Markus groaned audibly as he stepped onto the parapet. *I must be out of my mind*… After some self-words of encouragement, Markus jumped off and into the skies. Then pulling the switch on his pack and releasing his Eagles-Wings, he went soaring through the air just like the Angels who continued to soar and shoot upon their enemies; who in turn fought back with such blood-lust.

He barrel-rolled away from some gunfire of a Hellhound and slipped beneath another. He was momentarily blinded by some smoke and didn't see a missile heading right for him. With a yelp, Markus dove down and away just as the missile collided with another ship, destroying it with a muffled *boom*.

Straight ahead, Markus caught sight of the Hunter Black whose grapple-gun latched on to one of the enemy's wings, pulling himself towards it. As he passed the hovercraft he swung his sword upward, and when he began to glide again over to another Hellhound. Markus saw the hovercraft's right wing fall clean off before it spun out of control and fell to the valley below.

When Black saw who was following him, he turned his body around and began to glide alongside the boy, his cloak keeping him aloft as he *glared* at Markus.

"What are you doing!?" he demanded. "I told you to stay back on the walls!"

"You can't do it alone!" Markus shouted back despite the words sounding just as mad to him as they probably did to Black.

"I told you to stay and watch!" the Hunter repeated with a snarl, his anger now clearly spread across his otherwise indifferent face.

"I'm not going to stay behind when I can possibly do something!" Markus argued as he ducked beneath an incoming Guardian. "You said you believed in me- so tell me what you need me to do! Tell me, and I'll do it!"

Black peered at Markus, studying him closely as they both delved deeper into the battle. Despite the carnage circling them like swarms of deadly insects, he only focused on Markus who had a little more trouble with his own surroundings. The thunder of guns and eruptions of ships were *deafening*, and the hectic speed of all the fighters both Angelic and Ninevite made Markus' heart slam in his chest like a beast in a cage. Still, he followed Black close behind, who then eventually groaned as he leveled his body out, probably seeing that there was no point in sending Markus back when he was already here within the fray.

"Alright, fine." the Hunter gave in. "Stay close to me, and we will get to the Leviathan. Do *not* get shot, and at the first sign of danger- you *flee*. Do you understand?"

"Got it!" Markus shouted and he cried out as a Dragonfly suddenly swooped towards Black who then barreled away and sliced at the driver, sending the Ninevite's head flying through the air before the aircraft buzzed to a sharp dive right into another enemy Hellhound The soldiers on board the hovercraft fell away screaming as their bodies were alit with flame.

Markus stared at Black who never once batted an eye. *He really is a dangerous Hunter…*

Passing by an Angel Dragonfly, Markus used the draft to swoop up towards another Hellhound. Taking aim with his staff, he fired a bolt at one of the turbines and the machinery blew in a flash of red before engulfing the entire craft in flames.

Black swung behind him, catching onto one of the Guardians flying for another enemy chopper. The metallic owl hooted robotically as it's rider guided it before leaping off as soon as it turned and suddenly smashed into the craft that Markus had shot. Then proceeding to swing his sword horizontally, Black sliced the strings of two parachutes whose riders were trying to escape the inferno. The men fell away screaming.

More explosions erupted around Markus, and he felt bullets buzz pass his body like angry hornets. The heat of lasers even scorched his own clothing as he proceeded to follow Black through the insanity. He yelped as shrapnel flew past him, and he managed to get knock another aside with his staff before he could be impaled. A sharp pain bit into his thigh and turning his head to look he saw a hole that was bleeding. He had been shot, and it didn't feel like it hurt as much as it should have.

This is what war is like... Markus thought as he maneuvered past another falling ship going down in flames and smoke; the driver's broken and bloody corpse caught in the shattered glass of the front windshield. *This... this is hell.*

Black glided past another Dragonfly and hooking onto the side began to fire his guns again. He reloaded his nine-banger and took a shot at an incoming Hellhound, shooting through the windshield and spraying it with red as the driver was struck by the large buckshot. The hovercraft lingered for a moment as the copilot tried to regain control but he didn't see the Guardian coming in fast. The robotic owl shredded through the front with a single swipe of its talons. The remainder of the ship spiraled.

Markus meanwhile banked around and caught onto another Hellhound's wings with the blade of his staff. He hung from there, his legs dangling in the wind as it threatened to peel him off the speeding hovercraft. A crimson-garbed soldier came up to one of the openings, his Gun-Sword aiming right at him. Markus felt a flash of fear, only to be overcome with a feeling of awe-struck as he felt energy pour from his arm into the staff and from the staff to the Crystal-

Which was touching the metal-plating of the wing by the blade's base. He suddenly imagined the Hellhound blowing up and he gasped as and he felt something like a pulse shock through his arm. He managed to get one of his own wings up just as the guard fired his weapon, the bullets striking the bronze metal but otherwise leaving Markus unscathed. Before he could even process what he and the Guard was witnessed, blue lightening coursed across the hovercraft from Markus' hand, electrocuting all of the passengers and frying the controls. Markus then pressed his feet against the wing and managed to pull and wrench his staff free just before the Hellhound exploded into many pieces.

Markus stared at the smoke above him and his hand in awe. *What was-*

He suddenly felt a chill, as if he knew something was coming and curled his wings around him to use them as a shield as he suddenly came under fire from another Dragonfly. Keeping the wings above him to protect himself from the gunfire, Markus was left freefalling at an alarming pace. But if he were to spread his wings again, then he would be torn to shreds.

That was when he felt an arm grab him, and Markus looked up to see Black swinging from another chopper and using the momentum, swung them both back towards the attackers as Markus shielded them. As they got closer he charged the Crystal in his staff and at the last minute opened his wings and fired another bolt; this one completely blowing the chopper apart as it struck the cockpits windows and the pilots within. A nearby Angel swooped in and finished off the gunners on either side with his own Gun-Sword. Markus watched the terrifying beauty take place as the woman stabbed the nearest gunner through and then pulling the trigger the gun-bit took out the one on the opposite side. With both gunners eliminated, the Angel pulled away with a wave as the hovercraft began its burning decent.

When he felt Black let him go, Markus spread his wings once more, flying for another target as the Hunter in turn released his grapple and continued to glide alongside him. As they passed by another Hellhound, Black then swung his sword at a mini-gun mounted beneath the hull. The gun redirected itself and fired at another one of their own hovercraft; the windshield it fired upon shattering in flashes of glass stained with crimson.

At this point, both Black and Markus had made it through the worse of the battle-swarming cloud, and the two were now closer to one of the zeppelins heading straight for them. There were still plenty of Dragonflies and Hellhounds buzzing around as protection for the gunships, but without the insanity of the battle to keep them busy, Markus started to actually have hope. Part of him actually believed that they would make it.

But part of him still believed that they were also doomed, despite the words of Abner slipping into the minor cracks in his thoughts.

You will survive.

Ashlyn

Inside the safe room, Esmerelda and Ashlyn sat together on the cot in the corner while the walls shook around them with the sound of gunfire and cannon blasts. With every tremor, the two would tense up and shudder as the rumbling died down only to stiffen again when something else collided with the castle.

Dust shook from the ceiling from time to time, and sometimes some dehydrated food would fall off the shelf that lined the wall to their left. Q-pid was taking cover underneath Esmerelda's dress, peeking out occasionally in nervousness. Ashlyn kept her laser pistol in her lap with a hand resting on it, just in case anything was to come through the doors other than one of the guards or the queen.

Being in such a confined place with the unknown happening outside, reminded Ashlyn of her days as a street rat back in Nineveh; always watching the entrance to her safe haven for the evening and ready to fight anyone or anything that dared to invade. Over an hour had passed and neither she nor Esmerelda spoke a word as more gunfire erupted suddenly. But this time it was louder, closer, not muffled by the walls outside.

As if someone was shooting *right* outside the door.

Both of the girls stared at the doors as the gunfire continued, only to stop for a moment followed by a scream of utter terror. As quickly as it had come however, the screaming ceased and the gunfire sounded once again. It then paused, and silence followed and hung in the air like a shroud.

Whatever had happened outside the safe room... it had stopped.

Ashlyn stood up. "I'm going to go check it out." she told Esmerelda as she took up her pistol.

The princess stood but otherwise remained planted where she was. "Shouldn't we stay in here?" she asked in a frightened voice. "We don't know what's out there."

"They sound close... they may need help."

"Mel is strong, he can handle it."

Ashlyn frowned. Though Esmerelda was right, it was never Ashlyn's nature to just sit down when something was happening. Besides, she wanted to make sure that Mel was indeed okay and nothing had gone terribly wrong. "Maybe. But I'm just going to take a peek."

The princess looked like she wanted to argue more, but she relented with a sigh. "Alright, fine. Just be careful." she said.

With a wink, Ashlyn walked over to the door, her pistol aimed at the locking mechanism. She entered the code the queen had given her, and the door slid open revealing the hallway, and the horror outside the safe room.

Two bodies were laying in a pool of blood. Bullet casings laid among one while the other was sitting against the wall with a gory smear around his destroyed head. Both of the men were Mel and another guard with the third missing. The one named Mel, Ashlyn recognized in an instant. However, the large hole in the middle of his forehead spilled blood all over his face, and his dead eyes stared hazily at the ceiling above him as he just sat there his comrade at his feet.

Ashlyn covered her mouth and turned away fast, looking back into the room in order to stop herself for staring at the bodies. She gagged but managed to control her stomach. This was nothing compared to the things she had seen in Nineveh, but she didn't want to see it. She looked up at Esmerelda, who was staring at her worriedly. "They're dead."

"Oh no…" the princess said gasping. She ran up to Ashlyn, and when she saw Mel she covered her mouth. "Oh my God…" She looked like she might just puke as well.

Q-Pid emerged from behind the princess and then buzzed over to the corpse to inspect it. After a quick analysis, she turned her head and blinked at the two girls. "Deceased." she confirmed.

Ashlyn looked down the hallway once again and saw the other guard pinned against the wall with a chunk of ice stuck in his chest. Blood was everywhere; none of them had been spared.

Who… where did they go? Ashlyn turned the other way to see some bloody boot prints leading down the rightward corridor, meaning that the intruder had killed Mel and the others just to get past them, not to stop by the safe room.

Looking back down at Mel, Ashlyn stooped down and closed his eyes, allowing him to actually rest. She then pried the machine gun out of the hands of the other officer and handed it to Esmerelda.

"I'm going to take a look around." she told the princess who turned the weapon over in her hands. "Stay here."

Esmerelda looked at her friend worriedly. "Are you sure that is safe? We should stay here…"

"I can handle myself." Ashlyn said turning her eyes back on the footprints leading down the hall. "Whoever this is took out Mel, and we need to stop them. I have to do my part." She paused, and then added, "But I'm more worried about you. If you don't want me to leave I won't." She said this while looking at crimson boot tracks leading down the hall. Each track was about a yard and a half apart, as if the wearer was running. "But I need to find who is in this castle. We can't risk more people dying."

"I don't know how to shoot… Well this type of gun anyway."

"It's like a laser pistol." Ashlyn explained. "Difference is it carries bullets, not energy cartridges. Now, do you want me to stay?"

"My mother told you to stay." Esmerelda said. "Mel and the others… they were trained soldiers. What makes you think we might have a chance when they didn't?"

Ashlyn looked at Esmerelda with a serious expression. "The men I killed back in Nineveh were Ninevite soldiers. Men trained to kill. In order for me to survive and escape, I had to fight. Mel was kind to me, just like all of you were. I will not just sit here and let whoever did this get away. I want to make sure that they can no longer be a threat in the castle."

Esmerelda frowned, looking like she was fighting a conflicting battle whether or not to agree with Ashlyn or not. "You could be killed…"

Ashlyn turned away. "I know. But I have to do my part."

Esmerelda sighed. "Fine. If you need to, then, go. But do you really *need* to?"

"I have to do my part." Ashlyn repeated. After all that these people did for her, she felt it would be an insult if she didn't find Mel's killer. It was obvious that whoever did this was tougher than the soldiers, but Ashlyn didn't want to back down from this.

She refused to just hide while many others die.

"Okay," Esmerelda said taking one step forward. "Then I'm coming too."

Ashlyn shook her head with an instant, "No."

"Don't bother arguing. I'm safer with you anyway." Esmerelda said this with a determined look in her eye. "You can't stop me, Ashlyn. Besides, you still don't know the castle that well. You don't know where you'll end up when you follow those tracks." She looked back at her friend. "We go together."

Seeing no argument around this, Ashlyn sighed. "Alright, but let me do the shooting first. Do not use it unless it is life or death, okay?"

"Okay."

"And if I say 'run', you run. You got me?" Ashlyn didn't think it was appropriate to give the princess orders, but this was no laughing matter.

Esmerelda merely shrugged her shoulders. "Don't worry."

Ashlyn started forward. "Let's go, your highness."

"Ashlyn...."

"Sorry." she said quickly as they ventured down the hall, not looking back at the horrible scene behind them. Besides from the gunfire erupting still outside, the castle was deathly silent. They continued to follow the tracks through the labyrinth of hallways and doors on their search to find the intruder.

As they continued on, Ashlyn would peek inside doors that were left open, leaving those that were shut alone. All the doors that were shut were locked anyways, so there was no point in trying to get inside. Most of the time the rooms she and Esmerelda did check were empty, but sometimes there would be the body of a guard or servant. The gruesome scenes would make Ashlyn sick but she pushed on. All the blood and the stench of death... it was unbearable, but she kept going forward.

Esmerelda stuck close behind, her gun pointed at the floor. For a princess, she carried herself now like a calm soldier. Despite the danger lurking in her own home, she remained calm and followed Ashlyn close from behind.

Eventually they came across the door to the main division between the hallways. Ashlyn remembered passing through here when Mark got up after being knocked out by Mel. The door was cracked open; the control panel seeming to be melted down revealing frayed wires that sparked in the dark green light around it.

A cry and a wet slashing sound came from inside. Q-Pid started buzzing audibly as she flew, hovering in front of the girls and waving her little arms back and forth in warning.

"Someone's in there." Esmerelda whispered holding the machine gun close to her chest.

"Yeah," Ashlyn uttered, aiming her pistol at the crack. "Stay behind the door and behind cover. I'm going to take a peek."

"... Okay." Esmerelda said stepping back as Ashlyn stretched out and took a peek inside through the doorway.

~ Abomination ~

Lameika

"No!" the guard in Lameika's path cried out as he was completely frozen where he stood. She removed her hand from his neck and chuckled as she turned about just before the last soldier could come at her swinging his Gun-Sword at her. She ducked beneath the arc of steel before accumulating a shard of ice in her hand and slashed at the man's exposed throat. Blood sprayed over her like a fountain as the guard collapsed onto the floor, gurgling and choking as he slowly died.

"Pathetic," she uttered as she allowed the ice to melt, the water mixing with the blood as it dripped right off her fingers.

After cutting down numerous guards throughout the main division as well as the hallway leading to the vault room, Lameika now stood before the massive door of steel and bronze, looking at it in amazement. Her veneration was not for the vault itself, but the energy seeping through it.

She could feel *him*. So much pain and anger within those walls, concealed behind steel and a shell of igneous crystal formed by the evil spirits of Mt. Nudushi.

The Eldest was calling to her. He was beckoning her to come; imploring her to open the door.

I am here, she heard him say, and as Lameika removed her own Crystal from her pocket, she obeyed her master. *Let me out…*

Pressing the Crystal against the steel, she muttered phrases of an ancient language, working the magic within her own spirit and transferring it through the Crystal and into the steel door. Within a minute the steel became liquid, and fell down in a mess of molten metal.

She stepped through the opening, her boots squishing through the tacky liquid beneath her, her eyes set on the little pedestal in the center of the room. Among the many chests of jewels, gold, and scrolls of royal parchment, it was there. Sitting on the pedestal resting in the clutches of a four-fingered claw behind a box of Plexiglas, was a Crystal similar to her own and the other Seven. Blood-red with a tinge of purple and dark matter, and also twice as big as all the other Crystals; and from it radiated tremendous power and essence.

The Eldest.

At last.

Using her own Crystal to generate lightning, she casted it onto the box, which shattered into a thousand fragments, leaving The Eldest open to her clutches. She walked over, and slowly, gently as if afraid it would bite her as soon as she touched it, Lameika nimbly placed her fingers on the Crystal.

She immediately felt a rush of energy seeping through her skin, and flowing through her veins.

Such power, so much pain and anger to create such madness… and it was all in her hands now. She took the Crystal out of the claw, and peered into it, seeing past her reflection in the Crystal's many edges, and seeing the dark matter swimming around inside it. The Eldest was still awake, and He wanted out.

Imagine yourself… in a place of peace… A place of rest…

"Soon my master." she said with a smile of ecstasy. Cath was going to be *very* happy to receive such a thing of power. With the Eldest in their possession, they would soon be ready to unleash the darkness within The Dreaming.

The Dark Queen herself might not have a chance against them.

As Lameika stepped out of the vault and over the bodies of guards she had slain to get there, she noticed that she seemed to be very… familiar with the Crystal. She felt it *pulse* in her hand as if she was carrying a slowly dying heart, the energy within fueling her body and mind. It resonated with her own heartbeat, syncing with her very being. She felt as if The Eldest was speaking to her; this time with a clear voice- her own.

She chuckled at the thought, closing her eyes as she entered the main division; the statue of The Great Owl staring down at her as she walked around it. She sneered at the bronze memory of a rebel who defied an empire; defied the ways of The Capitol and all it stood for. The founder of the City of Angels, and she was expressed as a majestic owl…

It made Lameika sick. Simply, just, *sick* to look at the statue. She wanted nothing more than to burn it down and crush it into dust with her bare hands. But maybe… instead, maybe it could be useful in a different way…

"Halt!"

She looked up to see a guard standing in the room with his gun-sword aimed right at her. "Don't move, or I will shoot!"

The soldier then went for his radio but he had no chance as Lameika suddenly lunged forward faster than humanly possible, and pressing her hand against the man's chest, she shot an ice shard right through him, tearing through his armor and body in a spray of crimson. The blood splattered all over her face, making her grin appear feral and even more dangerous. She had come so far to get The Eldest, and she wasn't about to give it up, no matter what the cost.

She wiped her face with a free hand as she laughed at the body that now crumpled at her feet. Swine… all of them, mere nuisances no better than *swine*. Soon, they would all fall before her.

They would all die at her hand.

When she looked up, Lameika saw someone else. Someone who had just come in by the sensation of the fear that the witch could smell. The girl standing in the doorway, shook where she stood; a laser pistol in her hands aiming right at Lameika's heart.

"You…" the girl said.

Lameika merely smiled as the blood from the soldiers continued to drip down her face like a melting mask. *How interesting…*

Markus

As they drew closer to the gunships, the intensity of the battle continued to grow thinner and thinner.

There were still a few Hellhounds and Angels buzzing around behind Markus and the Hunter Black. With the worst of it now behind them, the two could now focus on only the guardian ships protecting the Zeppelins and the Mothership.

As they got closer, Markus hung back and clutched onto the bottom of the nearest hovercraft to catch his breath. His wings were beat up and some of his clothing had been scorched in the laser-fire and explosions that were still going on in the mass of the battle.

The battle fatigued him, and the weight of thinking about how many people were dying right now wore him down like a heavy burden.

These were not monsters, nor androids they were fighting. These were *humans*. His own kind. People who had families, dreams, and their own lives to worry about. What could be going through their minds when their life is suddenly taken from them in the midst of the bloody battle? Was it the loved ones they left behind? Were they wondering where they would end up in the Afterlife? Or... did they just not care anymore?

I always fought to protect Ruth and myself, and threatened to kill many. Even Ashlyn... but would I have really done it? But even Markus knew that in the heat of the areal battle, he didn't have a choice this time.

Whether they were falling to their deaths below, of combusting in a ball of fire up here, being shot, stabbed, or even ripped apart by the Guardians, many members of the Guard were just being slaughtered along with the Angels of Levitika. Normally, Markus thought he wouldn't have felt so bad because of how cruel the men and women of The Baron were back in Nineveh; and yet, sight of so many life auras flickering and then suddenly going out like candles before his eyes made him sick.

Through his eyes, Markus watched as the flames of life in many men, both Ninevite and Levitikan, were quickly snuffed out as the battle raged on. So many were just disappearing in the flurry of bullets, fire, and steel.

How many lives have I taken, so far? He thought it was too many judging by the weight of his heart and stomach.

This... this what war really is. War, is hell.

But despite the burden and the fatigue, Markus knew he couldn't just tuck tail and give up.

The people in Levitika were still alive, and they needed to be protected. The queen, Esmerelda, they all had to live to take the fight back to their enemies. Even Ashlyn... the only family Markus now had. He had to protect her too.

He had to survive.

I have to.

You will. Abner assured him from the depths of the void of carnage and hellfire.

As he released another pulse of energy into the Hellhound, Markus ripped his staff out of the hull, kicking off with his feet a good twenty feet away before the hovercraft exploded in a flash of red sparks. Markus felt the eyes of the pilots on him before the flames consumed them, and he could feel the guilt once again gnawing at his belly.

Still, he couldn't stop now. To stop was to die, and if Markus died, then he would have failed everybody.

I won't allow that.

Markus spread his wings again and began to take flight once more towards the nearest gunship; the sigil of the wolf's skull staring down at him through the sockets sewn into the blimp's front.

"I'm not done yet." he told himself as he tucked his wings, and dove towards the windows of the cockpit. Ignoring Black's shouting as he neared the ship, Markus cried out while holding both of his arms around his head as he dove headfirst through the glass.

A shower of glass fell to the floor with him as Markus landed. Gunfire erupted almost immediately after. His wings reacted quickly almost on their own, curling around in front of him to prevent the bullets from tearing him apart. The bronze feathers offered great protection, even as he felt the force of an energy bolt strike the wings with enough momentum to almost knock him off-balance. Still, Markus held firm.

Even though he was unable to see the attackers due to the wings in front of him, Markus knew where they were. Not because of where the bullets struck his wings, but because of their aura. Their flames of life were swirling across the floor, telling Markus exactly where they were. Through his eyes, he saw them all standing there; all the pilots as well as a few soldiers who were flying this ship.

A thought came to him and Markus pressed his free hand against the metal floor and in the other, the Crystal in his staff began to glow bright blue. Sparks flew from the tips of his fingers, traveling across the floor and to their targets. Markus heard cries of pain and then the thudding of bodies hitting the ground. He retracted his wings into the pack and stood up.

There were ten men inside the ship, all now tangled by wires that stretched right out of the floor and around their bodies. Many struggled against the wired binds but some were whimpering as pools of urine formed beneath them where they laid. Markus saw the tallest one's arm band and recognized it as a captain's band. The man had been speared through by a bundle of wires, that held him in place by the bleeding shoulder. He hung there, panting and hissing in terrible pain as he tried to keep himself up with his free arm in order to relieve the pain.

Markus walked over to him, hearing the boots of Black landing behind him. Markus then stopped as the Hunter suddenly rushed past him in a flash of light. In a blink of an eye the boy saw Black holding his blade up and pressing the tip against the man's throat. The captain froze immediately at the touch of the metal, and began to shake and shiver as if he was cold.

He was scrawny- too scrawny to be a captain in Markus' opinion, but then again, he had seen stranger.

"I want you to drop the bombs, *now*." Black told the man. For a moment, Markus thought he saw Black's own aura flicker from maroon to a dark orange color like molding fruit.

"You-" the captain swore and then grimaced as if the Hunter had struck him. "I cannot."

"Yes, you can." Black said now with Markus beside him. His voice was dangerously low with the untold threat hanging heavily in the air as the wind continued to rush in through the shattered windshield.

The captain gulped audibly. "You don't understand-"

"No, *you* don't." Black said. "You will drop the bombs *now*, or we will leave and take our chances blowing them up and you with them."

"Okay, okay!" the captain held his hands up which caused all his weight to be dropped back onto his speared shoulder. Thankfully, Black had cut the wire holding the captain in place, allowing him to drop to the floor with his wound now bleeding profusely. He then proceeded to place his sword against the man's throat before leading him to the control panel.

"Get to it." the Hunter demanded shoving the man into the control console that was for the release switch on the mini-nuke the Zeppelin carried.

While he got to work, Markus ran to the window to survey the carnage. The battle was still going strong; with neither side willing to back down despite how many ships and bodies were falling from the skies. All the while Levitika was closing in fast; the shots from the cannons and Gatlings along the massive walls flashing brighter and brighter as each shell took down a hovercraft or soared right past them. Some managed to crash into the Leviathan, but the massive ship continued to move on unhindered by the obstacles crashing into it; and their retaliation was merciless and unrelenting.

"All right," the captain said and Markus turned to see that he had his hand placed on a lever just above his head. "This is it."

"Do it." Black commanded.

The man flipped the switch, and then curled his hands around the lever. He hesitated for a moment, and then sighed as he pulled the lever down.

Markus turned away to look outside the window. He could not see the bombs fall, but he *did* see the flash of light beneath the clouds; too big for a small explosion like they could see up here. It was a flash of light that could only be made using a nuke. The gunship suddenly shook violently as the shockwave passed through them, but eventually the ship evened out and they were sailing smoothly again.

"It's off." Markus said turning back around to face the two. "The bombs are gone."

"All of them?" Black asked the captain.

"Every last one- I swear!"

"Good."

"Captain Ross," Ovid's voice suddenly came over the intercom; the voice that terrorized the citizens of Nineveh and even now sent shivers down Markus' spine, making him tremble in his boots. "What's going on? Why have you released your bombs?"

The captain looked at Black fearfully, unable to speak to either him or his dear Baron.

"Captain?" Ovid shouted worriedly now.

Black reached for the intercom button and pressed it. "Hello, Ovid." he said as he ran his sword through the captain's torso. Markus turned so that he wouldn't see the act, but he could still hear the gasp of surprise as Captain Ross was killed without a moment's hesitation.

"Captain!" one of the trapped soldier's cried out. The terror in his eyes were all too real, and it made Markus even more sick than before. He did not look until he felt Black grab him by the arm and marched him towards the shattered window; the wind pushing against them as they moved.

"Time to go." he said swinging his sword and flicking the gore off the steel.

"You killed him…" Markus whispered. "He surrendered though! Why did you do that?"

"No choice." Black said walking past him. "He would have been killed anyway. I made it quick; a mercy kill."

"This is wrong…"

"War is wrong. But it is killed or be killed. If you hesitate, you die." the Hunter turned his head forward as they continued to walk away from the men shouting horrible things at them. "We're wasting time. Let's go."

He still wanted to argue, but Markus relented. "Okay," he said unhappily jumping out of the broken window after Black, the last thing he heard from the gunship was Ovid's frantic voice.

"Men! Focus your fire on BlackRose-Two! Open fire!"

As he and Black soared away from the blimp, Markus saw shells and bullets fly in from the Leviathan and clash into the ship, tearing the fabric and shredding metal until the gasses within ignited, and just like that, the gunship was destroyed in a muffled explosion. The heat from the blast propelled them both forward and they managed to escape unscathed- though Markus couldn't say the same for those still left inside the ship.

They are all dead…

They glided low beneath the Leviathan so that no one could see them. Black would use his grapple underneath the belly from time to time to gain more altitude and keep up with Markus as they crossed over to the second gunship; the bombs directly in view. The mini-guns along the bottom of the Mothership ceased firing on the burning wreckage of the Zeppelin that was now sinking out of view, and Markus didn't relax until they passed by the massive weapons without getting spotted.

They were a third of the way there. Now if only they could make the entire journey without any more bloodshed than there already was.

Though it was unlikely and impossible, Markus still hoped.

Ovid

"Damn it!" Ovid bellowed angrily while slamming his fists onto his personal console hard enough to create dents in the metal. "Damn you, Damion Black! *Damn* you!" He reached out for the microphone marked 'BlackRose-1' and spoke into it. "Number one, this is Ovid. Number two is down in flames."

"We know; you directed fire onto our own ship, what is going on sir? Are we under invasion?"

"We had a few *rats* on board the ship." Ovid hissed still livid with anger. "They should be dead now, but keep your guard up. Keep sharp and shoot *anything* that gets too close- even if it's our own ships."

"But sir-"

"Are you questioning me, *Captain*?" Ovid demanded coolly. Even the men around him shifted uneasily at this. All the pilots kept their faces glued to their monitors, unwilling to risk getting pulled into Ovid's dangerous grasp. To disobey the Baron, meant disobeying the devil himself with the power to extinguish your life without remorse.

He was the master here; *he* was in control here. No one else.

The coward's pathetic reply came back over the radio. "No... no sir... I'm not."

"Good. Then carry out my orders- *now*." He turned the radio off and sat back down into his chair rubbing the bridge of his nose in an effort to calm himself down. There was still time.

That damned Hunter Black was close, but that mattered little. Even if he survived and managed to get the last Zeppelin, he still had The Leviathan. He would destroy that city regardless the loss of his blimps. He would recover what was rightfully his.

But should he fail, then *no* one would find Levitika again. He would make sure of that personally, before Death takes him away. Levitika would remain nothing more than the legend the world has made it out to be.

At least Ovid himself, would die knowing he was so close to seeing the City of Angels.

"Keep moving forward!" He ordered his men through clenched teeth. "We aren't done yet!"

"Sir!" everyone barked as they continued on course for the floating city beyond the thinning battle of machines and angels.

We are so close...

Ashlyn

"It's you..." Ashlyn said to the woman in black before her. She kept her Laser Pistol on the witch despite how terribly her hands shook. Despite having held many people in Nineveh at both gun-point and knife-point, she couldn't help but remain terrified.

This was *her*... "You're the witch who sent those Hunters after us. Those Woodies... It was you..." Despite how angry she felt, Ashlyn couldn't stop her arms from shaking as if her body had a million spiders crawling all over her.

The woman smiled cruelly as she rubbed the Crystal like it was a precious pet. "We never got the pleasure of meeting properly, did we?"

"Put that down." Ashlyn said hoping what she thought wasn't the case. That what the witch had wasn't-

"What? The Eldest? Just, let him go?" the woman chuckled. "Then this whole thing would have been a waste of time. He wants to be free, and not belong to anyone now. Like a caged bird, he must be freed, by me. It is my calling after all, it is the reason why I was born."

"Don't!" Esmerelda said jumping out from behind cover. Ashlyn resisted the urge to turn to the princess and yell at her for coming out. If she turned around now the witch might try something. It was a miracle she hadn't already. "If you set him free, the region will perish! The Dark Queen doesn't know how dangerous that thing is!"

"Who said anything about Lamia?" the witch asked. "That pitiful woman could never hope to master the powers of her grandfather. No, He shall be released where He was born, with the people who wish to serve Him for eternity."

The witch then removed a second Crystal from her pocket; this one greatly smaller than The Eldest. "I can't have you *children* get in my way."

"Drop it!" Ashlyn screamed gripping her weapon tighter. "I *will* shoot you!"

"I'm counting on it." the witch said as she slammed the smaller Crystal against the side of the owl statue.

Immediately dark red lights that looked like veins spider-webbed across the statue's torso and wings, and as the light reached the head, the two eyes began to glow bright red. Before the girl's very eyes, the bronze owl moved, the statue moving as gracefully as if it was real. It flapped its wings once, and then screeched with such sonorousness that the room seemed to shake.

Ashlyn felt her knees quiver beneath her, and she was not surprised when Esmerelda fell back screaming, her gun forgotten. The witch then began to pet the giant metallic bird while turning back to the children; a sinister grin stretched across her pale cheeks.

"Stay out of my way, or I will kill you." the witch then leapt onto the back of the owl, nimble as a cat.

"Stop!" Ashlyn shouted bringing her weapon up again and firing at the witch. With a swipe of the woman's hand an arc of ice appeared out of nowhere, catching the blast before it could connect with her own body. Snowflakes sprinkled down to the ground to Ashlyn's dismay. "You will have to do better than th-"

Brr-brr! The sound of a machine gun went off and the witch's head was thrown back with a hideous howl. Ashlyn turned fast to see Esmerelda still on the ground, her own weapon still in hand.

The witch sat back up snarling wickedly. Her right cheek had been grazed by the bullet and her ear had a hole punched right through the lobe. It was dripping heavily with blood that dribbled down the side of the owl.

"You little bitch!" the witch snarled and then raising her hand a large icicle formed into her palm. "Die!" and with that she threw the shard right for Esmerelda.

"Look out!" Ashlyn screamed, diving and tackling the princess out of harms' way just as the shard stuck right into the marble floor. At this point, the witch's bronze owl had taken flight and was now hovering slowly in the air.

The witch was about to hurl another ice shard when something buzzed right at her and grabbed onto her face. Q-pid clung desperately to the now confused witch who went to grab at her only to miss as the robot took flight again and stuck her little tail into the madwoman's ear. With a howl or annoyance the witch finally grabbed the robot and freezing it with her ice she hurled it onto the floor where it shattered into many pieces.

"Q-Pid!" Esmerelda cried out.

"You shall all fall!" the witch screamed clutching her ear and the owl flapped its wings, propelling the two of them forward towards the two. Ashlyn grabbed ahold of Esmerelda and threw her aside and then tossed herself back before she would be crushed by the massive owl that barreled past them. As the owl banked around the room, she rushed back for Esmerelda and the two ran back for the door, taking cover as the owl stuck its massive head though the doorway, thrashing as shards of ice continued to shoot past it.

Ashlyn kept far enough away from the head that continued to rock the hallway and create cracks in the floor and walls, just like Esmerelda who remained perfectly still on the opposite side. With a stiff 'hoot', the owl then backed away, and then spreading its wings again, it shot straight up like a rocket towards the ceiling. Ashlyn ran outside and fired a few shots at it, hitting the bird but causing no more damage than the ceiling did as it smashed right through the glass and causing an avalanche of both glass and stone to fall.

"Ashlyn!" Esmerelda screamed out grabbing ahold of Ashlyn by the arm and yanking her back just before she could get smashed by a large chunk of stone that had fallen. If the princess hadn't pulled her away, Ashlyn would have been killed. But she had far more to worry about, and looking back up at the hole in the ceiling, she feared what could happen next.

"Call your mom, *now*!" she screamed at Esmerelda. *She's getting away... Markus, she's getting away...*

Esmerelda nodded frantically as she reached for her radio. As she tried to contact her mother, she had hurried over to where Q-pid had been discarded and managed to salvage one of the major pieces which consisted of the little body and head. The wings were crushed and she was missing her tail and one of her arms.

"Damage..." Q-Pid buzzed.

"Thank God..." Esmerelda breathed as she continued to try the radio. "Hello? Mother! Come in..."

Ashlyn looked back up towards the opened ceiling in despair. "Please... hurry."

~ A Bond ~

Elizabetha

Elizabetha watched the battle continue to roar through the windows of the tower, a look of fear so great her own guards began to fear for her health.

She watched the enemy Hellhounds linger dangerously close to the city walls, with the Leviathan right behind them. One blimp was gone, but the Baron was still firing upon her city without mercy and was rapidly closing the distance between him and his goal. Some of his Dragonflies broke free from the battle and attempted to sail right over the walls only to be shot down by the Gatlings on the walls. Still, it didn't ease Elizabetha's anxious heart.

We'll make it, she thought trying to calm herself. *We'll be okay. Damion will-*

"Mother!" she heard Esmerelda's sounded over the intercom. Her voice was so frantic it came out like a screech, scaring the men in the control room right out of their seats.

She took the mic from her armrest. "Esmerelda, what is it? I don't-"

"The witch! She has The Eldest! She escaped and she took it! Everyone's dead!"

A witch!? Her motherly instincts screamed at Elizabetha to tell Esmerelda to return to the safe room. To have Ashlyn protect her, or take an escape pod and get far away from this place as possible.

"My daughter..." her voice faltered as the owl statue of her Great Hall suddenly flew past the tower and over the walls, smashing through a tower before heading towards the battle, a woman riding its back. Whatever she had to say to Esmerelda, was lost on her tongue. "Oh no…" she turned to her men. "Shoot it down with everything we got, leave our troops to deal with the Baron!"

"We might be overrun your majesty!" one protested.

"If that witch gets away it won't matter *who* wins this battle. Now do it!"

"My Queen," Slagar said who was watching the battle through a telescope. He turned his bright red eyes to her, his expression brooding. "We may have to use The Ray."

"Not yet." Elizabetha said shaking her head. The last thing she wanted to do was use the Shi Ray, especially at the height the island was at. "We can't afford to, not yet. If we do at this height, we will crash."

"But-"

"No." Elizabetha said sternly. She then felt something brush against her mind and she snapped at Slagar angrily, "And get the hell out of my head!"

To her pleasure, the mage suddenly staggered as if he had been violently shoved.

"I'm just as worried as you are Slagar, but if you *ever* try digging for answers out of me again, I will have you shot before the Ninevites kill us!" Now ignoring the man, she turned back to her soldiers. "Focus your fire on the woman in black; don't let her get away. And get Black on the mic, now!"

"Ma'am!" everyone said in unison as they scrambled to carry out her orders.

Elizabetha then took her mic again and called for her daughter. "Esmerelda?"

"Mother," her voice came back on. "What's going on?"

"Return to your room right this instant. Lock the doors and don't answer for anyone unless it is me, you got it?"

"A-alright."

"Your Majesty," Ashlyn then spoke up. "What about the witch?"

"We'll deal with it." Elizabetha said hoping that what she said wouldn't end up as a lie. "Right now, you're only priority is protecting my daughter. So… please, Ashlyn. Keep her safe. Both of you, stay safe."

Markus

Markus attempted to enter the next gunship as he did the last, but the ship's turrets would not allow him to get above the rope tethers.

So instead, he stood on top of the nuclear weapon, the wind threatening to blow him right off so he kept his Eagles-Wings straight out so he would not be carried away. Keeping a hand on one of the claws holding the tethered bomb in place, he braced himself against the wind that probably would have blown him right off had he not have the Crystal in his possession.

Black was up on top of the claw, at the base of the hull. He observed something, and then slid down and landed with ease and landed next to Markus. Despite not having a grip on anything to hold him steady, he remained sturdy without any fear of being blown away by the winds.

"There's no way to cut it." he said looking around, thinking fast. "See the tail?" he asked pointing to the rear of the Zeppelin whose bottom part of the tail was visible.

"Yeah?" Markus said looking back at it, his hair whipping around in his face as he turned back.

"If we can damage it, we can steer this blimp into the Leviathan."

Markus smiled. "And blow them both up."

"We can only hope. Let's go." But he did not move, for something caught his eye.

Markus turned to look and was immediately struck hard in the chest. He felt the bomb disappear beneath his feet as he began to freefall down to the clouds below. He began to extend his wings in search for an updraft to slow his fall, but all Markus was doing what slowing his decent little by little. As the ships above disappeared from his view in a *poof* of the clouds, Markus began to scream out as he tried frantically to turn his body and extend his wings before he struck the ground below.

Black

Black felt the air flush out of his lungs as he was struck as well, and *carried* across the sky, the metal plating in the shoulder of his attacker driving right into his belly.

He saw that he was being taken towards the Leviathan, and bringing his fists and the hilt of his weapon into the back of his attacker, he was suddenly thrown onto the roof. He tumbled across the metal and began to slide down the side, but he then caught himself on top of one of the wings using his sword as an anchor; the turbine behind him pulling him back, threatening to swallow him.

With a click of his heels, the magnetized plating within the soles of his boots activated, holding him in place and keeping him from flailing off the wing and into the engine. He stood straight up, his sword out and his cloak flapping in the wind as his opponent landed in front of him.

"Lee." he said to the rogue Hunter.

Lee stood straight up, his boots squealing against the wing of the Leviathan as the wind pushed against him and grinded against the studded plating in his own soles. With the tinted glass obscuring the Hunter's face, it was impossible to see whether Lee was smiling or not. His suit's gauntlet was covered in splattered crimson, with some speckles dotting his helmet.

Black began to circle Lee, who was eyeing the Hunter and seemed to be taking his sweet time as he took large steps like a child.

"Funny, isn't it?" Lee said with his hands spread out as he walked casually forward as if he was about to embrace a long-lost friend. "We go through all this trouble, the Baron, you, all of it; for a couple of stupid kids. And in the end, it wasn't even our concern as long as we found the place."

"Where is your sister?" Black demanded.

"She'll be here soon." Lee said. By the spark in his own life flame, Black knew the man wasn't lying but he wasn't sure either. He repeated, "Very soon. You know, the plan was to destroy as many Angels and the Baron's men as I could before she came, but I've had enough fun. I came for you, Black."

Black narrowed his eyes, keeping a close watch on Lee who came for him.

"The famous, 'Hunter Black'." Lee lowered his hands as he did his voice. "You are a legend throughout the Wastelands and the Southern Sands. Between you and me, I always resented my sister; the powers she grew with as well as how she could bond with our father's Crystal. I could do none of that. And knowing that you could, the Hunter I looked up to, my heart sank. I had no hope to becoming like you; the Hunter who I heard of growing up since you emerged from the Seifkr Empire. So, I did something else. For many years I have trained to fulfill my destiny. For many years I have trained body and mind to handle even the toughest of opponent and contracts. Years of hating myself, forcing myself to grow stronger. All of it, was to be able to kill you."

"I will give you one chance." Black said no longer interested in Lee's speech. "Leave now, escape while you can, and you will not suffer the same fate as your sister will."

"Ha, that's a lot of talk, Black." Lee said and with a flick of his wrists two blades shot out from the wrist openings in his gauntlets below his palms, as well as two machine guns over his forearms. "You're mine. I wanted the pleasure of cleaning your clock myself. I knew the others would not be enough, and you took care of them. You have my thanks for that; three less shares. A shame, but necessary."

"You're a monster."

Lee chuckled. "We're all monsters, my friend. Thing is, Lameika and I, we're the ones who are gonna survive. We are the ones who are gonna win. Because we have The Eldest now. And soon, everyone is going to know who we are. And you… you're just gonna be another faceless corpse among the fallen angels you deserted your Baron to protect."

Markus, Black thought as he gripped his longsword all the tighter. "Let us see who is the best then." he said. *If you can hear me, then listen well. Go for the tail as planned, do* not *stop, and do* not *give up. Levitika's fate rests in your hands.*

"Only the strong survive," Lee said. "So it is not the best we must see. Let us see who is *stronger.*"

And in the midst of the upcoming battle, Damion Black felt the brush of a conscious against his own, and he smiled. "Let us fight." he told Lee as he lunged for the Rogue Hunter, who let loose a flurry of bullets at his adversary.

Markus

Markus' eyes snapped open when he heard Black's voice clear as daylight as he continued to fall to the world below.

Despite the wind blasting all around his body in a fury, hindering all other sound even over his own screams, but it was there. As if the Hunter was falling beside him, Markus could hear his voice. It was then when Markus realized that he was not hearing with his ears, but in his very own thoughts.

Markus, Black said. *If you can hear me, then listen well. Go for the tail as planned, do* not *stop, and do not give up. Levitika's fate rests in your hands.*

Easier said than done. Markus thought as he continued his fast descent; the ground rushing up to him way too fast for him to catch a strong enough draft. He was slowing down, but for some reason Markus could not get his wings to cooperate and angle in a way that could help him dive out of harm's way.

So, he tried something else.

Straightening his body out, he turned so that he could face the ground and bringing all his weight forward, he turned into a stiff dive like a diver into water. His wings were angled and he picked up speed, and after a few seconds he snapped his wings open and angled them in a pitch that could send him skyward.

The end result allowed him to seize the wind and carry himself away from the ground that was mere seconds from catching him. He swooped upwards and hollered loudly as he flapped his wings again and started for the clouds above that flashed bright as if lightning was striking within the storm. Focusing on just breaking through the clouds, Markus rejoined the battle that was still raging as he pushed through the clouds and once again back into the fray.

He felt bullets whiz past his head and he had to dodge falling debris whether that be machinery or dead bodies. Eventually though after covering some more distance, he made it to the tail of the blimp he had been knocked off of. He retracted his wings and stabbed his staff into the tail flap that stabilized the aircraft, the steering flap above him turning to and fro against the wind.

Markus turned towards the Leviathan and saw two figures fighting on the wing of the massive ship. Gunfire was visible, as well as light from magic caused by Black no doubt. The other figure Markus could not see who it was, but judging by how much of a fight he was putting up against Black, he was good.

I can't worry about him now. He looked back up at the tail flap. He had to break it and somehow make it turn into the Leviathan, or at least steer it away from the city. Either way, this ship could not make it to Levitika under any circumstances. He then began to let the Crystal release its energy from him to the staff, hoping to at least damage the rotor. He imagined it just falling to pieces, believing that it would happen.

It was before he released it when Markus heard a loud screech. He turned his head to see a massive owl of bronze flying towards the Leviathan at break-neck speed, and riding on top of it, was a woman. A blast of ice engulfed a passing Angel, and the frozen figure fell as the witch laughed at the unfortunate soul.

Markus felt his hope extinguish like a flame as the witch continued to fly towards the Leviathan.

She was heading for the ship, but where exactly? The cockpit? Black? Did it matter?

No.

All that mattered was the blimp. Markus had to get rid of it here and now; he couldn't let anything stop him. He turned back to the tail and released all his energy and breath, letting the Crystal take over from there; and as he felt the presence of the spirit within the Crystal awaken, letting all of its energy become released like a dam letting water flow.

But a thought suddenly occurred to him. If the witch was here and no longer in the ship that crashed back in Levitika, then… could something have happened at the castle? Worry and dread clung to Markus' heart like a cancer, as he envisioned the faces of Ashlyn, Esmerelda and the queen crying out for help as their lives were in danger. If something happened to them…

Markus suddenly cried out as he felt the energy slip away from his control and it was suddenly released in a flash of blinding blue light.

Markus felt himself, leave himself.

It was strange. This feeling, it was almost like Markus was releasing all his worries again, letting his mind wonder as he had done so in the courtyard earlier that day.

But this time he felt no peace in his mind; only terror and destruction, similar to what he did in the Wastelands against the Woodies. Paralyzed it seemed, he now felt the power for the Crystal releasing through him and the staff like before, but the terror he felt within was almost unbearable.

He saw their faces. The agony the spirit felt, the monstrosities within. The kind spirits of the heroes of ancient times, but now broken, their will corrupted by the forces of darkness mankind all felt within them. Their demons, their fears, Markus felt them all. The sins that haunt them, the regrets that shroud them in their menacing lore, their very weaknesses floating around him as if they were the sea, and Markus himself was the one drowning within their embrace.

As he felt the energy within slip away and shroud him like a shadow, Markus felt himself succumb to their melodious cries until he was gone; and within the darkness, he heard a cold and harsh voice echo in his head, reaching out with crooked hands of darkness to pull him deeper into the void.

I see you…

Black

Black fell back, catching himself from falling off the wing by driving his sword into the metal right down to the hilt almost, stabilizing his balance as his boots reconnected to the metal beneath him.

He had driven Lee back over the bulk of the ship, and they now landed upon the other wing after their little spar. But still, he had to admit now; the Hunter was good.

Black was bleeding badly from multiple wounds, and his arms had been grazed just as well. He wasn't too hurt, but if this kept up any longer then he would be in trouble. Taking advantage of Lee who had dropped to a knee after a deadly blow to his gut, Black lunged at the Hunter who immediately held up his blades to deflect the blow. Black swung downward, and when the blades struck, sparks flew into each other's faces. Even with the aid of his own Crystal, he could not break Lee's stance; and when he disengaged to swing again, the Hunter caught his attack a second time, thus delivering a kick to the ribs- a dagger emerging from the toe and piercing through the gaps in his armor.

"Gah!" Black gasped as he pulled away as blood spilled from his torso. Lee backed away as well, his foot now covered in his enemy's blood. Black came at him again, this time attempting to stab but at the last minute changed his course so his blade passed under Lees arms and into his side.

The blade slid off the armor hardly making a scratch on the metal. If Black was surprised he didn't show as he leapt back from Lees arms which swung at him, the blades missing his torso by mere inches. He flicked a switch as he leapt away, the metal of his sword delivering a shock into Lee's armor, which other than a sharp snap and a crackle remained unscathed and Lee was still doing okay considering.

"Impressive, isn't it?" Lee asked laughing. "This armor's too tough, even for a sword like that. I'm pleased that you are putting up such a valiant fight, Black, really I am. You've gotten slow in your old age though." Lee crouched and repositioned his blades again. "Play time is over, old man."

"Indeed." Black heard the unmistakable voice of the witch Lameika and when Black peered through his peripheral vision, he saw her riding upon the back of the statue of the Great Owl. She was laughing hysterically, and in her left arm cradled a familiar dark gem.

Black immediately felt a dark consciousness brush against his own, and for the first time in his long-lived life, he felt fear.

"HA! You've lost, Black." she cackled as the massive bird hovered in the air, its glowing eyes staring Black down like he was prey. "The city is doomed, and soon the Baron shall be as well. But now…" The witch's face suddenly turned into a look of confusion.

"Sis?" Lee said lowering his arms in alarm.

"Something…" she said dreamily. "He's… He's telling me…" Her eyes then widened. "The boy!"

Suddenly a blinding light filled the sky and casted upon the Leviathan and all who saw it. Black shielded his eyes and tried to peek, and saw what it was. Against the final blimp's tail was Markus, a bolt of blinding blue light shining down upon him from the sky as if the heaven's themselves had opened up, his body appearing as bright as a sapphire in sunlight.

Suddenly the light became so bright it all came as white, obscuring the blimp before a deafening blast came from where Markus was. When the light faded and a hot blast of air pelted the side of the Leviathan, Black saw that the back half of the Zeppelin had disintegrating before their very eyes, and the bombs that were so close, were ignited. The mini-nukes went off in a blast of radioactive fire, causing the entire world to tilt beneath Black's feet.

He felt himself thrown back by the force of the explosion, and Lee too was shoved aside, nearly sliding off the wing in the process. The Great Owl faltered in mid-flap before it steadied itself. It wasn't a big enough bomb but the intense heat Black felt from the blast felt like he was being cooked from the inside out. He looked further down the length of the wing to see that a good chunk of it had been shredded with burning flaps of metal and engine-pieces now peeling off and flying off into the night. The Leviathan trembled beneath their feet, and Lee then turned to see what was happening-

Leaving an opening for Black to take his chance.

As the Leviathan shuddered beneath him, Black lunged forward and struck. He swung out with his sword, not trying to cut through the armor, he knew that he and the Crystal were not powerful enough now for that. Besides, he would need it to take care of the witch. So instead, using his sword and his own strength, he struck. He struck at Lee's side with such force the Hunter fell back to his knees, clutching his side. He held up a single arm to defend himself but in a flash of black fabric, Black was already upon him.

Grasping the man's arm, Black pulled him close so he could look the man in the eyes beneath the visors of his helmet. He then threw his head back, and brought it forward, smashing his head against Lee's and the helmet cracked beneath the force of the blow.

When he did so however, he had disengaged his grapple hook from his arm, and attached it to Lee's. He then struck the man again with the butt of his sword, breaking the shoulder where it landed. He then twisted the arm around so that Lee could no longer use it to defend himself and pulling the Hunter's head back again, he stared into the man's eyes, and immediately, Lee began to tremble.

"Look into my eyes," Black said allowing Lee's darkest fears to pass through him, feeding him, and giving him the upper hand to mentally break the Rogue before him. Lee began to moan as he saw whatever it was that frightened him the most. Black didn't dare go too far for there was little time left. But Lee was now caught and at his mercy, and he had to end it all here and now.

He then cried out to the heavens, but searching for only one person to hear him. "Markus, now!"

But he was cut short by a searing pain in his back as he flew over Lee, and landed a couple of yards away. Lee stood up rubbing his shoulder while his sister extinguished the frost from the hand she had casted the spell with. She had speared him through the back with an ice shard that was now sticking in his body!

Black tried to get up but found that he couldn't. He coughed out and blood splattered before him as his internal injuries began to make their way out. His arms were so weak he could not bear the weight of his own body and as he reached for his sword and grabbed it, his hand was crushed beneath the heel of Lee who now stood above him laughing behind his cracked helmet.

"Thanks, Sis." he said as he pressed the point of his bladed gauntlet against the base of Black's skull. "That magic… where did you learn that from? How did you know, about my father?"

Black said nothing, but glared defiantly at the Hunter who had quickly recovered from the illusion Black had casted upon him.

Lee bared his teeth in anger. "This is the 'famous', Hunter Black." he said shaking his head in disappointment. "What a bother. You weren't even worth the time. Your fangs have dulled. The boy's gone, Damion, and you are all alone. That little trick you did, I don't know what it was and I don't care. This is where it all ends."

Black stared at him defiantly.

"Prepare to die."

Suddenly Lee's eyes flickered and he looked up from Black as if he saw something. "What the-"

Bam!

A bolt of blue light suddenly struck Lee in the chest, blowing him across the faltering wing. He nearly flew off of it but he managed to catch himself by stabbing the wing with one of his blades. Another bolt of light struck the owl statue, disintegrating the left wing. The owl screeched as if flew at an angle, only to turn and crash through the cockpit windows of the Leviathan with Lameika still riding it. A massive explosion sounded inside, blowing the windows and whatever was inside out.

Black suddenly felt the Leviathan change in pitch as it suddenly began to slowly drop into a steady dive.

They were falling out of the sky!

As Black turned to see what was happening, he was shocked- no. Not shocked, *terrified* at what he saw. For Markus stood on the wing of the ship, his skin bright blue and his eyes glowing white. Despite not having any magnetized boots to keep him stable, Markus walked across the burning wing with ease.

Lee, who was trying to get up raised his fist and closed it tight to unleash a flurry of bullets towards the child's direction, but nothing was coming out. Angry, Lee sliced off his guns and squared up to the approaching teen, his blades ready for an attack.

"You are more trouble than I thought." Lee called out to the child who remained indifferent as he walked his steady pace, his staff ready and glowing brightly. "Die!" and Lee's rockets were lit, propelling him at the teen who stood still as ever as the two blades crossed each other, ready to slice at the boy's jugular.

Black took up his sword and attempted once again to get up, but still couldn't. So still stuck in place, he began pulling out the ice shard from his back which was now stained red. Tossing the ice away, Black then turned to see Lee almost upon Markus and in a last minute attempt to save the boy, Black placed his palm flat on the wing of the ship, and pulsed with whatever energy he had left as he beckoned Fethawit to help him.

Markus...

~ Possessed ~

Markus

Markus' staff moved fast and fluently, catching the Hunter's blades and then continuing to do so in a flurry of movement that just came to him like muscle memory. His body moved with such speed and strength that the Hunter Lee just couldn't keep up with the boy, and as a result earn a few good gnashes in his armor.

But something was terribly wrong.

Markus wasn't doing the moving.

Even the power the Crystal had given him in the Wastelands was nothing compared to now. Like a wizard or a witch, Markus extended his hand out and a flash of blue light momentarily blinded him and when he was able to see, Lee was on his back and sparkling as if he had been struck by lightning. With a hollow cry the Hunter leapt and spun into the air to kick at Markus, who just as quickly grabbed ahold of the Lee's foot and energy immediately flowed from his hand to the limb, and Lee's leg exploded in a flash of metallic shards and flailing wires.

Lee jumped back and caught his footing again before squaring back up before coming at Markus again despite the loss of his Auto-Limb foot. Even with the dismemberment of something, he was still very much able to fight. Every slash of his blades ended as quickly as they came as Markus spun his staff, catching every single blow he with ease that shouldn't have been possible.

"No!" Lee angrily shouted as he stabbed at the boy again.

This'll be fun.

Markus watched as his own hand lashed out and grabbed ahold of Lee's wrist. With inhuman strength, he suddenly twisted Lee's arm, snapping the wrist and tearing the armor. Lee cried out as he fell to his knees and as soon as he looked up he was looking down the length of Markus' staff, the blade-tip pressed against his jugular. There was no hope for the Hunter now. Markus could easily put an end to him once and for all.

But Markus was afraid. His body... it no longer belonged to him. *This is not me...*

Oh, yes it is. a darkness seemed to say, smiling at him through the veil his eyes peered through. *This is you, and so much more.*

What was Lee seeing, as he looked up at Markus' face? He could not see the Hunter's own expression through the helmet, but Markus could still feel him through his life essence. Anger and jealously fueled his rage and his actions, however those feelings seemed suppressed by an even more powerful feeling.

Fear. Fear for his own life, knowing that he was about to die, and at the hands of-

A monster.

Markus felt something shatter inside of him. *No... I don't want this. If this is what the Crystal can offer, then I don't want it!*

Oh, but I do.

Without words, Markus tried to scream. *Abner... what...*

You are mine now, son of Johnathon.

Are you sure? The feeling came without warning. It was cold, alien even. But Markus knew in an instant that it wasn't the darkness that had seized him, but a warmer and more recognizable presence.

Abner.

The Darkness, seethed. *Begone, Wolf of Eden. All this anger inside of you, you can't hide it. Why not let it run free? Let me take it from here, let the animal you kept caged inside free, and destroy him. It'll make you feel better. It's good to let the demons loose, once in a while...*

Suddenly Lee began to cry out as if he was being stabbed and Markus' eyes lowered to see that the blade of his staff was changing. Beneath the Crystal, the dagger-like blade of bronze shifted and stretched, turning into razor-thin shears that circled around Lee's neck, ready to slice the man's head clean off.

Allow your imagination- your desire to kill him, destroy him... Don't deny what you want- what you wish, you can make it come true.

No... no, this is not right! Markus tried to scream despite the crimson darkness that shrouded his mind, coiling around him like a serpent ready to suffocate him. *I am Markus, son of Johnathon. Brother of Ruth, friend of Ashlyn- I am me!*

The darkness growled, *You are mine!*

It doesn't sound like it. Abner's voice answered, embracing Markus like a long-lost friend. *This boy, is The Keeper, and the hope of The North. He won't be bested by the likes of you. Never.*

Markus felt something like a warm hand peeling away the coiling darkness, allowing him to really feel his own body again, and regain consciousness within his limbs. As he fought the urge to drive his staff into Lee's throat Markus began to feel his body growing weaker, as if all his energy was merely a rope being pulled by two beings.

Markus, don't let go.

Markus saw the glow from his skin slowly dim and his focus began to grow stronger despite his fatigue.

This is not you. Come back, let it go.

The cold voice came back with a curdling anger that felt like a gong going off in Markus' brain. *You... Release me... RELEASE ME!!!*

And then, Markus felt like all the blood was rushing into his head as the Crystal's grip on his spirit dwindled, and the world began to slowly fade to black.

Lee

The child appeared to be fatigued by whatever he had just done. The color in his skin was fading to normal, and those dangerously bright eyes that once glowed blue like that of the Crystal in his staff suddenly went dim as they transmuted back into their original color. Not only that, but the blade on the boy's staff slowly returned to normal, releasing Lee's neck as the boy began to sway.

Lee saw no better time to take his chance. As the boy began to falter, he swatted the staff aside and punched the kid in the chest, sending him flying back and tumble across the wing almost to the edge where he would have blown right off if he had not managed to grab ahold of a piece of shrapnel sticking out of the metal.

As the kid tried to keep his bleeding grip on the wing piece, Lee strolled over and grabbed the staff off the wing. He took it in both hands, and brought it down onto his knee, snapping it in two. He then tossed the bottom half over to the boy who looked up in a daze. He reached for the broken piece, holding the jagged edge out like a dagger.

Lee smiled as he strolled over as the kid was now attempting to get up on his knees ready to fight. He had to give the boy credit; he was tough and he was determined. But it wasn't going to save him, and as the ship continued it's decent to the valley below, Lee stood above Markus as he kicked his arms out from under him, dropping the child back onto his face; and with one heavy boot, Lee stomped on the back, pinning him down right between the Eagle's Wings he wore.

"Enough," Lee said allowing his footless limb to slide down to the kid's shoulders, and then grabbing a lock of the boy's hair, he lifted his face up and exposed his throat. "You really are more trouble than you were worth. We should have killed you when we had the chance." He began to lower the Crystal-blade down towards the throat, not seeing Markus' grin.

"You should have." Markus whispered in agreement.

Before Lee could say anything, something shot out of the wing of the plane and impaled him right under the armpit. Thankfully, it wasn't his real arm otherwise he would have bled out. Looking down the spike that had protruded from the ship, Lee turned his eyes to Black who was still laying down with his hand flat on the ship. From his hand, was a jagged crack that led right to the spike that had him trapped.

Lee sneered. "You son of a…"

"Gotcha," Markus said as he lunged out grabbing the Crystal and in a flash of blue light and in one fluent motion, grabbed ahold of Lee's shattered left ankle, and pulsed.

Having an auto-limb for his leg, the dismemberment did not hurt as bad as it would've if it was real. But since the little wires and circuits within the robotic limb were connected to the nerve endings where his stump was, Lee still felt pain, and as he fell back gasping in pain he had foolishly released the boy. Markus then suddenly grabbed ahold of his head, and those eyes flashed bright and blue once again.

At that moment, Lee saw flashes of something pass over his eyes. Shadows and memories of the past, that delivered heavy blows like the fists that used to beat him to a bloody pulp as a kid.

What is this? he thought as he tried to shake the horrible memories from his brain. He raised his hands up, as if he could try and stop his father's fists from striking him again. *No…*

"Aaarrgh!" He swung blindly at Markus, who rolled aside and the blade stuck right into the wing of the Leviathan. And then the boy reached for something on Lee's wrist, something he did not recognize, nor realize what it was until it was too late.

Markus had flicked a switch after jerking Lees wrist to the side, and a small grapple hook shot out of the little launcher, sticking into the metal of one of the turbines on the ship which was slowly breaking off.

"Black sends his regards." Markus grinned.

Lee's eyes went wide, and he tried to take the wrist-clip off just before the turbine blew off, and with it, Lee who was ripped off the spike and pulled by the arm right off the wing of the ship and down into the valley below, screaming for dear life.

He desperately tried to turn on the rockets in his boots, but in his panic, he forgot a critical detail; he no longer had a left foot, so the rocket in his right only sent him in a spiraling flurry as the turbine pulled him under the clouds miles beneath the Leviathan, which was now descending at a faster rate.

Ovid

Ovid coughed as he shoved a piece of metal off of him.

Dust and sparks were flying everywhere under the influence of the wind which tore through the windows and into the control room after that giant owl-thing smashed through it. It had damaged all the controls and crushed all of his pilots. He tried to steady himself on his knees as the malfunction alarm blasted throughout the ship. They were sinking, this much The Baron knew was inevitable. The bombs were gone too; he was losing and had no way to prevent anyone else from seizing the ancient city.

He had failed.

No… no…

Ovid shoved the hunk of metal aside and standing up he limped towards the windows. He heard a squishy sound beneath his heel as if he stepped in something wet, but he did not look down. The statue bird laid across the smashed consoles and monitors, the magic that possessed it was gone, making it as solid as the hunk of bronze it once was… well, now it was simply shattered pieces now.

Sparks flew at Ovid's face but he did not flinch, even when he felt the flesh on his cheek burn from a spark. He kept going towards the window, to the left of the massive hole as the wind continued to push back. Upon reaching it he looked down towards the wing of the hovercraft where he heard his men shouting about earlier. They had been saying something about Black and that kid fighting the boy-twin before the blimp crashed into the Leviathan.

Sure enough, they were there.

Black was struggling to stand up, his hand on one knee while the other held that deadly sword of his. Blood was smeared across the wing where he once laid, and more fell like rain with every step he took; the wind carrying off most of the crimson droplets like rose pedals.

There was no sign of Lee, and what surprised Ovid even more was the child with golden wings who was standing up as easily as if he was standing on solid ground. He held only a knife which held the blue Crystal within. That child of Johnathon, he was still alive after all- and he had the Crystal all along. When his men shouted out about the explosion and the blimps and even the bronze owl flying with the witch on its back he thought they all were just going insane.

But it appears that they were right. Everything was falling apart. It was quite apparent now that he has lost. He had miscalculated, and his entire fleet was going down in flames.

But he would make them pay. Black, and that damned kid- they would *both* pay!

At his belt, Ovid removed two small machine pistols, but clicking them together and extending them, the combination turned into a large assault rifle which he pulled into his shoulder and aimed down the sights. Peering down with an eye full of hate, he rested the crosshair on Black's torso, right where the heart should be. The Hunter was bleeding out, but Ovid would help him bleed faster.

"Goodbye." he whispered as he began to apply pressure against the trigger of his weapon, tensely awaiting to see Blacks' damning calm demeanor twist and turn as his body was pierced by many bullets.

But before he could squeeze the trigger any tighter, he was suddenly grabbed and was quickly swung around before getting slammed against the wall hanging by the small hand that curled around his throat. He had dropped his gun in the whiplash and was now lifted a good foot above the ground. He kicked and gasped as he clawed at the witch who held him, her eyes glowing bright red with half of her face smeared in blood.

"You-" he struggled. He punched out at her and Lameika grabbed ahold of the Baron's fist, freezing it instantly in a block of ice. Ovid moaned at the discomfort but then screamed as Lamaika applied more pressure, shattering the ice block into thick red chunks.

"Me." Lameika said with a sinister grin. And then she tilted her head back and opened her mouth wide enough for her jaw to dislocate. To Ovid's horror, a black double-edged sword of ice slid through the witch's gullet and past her teeth, gleaming wickedly in the sparks light.

"Wait!" he cried out. "This is an outrage! Release me or... or..."

And with one swift movement of Lameika's neck, she beheaded Baron Ovid, son of Akuta, and fallen leader of Nineveh.

~ Falling Angels ~

Lameika

Dropping the headless body of Baron Ovid onto the floor, Lameika 'swallowed' her blade and began to cross the shattered cabin towards the windows where he was originally looking.

She could feel The Eldest digging into her head, reading her, whispering in her ear, but she ignored Him; instead letting His influence, Hatred and pain flow through her veins. He was feeding her the saturated anger and lighting the fire within her. Though He commanded her to flee, His very presence and influence drove her into such bloodlust and rage. She had unfinished business to take care of before setting off with her master.

Black was a constant nuisance, always ruining everything, and the boy- that *child*! All this trouble, all of this chasing and planning to retrieve The Eldest, ruined by the one the foolish Ninevite Baron was so desperate to find.

Oh well. Ovid had nothing to worry about, not anymore. But Lameika was seething as she looked down to the wing and the now two passengers along it.

Lee was gone, and Lameika could only assume that he was dead. Otherwise he would have flown back up. Black was down, crouching closest to the ship's body, while the boy was walking along the wing towards him, his staff gone but his blade still there with one of the Crystals. He seemed to be calling to Black as his careful walk slowly broke into a light jog towards him. Despite how fast the wind blew or how much the Leviathan was still falling, he just wouldn't fall away and take flight like the pathetic bird he was. The bright and blue light that emitted from his skin like a glowworm faded back to his original form, the overpowering essence coming from him seeming suppressed once again.

At this, Lameika began to smile. The boy stopped beside Black, and was attempting to help him up. His life essence was tinged with worry, while Black's was full of pain and weakening spirit as he bled out all over the wing. And as the kid began to help Black to his feet, his side was open to Lameika.

She grinned as she crouched like a cat, her hands out wide with her fingers spread. Frost accumulated between them and two ice shards appeared like swords in her hands. With a sharp leap using the energy of The Eldest, she charged out the window and lunged towards Markus; her blades aimed for the opening below his armpit, where his heart lied beneath the ribcage.

Black's head suddenly turned and a look of alarm spread across his face, and at the last minute, he spun Markus away; an invisible force seeming to throw the boy away in a blast of maroon light and placing himself in front of Lameika as Markus was tossed away like a ragdoll.

Lameika's ice slid into the Hunter's back between his shoulder blades, only to emerge through his chest in a spray of red.

"NO!" Markus screamed as he pushed himself back up with his wings outstretched ready for flight.

Seething but at the same time greatly joyous to see Black's blood across her ice and soaking her hands, Lameika pulled back and slid the ice right out of the man who dropped to his knees. She shook her hands and let the ice melt away, dripping with water and blood as Black breathed raggedly as a fountain of crimson began to dribble from his wounds. He coughed out suddenly, spitting out more blood.

He turned his face towards her, weak and dying. This was not one of his illusions; he was truly dying right in front of her.

"You, idiot." Lameika sneered at Black as she looked up at Markus who was standing up, his blade aimed right at her. Her fingers still hissed of frost and she held them up towards the boy. "There's no more hope for you, *boy*." she snarled her voice no longer her own but that of a demon that had long since been suppressed. Her eyes glowed blood-red as did her sight as she looked at him with such hatred. "You are dead. Both of you shall die, and you will join your stupid sister." she started forward, keeping a hand on Black's shoulder as she started to move towards Markus.

Markus' eyes seemed to glow dangerously at that comment. "Get away from him."

She stopped. "Oh, so you *do* care about him? How... poetic." Lameika taunted some more. She grabbed out at Black's hair and pulled it back, exposing his throat. He was still choking and his breathing was labored but he was still holding on. The man *was* indeed as tough as the legends read. But his eyes were no longer cold and indifferent, but soft and moist as he seemed to be silently pleading with the boy to run- to flee for his very life. Even now, Lameika could tell that Black's heart had stopped beating.

"I'm warning you." Markus said his eyes glowing brighter. Was it just Lameika, or did it sound like some other voice was speaking the same words in unison?

"Oh, I see." Lameika said seeing the truth. "You've created a bond. Well, you're not the only one who has."

Lameika was so focused on Markus that she did not see Black place both hands against the wing, his thumb and index finger holding his own Crystal as he began to channel his life essence through the Crystal, making it stronger.

"You're right," he gasped as blood seeped from his lips. "He's not." And Lameika felt a spike of energy pulsate through the man as he released his own energy into her ankle which he grabbed.

Lameika felt her back arch back and her head shoot back, cracking her spine as she screamed towards the heavens above. The very cells in her body felt like every single one was on fire, and the muscles contracted violently enough for her body to jerk in great spasms. Through her eyes, she thought she saw tentacles of bone ripping through her chest, spraying blood everywhere while in reality it was her very own ribcage that had ripped from her chest.

The blade in her body shot out from her throat as she screamed, grinding against her teeth as it did so. She felt blood and tears drip from her eyes and nose as she felt invisible hands dragging her spirit out of her very body.

But she was not done, she would not succumb to Black's illusion, not yet!

She snarled past the blade in her mouth and twisting her neck like a serpent she lashed out at Black and swung downward with whatever strength she had left. But then, the boy suddenly cried out and held out his hand towards the witch. Some sort of force shot through his hand which knocked her head back, snapping the muscles in her neck.

"Gah!" she cried out as she suddenly dropped down to Black's level, the Hunter right beside her the entire time the illusion broke her very body.

Black then spun his leg around, kicking her feet out from under her; and in what felt like one swift movement he had gotten around her and removed his own cloak before strapping it around her neck with the magnetic clips. She screamed as she spun around towards him, casting another ice shard in her palm to try and run the man through. But the Hunter merely stepped back at a safe distance from her clawing hands, while at the same time releasing a strap which was connected to the clips that held the cloak around her neck.

The fabric then expanded as an electric current shot through the fibers and opened the cloak like a pair of wings. It was not the wind that caught them however, but the remaining turbine on the wing which had caught the corner of the expanding cloak in its rotors. Lameika managed to make a sound between a choked scream and a gasp as she felt herself pulled by the neck into the turbine. The last thing she saw was Black who stood watching as calm and unexpressive as ever, like Death himself.

You fool.

Markus

Markus shielded his eyes as the turbine that sucked the witch in exploded, causing a chain-reaction as the flames seeped through the windows of the Leviathan, detonating the cockpit and tearing the wing to shreds.

It all happened so fast; the witch began screaming, throwing her head back and staring out in front of her as if she was seeing something he wasn't. Then all at once, because of Black, she was sucked into the turbine and the explosion destroyed the entire wing beneath their feet.

Black was thrown off the wing by the force of the blast, and then Markus too was blown away as the wing of the great ship fell off completely, breaking up as it followed him down to the clouds below.

Markus felt the wind rush past him, turning his body around as he free-fell among the tumbling debris around him, the ones on fire bellowing tails of smoke as if they were falling stars. He tucked the blade-end of his staff into his belt and tried to flatten himself against the force of air beneath him. He had to spread his body, catch as much air as he could so he could slow down his fast decent.

When he finally managed to catch himself in the air, Markus began to frantically search for Black as the wind blew into his face. He continued to search among the falling debris and flames until he had found what he was looking for. He straightened his body out and tried to angle it so that he would fall towards the broken figure, passing numerous metal fragments in the meantime. Markus called out but the Hunter did not respond, and as he got closer, Markus saw that the man's eyes were shut, a look as serene as ever was on his face as always.

Markus reached for him and upon grabbing his shoulder, turned him so that he was facing the clouds below them. Markus hooked his arms beneath the Hunter's armpits, and pulled him in close and as they struck the sea of clouds. Markus then spread out his Eagle-Wings in order to gain more control of their fall.

Their decent decreased as they began to glide at a sharp angle towards the valley below. The danger of the debris was still very high as Markus felt the wings get struck by small bits of metal. He turned his head to see the bottom of the Leviathan appear from the clouds far behind them, like a dreaded dragon chasing down its prey. The wings were nearly burned completely off and the nose of the ship was smoking tremendously.

Returning his gaze to his front Markus ignored the falling ship as he attempted to turn and glide himself and Black down to the surface and away from the ship without having to carry his entire weight. The Wings were strong, but they were built for only one person, and if they took too much weight…

Markus didn't want to think about falling at the time being, so he had to use the updraft as much as he could as they continued to glide down to the ground below. However, as the two got lower and lower their decent only began to pick up in pace. Markus desperately began to flap the wings but the weight was too much. Some of the metallic feathers flew right off against the current of the air and before he knew it they met the ground in a tumbling crash.

Markus *bounced* across the ground, kicking up puffs of fresh snow as he eventually came to a stop. Markus knew by the sudden pain that shot up his forearm that it had been broken in the fall. Other than that, he had survived with minor scratches.

With some effort, he undid the now-smoldering pack, letting it fall off his shoulders as he ripped the neo-connector off the back of his head. He rolled over to his side so he could pick himself up. His legs were a little wobbly from the fall, and as a result when the Leviathan finally crashed a good few miles away, Markus fell on his bad arm from the tremor of the impact. He cried out in searing pain as he felt his very bones pierce muscle.

When he got back up onto his feet wincing, Markus began to survey the landscape. The cold and the pain hounded him without mercy, but he had to find Black. It was so dark that the only thing he could see was the burning ship miles away from him. It looked like a giant bonfire, the flames practically reaching for the heavens it seemed. Reaching for his blade, Markus seeped some energy from the Crystal, alleviating the pain and he began to scan the life essence around him.

Back again, I see…

Markus ignored the voice, focusing on the area around him. He saw the beasts beyond the valley on their hunting rounds now fleeing from the sudden crash. He saw bugs and snakes beneath the ground, and the flickering life auras of the men and women who fell from the sky above, their ships and choppers around them a burning inferno.

But about a good couple of meters from him, Markus saw the broken figure laying in a pile of snow, his leg broken and the life essence seeping from his bloodied chest. Markus half-ran half-limped over to Black and fell to his knees before the Hunter, who was alive but in terrible condition.

"You made it…" the man managed with a cough, his very essence flickering like a dying candle.

"You're gonna be fine." Markus said holding his shoulder. It was funny, he had never worried about Black like this before. The Hunter had always been so calm, so sure of himself, and he always managed to survive. Despite what he had done, there was no denying it anymore: Markus was indeed worried that the man was going to die.

He reached for his radio. "Don't move, I-"

Fast as a viper, Black's hand shot out and seized his wrist, stopping Markus in mid-sentence. "It's no use." he whispered despite the firm grip. "I'm done."

"No, you can't be," Markus said. "What about the war? Who's going to train me? What about the queen- you can't just die, Black! Damion!"

Black merely chuckled, as if amused. "You actually used my first name… Listen to me," he croaked. He held up his other fist, his sword still within it. "There is a grove in one of the western islands of Kaiken. Seek out Abram, my old teacher. Show him my sword, and he will train you. You are good with the staff, but you need to know the way of the sword. You must also, learn how to Dreamcast. Seek him out. You will know Abram when you see this."

From his other hand, Black revealed his own Crystal, pulsating dimly with maroon light. "Take them both."

Markus slowly reached out and grasped the Shock-Sword first, not pulling it away from Black who still held onto it until Markus finally pried it from his fingers. Markus felt that it was light despite its length. In fact, he was afraid it was going to shock him at first.

"And this," Black said again, placing his own Crystal in Markus' other hand, careful not to disturb the broken forearm. He closed the fingers around it, and Markus immediately felt the power within the new Crystal flowing through his veins.

So much pain, and sorrow, it made his own Crystal's influence seem childish almost.

"You *must* find the others," Black whispered. He then grabbed Markus by the shirt, and gently pulled him closer to his lips which were now dribbling more blood. Through his own power, Markus was able to see that the Hunter's heart had stopped. "Listen to me, Markus, you *must* find them all, and retrieve The Eldest. Use them, to destroy it. No one should carry such horrible power, especially with the Mad King among the evil spirits of old. Find them and destroy them all, so that no one, good or evil shall ever use The Dreaming again. Promise me, Markus."

Markus was trying so hard at this point not to cry. He couldn't cry, not now, not like this… It wasn't fair. "I can't." he said trying desperately to hold himself together. He felt tears threatening to break free of his eyelids, and eventually, they did without him being able to stop them. "I can't do this. I'm… I can't."

"You *can*, Markus. I believe in you."

"I'm too afraid. I…"

"Don't be afraid. Trust in yourself, trust in your friends. Promise me, Markus. Promise me that you will trust in yourself, and find the others. Destroy them all. You are our only hope."

Markus wanted to argue. He wanted to deny that he was the one who had to do it. Deny that he was The Keeper, and the one to stop The Eldest. He was too afraid, and after all that has happened tonight, he had absolutely no faith in himself.

But still, the words came out despite the conflict that grasped his heart. "I'll… try."

"Go to Abram," Black said as patiently as ever. "He knows where some are. And the other rulers of the kingdoms may have leads. Elizabetha will assist you there. Find the Baron's Crystal, find The Eldest, and then seek out Abram. From there, destroy all the others. Promise me Markus."

"Didn't you hear me? I'll…" Markus sighed, no longer having the strength to argue or fight it with Black any more. The man was just going to keep insisting until he agreed. "I'll do it." he finally gave in.

Black smiled as he relaxed and laid into the snow. "I'll give your regards to your father." and with that he closed his eyes.

"Black, wait!"

Slowly, Black opened his eyes into slits as he gave Markus his full attention.

Markus swallowed the lump in his throat, his tears now dripping down his chin and soaking into the bloodied snow. "You can't leave us. I'm so scared…"

With what little strength he had left, Damion then reached out and grabbed Markus' shoulder, pulling him towards him so that his lips were next to Markus' ear. When he had his saying it left Markus feeling just confused on top of feeling so hopeless.

Why is he telling me this? What…

Black then released him and laid back into the snow, and with his last dying breath, Black sighed. "Believe in yourself."

And he was gone. Just like that, the life essence within him went out like a candle extinguished in the dark, and the aura around him dimmed into the black.

Markus sat back on his legs feeling defeated. Black was gone. He always thought that he would rejoice when the Hunter wound up dead. But now that he laid here in the snow before him, the life seeping out of him in a river of crimson, Markus only felt horrible. It was disturbing and sad to think that he was actually caring for the man, despite how much things have changed in the last few days. Now Markus would be practicing on his own until…

The Kaiken Isles… Abram…

Markus heard garbled talk in Black's radio; breaking into his thoughts. What the words said or who they belonged to mattered little to him as he reached for the dead Hunter's belt and removed the radio.

He clicked on the speaker, silencing all sound as he spoke into it. "This is Markus," he said sullenly. At this point, his very tears had frozen upon his cheeks.

The radio suddenly blared, "Markus! This is Elizabetha. What happened? Where are you? We saw the blimp go off and the Leviathan fell out of the sky! Are you alright?"

"A little hurt," Markus spoke again. "But I'm fine."

"Good, the Ninevite army has been defeated and many of them are retreating. A few choppers are coming in near the crash site. They'll pick you up around there."

"Fine."

The queen could obviously tell something was wrong because she then asked, "Where's Black?"

Markus looked over at the broken figure whose blood turned the snow red. He then sighed before answering in a brooding voice.

"He's gone. He's dead."

When the chopper finally came and picked them both up, Black was wrapped and strapped into one of the garners across from where Markus sat. The whole ride back to the island Markus studied the figure wrapped in the sheets of white cloth now stained in some spots with blood. The cloth had been wrapped so tight that he could see the outline of Black's angled cheeks and nose over a pair of thin lips that would never draw breath again.

It made thinking of everything that had happened both in the past and present all the more depressing as Markus rode in silence not willing to talk to anyone.

Black had saved him and Ashlyn, he worked with Markus' very father, and had just given him one of the very things he needed to help in this war. Markus looked down at the blood-red Crystal he now held in his hand, twirling it in his fingers as he studied the exquisite gem full of mystery, and darkness.

The energy this thing possesses… Markus thought as he looked at it. It was like his father's own Crystal, but the energy emitting from it was not noble in the slightest. They were all painful. Fear, rage, anger, worse than his own and with no sense of righteousness.

This was an evil artifact, and even holding it made him very much afraid. Hatred, pain, fear, was this all that Black felt all his life? Markus turned his attention back to the dead Hunter.

Am I really going to continue with this?
What am I going to do?

~ The Prophecy ~

Ashlyn

Ashlyn waited outside on the steps leading to the castle with Esmerelda and Queen Elizabetha as the rescue choppers who had gone out to collect the wounded from the valley began trickling in. She scanned the skies, searching for the one that held Markus and the Hunter Black.

Everywhere around them, small fires were being put out by the Angelic Legion and the city residents; everyone working together to put their home back together after the barrage of fire and steel. A few Hellhounds and choppers had crashed into the walls and some men were using large equipment such as small Behemoth-like mechs to remove the wreckage; sending them over the wall and watching them fall to the world far below. At this point in time it was now nearing morning and the sun was just starting to peek over the mountains beyond the Northern Wastelands and further.

The men and women who had been injured were taken into the castle to receive treatment from Slagar and the other sorcerers; some with their children close by to see them through the treatments. Vic was there as well, with his box of tools to help those who had lost a limb or two. Too many people were hurt in the battle, and too many had died. The deceased were taken away in carts to who-knows-where. Ashlyn didn't bother asking the queen. She didn't want to think of the worst, not now.

Besides, Elizabetha appeared to be greatly concerned enough as it was, same as her daughter who sat with Ashlyn on the steps while hugging her knees in anxious waiting. Q-Pid laid beside her, twitching every once in awhile as she tried to speak.

Ashlyn scanned the fast-departing night sky in search for the specific chopper that had gone to retrieve her friend and the Hunter. Sometimes she would turn fast at the sound of chopper blades only to be disappointed that it was only a fighter's chopper or even a Dragonfly. She was glad they had made it safe and sound and all, but she was so worried about Markus, and when she heard about Black...

She just couldn't believe it.

She looked to her left where Esmerelda now stood, looking just as worried as she was. She was thinking the same thing most likely. When she had heard that Black was killed, she cried. She didn't flat-out sob, but only shed a few tears that had manage to slip. She was trying to be strong for her friend and for her mother. Two weights, that had to be difficult to bear. Ashlyn could never have been more grateful and more honored to have a friend such as her.

She then heard the sound of distant chopper blades and turning to look she was overjoyed to see that it was the rescue chopper she was waiting for. The three of them shielded their faces from the rush of air as the chopper landed in the street in front of them. The guards remained idle as they awaited new- if any -orders.

Soon some men climbed out of the cockpit of the craft and walked around to the sides where they disappeared, only to reappear again with a stretcher-

With a pile of cloth in the shape of a human lying across it.

It was the bloodstain that gave it away that it was Black wrapped in the cloth. Queen Elizabetha gasped as if she had just been punched and she ran over to them, ignoring the guard's words of distress. She rushed past another figure who hopped off the aircraft, and Ashlyn was overjoyed to see that it was Markus. He walked away from the chopper as Elizabetha and a few guards walked Black to the castle to where the hurt and dying were being taken.

Ashlyn rushed over to Markus and tackled him in a hug, catching him off guard by the sound of the air rushing from his lungs. She hugged him tight with her head against his chest. She could hear his heartbeat as she squeezed all the tighter. It was beating slowly, and heavily. She never realized how much relief it would bring her to hear such a beautiful sound. 'Joy' was an insult to what she felt at that moment.

"You're okay..." she said with a shudder. "Thank God, you're alive."

"Crushing me..." he gasped. "My arm... My arm!..."

She quickly released him, letting him suck some air back into his crushed lungs. "Sorry." she said. She looked down at Markus' arm which he hugged to his side. She felt bad for hurting him, but she was just so happy to see that he was still here, with a beating heart.

Esmerelda appeared beside her, a look of relief also on her face as she nodded at Mark. "You made it," she said with an obvious tone.

"Barely," Markus groaned. He held his injured arm in his good hand as he looked down at his feet, a frown settling on his face.

"We heard." Ashlyn told him. "The Leviathan, everything. But is the Baron...?"

Markus shook his head. "Dead, I think. I didn't see him come out." he said this in a low monotone.

"Well..." Ashlyn had nothing to say. What *could* she say?

"Black died a hero." Esmerelda stepped in when she saw that they were getting nowhere. "He... he fought hard, for all of us."

"Right." Markus nodded. "The witch got him, but... she's dead too."

Good riddance. Ashlyn thought. "What happened to your arm?" she then asked reaching out and then pulling back before she touched it.

"Broke it when Black and I crashed. I'll be fine." Markus looked at Esmerelda who was cradling Q-Pid, and asked to take a closer look. "What happened to you?"

Q-Pid buzzed, "Bad... woman..."

Bad woman, indeed. "The witch did this." Ashlyn said.

"Oh man..." Markus groaned looking at Esmerelda. "It's okay, I can fix her."

"You sure?" Esmerelda asked.

"When I get a chance. I promise."

Esmerelda appeared to relax just a little. "Just make sure you take care of yourself first."

"Right."

"Well, now what?" the princess asked as she looked past Markus to the entrance where her mother disappeared. "We won the battle, but we lost a lot of good people. Even... Damion. What are we going to do now?"

"Your mom will let us know soon, I guess." Markus shrugged. He then looked at both the princess and Ashlyn with a serious expression. "I gotta tell you guys something soon. After everything's said and done."

The two got the message and nodded in understanding. "Okay." Ashlyn said.

"Okay," Mark groaned as he tried to move his bad arm. "I better get this wrapped up."

"We'll go with you." Esmerelda said leading the way.

"Yeah, we're here for you." Ashlyn said walking beside her friend.

"Thank you." Markus said morosely. Ashlyn could tell he was troubled by Black's death, but something told her that something else was on her friend's mind. And beneath her heart, she felt that she was very afraid for her friend.

What had happened out there? What is he dwelling about now?

What was going to happen now?

Esmerelda

After watching Markus get his arm wrapped in a cast and into a sling, Esmerelda and Ashlyn led him up towards the main balcony, where the queen was going to deliver her speech.

Watching Markus get treated was painful enough, through his wincing as Slagar set the bone and wrapped his arm, Esmerelda could feel his pain. It was amazing her friend didn't scream considering how rough Slagar was. The sorcerer didn't even give him any pain medication or a potion to alleviate his suffering. What pained Esmerelda more, despite it being a silly thing she realized, was how Ashlyn was around him.

The way she looked down upon Markus and held his hand while he was being treated, the pain and sadness on the brim of her eyelids and the way she held her breath with each wince escaping her friend. Esmerelda could understand Ashlyn's concern, but it still bothered her to be so close to The Keeper.

Was this jealousy?

No, that was silly. Esmerelda thought she was being ridiculous at even assuming such a thing. Did she seriously *like* Markus?

He was cute and brave, yes, but she barely knew him other than from the so-called prophecy her mother and the Elders spoke of. Could she really feel a sense of jealousy towards Ashlyn, the closest if not first real friend she's ever had? Besides… it was stupid, and childish to feel such things after everything Levitika had just gone through, and Esmerelda felt ashamed at herself for even thinking such things.

Also, there were her *relations* to him as well. The news both Markus *and* she got about the man who raised Markus. If Johnathon was her mother's half-brother, that made her and Markus half-cousins. And so such feelings were not only inappropriate at this point in time, they were inappropriate in general. Still, she couldn't help but think…

There was no time to ponder these thoughts however, as they entered the courtroom, where the Elders stood in huddled groups whispering amongst themselves. Esmerelda saw that Markus did not fail to notice the way the men and women changed their pitch as they saw him. Was it fascination, or fear that they saw through him? Either way, none of them seemed eager to speak with the hero, least of all his company.

They soon stepped outside the doors to the balcony where Elizabetha stood near the marble parapet, the entire city- or whoever was left standing below in the streets cheering her name. The queen turned as if she had heard them coming and smiled at them, beckoning them over to the balcony. As soon as the three were in view of the city they began to cheer once again.

"Markus!"

"Markus!"

"Markus!"

Markus waved solemnly at the crowd, as if he was not sure if he should say anything or not. In fact, he actually took a step back to try and hide behind Esmerelda and Ashoyn. It was kind of cute, actually.

Luckily for him the queen held up her hands, silencing the crowd before she spoke.

"My friends," she said in a loud voice that echoed against the castle to the crowds below. "My greatest thanks to all who did their part during this horrendous attack against our great city. The enemy is either dead, captured, or fleeing, For through our magnificent Angels, the brave citizens of this city, and young Markus here, Keeper of the Seven, we have won this battle!"

This was met with more cheering that thundered across the city, but Elizabetha was not done yet. "We have lost many brave men, women and droids tonight. Today, shall be known as The Day of Mourning. My men will be scouring the surface below, and will take up any of our deceased to their families where they shall burn them in their ceremonial cremators."

Esmerelda knew her mother was talking mostly to herself at that last sentence.

"We are blessed my friends, for we are still standing, the hope of Levitika is still strong, and we shall rise victoriously as we take back The Northern Wastelands once and for all!"

The crowds thundered with cheering and whistling at that remark, and with that, Elizabetha turned around and began to walk inside, beckoning the three children to follow. And as she followed her mother into the castle, Esmerelda had never felt more proud of her mom despite the pain and grief she was feeling at this moment.

Why... out of all the feelings I should feel, why do I feel this way?...

Markus

Markus followed along with Ashlyn and Esmerelda close behind Elizabetha as they entered the Throne Room, where all the Elders and scientists were waiting patiently for their ruler.

The queen however paid them no heed as she crossed the room to a table, where a glass coffin similar to what Ruth was put in laid across, and inside was the Hunter Black. His armor had been cleaned as well as his face, and his hair had been combed and tied into a ponytail, giving him a fresher look. He too appeared to be just asleep, but everyone here was not fooled by the magicians' art of making the dead seem as such. Black was gone, and as Elizabetha placed a small hand over the glass as if trying to reach him, the whole room went silent in respects to the queen who was saying her final farewell.

Markus swallowed and bowed his head, the girls following his example. For what felt like forever no one moved or dared to speak as the queen muttered silent prayers of safe travels to Black as small crystal tears dropped from her sullen eyes.

Eventually she raised her head and blew a puff of air between her lips. She turned her head so she faced everyone in the room, eyeing them all before she spoke. "He wanted to be cremated when he died." she said, which caught everyone including Markus off guard.

Out of everything she could say… why did she say that in particular?

"I shall do it myself." Elizabetha continued. "You may all go mourn the losses of your loved ones for now. We will speak tomorrow."

"My lady," Slagar said stepping forward, his fingers intertwining as he played with them. He appeared nervous. "We are all, very sorry for your loss. But we should discuss-"

"Tomorrow." the queen sternly said turning her back on the man. "Please."

"As you wish." Slagar bowed stiffly and clearly unpleased. "Come." he told everyone. Everyone then started to go but Elizabetha then called Markus' name.

"You, stay." she said.

He looked at Esmerelda helplessly, who just shrugged seeming nervous as well. Markus then turned and walked back to the queen, stopping about six feet from her, not saying anything as the doors to the main hall slammed shut behind him, leaving him alone with her and Black.

For a long time, she didn't say anything and Markus began to feel skittish. Was he supposed to say something? Wait? He debated for another minute and when she still didn't say anything he spoke.

"I'm sorry."

Elizabetha shook her head, not turning to him just yet. "Don't be. I just…" She stopped herself and stood upright, taking a deep breath before turning to him. "Never mind. How is your arm?"

"Fine." Markus said shifting his arm slightly. It still hurt terribly.

"Slagar did a good job I see, as usual."

"I guess." He still remembered how rough the wizard was setting the bone.

"So, you now carry Black's sword, yes? I assume he has given you his Crystal as well?"

Markus nodded, looking down at the sword that hung at his belt. The tip of the scabbard nearly touched the marbled floor it was so big. "Yes ma'am."

"Good. And after we find The Baron's Crystal, you shall have three." The queen looked away in thought. "We will continue as planned. Nineveh is less defended now, so taking it will be easy. It will be useful as our base of operations. Now if only we can find The Eldest among the wreckage…" She looked back to Markus. "I'm sorry, I am trying to keep my mind busy."

Markus could understand that all too well.

"So. Have you decided to stay with us?"

Markus nodded, slowly. "After all that has happened, I can't just turn my back here. I want to protect this place, and do my part to achieve piece in the country. Besides… Black asked me to."

Elizabetha smiled softly. "I see. I am glad to hear that."

Markus swallowed the lump in his throat before saying, "After Nineveh though, I have somewhere to go."

The queen gave Markus a peculiar look. "Oh?"

He nodded. "Black told me of a grove near the Kaiken Isles. Apparently, his old teacher lives there."

"Abram… I remember him. My father had sent both Black and your father to see him, to teach them how to manipulate The Dreaming. So, you will go there to continue your own training?"

"You read my mind, your majesty."

She offered a small smile. "You don't need to keep up the good manners when we are alone, you know."

"It's always good to have manners." Markus said. "But seriously, after we free Nineveh, I have to go to the islands."

"Have to, or want to?"

Markus shrugged. "It doesn't really matter. I *want* answers, but I also have to go, if I really am The Keeper. Black said I would have to, if I were to become stronger in terms of magic."

"Well, I don't see any reason to stop you." Elizabetha shrugged. "We will be safe in Nineveh, and the residents would be sure to help us when the yoke of their newest tyrant is removed."

"No kidding." Markus said thinking of how great it would be to see everyone at the Badrat. To see Aventis' face when he finds out Ovid was dead, the whole city would fight back against the loyalists of Baron Ovid. "Sounds like a plan."

"Good." The queen looked back at Black, her smile completely vanished now.

Markus shuffled his feet, thinking carefully before asking. "I *do* need to know something though."

Elizabetha looked at him questionably.

"The prophecy." he explained. "I need to actually hear it. Black, mentioned a little of it while we were sparring… but I never actually got to actually *hear* it. If I'm going to keep on going with this, I need to trust you. I need to know about the prophecy. I *need* to know, your majesty."

"You think I made it up?" she asked.

"To be honest? Yes. I think you all made it up; you've given me no explanation of it. And besides… I've never believed in fate. Not like that."

Elizabetha smiled as if what he said was exactly as she had expected. "We haven't told you, because the less people to know about it the better." the queen said simply. "We had to know for sure if you were ready. If you heard it all too quickly, you would not be able to understand. And besides, if the trusted words got into the wrong ears, it would be disastrous, not just for us, but all of Levitika."

"Guess trust is a major issue here." Markus noted. "But I'm already neck-deep in this. I want to know, before I go any deeper into the wake."

"Indeed." Elizabetha nodded. "Keep that careful mindset. The Elders are power-hungry and malicious. They are not to be completely trusted, not even some of the citizens here who only seek great fortune from such knowledge." She paused and then spoke. "If I tell you, you cannot utter a *word* to anyone. For the sake of your own safety, as well as those who keep this rebellion going in balance, you have to keep it to yourself."

"You know I cannot completely agree to that, right?" Markus asked.

"I expected much." she sighed. "You have Ashlyn and my daughter after all. Very well. But first, let me explain."

Markus remained silent, listening to Elizabetha who began to weave a story for him.

"After a terrible battle within the borders of Xerxes, another Crystal was found in the possession of the Great Owl. Using it, she took the entire kingdom away from the world and with it the survivors and to the mountains where they were able to hide this floating island for many years. Because of this terrible power the Great Owl found possible with The Dreaming, she knew that it was better to hide and live to fight another day. It was then she told my grandfather of Levitika's fate, including the prophecy concerning the fate of the entire Region. She spoke it, and then wrote it down so my grandfather could keep the hopes of the survivors alive, as well as the hope of the rest of his descendants."

Elizabetha paused for a moment before slowly continuing, "She said that the… the son of his only considered grandson would be the final piece to freeing the Northern Wastelands and bring peace to the country. For many years, the prophecy has been spoken and heard by few, in hopes that sooner or later it would come to be as true. It read as such:

> *"Angels of Eden will fall,*
> *From the depths, nightmares will crawl,*
> *Nightmares from the past meet new,*
> *The Eldest's strength, and fear grew.*
> *Gateways must be shut, destroyed,*
> *Both by Dreaming, war, and droid.*
> *The Seven that closed the gate,*
> *Can no longer stay in wait.*
> *The one who can speak to all,*
> *Can prevent the world's great fall.*
> *Whether locked up, or set free,*
> *The Eldest rules all we see.*
> *Through fear, despair, and hate,*
> *He shall bring all from his wait.*
> *But before The Night shall fall,*
> *The Keeper, shall free them all.*
> *And to the end of this tale,*
> *Whether trapped or free, He shall fail."*

Markus took in what he had just heard, repeating every single line carefully as he played the words over and over in his head. Elizabetha stood patiently as he looked down in thought.

There were a lot of twists in the quagmire of words. What did all of it mean? It was all jumbled it seemed, a mix of present and future; and all Markus was able to get out of the end was that the one who is supposed to save the Region will either bring upon the destruction of the land or peace. Basically, saying that if he indeed was the one, there was still a chance that he would fail.

In the end, 'trapped or free, he shall fail'... Not very encouraging. Markus could understand why no one told him at first, second and foremost that if someone else got that information they would stop at nothing to witness his demise or even hunt for the Crystals themselves. Or, worst-case scenario, it makes the people of Levitika fear the future rather than striving for it with a desire to fight and make a new path for themselves. It was obvious enough for whoever stumbled upon them that they held great power and importance, but to find out what their sole purpose was, if fallen into the wrong hands, who knows what could happen?

"Guess I need to sink that in." Markus finally said after mulling it over a few more minutes. "Thank you, your majesty. I'll do my very best, and keep looking to the future."

"Very good." Elizabetha said. "And please, when you are alone you can talk to me normally. I like to think of you as a friend, Markus. Black held you under high standards, and I've always trusted his judgement."

"No kidding." Markus said finding it somewhat hard to believe but did not dare to say it. That was the last thing she needed to hear. "I'm sorry, again."

The queen nodded in appreciation. "All we can do now is make sure he did not die in vain. But I'm sure I don't need to tell you that."

Markus shook his head. "Like I said, I'll do my best. That much I can promise."

"We'll find the Baron's Crystal and The Eldest, and then after Nineveh we shall send you to the grove."

Markus nodded with a smile. There was still so much to do, especially considering all that has happened recently and what would be expected in the future. At least he would be heading for Nineveh, and through this entire journey, they would be able to free his home. He never liked Nineveh, but it was still his home as much as everyone still there. If there was a future in the world today, it would be through Levitika and their ways. And Markus was determined to find that in the purpose he was called to have.

He then remembered something important, and looked to Elizabetha once again. "If it's all well with you... Elizabetha, I do have *one* request- regarding my sister's burial, if the offer is still available."

The queen nodded. "Of course. We would not be able to stop the island but we would send you in a Firefly or chopper. What is it that you want, Markus? Just ask, and it is yours."

And so, he told her.

~ From Another World ~

Ashlyn

It was now mid-afternoon and Ashlyn was pacing her room while Esmerelda sat on the bed, worrying with Q-Pid in her hands.

Markus had been with Queen Elizabetha for a long time, and Ashlyn was beginning to worry greatly. Though she was exhausted, she felt that if she didn't stop moving she would just go crazy. She wasn't about to rest until she was sure Markus was okay- both physically and mentally.

What is going on out there? Is he okay? What is going through his mind? And what is going to happen next? All these questions invaded her brain as she continued to pace impatiently; the waiting alone was the absolute worst part. Though Esmerelda had urged her to sit down or even lie down, Ashlyn wouldn't stop. Regardless of how tired she was, she would not rest until she was sure Markus was okay.

Luckily, she did not need to wait too long, for the bedroom door opened to reveal a worn-out shell that represented her friend. Ashlyn grinned and went over to hug Markus but soon stopped herself as she remembered his arm.

"Is everything okay?" she asked.

"Not entirely." he said coming inside. "But it will be soon, I hope."

Esmerelda appeared beside her, she studied Markus before talking. "What did my mother want?"

"Plans for the invasion of Nineveh, and asking if I will now carry Damion's sword."

Damion… not Black. "Will you?" Ashlyn asked.

"What choice do I have? After all, I'm going to need it, if I want to be the man of the prophecy."

"You will do it then?" Esmerelda asked almost hopefully.

"Yes. But… Let me tell you…"

For nearly an hour they all sat on Ashlyn's bed while Markus told them about his conversation with the queen. Ashlyn watched with intense interest and her ears listened to every word escaping her friend's lips. By the looks of Esmerelda, she was just as interested and scared as she was.

Hearing the prophecy for the first time sent chills down Ashlyn's spine. She wondered what it meant, and understood Markus' confusion. It was all just vague; a quagmire of the present and future collided with trials and warnings. How was Mark supposed to evaluate the riddle?

It was when Markus mentioned about The Kaiken Isles and Black's old teacher when Ashlyn's eyes grew wide. Thankfully before she could say anything, Esmerelda beat her to it.

"You're kidding, right?" she demanded. "The Kaiken Isles are full of monsters and the Pirate Lord Ronin- he's a dangerous man and controls most of the islands; I can't believe my mother is allowing you to go after we take Nineveh!"

"What choice do I have?" Mark retorted. "Damion's gone, and the only one who might have a chance to teach me what I need to know to go against the force we face now might be this teacher, this Abram guy. Besides, I want answers."

Esmerelda shook her head. "I've never heard of him, so how can you know for sure he would help, or is even still alive?"

"Your mother trusted Damion. So apparently that is good enough for her. That, and he taught me as much as I know now, so why not try? What do we have to lose?"

"*You.*" Esmerelda said coolly which made Ashlyn's own heart stop.

"See, that's what we thought when we left Nineveh." she said speaking up. "We all thought we would either be captured or killed trying to find this city and you guys. We went through a lot to find you, and now we are here. So there is always hope, right?" This went against everything that Ashlyn felt, but she knew by the look on Markus' face that there was no way Esmerelda could change his mind. As long as he was safe, that was all that mattered. Ashlyn understood that, but in the world they lived in, you couldn't live in safety forever.

The room fell into an uncomfortable silence. No one daring to speak, as if afraid of what to say after what Ashlyn had just said. At some point with some effort, Markus spoke up.

"That's right." He licked his lips looking at Esmerelda with a more determined look. "She's right. There is always a chance, even if it is small."

Esmerelda looked down at her pale feet, grumbling distastefully. "I suppose you are right." she looked back up. "Do you really want to go?"

"Not at all. But I want answers, and I want to do my part."

"You are not going alone, are you?"

"No, your mother said she would send men with me before I left."

"Then I'm coming with you." Ashlyn declared. Esmerelda gaped at her but Markus shook his head.

"No." he said in a firm but not cruel way. "You might be needed here, and I don't want you to get hurt."

"I don't care," Ashlyn said standing her ground. "You're my friend- the only family I have left. I don't want to leave you behind."

"Besides," Esmerelda pitched in. "Who better to trust than Ashlyn?"

Ashlyn gave a nod of appreciation but Markus was still firm. "It's not a matter of trust." he said. "Like you said; it is dangerous, maybe even a fool's errand."

"I don't care about that now," Ashlyn retorted. "Friends stick together 'til the end."

Markus nodded finally but she could still tell he was not convinced in the slightest. "We got time, we will discuss it later." he said. "We got other things to worry about." He looked at them both in the eye before continuing. "This prophecy, this war… It's all a part of something bigger."

"Bigger?" Esmerelda asked.

Markus nodded. "While I was up there, I felt *them*."

"Them?" Ashlyn asked.

"The spirits, heroes and villains. While I was releasing my power, I was almost possessed by those things… and for a while, I understood. They are all a part of realm not of this world. And their energy is passed through the Crystal, and through those who can control them, and vice versa. That is why I am able to make myself stronger and… and use magic. It is all from somewhere else."

"But where?" Ashlyn asked.

Markus was silent for a minute as if he was in thought. And then, "I don't want to know. But I have a bad feeling that if the prophecy is word for word, and if this war is exactly how it is playing out to be, then I might find out soon."

"What do you mean?"

"When I was up there, during the fight... I thought I heard someone speaking to me. Like in the Dark Forest."

"What are you talking about?"

"I-" Before he could say anything however, a guard had busted through the door, interrupting all conversation and scaring all three of them to death with how sudden it was.

"The queen wants to see all of you, immediately." he said through his helmet.

Markus groaned, and Ashlyn could not blame them. It had not even been an hour yet and Elizabetha wanted him again?

"What is this about, Matthew?" Esmerelda asked. "The Keeper is very tired."

"It's about the witch and the attacking ship, your highness." the guard explained. "No Crystal was found among the wreckage, so we believe it might still be in Nineveh."

"Is that all?" Markus asked.

"No. The witch's body? The Eldest was not found anywhere near her, and her brother is nowhere to be found."

To this the three children's eyes went wide with dread. "Oh no..." Markus spoke their thoughts.

Markus

Markus and the girls took off down the hall leaving Matthew behind in the dark.

He was huffing due to his lack of energy but still Markus urged his legs to push on. He had to hurry. He had to hear this for himself. If the Eldest was indeed gone, then what was going to happen? He didn't need to look behind him to see that the girls were just as worried as he was. Maybe not as much but still worried nonetheless.

They didn't quite understand what Markus knew. There was no doubt in his mind: These Crystals, were alive; and if that's the case, then they're the key to life and death itself. But right now, the most dangerous of them all was missing. It needed to be found as soon as possible, somehow.

As the three busted through the main doors to the throne room, the queen and Slagar both jumped at the sound of the doors slamming against the walls.

"Is it true?" Markus asked straight to the point as he slowed his pace to a brisk march towards them, the girls following close behind. He felt so light-headed for running so hard he nearly fell over and was forced to grab ahold of one of the chairs at the tables still set to keep his balance. He needed to stay focused. "Is the Eldest gone?"

Elizabetha nodded hesitantly. Seeing that she obviously did not know what to say, Slagar stepped forward.

"Our Angels found nothing among the wreckage of the ship." he explained. "We had found the corpse of the witch that rode our dear statue… or what was left of either. We could not find anything; not her Crystal that your friend Ashlyn described, nor the Eldest. Not only that, but we also could not find the brother's body anywhere, and the freshly fallen snow from this morning had covered any tracks. We believe he is still alive, and may have the Crystals with him."

"No, no…" Markus said shocked at the shortage of breath he had as he spoke. "We have to find them, and destroy them."

"What!?" Slagar demanded in a sudden snarl, all respect and care completely forgotten. "What do you mean *destroy* them? Find them, yes, but destroy!?"

Markus' mind went back to the crash site, while Black was slowly dying on his finally breaths of air. He grabbed Markus and pulled him towards him and whispered in Markus' ear with his last dying words.

"Keep those two crystals only, destroy the rest, and leave no trace. The Eldest must not be revived, and The Elders must not get their hands on them. Destroy them all, break every portal to The Dreaming, and then destroy the Eldest. You must not let such power fall into anyone's hands. Use your power to destroy them all, that is your purpose. A mission, I give to you. One Hunter, to another."

"Slagar," the queen spoke up, breaking into Markus' thoughts. "I think I know why."

Slagar turned to Elizabetha, his expression still hostile as he waited patiently.

"Damion said something about the Crystals being needed for the Eldest, and in the case that the Eldest disappears, destroy the Crystals." She said this with a somber tone, carefully as she recollected whatever conversation this had been.

"That is *preposterous*!" Slagar argued. "Such power should be handled by the most respected carriers here in Levitika! We could win this war sooner and save more lives. We could heal more of the wounded faster and increase weapon and soldier production tenfold! Besides... we can't break them. We couldn't even scratch The Eldest for the love of all things still holy!"

"Markus," the queen said to him ignoring the rants of her magician. "Why did Damion tell *you* to destroy the Crystals?"

Markus gulped as he spoke. "He just said; 'don't let the Eldest use them, and destroy them'. He did not explain." He did not dare speak of the Elders, should Slagar react as expected to it. He promised himself that he would tell Elizabetha later.

"All the good reason to *not* listen!" Slagar spat. He turned on Elizabetha furiously. "My Queen, think for a moment if you please; the Crystals are evil creations I agree. However, they are useful tools in destroying our enemies. In our possession, and under the control of yet another carrier, what danger do we truly face? The Crystals are dangerous but *necessary* to free this Region and stop The Dark Queen and her armies!"

"That's enough, Slagar." the queen said firmly. "We will discuss this no further. I am tired, and so is Markus. Damion believed that if the Eldest was taken from our possession then we must destroy the Crystals. Whatever reason that may be, we cannot allow our enemies to use them however they wish. If Damion told me long ago and Markus the exact same thing, it cannot be a coincidence."

"I thought the plan was to collect them all?" Slagar demanded now seeming to change tactics. "Is that not what the prophecy says?"

"Well, rules are made to be changed." Elizabetha said standing her ground. "For our own safety, we must do what Damion believed was best. I trust him."

"More than your own servant?" Slagar demanded.

"Markus, what else did he tell you?" she asked him once again ignoring Slagar which made the wizard seethe even more so.

Markus gulped again. "To keep mine until all of them are gone." He didn't understand why he felt the need to hide some of the things Black had told him from her, but for some reason Markus felt as if Black was telling him not to utter a single word- especially in front of the infuriated magician before him.

"What gives *you* the right?" Slagar asked in a low and dangerous tone. For a second there, Markus thought he saw a flash of light flashed through the magician's eyes and for that moment, Markus nearly opened his mouth to tell him.

"Get away from him!" Ashlyn snapped stepping in and shoving the magician away. Immediately whatever spell was cast upon Markus was broken, and he stared at Ashlyn who was just about to get slapped by Slagar for her intrusion.

"Slagar, stop it!" Suddenly the light died in the magician's eyes as Elizabetha stepped in. "Don't you dare." Elizabetha said pointing a finger at the wizard. "You are out of line. Back away, now."

Slagar was about to say something, but the threat of the queen's words were much too heavy, and he withdrew with a hateful glare at Ashlyn who also retreated to her friends' sides.

Markus glowered at the magician. "You were trying to *hypnotize* me?" he demanded.

Salgar turned form Ashlyn to Markus. "Listen here you little sh-"

"No more, Slagar." the queen demanded. "You have said enough, now this discussion is *over*."

Slagar hissed in anger but soon calmed down- almost too soon. "You are right. I still say we should use the Crystals to crush our enemies first. You all understand that I only hope for the best for our kingdom."

No one said anything to the magician, who either didn't care or thought it didn't matter if anything was said at all.

"What do you think, Markus?" Elizabetha asked.

"I don't know…" Markus said feeling light-headed again. The further he got dragged into this, the more he realized that he was the one being asked a lot more than ever before. *They trust me so much…* "I'm sorry your majesty, but it is so hard to think. What happened out there took a lot out of me. I can barely keep standing."

He thought he sounded so pitiful and weak when the words came out of his mouth but they were true. Markus was so tired and drained, what had happened up there in the battle, was just too much he thought.

"Maybe someone stronger should carry that burden then?" Slagar said teasingly.

"Let us not worry about this for now then." Elizabetha said dismissing the conversation. "After what has happened, I do not blame you, Markus."

"Neither do I." Slagar said obviously still grumpy. "You are definitely… 'fatigued'."

"The battle is won," the queen said quickly. "Let us just enjoy the moment of your success. Rest, do what you need, train yourself a little but at a time, but make sure that you are healed."

"Magic is like running a marathon." Slagar said. "Run too much and you grow too tired to move. And you definitely need a day of rest."

"Thank you, *sir*." Markus said distastefully. The man had scratched him the wrong way, and what he had just tried to pull – both to him *and* Ashlyn, only made Markus distrust the man more. "But that still does not help us find The Eldest."

"Our men are scanning the landscape as we speak." Elizabetha said. "If it is still out there, we'll find it. Somehow."

Slagar said, "Yes, if the witch's brother is out there, we'll find him and recover The Eldest." Until then, worrying about it won't help us find it. You need to regain your strength."

Those words weren't comforting in the slightest coming from the wizard. "But what if-"

"You are going to have to trust us, Markus." Slagar insisted. "You cannot do everything on your own. I don't like you or where this is going, but I will say that it wasn't your fault we lost The Eldest, and we *will* find it. And if not… well, there is always Black's plan, yes?"

Markus gave him a dirty look, hoping the old man got the message that he was not satisfied. Slagar was acting all too friendly now.

"You did well, Keeper." Elizabetha said smiling. "Levitika is forever in your debt."

"Thank you." he said meaning each word.

"No," Esmerelda said speaking up again. "Thank *you*."

"Yeah," Ashlyn said smiling. "You're a hero."

Markus blushed a little, but thankfully he did not need to say anything, for Slagar was listening to his radio. He thanked whoever was on the other side and then turned to Markus. "Our pilot says we are nearing the Dark Forest, says the whole area is burned to the ground."

"That would be for Markus." Elizabetha said softly, almost sadly. She then asked him, "Are you ready?"

Markus' expression turned somber once again. "Yes, ma'am. And thank you again."

"For what?" Ashlyn and Slagar said in unison, Esmerelda stayed silent as she watched her friend.

It hurt to say, but his friends had to know. After all, Markus wanted them all excluding the magician to join him. He needed his friends, now more than ever. "One more funeral."

About an hour later, the three friends stood before the forest which was now a smoldering scar among the snowy landscape. Fresh snow was falling upon the burnt trees that seemed to reach out to the sky like crooked hands of the damned.

It was funny, only a few days ago, Ruth, Ashlyn, and Markus were running through this very forest, racing away from Slitzar and fighting an Arachnard among other terrifying creatures. What had happened to them all? Did they make it out in time, or did they burn with the rest of their home? Markus guessed it didn't matter now, but the thought still stuck with him.

All you can do is hope, not worry. As he looked down at the freshly dug grave where his sister now lay, her demeanor silent and peaceful beneath her glass coffin, Markus felt truly idle looking at both beauty in death and repulsiveness in life. He felt neither alive nor dead as he looked down upon dear Ruth, who appeared to still be asleep. He wondered what she would think of this place now? Seeing the forest burned to the ground. But this is what she wanted, before she died...

I want to go back to the forest... she had said as she died in his arms. *I want... to see the trees again...*

"You are back." he said to her knowing that she could not hear him, at least from where she was now. "You are back, but the forest is gone..." His voice cracked at the word 'gone', as if even himself didn't want to believe it.

Markus felt Ashlyn and Esmerelda press up against his sides, as if seeking protection from the cold winds now blowing in from the north, both of them looking down into the grave muttering silent prayers. The queen stood beside them, her eyes closed as she prayed for Ruth a second time. Markus was truly grateful for them all to be here; and as the guards who took them down in one of the choppers began to dump the dirt back into the hole, he held back his tears. He had done all the mourning he could, and now he had to be strong as he said his final goodbye to Ruth.

He watched in silence as her face was soon completely obscured by the mountains of dirt, and the grave was filled, leaving a scar in the ground once covered with grass among the snow. Elizabetha walked over to Markus, and placed a hand upon his shoulder. He looked up to her to see her give a small smile before she walked away, back towards the chopper and leaving him alone with Ashlyn and her daughter.

After some time, Markus had scooped up some scorched branches and using one of Esmerelda's hairbands, he tied two branches together to make a makeshift cross before planting it at the head of the grave.

Goodbye... he prayed again for the thousandth time.

You will see her again. a voice suddenly replied.

He looked to both Ashlyn and Esmerelda but both of them seemed still focused on the grave. They had not heard a thing. So, either by some sense of curiosity or fate itself, Markus looked up, peering at the forest of dead trees beyond and saw it.

The wolf from the forest stood out from among the trees, standing tall and bold, and seeming to stare directly at Markus. He stared back at it, feeling the weight of it's powerful eyes remaining on him, and with the little boost from the Crystals residing in his new satchel, Markus could tell for a fact that it did indeed talk to him.

The wolf pawed the ground and next to its muscled foot was a small green bud that stuck up and out of the ashy dirt.

Markus looked back down at the grave, wanting to ask Ruth what that was all about but realizing the pointlessness to it. He then looked back up and the wolf was gone; vanished without a trace.

But for some reason, Markus was not surprised. So after giving up the search for the beast, he returned his attention back to Ruth.

I will succeed, for you, sister.

And then upon taking Ashlyn's hand and bumping Esmerelda lightly with his injured arm Markus sighed.

"Come on." he said. "Let's get back." And then they all left, a new team, a new family; ready to take on the world as they plunged back into reality, back into the horrible world they wanted so desperately to leave behind with all of their pain and sorrows.

But still at the same time, they were ready to rise above the sorrowful darkness, and come into the light.

"Markus?" said Esmerelda.

"What?"

"Did you know, that if a forest burns down, a new forest will grow back?"

"I didn't."

"From the ash in the soil, new life will grow. New chances, new life."

Ashlyn smiled. "That's right. Well said."

Markus couldn't help but smile either. He felt so happy that his friends were here for him. "Yeah, well said."

When they all had returned to the castle the sun was already starting to set, casting shades of purple and orange across the darkened skies. A heavy snowfall started to come down and it refused to let up, pouring down in what felt like thick feathery clumps.

They say that the final snowfall would be thick and unrelenting until morning, which would be the beginning of spring. The season of hope, and Markus felt there was a small glimmer of hope within him. In his heart, he felt the smallest spark of faith. It was faint, but by the looks of the girls who walked the halls with him, he was able to tell himself that he was not alone in the unknown future ahead of them.

He had decided to sleep the rest of the day, so Markus went up to his room, letting the girls go to their own as they passed. They hugged, which was awkward concerning his injured arm but it felt good to be hugged in such a time. He then told them both goodnight, watching them both turn to their doors. Esmerelda took a gander back at Markus before shutting herself in her room and he could have sworn they both made eye contact before she had departed. When they did, did he feel something, or had he imagined a tense connection all of a sudden?

Markus then turned to Ashlyn who was entering her own room. "Ashlyn?"

"Yeah?" She backed up with the door open to hear her friend, her eyes locked with his.

"Thank you." he finally said. "For everything. I wouldn't have had the strength or the will to continue without you." Markus meant every single word, and his heart was lifted when she smiled.

Ashlyn smiled. "You're welcome." she said softly. "And thank *you*, Mark."

"For what?"

"For saving me. I would not have been here if it had not been for you."

Markus smiled at Ashlyn. "I'm glad Ruth talked me into it."

"Me too." she said sadly. She ran her fingers across the wooden doorframe in thought. "Hey, you need anything, I'm always here. Just wake me up."

"I will. Thank you." Markus said meaning it with all of his heart once again; and with that Ashlyn gave him that cute smile of hers, and disappeared behind her closed door.

After entering his own bedroom and closing the door behind him, Markus locked it. He then crossed the room to his bed, where he removed his clothes- save his pants -and rested Black's sword and the two Crystal's upon his nightstand. He then sat on the edge of his bed, ready for sleep but could not help but think. Something was chewing at him for the longest time; a thought that would not go away until he confronted it. That voice he had heard during the battle... what it had said.

Release me. That was what it had said, when Markus released that powerful blast onto the blimp, he had heard someone speak, controlling his body, and speaking through him. Seeing everything through his eyes, as if Markus was not just Markus, but two people in one. As if 'Markus' did not exist, but a shell containing two beings.

Not quite. Markus heard a voice say inside his head. He looked up with a start, and gasped at what he now saw.

Two animals stood before him in a whisper of silvery shadow. One was that of a golden owl, staring at Markus through eyes that blazed like the sun. The other, a wolf, but not just any; the *same* one he had seen in the woods. Both creatures stared at him with glowing eyes, their demeanor both dangerously threatening and shrouded with mystery.

Before Markus could even process what he was looking at, the shadows around the creatures churned, clouding his vision from them; and when the shadow completely blacked out the room, a bright light suddenly pierced through the darkness, dispersing the shadows as if they were mist.

Where the two animals had been, now stood two men. One in golden armor, a black goatee hanging from his chin, and his eyes glowing bright and blue. His hair was black as well, hanging as low as his shoulders sat broad and strong. The man beside him was thin, like a scarecrow with very little fat and muscle. He was bald and clean-shaven, his eyes glowing bright and maroon in color. He wore black leather armor, tied with straps of animal hide studded with golden buckles. Both appeared to be smiling at him, but their kind gesture did not overcome the fear in Markus' heart. Their very presence, felt *suffocating*.

Fear not, young one. the man in black said in an icy cold voice that sent shivers down Markus' spine, as if an icicle was pricking the back of his neck. His lips didn't even move!

Yes, the golden warrior chimed in a booming voice deep and strong. *For we mean you no harm.*

"Who are you?" Markus demanded in a soft voice feeling both scared and somewhat awakened by these beings' presence.

I am Abner. the man in gold said softly.

And I am Fethawit. said the man in black.

We are the ones trapped in your Crystals. Abner sighed.

Markus' eyes went wide with the sudden realization that he was right. Looking over at the Crystal's on the nightstand, he saw them both glowing brightly.

Yes, young one, Fethawit assured. *We are calling to you, from The Dreaming.*

"The Dreaming?" Markus gulped, not knowing exactly what to say. So many questions buzzed through his head like a swarm of hornets; so much to say, and yet, he could not find his voice to even say anything. So, he merely sat there, gaping like a confused fish at the powerful entities before him for what felt like hours.

Finally, with some effort, Markus asked, "What do you want from me?"

Abner looked down as if sad, while Fethawit seemed oddly amused. *What do we want?* the man in shadows whispered as if the question amused him.

We want to be free. Abner said. *And, you seek the Eldest, and the conquering of The Dark Queen.*

"Yes," Markus nodded dreamily. He wasn't even thinking, nor was he processing the words as they came from his mouth almost too easily.

Then we have much to discuss. Fethawit said.

Time is running out, young one. Abner said. *And a great evil is on the horizon amongst The Dark Queen's forces. The prophecy has begun.*

"But, what does it mean?"

We cannot say much for we do not know much ourselves. Fethawit explained. *We only know what we had heard from our journeys through The Dreaming.*

There was that word again, that place they were describing. "What is The Dreaming?"

We cannot speak much longer, Abner sighed. *I am afraid that this form we hold before you, cannot be held for much longer. Even now we can feel it draining us, dragging us back into the realm of Dreams. And He, is looking for us.*

He? Even as they spoke, Markus could see them flickering as if they were about to turn off like a light. "But I have so many questions… Who are you? Who am I? What is going to happen? What exactly am I supposed to do and why can't you explain further? I-"

Patience. Fethawit urged. *And trust in what Damion Black had said.*

That caught Markus' attention. "You know him?"

Go to Abram. Abner said as if he had not heard what Markus had asked. *Go to the Kaiken Isles. Learn how to channel the powers of The Seven, and learn of The Eldest and The Dark Queen. He will help you find the path you are to take.*

The fate of your Region, and those within The Dreaming, rests on your shoulders, Markus. The fact that the one garbed in black knew his name made Markus even more unsettled. *Remember, you are not alone.* Fethawit then whispered and before Markus' eyes the two beings seemed to dissipate into shadow once more. Blowing away like dust into the air of his bedroom; and as fast as they had come, they were gone; leaving Markus alone to ponder his own questions, and the many possibilities of what he would be facing in the near future. The prophecy seemed so much bigger now, and his destiny much broader than ever.

But Markus knew that he wouldn't be traveling this road alone. He had his new family, the Levitikans, and now… Markus had the feeling that he now had them: the spirits inside the very Crystals sitting on his nightstand.

Abram…

You are not alone. he heard as he closed his eyes.

It was like walking into a dream, that was just beginning.

"I will come."

~ The Cyborg's Fall ~

Lee

Lee panted and groaned as he continued to trudge through the snow, getting as far away from the battlefield as possible.

He had hiked all day now, and even with his cybernetic limbs he was growing more exhausted with every labored step. The heavy snow fell in large flakes like clean white feathers, covering the entire landscape as the wind bellowed all around him.

He had already put up many miles between him and the search party scanning the wreckage that seemed to stretch for miles on its own. Even with his foot gone, he was able to make the trip. Though unable to fly, the journey north was going to be awhile, but Lee was content. He was alive, and from his sisters' corpse- or what was left of it anyway- he had removed her Crystal and in his hand along with it, was the Eldest, glowing brightly and giving him the warmth he needed to endure the dangerous climate.

It was a shame really, losing Lameika like this. But even if he was unable to speak to The Master, he could still hear Him. He had made it clear as to what Lee and Lameika were to do once they recovered Him; and Lee would do his best to achieve his objective, and hopefully the Snake shall let his sister rest in peace.

He shivered despite his suit's heating mechanism, and his damaged auto-limb leg did not make it any easier. Even his arm which had been speared through by Black's witchcraft sparked every so often. If he was like Lameika he could draw strength from the Crystal she was given, or even The Eldest.

But no. He would have to rely on his own strength, as he always had. It would not be easy, making it to The Well, but he was determined.

Lee *would not* fail. He was trained to survive in even the harshest of winters, and the most desert of lands. He may have lost some limbs and suffered much already, but nothing would stop him.

Nothing at all.

Raki

Raki sat upon his steed, an Ahool he had acquired after returning back home to his tribe.

He had received many lashings from his Great Leader, but they were whippings he had very well deserved. The pain was already a distant memory as the many cuts that riddled his back were now solidifying into scabs beneath his Werecat cloak which protected him from the cold. He had watched the battle in the sky take place, and even sent some of his own crew out to scavenge for supplies from the dead.

That was when the man in torn armor appeared in the sudden blizzard.

The Ahool clicked its teeth, its pointed ears turning upon its head as it searched for prey. It shifted its wings to protect both it and its rider from the wind. By the look of the beast's behavior, it too noticed the man walking in the valley below the hill they were perched on. It scratched the ground with the claws in the knuckle of its large leathery wings, ready to lunge but Raki placed a firm but kind hand against the giant bat's flank and it finally calmed. The beast always obeyed the commands of it's Metal Head rider, and this one was as loyal as any Dragon or Dreadwolf; and Raki could not be happier, *especially* with how fast the beast flew.

However, seeing that man, and the glowing gems in his hands gave Raki a new sense of desire. Feelings he had not felt before.

It was as if, the gems themselves were calling to him; like a warm hand reached out for him against the cold harsh winds of the Wastelands, and was beckoning him forward, to save them, to collect them. He was so compelled to do so, to give up on his hunt for that Hunter Black who humiliated him and got him punished. To just go and free those gems from their captor...

Release me...

Raki smiled as he spurred his steed towards the man, ready for the attack.

The Legend continues in…

The Legend of Levitika:
   The Evil Angel

CPSIA information can be obtained
at www.ICGtesting.com
Printed in the USA
LVHW080141100422
715792LV00010B/584